QUESTIONS TO ASK
BEFORE PROCEEDING

ALSO BY MARVIN COHEN

The Self-Devoted Friend (1967) Rapp & Carroll (UK) and New Directions (USA); *Expanded 50th-Anniversary Edition* (2017) Tough Poets Press

Dialogues (1967) Turret Books

The Monday Rhetoric of the Love Club and Other Parables (1973) Rapp & Whiting (UK) and New Directions (USA)

Baseball the Beautiful: Decoding the Diamond (1974) Links Books; Second, expanded edition as *Baseball as Metaphysics* (2017) Tough Poets Press

Fables at Life's Expense (1975) Latitude Press

Others, Including Morstive Sternbump (1976) Bobbs-Merrill; *Expanded 40th-Anniversary Edition* (2016) Tough Poets Press

The Inconvenience of Living (1977) Urizen Books

How the Snake Emerged from the Bamboo Pole but Man Emerged from Both (1978) Oasis Books / Earthgrip Press

Aesthetics in Life and Art, Existence in Function and Essence and Whatever Else is Important Too (1982) Gull Books

How to Outthink a Wall: An Anthology (2016) Verbivoracious Press

Five Fictions (2018) Tough Poets Press

Inside the World: As Al Lehman (2018) Sagging Meniscus Press

Women, and Tom Gervasi (2018) Sagging Meniscus Press

Run Out of Prose (2018) Sagging Meniscus Press

Sadness Corrected: New Poems & Dialogues (2019) Sagging Meniscus Press

Life's Tumultuous Party: Reduced to its Essential Partycycles (2020) Sagging Meniscus Press

Plays on Words (2020) Tough Poets Press

Conversations and Versifications (2021) Tough Poets Press

QUESTIONS TO ASK BEFORE PROCEEDING

Marvin Cohen

Compiled by Colin Myers

Tough Poets Press
Arlington, Massachusetts

ISBN 978-0-578-89963-3

Tough Poets Press
Arlington, Massachusetts 02476
U.S.A.

www.toughpoets.com

For beloved Candace Watt

Contents

Preface

The episodes in this collection have been taken from Marvin Cohen's shoebox of unpublished typescripts written in the 1960s and 1970s. Marvin says that the title: "will inspire more lawyers to buy the book. No, I'm kidding, but the book is after all in its contents ideal for the thinking and reflective class as its natural readership."

Questions to Ask Before Proceeding, as Well as During and After

How much of a story can this given idea withstand? Is the story too bulky for the conception, or too slight for the conception? Is the verbal style appropriate to the idea? Is the narrative order fitting? Will there be a clarity to do justice to the conception? Will the unfolding *reveal*, rather than obscure? Will the way and the thing unite? Will the way parallel the idea's utmost revelation? Will words bring forth, and be the *act* of conception? Are the means to be productive? Will the working words combine into their chosen work? Will the work be what it has to be? Will the creation have illuminated its intended territory, just that and no more? Have the relevant details of the territory been brought together by a single vision? Is that all there should be; and nothing of anything extra? Has the work accounted for what it meant to gather into one harvest? Has sufficiency been served, and precisely that? Has the waste been stripped off? Does everything crystallize? Will it be valuable to others?

THREE STRENUOUS ATTEMPTS TO CHANGE HUMAN EXISTENCE AND THEREBY ALTER THE WHOLE WORLD

A Sincere Scientific Attempt to Free Human Immortailty from Physical Aging, Cellular Decay, and Death's Incessant Interference

PART ONE

I

To retard, arrest, ultimately to forestall the process of human decay, thus averting death, is Lenny's confirmed preoccupation. High stakes attend the solving of this nasty riddle, this knotty problem, this supreme obstacle to secure and complacent well-being.

Having no medical background, fundamentally ignorant of biology and chemistry, and not in general superabundantly intelligent at any rate, Lenny is basically handicapped, unarmed, powerless, for coping with or even approaching this insurmountable barrier to the human immortality-wish: physical decomposition, the fatal path of entropy in each isolated organism.

"By all standards, death is deplorable," Lenny whines to a friend who's heard it all before but who's too lazy—and polite as well—to stop Lenny from reiterating his morbid commonplace obsession in dreary plaintive predictable helpless melancholy.

"No-one has yet stopped it. How can you?"

"There's always the first time. True, I'm no scientist, I don't even know the first thing about science. Even anatomy fools me sometimes. I seem foolishly unqualified. But my horror and indignation at the prospect of death is my arms, my weapon, for opposing that grim spectre that stalks us all."

"Horror and indignation? Are they enough?"

"They motivate me."

"Don't you need a method, instrument, technique, for even beginning to go to work on this primary problem that covers the cosmos with human worry? Lenny, you're most farcically unequipped. Can you realistically hope to overcome shortcomings so drastically catastrophic for the stupendous scope, the inconceivable difficulty, of your all-consuming undertaking?"

"My means seem slender, with narrow resources and slim chances at most for any possible breakthrough. But I'm willing, I'm game. Others far better equipped to deal with the problem have never attempted it, with the odds laughing them in the face. Me, though, I'll be tenacious, and not give up."

"Persist, endeavor as you may, nevertheless to what avail will it be?"

"I won't know till I try and try."

"And try, and try, and try again? Poor Lenny. People will call you crazy, for the futility of your sheer trying."

"People need not know."

"You won't tell them? You can't work in secrecy. You'll need assistance. You'll have to rely on material agencies, banks of information, points of reference, manned by specialists in various fields pertaining to that distant object you bear so firmly in mind. Or will you be mystical, and occult?"

"I don't quite know how to go about all this business. It looks so bleakly remote. I'm quite beside myself, for it's so beyond me."

"So already you despair, Lenny?"

"Not despair (which leads to inaction), but *desperation's* active force, compels me, impels me, to a strenuous feat of urgency."

"Be concrete. *What* feat?"

"I haven't found a way. Don't mock. Grant me all the time I need, for this major enterprise."

"All the time? The rest of your life can be thus so vainly employed. Years, ahead of you. The vast shrinkage of your future itself."

"My brittle future against this terrific challenge. I may die trying to end death. I'll meet death head-on: winner-keep-all."

"What a tussle! You lose."

"I don't *presently* lose. I *might* lose—but later."

"There's no stopping you. Good luck, Lenny."

"I need luck to direct me. I'm at a loss—where, how, even what to begin. Death is terrible. Even now, it mocks me."

"Well it might. It's fiercely inevitable. You're pathetically frail. What craft or skill can you bear, to stop the unstoppable? 'Task Impossible,' you've assigned yourself."

"If that's its name, it'll be renamed if I win."

"If you win, more than names will be changed. The whole earth, all of existence, the face of creation itself, will be altogether else."

"I've aimed high."

"Too high even to call it lofty or noble. You've merely touched the height of the ridiculous; you'll come down empty, in a fearful fall from a flight so foolhardy that dooms you desolate and low even before the rise you'll never attain."

"Is that your professional opinion? For you, Jason, by profession being a biologist-chemist, have earned a right to critically disparage what I only profess to claim can be done. You damn me with force, for you're mechanically in the know about the science behind it all."

"As a specialist in the field you somehow magically hope to cover, I pronounce this verdict from the weight of my considered knowledge, having risen to the rank of expert in cell chemistry and biological human structure: you have no hope. You've spun out a fantasy impossible—by the very nature of things, inherent in our very beings—of ever achieving a corresponding realistic result in the world outside your deluded little mind. I'm convinced that science will refuse to yield to the gleam of will that reposes in your ignorant head."

"Enough, Jason. You've said enough, on this rather sore point that mars our present friendship."

"It was opinion, not unfriendlinsss, on my part. You're free. Go ahead, ruin yourself."

'Well, I'll set to work. You don't encourage me. Nothing in all past time does. I'll have to create a precedence, and let emerge so original a novelty, as to defy what evolution and history have thus far recorded or been the events of. The past doesn't support me. I'll do without its support, as I'll do without your encouragement. To end death, I must inaugurate Change by no means yet devised, in the combined talent, inspiration, and despair of people gone and here, the total work force of intellectual human labor on our rather eventful earth since prehistoric cells first oozed and graduated into source colonies at the origin and inception of the later takeover by masses of mankind in sheer technological dazzle."

||

"You've undertaken what no-one has been capable of bringing about. I laugh now."

"The test will be, will you also laugh at the end?"

"Let's assume that you succeed. A crisis of new problems would come about, by consequence."

"To kill death, to end mortality, is eminently desirable. The consequences thus given rise to, could be readily soluble, by comparison. Mere child's play, in the giddy aftermath of so heroic a conquest."

"But will the earth have food for immortal people and all the future newborns? Already its resources lie drained. What would people be like at two hundred years old? Consider."

"They wouldn't *look*, or *feel*, like their official mathematical chronologies, if their decay can be arrested at a much earlier age by the miracle of my steadfast work. A planetary food shortage? Overcrowding by massive overpopulation? I'll take responsibility, and head off disaster, impede catastrophe, by, if not one explored method, then some other. I'll look into it all. This is not a grandiose scheme pretentiously assumed on my part; just one human's humane contribution to the humanity he's a cell of."

Jason turned angry. Why was he a part to this ridiculous dialogue? It offended his scientific sensibilities. He gently exploded. He'd be firm with Lenny; yet, if he could, caustic.

"That's darn modest of you. Back up your boast with results on a long-term scale of spiraling widening of unforeseen effects on a cosmically primary order of foremost importance in the priority hierarchy of values and needs essential to life's physical and ethical perpetuation on a collective framework for the maximum quality standard of each person's personal sacred actual living."

Was Jason now identifying with Lenny's proposal, getting carried away, swept into Lenny's own mental scheme?

Now it was Lenny's turn, to be firm with Jason:

"You're drooling in the morass of your own rhetoric. Let's get back to basics. One step at a time. Universal immortality and the attendant adjustments necessary to its installation can't be the product of just one day's labor."

"True. There *are* limits. How do you propose to go about these sundry matters pertaining to everybody's body and soul in their joint overturning of time's traditional cold hold of terror over anxious people in thrall to overhanging doom?"

"I'll reduce complex disorder to a simple theoretical pattern by a succession of logical steps."

"What, in the essence of precision, shall they be?"

"Let me first arrest decay, which would be a monumental task in itself. Once bringing *that* off, I'll tackle what next should arise by virtue of my stroke of glory. First to benefit. Then to remedy the defects. I'll follow that sequence. I'm only, after all, human."

III

"The first step is your current stumbling block. Where shall you turn, even to scratch the outmost surface of depths darkly unknown?"

"I must make a start. Just slight headway, to entrench myself in a fruitful pursuit from which momentum may get rolling, carrying all before me toward my galloping goal."

"Lenny, you worry me. Are you perhaps not quite sane?"

"I'll ignore that disparaging insinuation. Nothing may deter me from my fixed objective."

"Fixed? It's uncertain, vague, undefined. For all your fixed resolve, your totally dedicated determination unwaveringly firm, you're stuck at an impasse from the start. Where will you go from here? Not even the flimsiest plan to direct your tangled energy."

"I'm middle-aged, but healthy. I'll devote my remaining lifetime to my sworn deed, or perish at the toil. Extensive, intensive work is ahead. *Effective* work is required, or all fails."

"Defeating decay, ending human death, are noble aims indeed. But they're only in the 'ideal' stage. You must break ground. Such vainglory, Lenny! Were it not for pity, I'd laugh."

The friend parted from Lenny, with those not overly hopeful words. He swirled away, angry but thoughtful.

Jason had had enough. His professional experience as a specialist, expert to the matter Lenny proposed to treat of, felt soaked with insult. Jason already knew the field. Lenny blindly assumed to know more, by audacity's shameful ignorance.

IV

The visionary, left to his vision, smarting from an adverse estimate from a real scientist but not less determined for that sharp rebuttal, folded inward to embrace, with touching loyalty, that vision whose banner fluttered tattered from the departed Jason's scientifically backed attacks.

Maybe *God* would protect and defend the vision? That last resort, when all else failed.

Thus, the need for prayer had arrived.

Hoping for enlightenment in his new solitude, Lenny prayed a fervid meditation from the brooding depths of his lonely plight.

A visitation of no inspiration arrived to cast a radiant light of mercy and guidance. Instead, grim mortality remained, with its "business-as-usual" no-nonsense practical process of dark inner decay. Worms were at work. Cells aged, toward decomposition. Relentlessly, youth was being broken down, internally routed in subtle undermining.

Time was against him. Bodies weakened; so that mentality must slump as well, deteriorate, lose force, fade, go dull, in remorseless spiral declining by vitality-reverse waning in decrepitude toward its own lapse.

A further pray-attempt. Summoned the second time, God might, miraculously, respond. Maybe he'd been coy before, playing "hard-to-get," like a maiden, whose pride requires persistent courtship and a repeated plea.

V

Lenny knelt down genuflectorily on both bony knees with trouser cloth between himself and the floor. He went through futile motions: foreshadowing the futility of what he prayed to be enabled to do, through divine intervention? Pre-failure failure, rehearsed in a vain prayer?

God was unco-operative, if he even existed. Faith crumbled into doubt; it had no hold for grabbing to clutch, grasp, cling on to, or tangibly at least to touch.

"Help!" Lenny shrieked. It echoed itself: "Help!"

Though frantic, an idle plea. Who or what could have replied? He was slowly dying, inside, wishing not to, not only for himself but for everyone else. But what's a wish? A wish is weaker than a want. A want implies practical possibility. A wish only indicates a dream. The dream is there, as an ideal, a distant value, only when the chances for action—effective action—are cut off. A wish is the residue of a hope gone barren from the hopelessness of surrounding circumstance, the lack of opportunity in, co-operation or concession from, the adverse environment. Then the want decays to a wish. Action barred, a dream-ideal-value is merely a mental substitution, meaning by mental, "insubstantial." Hope abandons wish so as not to waste its forceful effect on what objectively stands, when stripped of sentiment, as too unlikely to entertain save by self-indulgent fantasy that has the place all to itself now that hope and want realistically have departed for more fruitful occasions where promise gives more favor to desire.

Lenny rose from his bootless meditations, his sojourns into the ruined realms of obsolete prayer. "I want so to eliminate death, to retard decay. An admirable goal but pointless of pursuit when nothing comes to hand of how even to go about a bare beginning that could implement a lone concept by bold actual striving and progress. I'm lost. Others *aren't* lost, simply by never conceiving this brainstorm project from which torment and torture will ensue to the extent that the project is conceived with serious dedication based in an all-out commitment at the expense, perhaps, of sanity itself, along with other sacrifices that crucially undermine one's social life."

VI

"Well, I'll do without prayer. Jason, representing the sound opinion of science itself, tried to discourage me; and God, or His lack, didn't exactly endorse my idea either, with some positive affirmation. Neither Jason, science, nor God backs me up. This puts undue stress on self-reliance, which in my case is sorely deficient in know-how, expertise, or a grounding in the fundaments of basic information pertinent to my bold schemeless plan that has incompletely formulated itself, being bare of systematic method that could be the first toehold toward an initial clue to solve what Jason would call the insoluble but which I maintain can be somehow detectively cracked, though the secret kernel is safely locked inside the solid shell that protects and seals the kernel of indeed an impenetrably hard nut that seems permanently to encase the kernel of the secret of everlasting life darkly tucked away at the very core of inaccessibility itself."

Renouncing help from God and Jason, Lenny now blesses his Mission from his own soul's consecration, to raise his fortitude for it.

The will, and the world. Given the world's "no," can the will still prevail?

PART TWO

I

To cut himself off from distractions and other seductive diversions from his "life's work—dealing death out," Lenny quit his modestly paying, somewhat inconsequential job, but in such a way as prudently to get himself fired, which rendered him eligible to draw financial assistance in the substantial shape of a year's dole from the state, under the official designation of "unemployment insurance," a form of pre-socialism compensation for managing, through hook or crook, to exchange "income from work" to "income from non-work," within the legal sanctions of the "labor" economy, thus simply put.

Unencumbered by such family responsibilities as a wife and children, Lenny had no ties, enjoying the free status of a bachelor. So he'll devote all his energies to stopping decay and hence death. The single-mindedness of his purpose simplifies, unifies, directs his life.

His work is cut out for him, but it's no easy task. Quite, in fact, beyond all his powers.

II

He sets aside a few preliminary days to chart his course, and mull over his procedure. The uninterrupted solitude of his apartment shall serve to environ, close in, condense, concentrate, and intensify the sharp bearings of his all-points focus to clarify the nature of his unique task and so touch upon the likely techniques, the "how's" best adapted for treating the awesome "what" of the case.

He pours his mental brains out gnarled in the knotty grip of toil by cogitation, furrowing the brows of his grim-set forehead, sternly applying himself to theoretical elaboration of what he broods analysis upon—cellular decomposition, and how to arrest it.

"But what *is* a cell? It's all so chemical. It fits into the category of physical biological science, which, though broad and informationally

popularized as an accessible educational commodity for the low-lev-
eled consumer's market, escapes the extent of my talent; for science I
have little capacity, and no aptitude.

"So I'm called upon to delegate my research to a fully qualified
assistant. I'll advertise and interview applicants for this key post of science consultant. He'll be my right-hand man, even associate and partner, in my anti-death crusade.

"He must, of course, be not only competent, but reliable. Without
him, where would I be?"

This was his first decisive decision. But before he could put it into
action, a certain worry hit him: in order to select the right candidate for
the post of his scientific adviser, Lenny had to know enough to know
whom to select. It was in this specialized brand of knowledge that, just
at the wrong time, he was wholly deficient.

What he'd have to do would be to hire a suitably competent, scientifically knowledgable selector to sift out from among all the applicants
just the right choice for Lenny's ultimate scientifically chemical-bio-
logical consultant, associate, adviser, and technician in ending morbid
human aging decay at a sufficiently flatteringly early enough age for
people to permanently retain that prime sexually attractive stage for all
the rest of their undying lives, unimpaired by any vitality-decrease in
tissue, organ, gland, artery, metabolism, respiration, digestion, mem-
brane, or other member of each person's privately managed internal
team of cogs and spare parts that strike the right combination in balanced adaptation to the force and pressures from without that shift and
change with challenges and retractions along the varying configuration
on the scenes of time's tapestry.

But he didn't know enough about science to be able to select a
selector who in turn would select . . . .

At this rate, would any work get done? Decay goes on, as before;
mindless, heedless, of Lenny's indefinite plot against that slow killer of
precious lives of the high human classification.

III

Lenny seemed stalled. He'd hit on a snag, and was stuck at the starting line. As for making progress—he wasn't. He was getting nowhere, and losing valuable time while so doing. Would he call it quits, pack it in, and drop the whole business? No. Life is at stake. (To be precise, extended life, prolonged, perpetuated, sustained.)

He can't back out. Not now, not ever. Not at such high stakes, for himself and everyone. It's a life-and-death affair.

You can't get less trivial than that.

Too much depended on his, somehow, piercing the dank murky depths of disease-bearing cellular decomposition, which ebbs life's flow and drains dry the rich fountain of sensation-conceptual existence peculiar to our incomparable but mortality-claused species that dominates and culminates the minute pains, the dusty details, along evolution's arduous path.

IV

How to pick first a pre-selector most qualified to select the one who'd materially assist in every way (in fact, do mainly the whole job for) himself, is what Lenny's current problem boils itself down to, in its lurching appeal for at least that much of a solution introductory to advancing into the early stages of work itself, buckling down in dead earnest in addressing the goal of death's early demise in a person's prime lifetime, leading to immortality with retention of sexual heights with the powers of attraction intact.

He phoned Jason, who had discouraged him in their recent conversation about Lenny's declared life's work.

"Do you know a scientist who can help me pick a scientist who, under my command, can find a way of stopping human decay?"

"Me. Remember I'm a biologist."

"So you are! You've changed your mind?"

"And I specialize in human chemistry. This qualifies me to select your working assistant. I'll start at once. Who are the applicants?"

"I haven't advertised yet. Once I do, we'll arrange for you to interview those self-appointed candidates with the confidence to respond to my notice."

"Don't bother. I know who I'll pick already."

"How premature, when no-one has anything to apply to yet, no public notice having been printed."

"But I know the right man personally."

"Really? Who?"

"Me."

"But you were cynical about my project. You called it hopeless, and discouraged me."

"I had no confidence in you, but I do in myself."

"Can it be done?"

"Not by you. Maybe by me."

"But you were to be a *pre*-selector of the man finally selected by yourself to man expertly this extremely vital post."

"Lenny, I pick my own self to be that key man. Spare yourself the advertising. I'm he."

"You'll team up with me, Jason? It's my program, my entrepreneurship, my administration, and you fit in as my technician. Those are our respective roles. Let's start work. Recently, by myself, I was bogged down. But with you as my right-hand man in charge of actual over-all detail work under my executive leadership, finally, at last, we'll get somewhere. Work exclusively for me. Quit the biologist job you now commercially have in the chemical outfit, to devote yourself full-time, intensively, wholeheartedly, to our joint campaign."

"But Lenny, I can't quit my commercial job. I have a wife and kids to support."

"But *ours* is a top priority program-in-the-rough, which needs immediate application to get right off the ground and refine itself into planned actual activity on an elaborately minute scale that takes pains over every last precision, even down to the tiniest detail to be firmly clinched into place on the broad pattern woven lock by lock into a stunning aggregate that eats away into decay to pry open death's ugly secret. Our race will raise itself into the erasure of death, thanks only to our dedicated toil, Jason: yours in the microscopic laboratory full of measuring instruments to rip open the cell's heart and soul to pare away all that rots into the crystal purity of an everlasting life. It requires all your stamina, energy, and time, under my cheerleading supervision, to pull off this labor of love, Jason. Quit your commercial job. I'll get a government or international grant from a benevolent foundation that assists humane endeavor."

"I don't want my wife and kids to go wanting by risking their well-being by leaving my secure job."

"Foundation funds will cover their expenses. Our program fulfills ideally the stipulations for receiving a generous grant, since we aim to benefit mankind in no small way. Eternal life is no petty matter. It means what it says. And we—Jason—mean to attain it for all. If *that's* no contribution to mankind at a fundamental level of importance for the welfare of everywhere our fateful species, at the essential primary core that directly concerns the condition and predicament of all people still and to be alive—well, then what is? We'll reign ethically supreme. We'll rise heroically to true greatness on the central stage of the world, pre-eminently historical once our partnership is inaugurated as a crusade to remove death as so far the most lethal obstacle to the old romantic yearning, dream-based, cloud-capped, for love's only rival as an ideal: immortality."

V

Jason was now thoroughly won over, even to vie in enthusiasm and ultimate commitment with that passionate conceptualizer, Lenny. The latter's influence over the former has been pervasively persuasive, infecting Jason with the roaring fever germ of wild, untrammeled devotion to the sacred divine cause to which his whole mind, spirit, and strength are wholly given over.

"Delighted to have you aboard, Jason. You've quite changed your tune from before. Glad you see things my way—you're my converted apostle, formerly my arch detractor. I value you the more for having first sinned against the true light you'll help us be guided by, with your new-found zeal that brings me ideally the scientific assistance I need, suffused with your loyalty and inspiration."

"Let's strike while we're hot."

"Not yet. We're still on the phone. Our game is still in the talking stage. We're paving a discussion path to the starting line; with strategy yet undevised, but the fire in our veins boiling to a mental pitch."

"I can't curb my eagerness, straining at the bit, ready if ever ready was for the prime ripeness of taking a direct target aim at decay's own awful rot, where death's foul worm hides its snakeward hulk to strike life away."

"Restrain yourself, Jason. This is only a preliminary phone call. We're too apart, as yet, to combine forces to conquer our concealed enemy."

VI

Jason chafed: raring to go.

Lenny would have to check Jason's exuberance, with uncontrollable heaps of energy gushing to the kill to strike a fatal blow, once and for all time, against the entrenched cunning of fatality's own stronghold.

Jason implores Lenny to "Let's go," but is held back from the blind excess of impetuous zeal.

"Calm down, Jason. Once you mocked the cause you've reversed yourself to espouse. Conversions like yours could be dangerous."

"Lenny, you convinced me. I'm game, we're in business. Direct me, and we'll buckle down."

"Let me caution you to be patient, Jason. Rome, that classical city, though all roads are said to have led to it, wasn't built in only one day."

"Death was present then, and still is. It's been around too long. Its time has come—through us—to give up the ghost, to kick the bucket, and go six feet under. We'll hammer nails into its coffin, once we get its corpse inside. Its demise or decease, of course, must precede the funeral festivities. If it doesn't go peacefully, let's commit murder!"

"Jason, watch your violence! This phone could be tapped by police authorities."

"My violence is all in a good cause."

"Life? Is life a good cause?"

"Sure. Look at the opportunities it affords."

"Death isn't easily gotten rid of."

"I expect a hard time, Lenny. We face a tough road ahead. Death is a treacherous, cunning old wheezer; his guiles and wiles and old bag of tricks are tricky with experience and sneaky to the kill. All the lives death has taken, through hook or crook! On a scale stupendously scandalous. People have become fatalistic about it all. They've come to stoical terms of acceptance with the horrid old bully who always gets his way. We just lie down and let him roll over us! I won't stand for it a minute longer!"

"Calm yourself. Outrage, horror, and indignation at death's long list of atrocities and other abominations may cause you to sputter, foam, froth; but not stop short that long list from lengthening on the ancient scroll, adding fresh recruits to the hordes, mounds, and heaps of all those whose doom has come to roost and are gone and done, whose lives are now a closed and unread book. Once, Jason, you called my own horror, outrage, indignation, insufficient by themselves to take power upon their object, to change or end it. We need means, a method, some way of operating to effect what change we want and make action take actual effect and redo matter to the preferred manner. Railing is not enough. Let's plan our course thoroughly."

"I'm for all due haste. Delay means more people will be dead—even us, unless we're quick."

"The scurry of hurry, the waste of haste, achieve nothing but con-fused bungle and compounded delay."

"Let's strike with swift dispatch. Death remains at large, loosely at liberty. Our decay proceeds further, and eats our youth away."

"Alarm can't halt decay. We must figure out just what to do—and how."

"I'm aging, Lenny! It's too late, soon!"

VII

They were still on the phone. "Let's speed up our rate of getting going if we're to get anywhere in doing death in," urged Jason. "We've been slow too long. What's it for?"

"We'll proceed methodically, at a deliberate pace—not frantically slapdash. Slow efficiency, Jason, ultimately outdoes the tempestuous carefree approach. Let's consider, ponder, meditate, with extreme caution, our crucial move."

"That's *your* job, Lenny. You're the boss. Exercise leadership. I'll carry out—put into practice—your high directorship."

"That's where *you* come in, Jason: advise me."

"As your consultant?"

"Officially. I place heavy reliance on you."

"I'm *technically* skilled, but at a loss just how to . . ."

"You can't initiate? It's up to me? But I'm not scientific enough. I've got to carve headway with an insight? I lack one."

"Then we're stuck? Has death already won?"

"You were fast to proceed, now you're fast to concede. Steady, Jason. Steady."

"Lenny, it's so discouraging! We're lost!"

"Despair won't help, either, Jason."

VIII

The partners paused on their electric circuit. First they got somewhere and then nowhere. From nowhere, the view looked bleak.

"Well, where do we go from here?" Jason mumbled, breaking the unproductive silence that had sprung up between them. The gloom took on a deeper shade.

Lenny took charge. He analyzed the situation:

"We're mired, bogged down, stalled, at the start, having hit on some stubborn snag that impedes the gradual building up of momentum. I can't foresee any sudden burst of progress to get us out of this rut of nothingness; at least not now."

"When, then? Must we *always* wait?"

IX

An idea occurred to Lenny. He offered it, though it would hardly shake the earth:

"Let's get off the phone. Let's confer again, but face to face."

Jason was all in favor of this: "Call a meeting, Lenny. We'll have a skull-session, to draft up a plot of tactics."

"Precisely, Jason. We'll put our heads together, to save them later from turning into skulls. I won't weigh you down with administrative responsibility. I'll make a plan, and you carry it out."

"Take charge, boss. I'll follow."

"Now we know our respective roles. So much, at least, is certain."

X

Theirs was an unequal brain trust, to outwit their sturdy foe, death. Who does death's dirty work? Its prime minister in charge of internal affairs, its viceregal chief on the domestic front, known technically by the name of Decay.

Decay can, if it goes far enough, slyly gradate into suddenly a lethal dosage.

"Let's turn the tides on Decay, and slip it a lethal pill," says Lenny, now in command as the sole head of their partnership.

"I agree," argues Jason. "In fact, I *more* than agree. Shouldn't, in finality, we terminate this phone conversation so that we can face-to-face get together jointly to outface Decay and its boss Death? This phone melts in a marathon of longevity to echo our unseen voices."

Jason's suggestion was promptly taken up through the intermediate stage of arranging a meeting at Lenny's flat and then they both hung up, in the fraternity of their accord.

Would they ever succeed in ruffling the decomposure of cells? Could somehow they bring about by means not yet known the organic purification of life indefinitely sustained? Life was not yet free to be tampered with. It was captive colony to a totalitarian despot. Could life be liberated from dominion status through Lenny's and Jason's joint utmost effort? Life was a subject state to death's tyranny, and was lorded over by its grim oppressor.

How could the two friends—now colleagues embattled against odds of impossibility to create the truest miracle—catch decay off guard, and perpetuate a fatality on life's most iron-clad dictator?

Death wouldn't just roll over and die. It would fight to retain its old rights over that quick, glittering prize it's always held captive. Life is the very life-breath of death, so why would the latter relinquish the former to a mere biological chemist and his supervisory boss?

Death wouldn't easily give up life. But neither would Jason and Lenny give up their silly dream to snatch life permanently in safety from its ruthless possessor.

PART THREE

I

Lenny applies for a grant from a foundation and it's granted. This enables Jason to quit his commercial job as a biological chemist to devote his full-time obedience to Lenny's brainstorm, should that ever come.

Lenny's free term on the compensation dole of unemployment insurance still isn't over, but when it is the foundation grant will amply cover his modest living expenses (mainly food and rent), just as it helps to support the more-than-bachelor family of Jason, his wife and kids.

The successful grant application, in order not to seem like a crackpot notion from a novice of a charlatan, and to be decked out in technical knowledgeable terms of authentic legitimacy, had been written, on Lenny's request, by his thoroughly competent assistant, Jason.

With the vast sums at their disposal, they rent out a laboratory and fill it with the instruments Jason will work with on their intricate project. *Which* instruments? They only guess. They haven't found an operational mode yet. (Jason had bluffed one on the application form for the grant, so as to let it appear that the partners had a definite scheme in mind, within reasonable margin for a shift in method should the advancing work suggest altered further forms in the process of revealed progress improvised fluidly in the course of work.)

||

"People are so apathetic about dying, it sometimes seems," Lenny complained to his technical assistant in the laboratory. "Religion, the promise of an afterlife, lull, appease, placate, console, solace, divert poor doomed fools from the starkness—unrelieved, disagreeable, unbelievable—of their lonely dooms."

Theoretical, theological chat like that came instead of concrete work, because concrete work was blocked off by their not knowing where or how to try to make an incursion or inroad upon empirical decay in the physical corruption of human matter. So idle philosophizing filled up the vacuum of their inability to arrest cellular decomposition due to the lack of a great insight, discovery, invention, to create a practical break.

"Maybe we're only mediocre?" Jason suggested. "Patience!" Lenny was obliged to reply.

"Has your inspiration at last arrived?" Jason would persist.

"You'll be under immediate directives, when it does," asserts Lenny, waiting somehow, with open hope grown old and cold, to fertilize a miraculous seed to bear a more-than-promissory growth on the objective plain of active work in measurable progress for the proof and truth of result actually achieved by standards of scientific validity ascertained as admirably legitimate by the specialized community of scientists concerned and thence by relays in popularized conveyance to the world grown groaning with the ignorant lay public everywhere, rejoicing at the news: "Human Death at an End: Decay Officially Defeated," emblazoned in headlines, proclaimed in banners, to disbelieving cheers, a universal amazement roaring, incredulous, having advanced their standard of living to the absolute impossibility-turned-actual of a supreme ideal entertained only in dream form but now an attained value: Immortality added to the life one already has, heaped on, by a generous turn of fortune.

Endless life, minus the aging disgrace. The partners merely thought about it. Their expensive, grant-purchased, finely delicate laboratory equipment just idled there, as they sat around, to while the time away (bigger and bigger chunks of it) in dreams of glory and success. Jason had nothing to carry out, since Lenny had no inspiration to set him about a definite task.

Human cells were looked at under the microscope. Only passive observation. No transforming vision, to work a radical change in the structure.

III

Years went by. The grant regularly renewed itself; for the Foundation thought it was a long-term project that required an infinite patience of time.

Lenny and Jason were personally aging, at the same rate that, in their chosen line of work, they quite plainly were failing, by the barren sum of their results so far in the course of their fruitless quest.

Jason sadly observed: "The older we get, the older we'll be at the stage our decay is finally arrested—*if* we ever achieve our object that's gone stale with years of no progress whatever."

"Don't despair *yet*, Jason."

"What's to *prevent* despair, then?"

"Eternal hope."

"Eternal hope is the substitute for eternal life, which, Lenny, by now looks just too beyond our moderately capable powers."

"Hold on. We've invested *years* in this project. Television, newspaper and magazine people, to whom the Foundation must have leaked the news of our proposed endeavor, are clamoring to interview us as to just how far we've gone. Scientists have expressed interest too, and editors of scholarly journals. We're being snooped for a scoop. With evasion, I've bluffed them all off so far, claiming the need for secrecy and privacy."

"But we can't hold the world *indefinitely* off, poor Lenny. It's got a right to demand to know. It's to *everybody*'s interest that we cure aging to end death. What more universal, popular concern can there be, of vital interest to reach anyone's heart with the most 'profound' emotional impact?"

"We're not ready to grant interviews. Experts would see through our bluffs, and expose us as frauds. We can't fool *all* those hounds, even with deceptive double-talk in your scientific jargon, Jason."

"Rumors and speculations are growing rife about us. Intense curiosity is centering on our laboratory den. I'm waylaid by the press when I leave or when I arrive; they lurk in wait, in competitive journalistic pressure to snoop a scoop out of us. I can't *indefinitely* be mute and curtly cut them off with that overworn phrase, 'No comment.'"

"Nor can I, my dear technician-in-idleness. The world is creeping in on us. We're the intriguing subjects of speculative publicity; as rumor and conjecture come closing in with circling shadows like vultures to swoop down and expose the rot and corruption, the pretention and deception, in what we've claimed, professed, behind our guarded pose of secrecy."

"They see through us in our postures, in a competitive conspiracy to debunk us as perpetrators of a hideous fraud on humanity's vulnerable hope?"

"The rumor grows, my poor Jason, that we're exploiters of the foundation grant game in order to be glorified in grand support and official sanction as base, parasitical idlers."

"Those rumor-mongers are, in effect, right. We've done nothing for years, except waste time in dreams and drain the Foundation a bit of its fund-letting. Rumor has grown correct. It's our bitter paradox, Lenny. Accusations are true, underlined in heavy irony, that we're a couple of frauds. Our identity is exposed!"

"Yet, Jason, we began in good faith, and undertook our project in the best intentions, fraught with passionate energy, the sincere ardor of our enthusiasm, such committed devotion that attested to purity of souls beyond reproach."

"Years went by, and no inspiration kindled you. My expert, precise hands, my veteran, practiced eye, grew cobwebbed dust and the stagnant stench of rust. We've grown old in this stifling abortion of our wills, and corrupted in idle habits. The hawks of exposure come swooping down, in dips and dives, having circled overhead for too long, in hovering suspicion."

"Then, Jason—I ask you, as friend to friend in our besieged laboratory that reeks of laborlessness: publicly, shall we admit defeat?"

PART FOUR

I

Having a long distance to travel, all the way from earth to Hell-heaven, a rumor turned false in transit and reached the ears of Death in this distorted form:

"Death was being threatened with extinction by the heroic joint anti-decay force of two human men: Lenny, the executive director of the task force onslaught; and Jason, the brilliant biochemical technician who was on the verge of liberating the human cell, forever, of its ancient slow gradual insidious destroyer, Decay."

Hearing this "news" from a messenger's panting mouth, and not knowing that it was wrong, Death was, in turn, appalled, mortified, scared, horrified, and violently upset.

"I'll have to go down in person to that laboratory on earth where this plot against me is hatching my destruction," Death swiftly decided. "I'm accustomed to destroying, not to *being* destroyed. Though below my dignity, I'll have to seek out Lenny and Jason and somehow bargain them out of their growing power to deal me a lethal blow and make things fatal for me—*me*, the source and origin of fatality through my agent and capable minister, Decay."

Death summoned Decay to go with him; travel arrangements were soon made, for what was pegged to be a fateful trip of decisive importance to the entire historical future of collective humanity in its absolute totality of everyone either living or unborn—but not including, unfortunately, those already dead, that numerous throng of people with only a past.

■

Death and Decay reached earth, refreshed themselves, and started out for the laboratory where they'd be so surprised—and relieved— were they to discover that there was no foundation whatever in the report of progress to kill them off.

With the aid of a map and directions, the two visitors from Hell-heaven located their destination but had to plow through a swarm of newspaper sleuths; radio hounds; television newscasters; obscure scientific research specialists representing technical or trade journals of limited (scholarly) appeal; a crew of sensation seekers who grub in celebrity proximity; humanitarians; philanthropists; crazed people in a denominational assortment and classified miscellany of types termed popularly crazy in roughly unofficial designations of that insanity-connected category for weird, erratic, unpredictable sorts of behavior-strange people; free-lance journalists; movie agents; suspicious Foundation investigators; a picketing bunch of well-drilled undertakers, cemetery owners, funeral establishment thugs, and others who gain a living off death and, even at the expense of their own deaths, are militantly opposed to their meal ticket Death's termination which would deprive them of their professional means of livelihood; biologists; chemists; physicians; philosophers; ministers; priests; rabbis; representatives from foreign governments; spies; underground characters; shady dealers; nondescript mysterious figures; pickpockets and confidence tricksters to exploit the milling crowd; plainclothes detectives and uniformed officers of the law for guarding the peace with law-and-order vigilance so that the crowd won't become an out-of-control mob charged with unruly anarchy and nihilistic seeds of destructiveness potentially inherent in the transition from crowd to mob; lawyers; representatives of commercial interests from industrial, public relations, and other fields either gigantically corporate or individualistically hustling and other states in combinations between; feature article writers and magazine columnists on a syndicated or exclusive basis; just plain people; and an assorted collection of others, just to mention a few of the types in the crowd blocking access to the laboratory to which Death and Decay (dressed nondescriptly in protective anonymity to look inconspicuously like anyone else and go undetected for what they in fact were) had expressly traveled all the way from Hellheaven precisely for the purpose of deliberately paying a delicate visit.

III

But they weren't able to gain entrance. (No-one else was, either; Lenny and Jason had taken careful security precautions, foolproof, iron-clad, privacy-protective, to be quite uninterrupted in perfect secrecy: their protracted, extended idleness—a potential source of embarrassment as well as outright of scandal—mercifully undetected, sealed officially off from unwarranted public intrusion.)

Death and Decay, in their incognito guises, were brusquely denied entrance by an armed guard at the laboratory door.

"Persuade him to admit us," whispered Death to his ambassador, Decay, who was polished in the art of diplomacy and other artful social dodges by a refinement of manner and urbane elegance in the genteel uses of the world, thus equipping him to be minister-at-large, with or without portfolio, and roving emissary, to his majestic master, Death, whom he served with such able finesse that he was considered—by those occultly in the know behind the political scenes of Hellheaven's fairly bureaucratic government—to be the logical successor to Death's presidential throne should that awesome incumbent ever accidentally surrender his reign and lose his crown at the helm by, of all things, dying.

With a sophisticated air, and with slightly a foreign accent (a faint one, barely discernible, certainly not pronounced), Decay addressed the bulky guard at the laboratory door with words mildly subtle with an air of understressed importance in the speaker himself and his well-dressed companion alongside:

"Sir, let us in. We've important matters to discuss with Lenny and Jason, although admittedly we're not expected by them. Are you corruptible by bribe? I'll give you a million dollars to let us in. That would enable you to quit your humble job of a guard—hardly a dignified post of worldly prestige or conferring of much status."

"My orders," the guard recited by rote in mechanical dumbness and dense stubbornness, "are to resist all bribes, whatever. Those orders are strictly to be obeyed. Previous attempted bribes by others failed. Yours can be no exception. Lenny and Jason expressly forbade me to let anyone gain entrance, whatever the pretext on any note of urgency. I'm hardened to all visitors, and deaf to their protests. Notice that I'm armed. I'm licensed by the Foundation to shoot anyone who tries by force to gain entrance once his verbal plea has failed to impress me."

While listening to the guard's prepared speech, Decay turned silently to signal to Death the query for a silent signal back as to what, in this tight situation, he should do. Death's signal was to the effect that they would turn back and not press the issue. They'd book a hotel suite and plan for the morrow their next move. What on earth could they do now? They'd swallow their rejection, the impersonal insult, and return tomorrow equipped with a strategic maneuver. They had to arrest, at all costs, the grave progress they assumed Lenny and Jason were making based on the false report they'd been given in Hellheaven, prompting their emergency journey to earth where they hoped to keep collecting lives at the standard old rate by preventing Lenny and Jason from disrupting and terminating their customary revenue of souls surrendered by an uninterrupted tradition of longstanding, deeply established mortality built solidly in, at the start, to the fatal biological nature of the cell.

"Sorry to disturb you," Decay politely replied to the guard, as Death and he turned away, through the jostling crowd, to find suitable accommodations in a hotel, preferably one of subdued elegance.

IV

Though rumors were rife and increasing that depicted Lenny and Jason as imposters on a lavish scale of living off Foundation funds for years with no justification whatever in terms of the least result to back up all their vaunted promise, thus bilking unfairly the Foundation as well as cruelly raising false hopes in the poor deluded breast of humanity, such rumors didn't yet reach Death or Decay, either orally by casual eavesdropping from clusters or passersby in crowds in the throbbing city, or by readable gossip in print by press, or on radio or television.

Usually observant and alert, Death and Decay somehow didn't pick up, get wind of, all this speculation so much currently in the air, electric with pulsation, a cloud of excitable static raining rays and impulses on the counter-murmuring populace caught up in the rampant welter of this scandal-in-the-brewing.

Still basing their attitude on the misleadingly erroneous report brought to Hellheaven, those two distinguished residents of Hellheaven (now on not a state visit but top-secret mission to earth to conserve their vested interests in the maintenance of a status-quo death quota in keeping with the increasing population rate on the mortal chain of human generations on the cascade or stampede of onrushing time to cover the moving belt of geography with new imprints from the broad press of history) considered Lenny and Jason to be definite threats to be taken seriously, carefully countered, cunningly dealt with, by bargain,

Faust-compact, Mephistophelean arrangement, transcosmical bribe, stealth, subterfuge, cheat, sneak, or exclusive personal-immortality clauses on the hush, on the side, under the table with a swift handshake to seal a secret deal of giving Lenny and Jason eternal life in exchange for letting everyone else die as usual by the natural code of disease and old age, the same old tragic load as usual at the inflationary rate of galloping giant overpopulation (keeping births' equation to deaths at fixed one-to-one, with Lenny and Jason solely exempt and eternally so).

V

So as not to be overheard, Decay and Death didn't dine in the hotel restaurant (where *they* might have heard stray gossip to the contrary of their fear-formed suppositions), but rather ordered room-service in their suite-retreat.

"Advise me, Decay. We've got to make contact quick with Lenny and Jason before their experimental scientific research finally discovers a way of killing us. Their telephones are unlisted; they answer no letters or even urgent telegrams. The guard won't admit us. Their laboratory is sealed off; they're incommunicado at unknown residential apartments. Only when they leave or enter that laboratory (potentially fatal for us) can they even be seen. Seen? Only just sighted, or glimpsed. Like obscurity-worshiping celebrities.

A surging mob of press hounds, telecasters, and other opportunists or gawkers tries to jostle them on their arrival at, departure from, their strictly private laboratory where such work is done against us that makes me want to scream—or at least cry out. They're sought after for multitudes of purposes, by eager, panting, pressing, beseeching, surging people, closing in frantically; but they're attended to, in tight protection: policemen and Foundation guards and detectives and government agents brutally form their bodyguard and keep them out of stray conversation's way; no casual question-answer in passing, and no impromptu interview by any loose informal accident in deliberately random reply-provoking remark to lure them from an implacable public solitude clenched in the firm policy of silence. Sealed off, barred to us, they have a free hand, my dear Decay, to seek our twin destruction cleanly licensed, Foundation-backed, in an open act of crime against us. And all so glaringly private! Secretly, we smart with insult. Yet we can't revenge ourselves!

"Oh frustration! We eat in a comfortable hotel suite. We're careful to remain unknown. But could this be our last meal? Is their breakthrough imminent? How many breaths are left to us, from our affording lungs?"

Decay remained glumly silent. Death ranted on, between edible chews, in grunting rage.

VI

"Those two mortal enemies of ours—we're denied access, as though we have no special right to them! We're treated like everyone else! Yet let's remain anonymous; this is not the time to identify ourselves. We're spies, in our own cause.

"Jason and Lenny—merely mortal enemies of us? They'll be our *immortal conquerors*, if we don't soon prevent it. How to stop them?! Think, Decay, think!"

Decay no sooner started thinking, but word by word his thought was accompanied by speech, slowly boiling to a haste.

"Jason and Lenny. How their birth curses us! They labor against us. We stand by, helpless to their access. And they work on. And on and on. Oh, they're getting close!"

This frightened Death. He burst out: "Too true, Decay. Too true. Now advise me. Your opinion, please."

"What on, dear Death? On what? Oh you poor soul!" declared Decay, in pity.

"On mainly those enemies. Clarify our predicament. What course of action to take? They want to retard and arrest you, Decay. How can we retard and arrest their progress to that end? How to cut them off, from cutting off us!? Advise!"

"I will! You'll choke on your food! Be calm, Death."

"Speak, fool! I wait!"

"For what?"

"For you to speak!"

"I think of Jason and Lenny. And they think of us."

"They more than *think* of us, Decay! They plot our active horror! I'm afraid!"

"Of what?"

"Dying."

"How contrary to your nature, Death. Fear not."

"But those enemies? What do we do, Decay? What?"

"I don't quite know."

"No? But you should. Aren't you clever?"

"I'm reputed so. You've found me so. But earth is a hell of a place. I'm confused now."

"Don't be. Can't we kill Jason and Lenny? Can't we?"

"They're safe from us."

"Are we, though, from them?"

"No. We're in danger. They endanger us."

"Must we let them passively? We're powerful!"

"Our power is great. But unusable now."

"Decay, this is outrageous! Have we no recourse, in our own defense!? They brood our end, in a well-equipped laboratory. Can't we shift? Decay! Let's act!"

"But Death—how?"

"That's the point I consult you on. It festers, while we eat."

VII

Decay ponders. Can they outwit Lenny and Jason? Two pairs, at immutable odds.

The visitors have come all the way from Hellheaven. Those for whom they've made this trip are still unvisited. The unvisited coolly plan the demise of the visitors—so think the latter. But Lenny and

Jason have given up. For years, they're idle. Secretly, they abandon their project. Public rumor catches wind of this. The press suspects them, and accuses. Thus brews a scandal, to catch a fraud by the tail. The visitors strangely don't sniff it out. In innocence, they still fear.

VIII

Assuming that Jason and Lenny are dangerously coming close to the kill to imperil himself and Death, Decay broods in the hotel suite, over dinner, just what to do. Such trouble, over only two humans! It's downright embarrassing. It's ridiculous. Decay's thought twists off, and comes to a new turning. First he refers to Jason and Lenny, over whom Death obsesses in such anxious turmoil that his meal is almost spoiled. He bites down and munches. He darkly listens. Dear Decay deliberates on their enemies, soon to veer off in pursuit of quite another point. Here's what Death hears, in near panic, by Decay's subservient utterance on their scientific stalkers whose quarry they are, or feel they are, in ignorant tension and fear.

"Death, our problem is how to reach those two men before we're much too late. The solution quite escapes me at the present moment. I'll carry the problem to bed, and 'sleep on it,' as the colloquial expression will have it. But Death, let me contradict you on a point, subordinate and technical, but hardly academic, which you let slip."

"Yes, Decay?" condoned Death, packing in his dinner, as was his loyal assistant who had rendered such reliable service, such devoted consistency, during the centuries of their legendary but actual collaboration; as the densely populated graveyards and other systems of cemeterriality so multiplicatedly attest in mute wide acres of their gloom.

IX

"Death, *I'm* in danger of being totally annihilated; you, however, are not."

"What an enigmatic assertion, Decay! Please explain yourself."

"Should Lenny and Jason diabolically succeed in their relentless laboratory experimentations to radically create a novel scientific precedence to notably modify man's historical condition, they'll eliminate *me*—Decay—by arresting cellular aging at a mature but still youthful stage. That would stop *me* from being your minister, Death; but you have others. I've brought about disease and old age; but *other* agents render you loyal service. You feed on disasters and catastrophes and deliberate or accidental violence in individual or group events. Natural havoc comes from hurricanes, earthquakes, tornadoes, volcanic eruptions, snakebites, inadvertent poisoning, and such other modes, conduits, vehicles to your great gaping greed as categorically are outside my own domain, ministration, or province. Fatal fires, whether by arson or inadvertently; drowning, falling from heights (whether a slip or a suicide or a push): those also have I nothing to do with, but are legitimate food for your endless appetite, my great Master. You have ways of consuming and devouring and gulping down your soul-morsels, to which I make no personal contribution. Violence, fatal crimes, wars (and the complicated machinery thereof, those surpassing instruments of almost aesthetic efficiency, masterpieces of pure objective destruction, so effective as to be economically beautiful to the coldly impersonal scientific eye): these, and such like, will keep the wolf from your door, and provide the plenitude of repast to hold starvation at bay."

"How true, Decay. I'll confine my worrying not to both of us, but to you. What would my life as Death be without you? Without you I'd manage to live on—but I'd lose my heart and soul and right-hand man. I can't contemplate it. My standards would be so reduced! As Death, I'd even contemplate suicide! For you, Decay, are my pride. Please be always at my side. Oh that infernal Jason and Lenny! Those brutes!"

"My mighty Master! I adore you, Death!"

They stopped eating to embrace and weep. As stones grow from pebbles, hacking sobs emerged from their mutual stream of tears.

What a touching couple! Sentimental Death, and his subordinate, Decay; of unequal rank but joined by noble friendship as true equals of the spirit.

X

Decay attempts to comfort Death. "Better you live, than that we *both* die." Death grieves bitterly, already, in advance.

"Let's prepare. Soon I could be taken from you by a successful breakthrough in Lenny's and Jason's great scientific struggle, which technically I must admire, though I should expire by it. An end to me is nigh."

Death groans. Decay continues.

"But in you, dear Death, I symbolically sort of survive, by our unbroken spiritual bond."

Death now wept copiously. It ruined the greater part of his dessert.

Decay saw Death choking on the gulping sob of misdirected food. The spasmodic fit almost quite undid Death, right there.

But he recovered, in slobbering gasps. The panic subsided. A pause ensued. Death grew morose. Gently, Decay prattled on.

"Should I die, dear Death, you retain a sufficient plurality of outlets—violence, disaster, catastrophe, and such other means—to subsist indefinitely on an endless diet of human fare."

This hardly cheered Death up. Death looked fondly on Decay. "You're my favorite!" came out painfully from Death's fluttering chest.

As though in farewell, Decay continued. "An ending creeps up for me, in time's anguish. But mine only. *Your* end, Death, will never be, until the final human being of that durable, hardy species has been born in the last birth and lives to be your last supper. Till then, even if I as Decay should breathe my last under Jason's instruments with Lenny's supervision, you'll manage to eat well and regularly, I'm sure."

Suddenly, Death took heart. In humorous optimism, he regained resolve. A gust of cheer broke out. He spoke with energy:

"At the moment, we're dining on the same fare that *people* dine on—instead of on people themselves. This hotel is too high-class for cannibals. Decay, how well you've enlightened me! *You're* in danger, but I have other means of surviving. That puts a new perspective on our earth visit. But I refuse to lose you! You're my favorite source of sustenance. Now we've finished our dinner, let's find out possible news about our enemies. I've ordered a newspaper brought up to our suite, as well as an informative magazine. Let's also put on the television; also the radio. Through these media we'll learn what's afoot by rumor and speculation or fact leakage concerning our hard-to-reach pair that strives to deprive me, dear Decay, of your invaluable service. Newspaper, magazine, radio, television. Let's go down the elevator to the lobby and get the drift of people's random conversations, as well: a cross-section or representative slice of the public rumor-mill. If we're barred directly from Lenny and Jason, we'll at least take opinion samples from the general consensus of the breathing mental air here, on the very earth where, dwelling and working, Lenny and Jason secretly concoct their threat. What are people talking about? Let's hear."

"We'll investigate, Death, what atmospheric climate radiates from the sealed-off laboratory as reflected in the random current of attitudes on popular tongues that wag out a kind of folksy drift. By print, television, radio, we'll detect how we fare, though Lenny and Jason try to conceal it. What's our state? How do we stand? Does elimination face me? Will we be violently forced apart?"

"Let's spy around, Decay. We'll find out a bit of intelligence. The free press, freedom of speech, unlock secret truth, revealing and expressing all hidden essences in liberal, wide-open democracy."

"Let's discover our futures. What's said here, written, and shown? It concerns us to the quick. Let's find out what's the reigning mentality. We'll wade in the stream. Clues will wash off on us. We can't guess till observations trickle in, from the multitudes and their spokesmen. Come, Death."

PART FIVE

I

In their laboratory retreat, Lenny suggests to Jason:

"Let's issue a public confession and declare our guilt, release how idle and inactive we've been in a fraudulent misuse of Foundation funds, exploiting grant donations as imposters who finally confess themselves after years hidden in a criminal false pretense of liberating humankind from death and decay's damn disease."

"Let's make a clean breast of what's been welling up in our chest. We're just a couple of cheats, Lenny. Instead of ridding mankind of pestilence, we've heaped on more. We're corrupt disease colonies, a bloated malignity of fungi. We've been a blight and a scourge, in a foul misplay now caught in the web of publicity by an unfavorable press of rumor. The media is right that we're wrong. Gossip has turned upon us. We're scandal's fools, for we've run out of fools to fool. We played on people's hopes: immortality; that's now played out. A hoax is where the hope had been. All people are bound to die. We're old, our time is near. We're close to our own ghost."

"So we are, poor Jason. As a family man, you've disgraced your wife and children. As a bachelor, I've spared others at least. Now we know failure. This is failure, Jason."

"Not yet. When official public humiliation comes upon our frank admission, then our failure will flower notably. Oh Lenny. When first you told me your schemeless dream, I laughed you to mockery. You challenged me whether I would laugh last. The last laugh is on us both, for I changed to belief in you and joined my scientific knowledge to your project. I share jointly now in our humiliation. Only our friendship has survived. Our names are blemished. The world already jokes. We choke on its joke. Let's throw ourselves on its mercy. We'll call a press conference. All the media representatives will attend, Foundation scholars, chemists, biologists, and public spokesmen. We'll open out in a full confession, an open purging of our crime. We'll fling our great old dream to the wolves that howl and snap at us. We'll be a public sacrifice, ceremonious in our failure. An indignant pious outcry will devour us. It will be our pre-death death, on the victims' altar. A fitting end to glory's sunrise. We'll harvest a rich failure."

II

Death and Decay did field research, to examine what was likely to be "up." They found out that they need have no fear. Oh, what a surge of relief!

They plan soon to return to Hellheaven. The threat has turned harmless. They're safe.

"Too bad we two couldn't have confronted those two, and 'had it out,'" said Decay, on a note of regret.

"It would have been dramatic, or fun, our little showdown. Face to face, us four. What we missed, Decay!"

They laughed. They were in a sweet mood. They own the world. They limit, define, contain Life. All will be, as before. Dear, dear. What an unnecessary worry it had proven to be! Plainly, they'd been misinformed by an erring messenger. Out of that, an adventure had come. A "tight scrape." Now, they're free to whoop it up with joy. They love the universe. Finite human life provides decency and order in the Scheme of Things. Death and Decay are conservative, by their natural interests. They love how things are, have been, remain. It's a dedication, a principle. Life is a wonderful voyage, floating Death and Decay on the blissful sea of their serenity. Ah, Creation! Constant creation. To replenish their destruction.

They live continually on, in Hellheaven. Earth sends them endless nourishment. A peaceful grandeur grips the Cosmos. Words fail. God endures. Death and Decay have faith in Him. How else to explain all this?

Lenny and Jason are dead, outlived by their infamy. It was a laughable episode.

The Struggles of a Free-Lance Genius

PART ONE

I

"I've got to make a break with my past; and to make a signal, sign, emblem, or symbol of the turning point of this change from the me of before to the me of from-now-on (till further notice), I now install (for the objective world to well note, the external realm of social impressions I make upon all the people who aren't me but who compensate for not being me by as least concerning themselves with me when they can) a name change. For all my life I was Janet—thirty-four years worth of that. Suddenly, now I'm Jane. Why? Because I will it so. I'm free to do it. So I've done it.

"I'll serve notice. Meanwhile, my subjective solitude continues."

Jane paused and thought. She was sitting down residentially indoors. Her past life passed before her, as though on review, battalions of squadrons past the inspecting general.

Did it pass muster—her Janet-life? Under Jane's new eyes, no. Jane didn't approve quite of what she inherited from Janet. She'll set it to rights, revise, rectify, replace, improve. She has "Janet" to work from, as the material base to build on, once some demolition work is done to efface this or that. By ending her old beginning, she'll make a new start—but not from scratch. She'll work over, patch up, repair, mend, alter; but install as well, introducing radical departures.

II

"During my being of Jane my life maybe will prosper with fruitful success in the good fortune of what I undertake. My career as a free-lance genius will perhaps 'take off'—crowning me with an increasing frequency of joy. Should that take place, then 'Joy' will replace 'Jane,' which now is the replacement for outmoded 'Janet,' in mutations and metamorphoses of my long-range evolution and short-range development along the wobbling span of the only life I'm granted. It's only one life. But by varying it within itself, I make the 'only one life' into a plurality of stages, phases, steps, periods, transformations, outgrowths, distinctive sequences that crowd into my life a rich mixture of dramatic romantic glamor to parallel nature's inexhaustible diversities as corresponding me-miniature to the sprawling macrocosmic universe 'out there.'"

She accompanied her last phrase by looking out the window and exaggerating the local view into immensity's enormity farflung into the total whole of All. This imaginative thrust expended her resources and left her in the vacuum of a shock, self-induced. She was jolted backwards, snapped faint, locked lame and loose temporarily in the flowing bonds of a swoon that liberate at the instant that they annihilate.

She gave herself over to it. When she "recovered," she was further yet from being her old self. "Janet" slid into remoteness. "Jane," freshly arrived, "took over."

"A resurgence as 'Jane.' I'll announce outwardly that name, and live up to what I'll make it mean, socially to manifest in the world's terms the charging new inner me emerged so suddenly but hardly in a transient role. It hardens out, and is durable. It takes on a life. It's not fly-by-night. It solidifies my present in an ongoing capacity. It historically terminates my 'Janet' past, defining it by the new retrospect chart it's drawn up while it assumes the urgency of its own life."

III

Being a free-lance genius required exceptional talent; to be gifted or endowed with this unusual promise was of course not the common lot of just everyone. But Jane was neither common nor "anyone." Someone as unique as she could only have one identity: herself.

In turn, that identity could only have one person to fill it: Jane. The two of them—her identity and she—were mutually bound up, together.

Without one, where would the other be? As counterparts, Jane needed her identity, her identity needed her. Fulfillment for those two needs was, fortunately, ever simultaneously at hand by automatic reciprocity within the single nature of that compound that derived double support from interfused components.

IV

Blessed with such rare promise, Jane needed a strong character, firm discipline, a "no-fooling-around" habit of work grounded in duty, commitment, principle, enthusiasm, inspiration. Lacking this, her "free-lance-genius" reputation could turn upon her and make her a mocked figure of scorn, a well-ridiculed fool for presuming the grandiose bombast of pretensions found unfounded. A preposterous imposter? No, she'd more than justify that lofty tag of hers—in the world's eyes and hence her own. In honesty to merit a title that sounded so flattering was hardly a petty task to take on as a facile trifle. So she boned up, studied hard, got a wide education, attended special classes, took advanced courses, read extensively, practiced diligently, and thoroughly applied herself.

Her successes have only been minor and tentative, sometimes even tenuous or dubious. Fame has somehow avoided her marked advances. That was when she was Janet. As Jane, though, she'll attract elusive fame. Hence the significance of her change of name.

V

Her parents had a lot of money and her alone as their favorite only solitary protected child upon whom to dote with parental indulgence to spoil her. So she had plenty of means and freedom to develop her gifts, unburdened by the draining time-wasting drudgery and exasperating toil of making a living. Not only was she her parents' only child; she's never had a husband or children yet of her own, upon whom to lavish "creative" energy. She's free to work at her range, then, of skills.

In her private scientific laboratory she arrives at a terrific discovery so far-reaching in its massive consequence as to be absolutely major, substantially first-rate: potentially, at any rate. One doubt, however, lingers: will it work?

If it doesn't, she'll *make* it work. That's called *marketing*.

Bearing this in mind, she arrives at the administrative office of a large maternity hospital, having arranged an appointment with the executive director of the whole establishment whose purpose was to expedite—cleanly, efficiently, harmlessly—the birth of babies from women whose pregnancy had reached an advanced stage suitable for labor to begin, to issue forth in the infant that embryonically had been carried in the expanding bulge up prominently at front.

"Come in, Jane. I run this hospital as its head. Come to your point. Why are you here?"

"Well, doctor . . ."

"Please, Jane, I'm so busy. Any further hesitation on your part, and on mine I won't hesitate to terminate our interview harshly on the spot, at once, putting an end to whatever your petition might have been had I permitted it to even begin, which I won't unless—sparing me details—you tersely condense what you have to say in terms of such foremost brevity as to cut short even the most relevant digression. Proceed."

"Doctor—"

"Jane—even saying 'Doctor' takes up too mush tine. Dispense with those formalities, those time-wasting courtesies that stall the pith of your message with the cumbersome paraphernalia of delay."

"You see—"

"No, Jane; don't 'you see' me. I have no time for preambles and overtures that ramble on in conventional phrasemongering. That's my last warning. Heed it, or I'll have you ejected from our busy premises. Give birth to what you want to deliver. Or to put it another way, deliver yourself most pregnantly to issue forth with your conception-turned-manifest. Yes?"

"I will!"

"Yes, but when?"

"Now!"

"Let Now haste swiftly to the past. Get it over with, Jane! I'm too busy to prolong our talk at length into a discussion or conversation. Are you tongue-tied?"

"No. May I speak plainly?"

"Please."

"I've invented something wonderful—or discovered it."

"Which?"

"Maybe both. Or else one."

"Let's not get bogged down in academic technicalities, stalled in semantics, knotted up in the intricacies of a rhetorical detour. Adapt your manner to the specific matter you have in mind. I'm not inclined to wait. Do you think I have all day?—Answer me, Jane!"

"No. Decidedly not."

"Good. Just what I wanted to hear. Go on, then."

VI

"May I, then, be brief, Doctor?"

"By all means. Just what is it you've intended all along to tell me? Put it proverbially in its own nutshell. Let's not dawdle or dilly-dally any longer. My responsibilities are so overwhelming, they drive me frantically to the pit of awe, where, in frenzy petrified, I—almost— despair."

"I understand your plight. Believe me, I'm sympathetic!"

"You *look* kind; undoubtedly you *are*."

"You *inspire* kindness, Doctor!"

"Do I? How pleasant to hear! It's lunchtime, I'm hungry. Let's go out to eat."

"But the duties that were weighing on you . . ."

"They can wait, Jane. *I'm* the boss."

VII

"The treat's on me," gallantly insisted the head doctor. He preened himself on being masterful, protective, now, in the restaurant, sitting at a table, having given orders to the waiter.

Why was the hospital head that way? Because Jane attracted him sexually, in spite of his being a husband and four-times father.

He'd never seen her before today. Their appointment was set up by his private secretary. Upon Jane's telephone insistence to the secretary that the matter was in the primary order of urgency at the forefront of priority's graded seals in the high interests of humanity itself, the appointment was made last week on a busy schedule for today. At first this director busied himself warning Jane he was too busy for any roundabout exposition by way of wordiness from herself in superfluous prolixity of phraseological redundancy. He had taken a severe stand, brusk and businesslike, firmly unmistakable, at the onset. This cowered her, and he got sexually excited in his high-pressure office by her fumbling attempts to acquiesce in old-fashioned female obliging meekness implying humble and awed obedience should he powerfully drive home a sexual proposition by the masculine prerogative of an overture.

His reaction to Jane was a not untypical case. She gave off such a little-girl aura of docile femininity—despite her also being so dominating a thing as a free-lance genius. It excited the hospital boss even more that he might dominate such a *talented* little sweet thing. Oh, he sat tall, at the restaurant! She was asking him a favor, probably. She was importuning him; beseeching even. (She hadn't said what for, yet. But that mattered less to the hospital chief than the fact that she was relying on him in a clinging way.) It inflated his importance, his power, his masterful position, and his cock bulging with the sweet wild dream of sperm, brimming ecstatically with alertness to the brutal control he had over this situation.

Drink, *hors d'oeuvres*, main course. During those he bantered some meaningless innuendos to this damsel-in-his-power. Oh, how he was taken with her! She before mid-thirty, himself fifty already. But still . . .

VIII

"Jane, you may call me Dick."

"Dick? But I thought your name was Harry."

"It is—or was. But I'm sort of done over, transformed, by you. I'm now just not what I was."

"Even nominally?"

"Yes. You aren't married?"

"No."

"Any constant steady boy-friend bond?"

"Not presently. But why ask me that?"

"Because I'd like us to become intimate, as lovers openly sexual—in private, of course."

"You're quick, Dick."

"Jane, you renew my youth, I'm excited."

"Dick, I thought you had a busy schedule today. The restaurant is empty of eaters excepting only us. The others ate and left, the lunch hour is long over. And still, you haven't let me come to my point."

"If you insist, Jane, then do. But first I had to come to mine. I find you unbearably sexy. Please let's go to bed tonight—no, why wait? Let's go to your apartment straight from this restaurant. I'll pay the bill."

"But our dessert and coffee aren't finished. You're so hasty, Dick."

"Hurry, Jane. My anger is boiling up, bulging with sexual impatience. I'll explode, before long."

IX

"Dick! You're a grown man! Control yourself."

"I do, ordinarily. But with you it's hard."

"But you're in charge of the hospital. Aren't you neglecting your responsibilities? You had so much executive detail to comb through today. And you're ignoring it—for me."

"Were it not for you, I'd be hard at work."

"I'm appalled, then, how much power I have over you. It terrifies me. I'm literally frightened!"

"Don't other men respond to you similarly?"

"Yes, often. I have to put them in their place, ward off their bold intentions."

"If you're frightened how much power over me you have, then let me suggest a solution."

"Do. I'm frightened of being frightened. What can you recommend?"

"Simply this, Jane. We'll reverse the power. It'll comfort you to hand the power over to me. *I'll* have the power, over *you*."

"But for that to happen, I have to be attracted to you."

"Well, learn to be. I'm strong. Appreciate it."

"But Dick—why *you*?"

"You insult me—why *not* me?"

"You're much older than me. And you said you have four children and a wife."

"So I do. But I'll leave them—for you."

"This is sudden."

"So are you. You crept up on me unawares. Our appointment was long ago this morning. Now the first *dinner* patrons are filing into this restaurant, long after the luncheon customers all cleared out. My decisively important running of the hospital, with a lot of complicated problems to deal with and decisions to make, of the first urgency today, have been disregarded. The Health Commissioner could charge me with negligence in my post of public responsibility. My neglect takes on the proportions of a scandal, if publicised. But my will, my firmness of character and devotion to duty and to my committed office, drained away, Jane, as I beheld *you*."

"Oh Dick—you scare me!"

"I do? Well, unscare yourself."

"How?"

"By submitting. Do just as I say. I need you."

"You're too abrupt. My answer is no."

"If you don't reverse that decision, you'll regret it."

"Is that a threat?"

"Yes."

"How?"

"This morning, Jane, you came for help?"

"Admittedly, that's why I pressed your secretary to arrange the appointment, Dick."

"Well, you're in my power. I won't help you, unless you give in."

"But Dick: it's not yet proven that you *can* help me."

"You're right: will I be *able* to help you?"

"Let's find out. Shouldn't I, at last, come to my point? It's night, it's evening. Our day has slid past."

"You transform me from Harry to Dick, and day from morning to night, and me from responsible to negligent in the execution of my duties, and me as well from loyal family man to lustful infidelity with relocation of love from longterm wife to suddenly upon you."

"Is all that *my* magic?"

"Upon me, yes. It's *your* magic. But I'm your chosen subject."

"Not chosen by *me*."

"*Self*-chosen, then. Self-appointed. I'm willing. I will you."

"To what?"

"To win we willingly. And to lose your will to me."

PART TWO

I

Jane defiantly and absolutely refused to submit to this hospital chief's high-ferocity force of bullying might. He had a commanding personality. But her marvelous invention or discovery needn't resort to *his* influential help; it could be made fit and workable for the world's market and her personal fame with assistance elsewhere. Why rely on this particular administrator, who'd first put pressure on her to hurry her point across that morning (they were still at the same restaurant table where they'd taken lunch, and now the dinner hour was long over and it was close to midnight closing time and still there they were, locked in the impasse of their struggle, crossing grimly opposed wills in the undecided contest of a confused stalemate), being too bluntly busy to hear her out?

Abruptly, the tone of his whole tune went whack out of key. He'd fallen spell to her unwitting spell she found herself passively casting. Her impact on him was so devastating—as well as violently instantaneous with the immediacy that gradually crept up on him to assault his senses and cause him to abandon his highly placed post of appointed office of primary importance to a crucial segment of the public—as to work a radical change in him to the extent even that from being Harry his name suddenly had become Dick. Such an explosive effect she had over him—was she scared in *his* power, to have transformed him so; or dazed numb and dumb by his writhing in *her* power?

Such a turn outdid nature's normal modesty by leaping gradual stages at a dizzy accelerated pace, knocking proportion out of kilter in stunning rapid monster rate in grotesque twisting freakage upsetting to stable regularity's course of secure predictability; and obtruding abrupt lust and tyrant love upon her independent prim prudery that recoiled at captivity to a man; the premium being fame and good work in the successful status of a free-lance genius, a difficult ambition requiring the sustained conviction of discipline in the pursuit of a glorious career.

Overwhelmed by her, this hospital director, at an instant, was Dick and not the Harry he'd always been. That nominal change paralleled the dynamic internal transformation he underwent upon radically "experiencing" Jane in her role of supplicant to his power and influence: barely had he glanced at her in his office and briefly exchanged words with this girlish grown woman of an unknown talent potential, but he was jolted out of Harry into Dick. He was overcome—enthralled. Now he wants conquest: she must bend to his will.

This proposed power reversal didn't enchant Jane. She was a recent

Jane. She'd *voluntarily* become Jane from Janet, with controlled deliberation. Dick's change from Harry, on the contrary, had been bewilderingly involuntary, an outburst based spontaneously on the unique tangle of their circumstance. He was a helpless victim to her. She'd sought his help at an impersonal level of scientific work; not his victimisation, his subjugation, on a sticky plane of personal clash and piratical romantic outrage: crude lust thrust upon her along with the stifling threat and possessive arrogance of love that would bullyingly clamp down hard on her jealously guarded precious individuality and independent pursuit of a difficult career blending an ambitious mixture of discipline and genius to offer the gifts of well-wrought work at the fashionable or immortal altar of female temple marketplace, where all the world's nobility congregates and critical verdicts are rendered, judgments and reputations achieved.

II

The head waiter came over to them. He both looked and was sleepy. "It's past closing time. You're at the same table where you were served lunch. How momentous your discussion has been so prolonged, if I may venture the liberty of an estimate. By this time, hasn't it concluded itself decisively? You shake heads no, in unison. Well, you're asked to leave, anyway. Unless you plan to stay for breakfast? Dawn succeeds night by stealthy degrees. But I've been on my feet all day, and am sleepy. Graciously, please, leave. The remnants of our staff must lock up. May I presume to suggest that the both of you—together or separately, that's your business—go to sleep after first going home? This is a bit of homely advice. By giving it, I don't mean to exceed in insolence my humble post as a serving waiter to your public and appreciated custom. You, sir, I've seen often come here to eat, we're on semi-familiar nodding terms, you control the maternity hospital near-by and stop in for lunch quite frequently. And madam, as for you, I've never seen you before. Now, however, I have: the whole day and all night, it seems.

"Please come again. But to come again, you've got first to leave.

Please leave together. Are you colleagues or collaborators or in a client relationship or are you lovers or what? Impudent of me even to ask. Such curiosity is unfitting to my post. I aim but to please and serve. This is a public restaurant, it's closed, go. I'm boldly direct, due to sleepiness. Courtesy will return to me, more freshly, When you two again confer your patronage on us here eager to serve you: but during—I must stress—our hours of being open. Work wearies us. Customers can be demanding eaters. As in your case, often they converse. Carry, will you, your conversation elsewhere. Ease us home from weariness, by courteous decency. I tire even telling you this. In fatigue, I can sniff the dawn. It's tired of waiting, as I also am. Pay your bill and leave a generous tip. Please. Odd that I *give* orders. Usually I take in them."

Dick did as told. He paid, the door was unlocked, they were let out, he and his companion of the day. On the pavement outside, on unfamiliar, unsteady feet, awkwardly they stood in late loiter-linger, languidly shuffling four numb legs in a league.

The clean-up crew and final waiters all left after locking up, to send their ways sleepily home at last, first passing Jane and Dick, who looked back at the darkened window pane behind which they'd sat practically all day deep in their unexpected talk.

Talk? But Jane hadn't accomplished her purpose. "Dick, in your office earlier this—rather *last* morning (the restaurant window—in front united of our bleary eyes—gradually lightens up to reflect the dawn that creeps slowly behind us from the morose sky of a city anxious not to resume the insomnia of another early waking)—yes, it *was* last morning: there's unconcluded business from my end. You recollect: in your office, Dick, you curtly told me hurry up get to my point in terse condensed brevity and the superfluity of no digression, to say what you'd granted me an appointment against your busy schedule specifically to say. Well, that point was never made. Is it too late now?"

"Never, Jane. Delay just slightly longer coming to the point. The place finally to have your say—the *logical* place poetically to conclude our long deliberations on the culminating crescendo of climactically the ultimately proper atmosphere is your bed. I'll hail us a taxi cab to your apartment, where privacy shall specially favor us, as opposed to my house where four children and a wife are; the latter probably worried where I am if she's at all conjugally decent and maritally concerned for my welfare. Well, I'll not ease her worry yet; I'll prolong the fit anxiety of that loyal mate, to appease my own anxiety to hear, dear Jane, at long last, the point you kept an appointment to make this morning. No, it was *last* morning. In roundabout cycle, we arrive at last. You'll come to your point in your bed, won't you? I'll go out of my way, to hear you make that long-delayed point."

"In a woman's bed, the *man* comes to a point. However, I'll *disappoint* your deception, Dick. I'll seek help elsewhere on my scientific invention or discovery I'd come to consult your assistance about. I won't be seduction-bribed, on that point. In point of preserving my chastity against your unwelcome intrusion, I hope my point is well taken, however disappointing to your lovelorn lust. I've made a point of pointing this out. My inclination-indicator points the other way, Dick, from your tricky point of 'escorting' me home. I appoint you out of my life. It's pointless to discuss this further. My puritanical integrity is intact. It points victoriously to you as my defeated assailant. We'll take separate cabs—you to your family, me to my home. Turn back, Dick, to Harry. I won't fulfill the name-change that involuntarily I caused in you. Administrate your hospital better next time. You abandoned your duties, you betrayed your public trust and would have that of your wife had I let you. *There's* a cab for *me*—I'll take it. *You* wait for the *next* one, and take that. I've stepped into the cab, and through its open window—Harry—I tell you how sorry I was not to have come to the point we'd made an appointment for. Other matters intervened. I meant impersonally to tell you of that invention or discovery I scientifically hit upon, and why I went to consult *you* about it. I'll seek assistance elsewhere. You weren't quite listening in the right spirit—objective impartiality, the quest for workable truth. My 'girlishness' got in the way. The Dick it made from Harry now reverts back to Harry. Personal interest muddled end you messed up with sloppy intrusiveness. My point remains untold till a better listener lets me come to it. Thanks for lunch yesterday, and your proposition or proposal. Did my little-girl docility excite you? But I'm stubborn, a free-lance genius. You might have midwifed the birth of a major work. Your job *is* to assist conception in issuing fruitfully forth."

Before the director of the maternity hospital could quickly reply, the red traffic light changed to green, and the Jane-bearing cab bolted off into . . .

No longer a city night. Into the morning rush hour. Office workers were on their way to work in a multitude of buildings. Each one knew *which* building, as the minimum competence requisite for anyone entitled to holding a job.

III

"Well, I'll try someone *else*," meditated Jane, slumping well back in the back of the cab. "My sexiness got in the way, with that one. To be sexy *and* a free-lance genius—what odd character companions are those two near-contradictory traits I hear embattled in the social striving of my private self. Work and love *can* be reconciled, in the full life. I'd like a man to marry. But not at fame's expense, or at my heart's compromise, or to prostitute my body and trifled affections for my career's fulfilled offspring of works that endure. Love and work, in juggled purity, each self-sustained from my same being. On them both, may equal blessings pour richly from fortune's fountain. Part passive, part active, I partially can control and regulate my fortune's generous flow. Helpless, I can also guide it. I'll take what charge I can, submitting to strange quirks of chance along the way.

"The way where? The made way, inside my granted future forged by my own efforts in the mingled course of chance luck along such unknown ways that as I sit here being driven, I can only slumber, and say, 'Not yet.' One day, I'll be somewhere else. I'll find it out then. Now, meanwhile, I'm closed in. Consciousness blurs. I sleep."

PART THREE

I

In new shapes, Jane's future rolled steadily in. A major new shape takes the form of Frank, the managing doctor director of, in a different part of the city, another large maternity hospital to help offspring meet their mothers at the incident of "giving birth" on the part of the mothers, "getting born" on the part of the ones whose embryonic service has been paid in growth to nature's miracle.

The phone in Frank's secretary's office, as it's built to do, rings. Frank's secretary, of course, answers it. She's paid a handsome wage to discharge such routine motions as picking the simple receiver up and into the mouthpiece giving formal tone to "'Yes?"

On the other end Jane's voice waited for the "Yes?" to end before explaining, "I'm Jane. Please make an appointment for me to meet Frank, the executive administrator of the hospital, whose secretary I presume to be speaking to, unless we're on a wrong connection, in which case I'll hang up and hope for a better extension on my next dialing attempt."

"No, Jane. Stay on. I know I'm Frank's secretary. So, now, do you."

"At a convenient opening in Frank's full schedule of busy-ness, please book an appointment in for me. That way, I can see and meet him. Is it your formal duty to ask me why?"

"Yes," Frank's secretary officially replied. That was Jane's cue. Here's her explanation:

"I'm a free-lance genius. I scientifically invented or discovered something. I'd like to consult Frank about it. He could help make the potential importance of what I've done actual."

"He has a free minute tomorrow morning at near ten o'clock. Arrive slightly before then, and I'll arrange to have you see him. I've duly noted down the appointment on the office calendar. Do you know the directions of our address?"

"Thank you," Jane assured Frank's secretary. "How should I dress?"

"Neatly. But be careful."

"Why?"

"Frank could sprout a lust for you. He's divorced and without a girl friend. To mix pleasure into 'business' is something I wouldn't be surprised to see him try."

"How can I heed the warning? By resisting?"

"Yes. But if you consent to be seduced, then that's your own adult choice. It would, of course, delight the director."

II

Frank was alerted by his secretary to the advent of his visitor. "Show her in," the hospital chief informed his experienced secretary who sprang up efficiently to carry out the order with bungling kept down to a minimum as she cleared the way to Jane's arrival in Frank's top executive hospital office.

"You're pretty!" gasped Frank, once that discreet secretary closed the silent door on Jane, standing but told to be seated by Frank who was already sitting.

"But there's only one chair. And you're in it," Jane pointed out.

"That's the whole point," Frank admitted. "If I'm in the chair, that's like the coiled springs on the bedstead framework. On top of that goes the mattress. On top of my lap, goes your nice behind."

Stubbornly, Jane remained standing. "Don't sidetrack me. I'm not here to feed your lust."

"You're a free-lance genius? What are your credentials?" Frank asked in frustration from his chair to the standing visitor he was attracted by but who sexually rejected him demoralizing to his proud code of instant masculinity.

III

"I've invented or discovered something which might prove to be important."

"That's *partly* informative, but not completely. What have you done? Why might it be important? In what position can I be to help? Those are essential things you must tell me."

"Frank, you're too demanding! First you want lust, using my body for the purpose. Upon my refusal, you then switch to another track: pumping information from me, as though I were a well and you dip in an empty bucket hoping to pull it back up full of water."

"What an old-fashioned country image you've just evoked! It has a bucolic ring, like a faded lithograph of some rustic setting, semi-pastoral, semi-homey. I just ooze with nostalgia for that forgotten corner of our dear old national history. It's so quaint! Ah, I'm in an antique mood. A country well! Dear Jane! I love you!"

"Intending matrimony?"

"Eventually we'll formalise it. Now, let's be casual. Remove your dress."

"Don't distract me from my point, for which we've agreed to this appointment."

"The point! I forgot what point you were going to make, before carnal interruption took imaginative hold on the mental lust I bear for you."

"In a little-girl way, do I entice you?"

"You needn't even ask. Of *course* you do!"

IV

"Overlook my being a woman. It's irrelevant to what I've come to consult you about."

"First, as a man, you insult me. Then, as a—what?—do you consult me?"

"As the head of this maternity hospital. You may be pertinent to what I discovered or else invented—maybe both. It's essential that you do what you can to help me."

"I will, if you marry me."

"But you're much older than me, even though I'm not quite young.

In addition, we shouldn't overlook the factor of your simply not 'appealing' to me. In a word, I'm not attracted to you, so I spurn your offer."

"I'm hurt, Jane."

"Despite my rejecting you, will you help me?"

"I'm not a saint. I'm only the chief head administrative executive of this large hospital to which pre-maternity patients in an advanced state of pregnancy are widely admitted in their full-bellied condition."

"You needn't be a saint in order to help me. Just be a generous human being. What I've done could benefit mankind, which is a goal we all must nobly have to pool our contributions to the common welfare to lift up our kind and improve their lot to alleviate what's not so good in the broad condition of humanity. Help me to help all of us. The opportunity for being a general benefactor is relatively infrequent, if not indeed really rather rare. Your opportunity is now. I bring it to you. Add your labor or advice to what I've done. I must give my work worldly application and market; confer the practical occasion empirically complete in concrete reality upon my theoretical concept that I've worked out so far to a brim and margin for the fertile overflow into humane general advantage. Favor this request, Frank. The greed of ambitious fame and career vanity may, in both our cases, take advancement from a great leap. But glorious ideals may be served, as well, in pure disinterestedness, to enhance the precious substance of human life conducive to a happier breed exalted nobly to finer prospects. Oh, I falsify by sentimentalizing or romanticising. I've inflamed my rhetoric to a grandiose inflation."

"Specifically, what are you driving at? Your point, Jane?"

"Are you pumping me again? I'm not a well, Frank!"

"I'm curious."

"You're nosy, too. You pick my brain to turn my work to your benefit and steal its secret."

"That's an unfair accusation. You requested an appointment with me, and it was granted. You've sought my assistance, approaching me for it. To be of any service to you, I must know facts."

"Yes, but *what* facts?"

"That's in *your* telling, Jane. Don't reject me professionally and intellectually, heaped on to the sexual disgrace you've already inflicted, having humiliated me at my masculine core. Did I agree to an interview to amass insults from you?"

"I've been standing while you've been sitting, Frank. Ask your secretary to drag another chair into this office. I crave comfort."

"I crave *you*, but you deny me that. In retribution, can't I deprive you in kind? You're so pretty, being obliged to stand so long and uncomfortably while I take my ease in a chair. Permit me this small sadistic indulgence, to mildly torture you somewhat for refusing sex with me. It's the modest form of revenge that I can take. Forgive the pun, but can't you 'stand' your punishment?"

"Frank, I won't stand either for your pun *or* my punishment. Relieve me of both. Afford me some ease. Get a chair in here for me."

"Let's compromise: Sit on my desk."

"But at its height, my knees might be in danger, dangling, of a flirtatious length of exposure to the thigh: which, fearing the lance of your lust, I'd take prudent, prudish care to avert, even at momentary relief's expense."

"Sadistically I say, then, Jane, sardonically I enjoin you, uneasily then to remain standing on legs stiffened to fatigue's knot."

"You villain! I'll seek help elsewhere. You're cruel."

"*Circumstantially* I'm cruel, by interaction with you. Normally, I'm a kind man."

"If you didn't lust for me to risk the rebuff I gave, would you have been kind, not cruel, to me?"

"Certainly. Inadvertently, you teased me, gave temptation without gratifying it. If I didn't find you sexy, I'd be kind, not cruel."

"Such is my misfortune—and yours. Now concentrate on our project."

"Project? What project?"

"The work I've done, and your bringing it into public light, applied market, actual worldly effect."

"First, Jane, *describe* your work. What did you do?"

V

Still, Jane stalled. Was she reluctant to "give away" her discovery or invention by divulging it, revealing it, to that very authority she chose to confide in as a condition for tapping him for, extracting from him, the critical advice, the practical guidance, she so essentially needed for putting her scientific breakthrough on a solid plane for effectual action to carry into practice her worked-out theory left dangling in only its proven conceptual stage?

They'd been in that office for so long! At least Frank had been sitting. Were her feet tired!

VI

The pain in her feet, in time, became rivalled by the pang of too much time having gone by in the absence of the act of eating. Jane frankly confided this recent pain to Frank:

"Ow! I'm hungry!"

"Me too. Despite my busy schedule: we've gainlessly been engaged in conversation since this morning at ten o'clock. The lunch hour has passed us by so fast, that we've fasted in it."

"I hold fast to my stubborn repulsion of your sexual advance. But I'd graciously yield to a kind offer of food."

"No. Stand fast in discomfort, steadfast in your fast, as you stand still there in hunger with no chair or food to relieve you."

"Torture is suitable punishment. For what?"

"For turning down the offer of my hand in the lust of marriage."

"Halt your sexual obsession. Between us, let's boost humanity's lot. I've yet to come to the point our appointment was made for. Shadows lengthen. My legs and my stomach acutely ache separately. The normal working hours for office employment have closed up shop for the day, giving labor leave to rest."

"Yes. I've wasted valuable time that I should have given over to my administrative duties—just on you, Jane, how can you compensate me?"

"Not by sexual means. I'll share my scientific secret with you."

"Finally! Isn't that what you came for? So that, by so imparting, you'd empower me to render substantial assistance in my specialised capacity and vast administrative authority. Avail yourself, then—though not exploitatively in abuse and violation of me—of the services I can render. I offer them, despite the insult to my sexual manhood you mercilessly tendered."

"What will *you* stand, then, to gain?"

"Shared fame in your workable secret. Glory, power, and the satisfaction of doing massive good for the world."

"Frank! I'm hungry! My feet hurt!"

"It's already late at night. While I've been sitting all this while in my office with the door closed, you've been all this time standing, since ten this morning. Your feet and stomach hurt you. Don't you also need to urinate?"

"Yes, Frank. I feel a terrific bladder pressure."

"Me too, as well as being starved. I share two of your discomforts—the need to eat and to urinate (the latter, of course, to be first in the sequence of those two reliefs). Your third discomfort—standing on your feet all day—I gloat to say that I don't share."

"I ask for mercy, Frank."

"Jane, I grant it. Let's change our states. We'll halt our talk, and take fundamental acts."

Frank was as good as his word, keeping all respects of his promise. Finally rising from his long-sat-in chair, he stood, walked over to the door, and opened it, signalling to Jane to follow him out of that all-day office prison.

The secretarial staff of the hospital has all gone home. Only nurses, doctors, midwives, remained, and patients, on other floors. Frank escorted Jane to an appropriate bathroom down the corridor which she entered in grateful haste. He entered another bathroom in similar haste. In separate privacy, each took the required relief.

They re-met in the corridor, took the elevator down, left the maternity hospital, went near-by to a restaurant celebrated for staying open late. (It was past midnight.) They chose a table near the window. Here was Jane's first opportunity to sit since the morning! What a load off her aching feet!

Frank had been sitting all day, so sitting was no great relief. But eating would be. And for her it would be. Oh joint hunger! Oh, the dear great need for food.

VII

God, did they eat! They ate without talking. They'd talked enough, already. They'd talk more later—to more co-operative purpose, it was hoped.

Food now. Stuff.

Wouldn't they ever stop?

Not yet. So vividly in the present is their tasted food by rapid forkfuls thrust.

VIII

They're full now! Good. Now to resume talk, to fuller purpose than before.

"We're closing," the waiter said. They had to go.

They stood in the street in the middle of the night. "I'm so tired, I'm sleepy," Jane admitted. "So also I am," joined Frank. This let their unison emit a gaping yawn, from two mouths so recently open to foodfuls of abundance and before then to talk's rambling discord.

"I'm divorced, there's only me in my apartment. Join me there," Frank slyly suggested.

"No sex, no intimacy," reproved Jane. "I'll to my home, you to yours, in chaste separation. Our talk will resume 'tomorrow.' To greater effect."

Sleepily driven apart, they'd made an appointment to meet the "next" morning—not in Frank's maternity hospital executive administrative office where Jane had felt imprisoned to an interminable standing sentence while her tormentor quite comfortably was sitting.

No; their appointment was to take place in Jane's laboratory. There, *she*'d have the territorial control. And she'd divulge her discovery or invention she'd scientifically come across in the active course of being a free-lance genius. To reveal that secret finally! To the right man.

Would Frank be trustworthy, in good faith, and not abuse the privilege, but liberally assist in a generous spirit the translation of theory concept into a world of practical good?

If he could, he would. Much depended on what Jane had discovered or invented. Would it hold up? Could it contribute?

First, separate sleeps. Dropped blackly into a dreamless fatigue.

PART FOUR

I

"I'm impressed, Jane, with your laboratory. What wrought your free-lance genius here among these instruments?"

"My discovery, Frank—or invention."

"Is your free-lance genius only scientific?"

"No. It's resulted in works of art, literature, musical composition, theater, and other cultural contributions, as well as critical essays, philosophy, psychological research, medicine—"

"Now we're getting to science. What is it, then, you consult me about? Withhold no longer that theory or concept you've fully worked out. If I'm to help you, then let me know your secret."

"You won't abuse it? You won't exploit little me? You'll take it in the best of faith?"

"In the critical spirit of open inquiry, skeptical; not on trust or faith."

"You won't bother me sexually?"

"I'll resist the yearning to. I accept your stern condition to relent on my lust for you; to concede your disinclination to requite my hot but lonely passion for you."

"Then the decks are cleared. So is my throat. I come—belatedly, following a detoured series of digressive obstacles—to my very point. Is your readiness for it ripe?"

"Its ripeness already gathers the rust of decay. Decay rounds off the interminable irregularity of our delay."

"Frank, shall I put it quite simply? But not so as to sacrifice its complexity?"

"Jane, precisely do that; or both."

"Has your listening turned its open ears on me?"

"To the degree that you'll be heard by my hearing if only you speak."

"I'll speak by made utterance. Now follows my communication. My open mouth, your open ears, mingle their open combinations in the admixture of transmission reception, in the organic mechanics of vocal oral audible . . ."

Was Jane breaking down? She needed calming. Frank must be gentle. Was she inspired, or just a lunatic? She doubled up troubled in silence, loudly coming to a screech. Frank would nurse her out of it. Did she *want* to hold back? Was her concept, finally, flawed? Was her theory loopholed? Was imperfection, if not failure, realized in internal turmoil? She wore a laboratory frock. Thirty-four and puritanical, she was so sexy! She seemed about to crumble. She had a girlish maidenliness that brought out Frank's protective strength, his despairing tenderness, his paternal forbearance.

Was she breaking down? Should he be gentle or firm? Coax her, bully her, baby her—what would work?

Had she been coming apart? Sweet, frail, and crazy? For all her "free-lance-genius" title assumed so blithely professed, so sweetly, endearingly proclaimed with exquisite mystery?

"I'll be hard," Frank decided. "I'll brook no nonsense from her. I'll take a hard stand—if necessary, seduce her, in her vulnerable plight. The control she's lost, *I'll* gain—over her. It's my chance."

II

"Convey your meaning. Where are the words?"

"I falter. In tongue-tied stagefright, I'm blocked off—stuck paralyzed in my congestion."

"Jane, my time is valuable, I'm busy, I'm neglecting my maternity hospital administrative duties with good will generously impatient to assess your message and help you work it out by interpretation to practical means. Do, Jane, get your point unstuck, and roll it off."

"I apologise. May I, then, speak?"

"I wait. Be free. Get uncluttered. Go."

III

Jane sought clarity. Her words finally untumbled themselves. In a flow, they found their audible shape.

"Here it is, Frank."

"Here *what* is? What's on your mind, Jane? Go ahead."

"You remember I referred to a discovery or invention? That's my subject matter. May I proceed?"

"I recall your alluding to an invention or discovery. Can you cover it—or them—in some detail? The impression remains vague. Can you impart a vivid picture? Do delineate with some clarity a fuller rendition of the precise point you wish to make."

"I'll honor your request—or is it a demand?"

"Either—or both."

"Frank . . ."

"To the point, Jane. No niceties of language nor forms of address, rhetorical courtesies, stylistic conventions, formalities of speech. Strike its heart!"

"*What* heart?"

"That point's."

"I'm in a metaphorical muddle. Heart?"

"No, point."

"Frank: I have something to say."

"Don't scruple on its delivery. Give telling utterance to what you say, on the tongued wings of your speech."

"Tongued wings? I'm lost, Frank."

"Be found, Jane. Be the verbal conduction of your own words."

"Is speech an act?"

"It's action-packed—an *inter*action. As a listener, I complete it. The cycle forms full, in my mental ear."

IV

Jane regained her fluency as abruptly as she'd lost it. Word by word, she piled up her temporal, linear content, and between pauses compiled an accumulating effect built on the crescendo of momentum in collective aggregate, the sweeping current flowing tidally across in swelling surge lifted and propelled.

"Clearly, Frank, the appropriate disease is needed to be found to fit the cure I've made."

"The cure without the disease? The cart before the horse? Effect going before cause? You've reversed logic, on the human frame?"

"This cure I've discovered—or invented—is tested and put to the proof. Only the disease is needed. That's all that stands between my historical contribution to human health and recovery, and the uselessness of my discovery in terms of its therapeutic inventiveness."

"What disease have you found a cure for? In what category of illness does it fall?' And how can I—director of a maternity hospital—at all help?"

"I don't know the nature of the illness for which my remedy was specifically devised or concocted. In your professional capacity as head chief of the hospital for women giving birth, you're uniquely situated for directly aiding my aborted project and easing finally its breakthrough into joyous workability. Your eyes mutely ask 'How?' All you must do is see that new children get born who bear in infancy the strains of the illness needed for which my remedy works. Can't you control the diseases babies bring into life? What sort of head administrator are you, if not? If you're an executive director, then execute, direct. I need a new breed of people who are plagued with what I can cure."

"Jane, you're sexy. If I do what you say . . ."

"Sorry no sex. I don't compromise."

V

"But Jane, can't we marry?"

"I don't fancy you. You're too old. I won't open my legs even as a favor to you. Have a pure motive: help humanity. Be a co-benefactor, with me, of the human race. In disinterested purity, not to grovel a sexual benefit from my helpless girlishness which teases you to distraction and corrupts you with enticement."

"Jane, I withdraw from our collaborative venture. Its difficulty simply saps my will. Even sex with you couldn't eradicate that difficulty. Your fame, reputation, and career will have to suffer by the curse of insufficiency, incompleteness, failure, flaw, imperfection, and ultimate futility. Be a free-lance genius by other means than by trying to get a maternity hospital head to induce a new disease strain—or stain—in human genetic evolution. Let the cure you've discovered or invented be wasted and slip down the drain. Let years of work empty themselves of further hope. You're more sexy than realistic. It's already late in the day. Our talk gathers no purpose. I'll return to my hospital to administrate it. I wanted to be your husband or lover. You inspire sex, but are not inspired by it. You were inspired by a theory or concept—which I won't even *try* to market. I pronounce that less than no value adheres to your discovery or invention, which is condemned not to take workable effect in the open world outside."

Having delivered himself of that, Frank made ready to leave. Alarmed, Jane stalled him. "I'd wanted to become 'Joy,' my name upon success in the glory of my career that wins fame. My old name used to be Janet. I became Jane, waiting to cap or crown my mighty free-lance-genius efforts by contributing to humanity's welfare on a scale of selfless heroism, taking on 'Joy' for a celebrated new name upon the successful completion of my heart's ideal work on behalf extensively of all my fellow beings. This ambition takes on a flat ring now that I've sounded you out and consulted you on your expert authority of being a social leader linked solidly to sober scientific endeavor. Frankly, you've discouraged me."

"Instead of advancing to 'Joy' for a name, return to 'Janet.' You'll approach middle-age, in little-girl sexiness. Will some man get pleasure from you?"

"I'll tighten up carnally, and be closed off. My sexual rejection of you is vindicated; even had I prostituted myself, you'd have been unable to help me."

"The whole point you worked so hard for was simply helpless from the start. Give men pleasure with your body."

"That's common. I aimed higher."

"The higher aim failed. The lower has at least possibilities. Pursue them."

"Can there ever accidentally by random chance be started the disease strain or epidemic plague contagion that would make the cure I've discovered or invented valuable and useful?"

"Perhaps. Wait and see. Finally I take goodbye and go from your laboratory back to my hospital office to supervise over women giving birth."

"But it's night. Your office is closed by now. It got late while we spoke."

"It *is* late. May I stay the night here?"

"No, you sly beast."

<h2 style="text-align:center">VI</h2>

They'd both been sitting, all that time. Frank hadn't been made to stand by Jane as a tactic of retaliation in reprisal for his mild bout of sadism in his office.

Jane escorted Frank out of the laboratory into an outdoor night of stars and the shiver of a little moon. Frank again felt drawn in romantic gallantry to his girlishly-retarded-seeming little bundle of withdrawn misguidedness so clinging and dependent, yet so brazenly self-sufficient in assuming a glorified destiny. "Before I find a taxi-cab, may I, in departing, for all my troubles, have at least a kiss?"

"Have I put you out?"

"I went out of my way, and out of my head. It was all one great big abortion."

This stunned Jane. She broke out weeping.

It brought out the beast in Frank, after all that went before. Under cover of the night, he took her trembling, sobbing, shaking shape in too paternal an embrace to be exclusively sexual.

She broke loose from his hold. In frantic resignation, and a toss of dismay, he panted. Purely sexual, the panting was in too early a stage to even approach the confines of climactic release. He felt unfairly teased. He was annoyed: angry. He could hurt her.

For *her* part, she gave in to misery. She'd never felt so sad. This sadness was the lowest low she'd ever been—or so it seemed.

"I'm romanticising how bad I feel," she told Frank.

"And I romanticize *you*—quite foolishly so. May I hurt you?"

"How?"

"Knock you down."

"How undignified! You're being a child. There's your taxi cab."

He waved from the open window—an unfriendly defiant gesture. The cab merged its blackness with the night's, the motor hum went out of sight, and Jane stood—alone.

"At this point, things are barren, bleak, and pointless in my whole life. 'Jane' hasn't turned out. 'Janet' is far behind. What's next? I'll assume 'Joy' for a name. That's only a nominal change. I require a substantial change. This life I have—I need a new phase, a whole metamorphosis. I want to make, build, do, create, find, discover, invent, form, shape, take effect. The world sleeps. I want to wake it. But it *is* awake. I want to shake it.

"But action is limited. How *talented* am I? Were I ever insanely gifted, what is there to do, to carry off, to put on, work out, to effect, to cause—that *counts?*

"I'll abandon *that* discovery or invention. What shall I devote myself to? Not some general cause or movement, some belief based on popular conformity, some dull outside doctrine.

"I want something dynamic—ripping with vitality. I'll start work on it. With all my brains and heart, I'll give it every ounce of my genius, in total dedication.

"But I'm not clear what it is I'm going about. It's too new as yet to define. It's so new, it's not even born.

"I'll give it birth. It's an ill-shaped monster embryonic to my concept, a mere fetus-theory. But I'll carry it through. It'll evolve.

"Dawn has arrived. I'll return indoors. Rather than go to my apartment to sleep, at a distance, I'll stay at the laboratory and lie down. I'll lock myself in. Alone. To dream, to hatch, to plot. To seize on to a work: one looking for its own definitions, to find the nativity appropriate to its novelty.

"I'll explore realms only of the new. To fasten definitely on a point, and drive home a new truth."

Newly self-named 'Joy,' lonely but no longer sad, she locked herself into her laboratory and lay down on the cot that was there. Day increasingly filled the window. Soon, it was almost next night. She was too much thinking, for sleep. The thoughts went through their flux and flow, shapelessly shorn of any concrete.

Then it was next night already. She'd gotten up several times, and returned to the cot. Hunger pains grew worse. The refrigerator was empty of food—it contained some scientific stuff that had to be preserved by cold.

"I need help. What can I do alone?" She was sitting on her cot. Her career faltered at loose ends. She was at a loss. A vacancy stared—*from* her, or *at* her? The outside world was the border where she ended. Her inside world was the border where the world stopped—or overflowed to begin?

Which was in, which was out? Oh, life is fading fast, youth is far behind, nights and days succeed in swift succession all the previous weeks that get swallowed up by their months that are devoured by their years that slide back into the old birth by which she first came here?

Is "here" a "where"? It's more "when," it's all the "when's." From whence? To whence? And in between, a dizzy blur.

She'd impose order, clarity. Via some work. To work in verb form, active, to make work in its noun form, final. To tear an absolute from all the relatives. To make something at rest.

VII

So searched her soul for itself and her identity. Which was she, or how? Here was a moving "now." She'll arrest something, wrest it, from all the restlessness that bounds about.

She'll ply her craft, her trade, her vocation, to follow the calling that summons her.

Yes, but what is she cut out for? Her freedom is too loose. It needs a lance, to penetrate . . .

To be free-lance? To carve out what?

VIII

Being a genius has its burdens, drawbacks, strifes. There's lighter traveling in mediocrity.

Is she truly mediocre? How dashing to pride, after genius assumptions. She'll investigate those two states, at their blending place.

IX

How excellent love would be! Her rich parents pester her to be married. She's resisted.

She'll be married, *and* do her work! Both!

Yes, but do *what* work? And to *whom* married?

She'll marry a man not yet met, when the love and sex are felt.

She'll do work that she decisively feels right for. It's not done yet, it's unknown. It's in that peculiar, intangible place, "the future," this impalpable work she's yet to do, this husband sexually active with her. They're "off," in the *somewhens* for which her life hangers its incompleteness in desire, want, need, lack, apprehension, hope, expectation, fear, the emotions referring to the new unseen, unheard, unsensed, unfelt, not yet lived through.

X

"Well, I'm still here. The world and I. Elastically I go between passive and active, accepting and trying to assert.

"I'm still here. In my laboratory. I'll leave it, go to my apartment, I need to eat. I'll eat. That much done, we'll see what follows.

"*We*'ll see? But who's the '*we*'?' There's *me* for one. And who's the other?"

Unanswerable. She let go of that problem. She went out to eat, it was daytime. She was looked at by men. What could she do?

XI

"I don't like 'Joy' for a name. I can't live up to it."

She needs a whole new change. The world rejects her old forms. "What would be suitable to current situations to which circumstances may confine her and so set off her condition to new definitions?

"There's work to do. I have loads of money, in unrestricted freedom.

"Men scare me. Work evades me. I need to settle on something. I'm at acute unrest. This readies me. Goodbye for now's me. If I can lay my hands on her, I'll take on my next me.

"She bears too much resemblance to the me I knew; I'm one lump my whole life through, all compact on itself; with tiny, exaggerated variations that are the phases and stages my motion touches on.

"Is life more than me? Not *my* life. It's quite closed in. Drenched, in the world."

To End Unhappiness Forever, in All People:
A Notable Goal, and Its Two Aspitants

I

Laura, a physician of the feelings, told her professional colleague Matty (another physician of the feelings with a different set of customers, clients, or patients) that seriously her humanitarian aim of her studies and working experiences in their field of therapy was to develop a practical theory eventually leading (if not during her own career, then in that of her leading disciples) to, if at all possible, the elimination of unhappiness somehow from all actual people still young enough or sufficiently as yet unborn to benefit from her findings which would provide a radical sweeping transformation of human nature altogether.

Those two physicians of the feelings were having a secret, private, low-keyed, unofficial exploratory conference of sorts, hoping to break ground and to agree on the terms of a collaboration on a dual project of ridding humankind of sorrow, suffering, and woe, lifting the race from bane to boon in changing the essential face of its total feelings for the good, a globally pervading breakthrough with electrifying colossal boost to the whole tone of existence altogether in the human form of our species, a major departure from the traditional sadness that has clouded our history with miserable internal conditions.

However low-keyed, theirs was a high-level summit conference on the top floor (observation deck, closed in by glass windows from exposure to winds, atmospheric currents, weather, and even the local climate) of a vertically towering skyscraper that soared heavenward from the rocky deposit of its city base. At the top of the tallest building, the two physicians of the feelings were literally lifted high above the awful travail of the plentifully saddened general populace that crept their unhappy lives along on the grim rounds of their low grounds, grounded grindingly to an underlying base of moody gloom at the emotional bottom of heartbreakingly just about everything, the blight and plight of the luckless.

Laura and Matty would, if they could, change all that, drastically for the better. They put their heads together. Modestly unknown to history, this conference might one day prove historical, if the earth-shaking results they hope for succeed in uprooting the whole tenor and frame of human existence as dishearteningly realised to date.

In their private, unprofessional lives, these two physicians of the feelings were separately married, with families, apart from each other. Their affinity for each other was strictly businesslike: each respected the other's views about psychology, motivation, behavior, and the ideal of "controlling" emotion instead of letting it fall where it may in the random course of haphazard lives and interactions, the events of chance that shapelessly befall everyone's social, love, family, business life in subjective related apartness to, free, the partially patterned flux of repetitions, variations, and surprising novelties in the strange realm of external occurrences as subjected to evaluation, analysis, interpretation by objective methods to serve the scientific or therapeutic objectives that try to treat of, deal with, all emotions, painful or pleasant, constantly undergone as the prize and penalty of being alive by each person feeling his way along the process of his own living by way of the yardstick of how he's feeling according to what happened and what he wants in what he finds himself doing in the life he happens actively to be leading by the accident of being himself of all the people to be, having solitary rights to that exclusive but dubious privilege and retaining himself for an identity as a stable constancy through his lifetime, whatever the changes that occur to make each moment somehow fresh and special in the crest of altered phases and new stages emerging within the consistency of his remaining the same person throughout by character or at least by nametag or by it all happening within just one life however varied free time to time to create radical aspects or outlooks dawning unprecedented on currents of constant discovery.

II

On behalf of all other people; acting independently of any organized body, official group, professional committee, or foundation grant, but strictly on their own initiative in the spirit and enterprise of private inquiry, research, striving, experimental work, partnership efforts to discover a framework or foundation for individual controlling of, instead of victimization by, one's own feelings; Laura and Matty met to discuss such elementary mysterious matters at the top skyscraper floor observation tower (glassed in) of the tallest modern building ever measured in the vertical world of space. At that level they concerned themselves as therapeutic professionals with dense undifferentiated hordes evolved by evolutionary "selection" peculiar uniquely to the miraculous dangerous fertility of the star-struck earth.

Sitting physically on a pinnacle above the city geographically (a topographically mountainous peak would be the natural parallel), would they cap and crown to a pinnacle height of record loftiness their aspirations as benefactors of the crawling, teeming mass of fellow beings below and offspring spawned therefrom by a future lateral generational multiplying of a greater rate of people peeked by swifter time in spatially shrinking packets at an increasingly crowded pace in a pastiche of thick layers around the globe's swarming surface?

Aside obviously from gender, how did the partners, who would strenuously collaborate on their extraordinary, humane goal, differ pertaining to their aptitudes and work dispositions, their capacities and attitudes, respective of each other and absolutely of themselves in taking on together this titanic task?

Laura had the more progressive notions of the two, a bolder optimistic audacity to defy normal average laws by outsmarting dismal "reality" with achievements so outstandingly positive that happy feelings would replace unhappy ones on a wholesale, sweeping scope in a tremendous lifting of so-called human souls from their extensive sorrow, their broad common woe, along the world's aching belt.

Matty was more cool-headed and moderate. But Laura's enthusiastic zeal happily infected him. He'd be her loyal comrade and ally in their joint undertaking, though he accepted designation for the "follower" role, respectful of her inspired leadership. Nominally equal, he realized, unresentfully, Laura's natural superiority for purposes of the goal they were dedicated to: eliminating unhappiness and allied terms in attendance like suffering, trouble, misery, anxiety, grief, anguish, discomfort, despair, depression, disappointment, dissatisfaction, displeasure, unpleasantness, irritation, morbidity, pain, worry, agony, disturbance, and such kindred words loaded with emotional meaning under the mathematical measurement of "negative."

"Laura, the 'negative' can't altogether be negated, nor the 'positive' posited by affirmative accentuation, as though we were giving a promotional 'pep talk' like a campaign of advertising publicity on behalf of a client whose 'line of goods' we want 'to get over' in market fanfare as public relations agents representing some vested commercial interest however philanthropically glossed into the glorified rationalization as somehow a disinterested 'service.'"

"Our scientific truth-search will purely be untainted by cheapening applications, Matty. Still, our discoveries will be practical, not academic, to take effect in feeling and action and of course in consciousness."

"Laura, what's our program? How can we collate case histories into a workable discovery that covers cases in general and can be carried out by even people who aren't our 'patients'—the general populace down to each particular individual?"

"A concretely inspired generalizing to penetrate the hearts of people's heads must carry us special seekers to the source and derivation of behavior, the emotions, consciousness, to shower our study with insight for redirecting and controlling of what so far just 'happens' to people."

"Laura, we're talking in circles, to endlessly redefine our goals without advancing a step to tackle the problem itself. So far, attempts to improve the happiness of people have been by way of changing economic conditions to provide people with better financial opportunities to get more money by more agreeable means and to acquire more time for enlightened ways of spending that money with consequences popularly termed happy."

"To change the outside world to change the inside world. Communism, socialism, utopia, labor unions, slum reform, low-rent housing projects, welfare, cheap medicine and medical treatment, guaranteed income, state liberalism, philanthropy, utilisation of the sun's energy, harnessing of atomic energy for peaceful domestic labor-saving functions, saving the world's natural resources from being drained and depleted, new agricultural methods for condensed foods and soil conservation, greater highway efficiency: these external improvements have been designed to make people happier. You and I, Matty, struggle from quite other angles to reduce sorrow, misery, woe, and the rest of that dark, foreboding catalogue. Let's survey progress of results, if any, thus far, to date."

"None, I regretfully must report, in all unhappy honesty, Laura."

"We've got to step up our rate. Let's get rolling."

"How, however? How?"

"Precisely, Matty. You've hit on our problem. We know *what* we want to do. The solution lies in lighting on just the right 'how' that'll turn the trick."

"That's your *job*, Laura. You lead."

"But how will you follow?"

"By what you lead."

"Oh, circuitous! *How* will I lead?"

"By what you're guided by. Initiative, inspiration; will you resort to *divine* guidance, Laura?"

"No. Happiness is an earthly matter. I'll deal in those terms: the now, the here, that environs us fast and fatal stuck to circumstance, bound by predicament, hemmed conditionally in to situationality and all its strictures. We rest uneasy on the contingency drift. We wrest solution from the furrows and fissures of those problems gnarled rootlessly in earth like teeth that lodge too loosely in the pulp and infirmity of sinking gums. Do I take courage from this? Or despair?"

"Alternately, in your quest. *My* quest too, Laura. Ours. But you lead."

"Lead? How?"

"Happiness in, sorrow out. That's our pursuit. But lead."

"By what base of how?"

"Are you failing us? You lead."

"I'm unhappy—I fear failure."

"Experimenting on yourself? Good. That's a start."

"I'm forlorn. The start could get stuck. A snag could be hit. We'd be stalled."

"That's a key, Laura: you lack optimism—on which happiness depends."

"But happiness can return, once optimism is finally abandoned and fully renounced. We reach a stage of being resigned: on those new grounds, a patched happiness may reform. *Other* hopes and desires crop up, to set up new conditions for subsequent happiness."

"Laura, we're being interrupted."

"What by?"

"A waiter is bending down over our table."

"I was caught in thought. Now I see him."

III

The waiter recalled them to "reality," so-called. "A mechanical accident happened unfortunately," he informed Laura and Matty, who were still sitting around their round discussion table with cups and saucers, spoons, knives, forks, napkins, glasses, table-cloth, sugar bowl, salt and pepper shakers, even a narrow vase of flowers, on it.

All over the whole top floor of that highest recorded of all vertical buildings from the standpoint of how tall it was, the room was surrounded by curving see-through continuous windowing affording so panoramic a view from all sides that the sloping contours of the earth itself, drifting in a mist of near-by outer space; would theoretically be visible to superb long-range vision by somebody gifted with eyesight at-tuned superlatively to aeons of immeasurable distance, assuming clarity of range and no weather obstructions such as glowering clouds, pale fog, dim haze, a light drizzle, and other confluences of the elements in the chemistry of physical matter along the stratosphere-topped atmosphere in which living things draw breath, expel breath, with lungs organically internal to the set-ups of their various systems.

That top floor had lots of other round tables, all alike to the point of being identical, which surpassed the state of being similar, in the mere measure of partial resemblances by the modest scale of comparison.

But the only one of all these tables currently in actual use was the one at which have been for quite a while now seated those physicians of the feelings, Laura the leader, Matty her follower, deep in a ways-and-means committee meeting or high-level conference on how to eradicate unhappiness from the emotionally laden human "breast."

A waiter had bent down to interrupt them, cordially gravely demeanored in his professional serving apparel and bland, impersonal manner.

"*What* mechanical accident?" his patron Matty inquired.

"Well, sir," continued the waiter, somewhat surly but impeccably correct by each external creak of his waist or fold in his crackling uniform signifying what a first-class establishment he was employed by at the observation deck dining room high above the tiny speck of earth below.

Judicially, the waiter paused, to build up the suspense for a telling effect upon his captive audience of two serious "types" at the table.

The pause durationally churned up too much silence in overprolonging the critical moment for speech ripely rusting past the right delay of its bursting out.

Time caught Laura and Matty looking up at the waiter, with expectancy and apprehension, from their sittingness to his stooped standing bendingness.

Time stopped at this tableau. Arrested to this fixed moment.

When will motion resume? When will speech get going again,

from the waiter on his cue?

Time is stuck. There's been a mechanical failure. The universal happiness project of the physicians of the feelings is bogged down in time's continual delay.

It's happened at the top of the highest building, and pyramids down to the level lowness of everything at the flat final base of the world, whose reputation, however, remains round, as a self-contained sphere swirling in swift space.

IV

After such a seemingly endless pause, the scene turned "normal" again. The waiter found the speech he lost, and took up the thread at once, which inexplicably he'd left dangling almost to tatters.

"We're trapped up here," he explained. "The elevators aren't working. There was a cable failure, caused by a motor failure, or power failure, or an energy stoppage. Till all is repaired, prepare to spend the night here. To wile the tedious time away, you can count stars that glow so close to our top observation tower where we are, at the height of the tallest building. If you go hungry I'll bring you more food, for it would go stale anyway if uneaten since refrigeration is an added victim to the over-all electrical compound stoppage at energy's mechanical source."

"What about the emergency staircase exit?" inquired Matty.

"Unusable," the waiter flatly declared, on a note of negative decisiveness.

Laura angrily protested: "Waiter, our predicament is outrageous. Where's the management I can complain to?"

"Safely outside this darkened building," the waiter blandly reported.

"Can't you pull an emergency switch?" Matty urged, in his restless pre-panic state.

"There's none up here," sadly answered the waiter, leaving his "guests" quite in the dark as to what they next would do, or even *could* do; as escape momentarily seemed barred from the fatalism of their lives caught up there, trapped helpless beyond the peaceful control of any intervention, at least momentarily.

But how long would "momentarily" last? That was, of course, another matter to be decided only in and by *time*—that ever-present element in the life of everybody human, no matter who.

"No doubt," the suave waiter pursued, "you've appointments to keep. Well, phones up here are out of order too, so you won't even be able to break your appointments to allay the worry and anxiety of whoever each of you is expected by, in your private social and professional lives and family lives if you're both married—are you?"

"Yes," assured Matty. "She" (nodding toward Laura) "has a husband and children, while, on my part, I have a wife and children. And *you*, waiter? Are *you* a family man?"

"As you are, sir; also with a wife and children."

"Waiter, are we in serious danger?" Matty went on to ask.

"I hope not, but I don't know," the waiter factually shot back.

Outside, the day got dark and changed to night. Inside, there was no artificial electric light in the observation deck tower where they were.

The rest of the building was dark, too, all the way down, with an internal power failure to keep compensation away for the natural sun giving way to night in the primitive great outdoors of a vast cosmic sky.

V

There was no moon to see by. Laura, Matty, and the waiter were all hungry. "Let's not waste the food—it'll rot," the latter warned, "due to the refrigerator joining in the over-all power failure. I'll bring the food, and we'll eat it all up."

He did and they did—all three. A crisis had joined them as democratic equals. In time of danger, snob rank class sometimes loses hold; people close ranks, in universal fastness, bound to their cohesive brotherness, having a common adversary.

From below shone the city's normal electric current in all the city's buildings save the one in which they were stranded so far up that it was at the top of it where they were, peering down. Light also came from above them, the stars. The moonlessness of the sky period was tolerable in their trapped night with no civilized freedom in the will of their motion. The sky was on a moonless cycle, just then, as an accidental coinciding with their being caught high indoors with no internal artificial illumination.

At their round table of the many in the observation room suite tower top deck, they gorged on the food that would have gone to waste had they not been so gorging on it so as at least to control its current intake where it could do some good.

They'll sleep on the floor, all three discreetly apart. They'll hope that the currents will be on by the morning. Mechanics and electronic technicians will surely repair the power failure in such a technological universe they currently found themselves in but locally with such a flaw, that on the floor they took their several rests, which they'd never expected to do when earlier that day Laura and Matty had ascended on the working elevator for their high-level, low-keyed conference and they'd outstayed the other patrons of the dining and snack room; and the waiter who served them was the only serving person to be remaining and so was trapped too with them in the unity of being three human victims all to the same godlike electric failure by minor or major misfortune.

VI

Crews of technicians were working through the night on the building basement dynamo transformer to mend what went wrong and restore rightful light and elevator service and phone use to the benighted structure of soaring verticality at a record height in a city of mighty artifice in hurling upwards its steep solid modern forest.

In the same clothes they wore while talking before, Laura, Matty, and the waiter (now their equal) slept on the hard floor, with heaving breath coming from recently bulging stomachs.

Meanwhile, the night was wearing on toward the next morning, as regularly occurs no matter where people are or what their circumstances, whether irregular like this one or by ordinary degree.

Next morning they were released. Happy day!

So much for *that* suspense. But what about ridding mankind of sorrow, woe, suffering, misery, and suchlike unpleasant emotions? Matty expected Laura to lead, to find a way of ousting unhappiness from what people are able to feel. Laura, though searching for inspiration, can't find any; and so the problem goes unsolved.

Were they arrogant to take the problem upon themselves; excessive pride presuming to scratch toward a scarce solution? They're back on level ground now, to take renewed bearings. They'd bade the waiter goodbye; thanked him for sharing their "ordeal"— a sharing which on his part had been every bit as involuntary as on their parts, upon the chance accidentality of a reliable environment perilously lapsing from the certitude of smooth function.

Well, the security is restored, on the outside level. Now internal tension takes over. The pressure of an unrealizable goal. The stress of vain forward strain again.

VII

What now? The two physicians of the feelings, free from being helplessly high up by mechanical building failure, were decidedly *un*free in fretting and floundering on the uncertain hooks of their self-imposed aspiration to free humanity from its low-flying, encircling clouds of sadness gradation.

They'd undertaken, perhaps, too stiff a task? This skeptical doubt held uppermost fore in Matty's less idealistic head of the two.

Laura bore the main responsibility brunt. Her failure loomed the greater for how high her humane hopes had outrageously risen at her stubborn onset.

She resolved, though, not to give up; forthwith informed Matty of her decision. They'd need to review their seemingly hopeless project from quite another angle, to get a fresh grip on it . . . though their grip on it before had been ever loose, tenuous—in fact, had not been a grip. They had no-where to go *from*, as well as *to*. This put them in a tight bind. They had nothing solid to struggle against, no ground to build on, having taken no previous steps of definite import from which to measure any further gain along the arduous road they'd jointly and foolheartedly undertaken in bold surmise of eventually, somehow, a miraculous triumph to crown an overcoming of heroic odds.

Intention as against results! They simply don't balance, by reckoning on any sober scale. The tally measures only naught, at latest estimate.

This unpromising non-beginning foretold an ultimate defeat in the making; a defeat already long underway, undermining the efforts they don't know how to make, at vague directionless purpose. The only progress being made was that of futility, which joined forces with failure to cut Laura and Matty off at the starting junction where premise clutches to hope in a vain enterprise.

Still, they were undaunted. Ahead!

What an imposing happiness condition on *themselves* they'd erected! But the sheer hopelessness took away desperate despair, to insure them against terrible sadness when inevitable failure overtakes their stern resolve, to dim their doomed strife in calm, resigned tranquility, the serene acceptance of the impossible not—despite desire—occurring.

VIII

"Happiness depends on desire—and so does sadness," Laura ventured in tentative firmness in the professional office of Matty after his last client or patient had been given appointed treatment or therapy for that day's list of sessions.

Matty reflected on what Laura's words meant, in due deliberate consideration of how much truth had been contained in them, as opposed to how much not-so-much-truth was packed falsely in, too loose, too tight, to what those words meaningfully could convey, in the verbal vessel of the sequence, the content-loading by the frame or manner that bears what matter it bares to the mind being communicated with.

"I think so too," Matty agreed, to his superior colleague in their joint undertaking to wipe out, quite eradicate, those feared feelings we hunch together under that dreary, dread, too-common terse "unhappiness."

"Our harmony is too mild and tame to help us make progress; we need more of a dialectic, or constructive dialogue, from opposed polar camps, to grind out truth between us from a clinch of strife, a struggle of discord," Laura decided.

"You're right!" again agreed Matty. This illustrated her point. Talk, talk, but no result. Slow or fast, "nowhere" seemed their only likely destination. This hurdle, or obstacle, impeded their progress. The obstruction amounted to a roadblock, of sorts. Faced with such an insurmountable barrier, what could Laura at all, indeed, do? Matty was stifled to follow by her want of direction. The impasse might quite undo their joint project, by proving it unworkable. They had virtually lost heart, already, thanks to a suffocating discouragement on the field of proven results. Further resistance would yield further despair. Only a miracle would suffice to save them. But who can plan a miracle? It can only happen by the purest accident, on a remote feather kicked up by the dust of stormy chance.

"Let's wait for the miracle," Laura suggested.

"It might never arrive," Matty warned.

Silence followed. The two physicians of the feelings watched, heard, followed the silence—as though it wasn't their own, their own responsibility.

The silence piled up time, in neat packages, in quiet bundles, in chunks of space.

While the silence grew, and time swallowed it with no ill effect, the goal of rubbing out sadness fell back from hopeful desire to idle wish or dreamy ideal. Unhappiness remained, in plentiful supply. More than enough to go around. But it alternated with happy periods. In the end, the feelings somehow "balanced out"—in many cases. Lives had to be lived; work done, and play. Laura wished to contribute something new and major, but didn't. Matty joined in her failure. Failure? No. Not enough work had been put into it, to call it failure.

They just never got rolling. It never got off the ground. There were no steps taken. There'd been a high-level conference, a low-level one, and it all leveled out. Precisely nothing happened—for the troubles they'd taken or hadn't. "Nothing" let everything else be. "Nothing" was non-interfering. It stepped aside. It watched.

THREE TALES FROM
LOVES UNNUMBERED
ENDLESS INFINITY

Bill Cole's Soul's Sole True Pure Love

*(Don Juan Takes a Cure in Heaven for his Well-Worn
Jaded World of Women: an Extravagant Romance)*

Notes:
1. *Boss's*, in the possessive case, is spelled *Boss'es* with deliberate intention to give it a solid two-vowelled, two-syllabled sound.
2. Some words, like *love*, *soul*, and *boss*, are capitalized in some places and not in others, due to different context in different places.

CHAPTER 1

I

Squirming under Bill Cole happened hardly to be the lot of only one woman. The most diversified breeds of women, a widely varied bouquet of types, claimed common sisterhood in thralldom to Bill Cole's strokes, which fixed them all exquisitely, but at different times, to the loving plunder of his lust.

"It's my sole unique privilege," claimed Alice, "to be his special girlfriend." But it wasn't. Janet was similarly deluded. "Bill Cole and I," she hinted broadly at a gossip feast, "make one continual pair." Maliciously, she was asked why, in that case, Bill Cole wasn't there with her, at that moment. Her silence was telling, and confirmed the point of her debunker with suddenly a private sob so publicly put to observation.

Those two examples were infinitely multiplied. Each of Bill Cole's innumerable women concocted the hopeless fantasy of being his one and only love. Reality brought such plentifully opposite evidence in refutation of that pathetically doomed romantic hope.

Woman swarmed around him persistently, at all the literary "do"s, society gatherings, cultural affairs, and commercially inspired parties of roughly professional polish. His tall figure could be seen emerging centrally erect at the top of a swaying incline of surrounding devoteries, like a tree trunk that finally goes vertically parallel to its own true sides after thinly divesting itself of, at bottom, a broadly spreading base of elaborately entwined roots. What was his magnetism, that earned the envy of his gender's less fortunate colleagues? He was direct to the women, but so were some of his rivals. He was subtle with the women, but so were many of his rivals. He was delicately handsome and immaculately groomed, with a bright amplitude of verbal gifts that sealed his reputation as an occasional wit; and only a few rivals could emulate such a formidable assortment of women-conquering traits; but other ingredients went into the compounding of that total assembled combination known under the personality of Bill Cole, a recognized identity lethal to many a fluttering woman.

II

The Bill Coleness of him constituted the instituted essence of himself, with the most indisputable authenticity of personal self-belonging. No one else had such a claim. Being Bill Cole was the ticket that opened the private key and lock to the admitted holy home of women's heavenly intimate holes.

Of course, those "holes" were all well furnished with surrounding flesh; otherwise, there would be a failure of enticement.

Stiffly, Bill Cole would go to work in there. That would be the perfect end to many a successful social evening.

III

As a glorified womanizer, a swain and rake of flagrantly irreproachable repute, a notorious Lothario so debonairly philandering, the cosmopolitan Don Juan local to the lively social set of a dangerously swollen metropolis all puffed out with cancerous tissue and fungus ferment of brimming revolution to radically explode such a decadent age—Bill Cole was Don Giovanni himself, nobly stepped out of old Spain and given a current New York setting for amorous escapades equally celebrated, for the lordly magnificence of discreetly publicized eminence in the high, dashing romance of eroticism elaborately conspicuous yet subtly toned down to adroit underplay.

Don Giovanni had his Mozart to musicalize the firmament to the monumentality of a Myth. His legend is revived with each performance of that opera, to a soaringly sonorous perpetuation more seductive of Immortality than any other work. Immortality has granted her divine favors to Mozart's celestial masterpiece with its darkly secular underside, the ascendancy of all the earthly carnal into the semblance of vast Paradise itself, the towering Dome and pinnacle spire to which all souls must bodily aspire.

Who, however, is Bill Cole's Mozart?—will he step forward, please, and reveal himself? Let's cap Bill Cole's lecherous career with lyrically lascivious music that tunes all planets in one melodious orb so dear and near to the loftiest sphere. Have no fear. Bill Cole's Mozart will, presently, appear.

IV

Margaret is luscious. She meets Bill Cole at a party and is promptly reduced to fawning flirtatiousness. He accepts. They leave the party and take a cab to Bill Cole's apartment approximately a city mile away. Without much prelude, Margaret strips down slowly, arousing him to the pitch of a raging bull, a rearing stallion, grown enormously potent. Then, he simply overwhelms her. She gasps down "dead," in the very bed.

Such an encounter, with its typical consummation, is an ideal rarity for most men. For Bill Cole, it happens to be a regularly frequent commonplace, a normal occurrence that he takes casually in stride. Margaret loves him, but so do many other women. Bill Cole submits modestly to his natural supremacy. He's simply superior, and that's all there is to it. His superiority goes without saying. He's the master. Women recognize this, instantly, and treat him as such. Courteously, he expects thus to be treated. That's the position life has placed him in. It's his, by divine right.

Linda wishes to reform him. He's just darting and bouncing around among women, like a headless amoeba in the random of endless colliding motion at odd electron angles like a pool ball out of control using four sides variously of the same billiard table forever. She would cure him of his perpetual amorous restlessness by affording him a settling-down nest—on the soft permanence of her own bosom. She's offering him this opportunity for his own good: stability, consistency, security. Politely, he declines. With gallant gratitude. He treats her like all the rest: one among many. His all-encompassing erotic democracy is glad to accommodate her, to make room for her. Not as a special concession, and with no fancy privilege denied his other women. Linda is pretty, so she meets his requirements. An aristocracy of pretty women is what his democracy really melts down to. Why deprive himself of his autocratic, exacting standards? He's a connoisseur of refined taste, and his taste covers the gamut of at least pretty, and preferably beautiful, women. He can carry off such a taste; other men can't, quite. Why not, then, indulge it? Women co-operate. He's rewarded, for his fastidious discernment. No thank you, Linda, no marriage. There are others, beside you.

Men who have difficulty with women are often glad to get one to marry. Bill Cole has no difficulty; constantly new women enter the social arena. He plays the bunch, and not singles one out.

V

There are so many of them ("them" meaning merely women), and so easily come by—met, wooed, and bedded—that Bill Cole has become jaded. His earlier enthusiasm has rotted away with the facility of his success. He plays the "dandy" role with all the bored ease of a lifelong actor wedded so to the role that personality and theatricality merge into the same essence.

Dapper, elegant, eligible, jaunty, rakish, somewhat cynical, urbane almost to slickness, yet gentle and humane: that's our Bill Cole. He has love down to a programmed technical pattern, with just the spicy margin of risk and unpredictability as to allow the mystique of daring escapade, the intrigue of the gambling venture, the freedom of lucky play.

He gets angry if he loses; yet quickly survives it. The importance and value of women have diminished; that is, the importance and value of a rounded-out love affair that deeply involves the committed partners to a bond that tenderly admits the loyal exchange of an intimate understanding. He keeps his soul out of it, and engages just his intellect. He has quite a quantity of "light affairs" going. He surrenders none of his whole Self, but employs his faculties for a fine superficial relationship to an astoundingly simultaneous degree in the broad, thinly spread field of women by interchangeable members, the numerically intertransferable, loosely sprawled empire of nightly juggled women on a rearranged, shifting pattern over the dissolving years.

Women climb on and fall off that revolving turnover scale. The years are wearing thin. Bill Cole has been aging, all this time. The concession he makes is in the average age of his women rising as well. So much handling goes through his process. Women, falling on and off his rotating spindle. Women, lit up one by one on his now autumnal tree, leaf by leaf, hoisted aloft by his graceful boughs, his arching branches, the delicate filigrees of all his nimble twigs.

Is love so quantifiable? There are too many qualifications upon its purity and simplicity. He seduces almost by rote and formula, now. This reduces romance to an ever recurring game, set by his own rules. Women are his sport. He's a professional campaigner, an astute veteran connoisseur, a champion player, an endless scholar and tireless practitioner of that eternal sport. But it's only a sport. But he's living it, wearing the random mutiplicity of its numerous flesh.

VI

Thus, he's evolved to a crisis. What is life's meaning? Where does love fit in, with so many lusts ripening and closing? Is life only lust—the conquest? To vanquish, conquer, kill, one after another, to slay and capture, to captivate and conquer, to win and then discard, all those women's hearts, with their built-in bodies? That's the life he's been leading. It's too pat. It's cut and dried, to his own stencil, to an invariable mold. The crisis has arrived, for soul-searching. To delve, and fathom life's meaning. Coated with renewed layers of fresh victims—women.

He's pursuing life's meaning. His life is himself. Who is *he?* Go to a psychiatrist, to find out? No, he's too proud, with too much sense, for that. Religion? No, he's far too sophisticated. A political cause? That's too irrelevant to *himself.* Who is *he?*—(laden with women). The *himself,* of his very self. Where possibly no woman has penetrated—though so many have tried. That kernel or corner of his inaccessible self, remote from his social affairs, his literary career, his extensive womanizings. That core of soul, unknown to everyone including Bill Cole. Inwardly, what truly is he? No psychiatrist or religious broker or political doctrinist or healer of any description could show him, lead him to self-revelation. It must burst upon him, by itself: from within. But he's led an outside life. The *world* owns him. That universe of women-dickering. That phenomenal globe, outside. Where his habits reside, his assets, his talents.

He wishes to be found. To be Saviour-bound. Let *one woman* do it. But who?

VII

No questionnaires to be filled out, no interviews. He'll just find her, through the pack. Finding her, he's found himself. She'll mate his soul, to a perfect fit.

His usual social life will yield his discovery. He'll keep up his party-going. Amid all the sparkling glitter, he'll chance on that rare nugget—his own.

They'll wed and be eternal. No more trivial frivolity. No more the merry-go-round of successive seductions. No more squandering his gifts on rounds of endless dissipation in the circuits of convivial socializing. He'll be pure, and true. In a holy vow.

Yes, but with whom? Let the candidates emerge. He'll sift them, through.

VIII

One by one, women may apply. Who will be the Chosen one? Destiny will be unfurled, soon.

The double destiny, of Bill Cole and his Soul's own true Wife. Two mates, dissolved in the same Fate.

He's circulating among the candidates, now. All are only too eager. He'll identify the Right One, perhaps, in a cosmic leap of recognition, by perversely, of all aspects, her—indifference!

That's the key, the code. But many *may* be indifferent—in probability's numerical law of combinations, considering the huge outlay of massive chances encountered. What *closer* signal to key in on, after the eager ones and interested ones and accessible ones and willing ones and game ones and open-to-invitation ones have been eliminated in this golden tournament, leaving only the finalists, in ever narrowing numbers?

Not alone by her indifference—an essential qualification, a fundamental prerequisite—shall he know her; but, more specifically, in refined subtlety, by some other sign—a sign uniquely hers alone, signifying that she was designated for him by Fortune's own sovereign authority. What will that sign be?—Which Love, stumbling blind, shall in due course appoint?

IX

The hunt is on. The search is underway. Missus Future Bill Cole—
no less—is being quested for. She'll turn up and come forward, in
Time's thorough passage to that end. She'll appear, presently. As unmistakably the rake's cure, putting Don Juan to rest and inserting, in its
place, Love's holy monogamy, the conjugal trust by divine mandate,
the fidelity of souls pre-wedded by destiny's ancient spell, which in this
dear lifetime achieves a radiant confirmation.

CHAPTER 2

I

Roberta was a dazzling blond. Would *she* fit the bill? Suitably
indifferent, was it she whom Destiny had in mind for Bill Cole's final
reformation?

Perhaps. But then again, perhaps not.

It's the Big Maybe. (Which can operate both ways.)

He met her at a cocktail party given to celebrate the publication of
an unimportant non-fiction book by a publisher that caused trees to
be chopped down for mass paperback and clothbound printing paper
purpose. He coolly walked up to her to begin a conversation which
might lead who knows where? By then, the party was already crowded.
"Oh, I heard of you. Are you Bill Cole the critic?" she replied. "Basically, you're a reviewer, but you've compiled and edited anthologies, as
well. I'm Roberta, an editor for the publishing house that's hosting this
party. I haven't personally worked on the book being celebrated, but,
being loyal to my firm, I hope you review it favorably, or at least give
it a glowing mention, implicit with recommendation, in your popular
monthly magazine column."

"I don't intend to. The book isn't important enough. So let's change
the subject. I like you. You look great. When this party is over, let me

take you out to dinner."

"No."

"Why not?"

"You don't attract me."

"No? That's unusual. I attract almost all women. Why not you?"

"You're much older than me."

"Yes, but other girls your age are in various phases of love for me. So don't let our age difference stop you from joining them. First have an infatuation or crush on me. Let it develop into a consuming passion. Adore me. It'll be fun."

"For you. But not for me. I'll only be a victim."

"Not if I love you back."

"Will you?"

"Love me, and see."

"No. You don't attract me."

"But can't that be changed?"

"No. I'm quite indifferent."

"And I can't prevail, by any further persistence?"

"It would be useless, and only demean you. Give up. Also, this conversation has reached the pointless stage. Let's separate. I want to talk to other people. So must you."

She drifted away in the crowd. Mentally, Bill Cole said goodbye to Roberta. Her blond, dazzling hair was now obstructed by hordes of people. She had rejected him. It smarted. She had cited their age difference, though that probably made no difference to her over-all indifference. He felt old, and self-unfulfilled. The female Saviour hadn't arrived yet, to personally complete him. It wouldn't be Roberta. Would many others have to eliminate themselves, before he found his True Mate? Only indifferent women would qualify. In one, unknown yet, the right Sign would gleam through. He'd find her, but when? It would be final. She'd define him, to the finest line, finally, of his Lovemost self divine.

II

One of the social events of the season: a magnificent buffet dinner party, for two hundred carefully selected guests, at the luxurious private town-house of an extensively connected, lavishly exclusive, culturally prominent matron of arts, letters, beauty, refinement, money, and class. Security precautions ruthlessly blockaded any would-be crashers, helped by bulky door-guards, uniformed and armed with a precise guest-list at check-point. Invitations had been limited and non-transferable. Those who *were* invited couldn't but feel special. This thrilled the atmosphere to grand circles of glamour within grandeur. A highly celebrated beauty was there: Anne. Everyone just simply stared and stared.

For Bill Cole, staring wasn't enough. Its results could only prove passive.

As a man of the world, scouring the world in search of his self's central soul (an abstraction for which he needed a concrete but as yet unknown woman to tangibly materialize a spirit imprisoned so far in its formlessness), he took action, and accosted Anne, in full but hushed view of that distinguished assemblage.

"I'm Bill Cole."

"Are you? Indeed! And who is *that* supposed to be?"

"You've never heard of *me?*"

"No. Should I?"

"Yes. I'm known in this city's artistic, literary, social, and other concentrically bisecting spheres."

"But I'm a visitor to these parts. It's all so strange to me, here."

"But, being the celebrated beauty Anne, surely your fame is well known here."

"As well it might. Television, films, magazines, and newspapers keep me prominently exposed. But Hollywood is my base of operations. From there, my fame has spread all over. In *your* case, my dear man (sorry, I've forgotten your name. Let's *leave* it forgotten, for the sake of my mental economy), you're only a *local* celebrity, of sorts, bounded by the city of New York. So why should I recognize you? How arrogant of you to come up to me! How below your station, to put on airs of presuming to talk with me. Go away. Neither to my life nor to my career (they're one, at times) can you ever matter."

"Then you qualify."

"For what?"

"As my permanent mate. You've passed the test."

"Was I taking a test?"

"The indifference test. You're suitably indifferent."

"I wish to remain so."

"Dear Anne. Let me persuade you to change your indifference to Love. Your indifference qualified you for eligibility as my Soul's True Wife. Having already served for the passport, your indifference may now be discarded, as we enter the second stage: give me the Sign, that you're my True and Only One."

Anne merely stared. This strange man's audacity could only come from a crazed mind. She turned her back, made her way past guests, and joined a conversational group at a remote corner of the next room, a group that joyfully made room for that stunning star, opening its ranks to include her most centrally in its worshipful midst.

Back to the momentary Bill Cole zone of the big party. He was left standing there—in his tracks. In front of plenty of listeners, including the hostess herself. Bill Cole had gone through a rejection process, a conspicuous humiliation closely attended by witnesses to that historic occasion.

Bill Cole was stunned. Would his reputation hereby decline? Had thus begun the reversal of his Don Juan's succession of conquests? A series of atonements for his career of previous heartless triumphs?

A blond publishing editor, Roberta, had rejected him at a literary party last week, but there'd been no witness to overhear it and churn it through the gossip mill. His rejection just now, by beauteous Anne, the television and cinematic performer, would assume alarmingly public proportions. It would get into the papers and be talked about. Would Bill Cole ever be taken seriously again, as a ladies' man? Had he, in effect, met his Napoleonic Waterloo?

III

From this predicament, with his life looking grim in front of him, rescue came from an unexpected source: the evening's grand hostess, whose well appointed house was the site for two hundred entertained guests to crown the very height of the social season in the rich splendor and gaiety of notable magnificence.

This wealthy ornament of society was known simply as Liz. She came over to console Bill Cole.

Guests milled around, straining ears to record this interesting succeeding event in the wake of Bill Cole's ignominious rejection by Anne, the show business star, on visit from Hollywood, whose heralded beauty was on personal display on this memorable evening, which journalists and photographers were now recording, on the spot, for posterity's topical consumption on the morrow, to thrill followers and nonfollowers alike of the fashionable world's carnivorous plunges and jumps in the fame and fortune bubble tank that swirls and pumps with illuminated fish effects, bladder-puffs, the fluid phosphorescence of treacherous appearance floating in and out to pop and burst, to bloat and pop, in brilliant shallow brevities along the rippling surface and illusory depths of the fame and fortune bubble tank, lit permanently for passing public inspection.

IV

"Don't worry, Bill Cole. Anne habitually rejects almost all men."

"But I'm not 'all men', Liz. My reputation was built on being a towering exception."

"But you've tasted defeat before, surely, Bill Cole?"

"In *private* I swallowed them. But here, my setback gets boosted by Anne's fame and glamour, and by the social prominence of your outranking party, to an unwelcome limelight to showcase my public humiliation. I'm damned, now. It'll be reported in the papers tomorrow, and over radio and television. I'm deflated to a laughing stock, a come-down to be widely belittled in all mocking circles. Formerly adored by adorable women, I'm now a gossip column's joke filler, at the expense, I'm afraid, of all my dying dignity."

"Bill Cole, you're taking this too solemnly. Do I detect the pompous note, in your usually measured tone? I'll restore you to your glory. Here's how."

"How, Liz? How?"

"I'll become your mistress."

"No, it's too late."

"Why?"

"I've reformed. I've taken a spiritual vow."

"How?"

"I'm looking for Eternal Love, with One Woman, to find the Soul I lost or never had when I was such a promiscuous philanderer as Don Juan's embodiment of that timeless myth. I could gaily have accepted you *then*; but not now."

"How serious you are! But if you are looking for True Love's heaven-high union of Souls, then why not take *me* on? Couldn't I be the a good prospect? Together, we'd go sublime, and lift the recorded summit level of passionate idealism a notch higher than any previous attainment of romantic legend."

"Thanks for my confidence, Liz. But no."

"Why? I'm wealthy and pretty. And well-accomplished. And I love you."

"No."

"Why?"

"The candidate for sharing immortality with me must, initially, qualify by virtue of her indifference. Which *later* I'd overcome and reverse. But *your* approach was *far* from indifferent: hot and heavy waxed your overture, moistly rapturous with the loftiest mating call. You've thus eliminated yourself, by demonstrating interest. I don't mean to insult you, or viciously to condemn you; the trial is impartial, impersonal; it's a secret contest, but fair. By those given rules, which I've sworn to follow to my soul's holy salvation, you, Liz, have failed. Anne *didn't* fail; she qualified—but rejected me: *I* failed. We *both* lose, Liz. Alas."

V

Liz wept, as openly as her dignity could afford. Some witnesses, touched in sympathy, wept along. Bill Cole, though controlled and masculine, wept too. A newspaper photojournalist fixed that tableau with a flashing camera. It would appear prominently, tomorrow, in the society page, or the culture section, or even on page one itself, than which there was no page earlier, unlike some books that have introductory pages roman numeralled before the official pagination that marks out the body text. At any rate, the publicity would be detrimental to what was left of Bill Cole's dwindling reputation as his era's perfect Don Giovanni who awaits his Mozart, as Doctor Johnson awaited his Boswellian biographer.

With public scorn to be heaped on him for so fallen a state among women, will Bill Cole be forced to lower the beauty and youth standards requisite in his women? Will the point be who will accept him, and no longer whom he will accept? But that's further complicated by the condition that the woman must first be indifferent to him, and later overcome that indifference, in order to qualify as his Soul's True Mate and Self's Finder.

VI

Bill Cole, rejected by Anne, the party's beautiful star; Liz, the party's bright hostess, rejected by Bill Cole (though for totally different reason's than Anne's for rejecting Bill Cole): laden with these key rejections, the party slumped, and never recovered. The atmosphere sagged, dragging down other guests to a somber mood unity. (A party is an organism. The component individuals each feel their own feelings, but the party as a whole has a collective feeling all its own.)

Bill Cole went home alone. He was almost suicidally depressed. It was just short of midnight, or just after. The lonely phone rang. It was a former girlfriend whom he neglected and then abandoned.

"This is Mary."

"*Which* Mary? I know several."

She pronounced her last name. Unremembering, Bill Cole puzzled it out in a pause. The pause was echoed by Mary, on her end of the line. Poor Mary. She felt ignored, dismissed, unconcerned with, the profoundly cold object of Bill Cole's barely polite indifference.

"Sorry Mary. I don't remember you. This is no slight. I have so much to remember; or rather—for economy's sake—to forget, if suitably unessential. As I've take the trouble to forget you, Mary, you must have been sufficiently unessential. But am I necessary to you, that you've bothered to phone? When did we last meet??

"Eleven years ago."

"The you're eleven years older. You must have lost your looks. Were you even *then* much younger than me?"

"Not much, but a few years."

"Why, after eleven years, did you phone tonight?"

"I'm lonely. I loved you once. I'm depressed. I'm depressed so, I've regressed. Through the years. Back to you. In love's fond memory."

"I'm depressed, too. I'm lonely, too. Ordinarily, I'd say come over and sleep here. But it's too late, I've changed and take a vow."

"*What* vow, Bill Cole?"

"Instead of cluttering my life with a multitude of women, I'm cleaning house—spiritual house—to create an altar or shrine, haven or temple, for the purity cleansing of a perfect union, soul to soul, with One Woman, whom I'll loyally wed."

"May I be she, please?"

"No, Mary—whatever Mary you are—no."

"Why? I'd devoted my life to you."

"I don't doubt that. But you don't qualify."

"What do I lack?"

"Indifference. The candidate for Oneness with me must first be indifferent. You've avowed love for me, and phoned me tonight with wooing intentions, however based on eleven-year-old reminiscences."

"I qualify."

"How, Mary, how?"

"I once *was* indifferent to you. Long ago."

"That's insufficient. It's only now, after I've taken the Vow, that the candidate for Soul-sharing must indicate her eligibility (unknown to herself) with pure, unfeigned indifference. Your indifference was ancient history: it doesn't count now."

"Oh Bill Cole, couldn't you waive you pure vow, just for tonight, just for a little erotic pleasure? Please?"

"You tempt me. But no. Thanks, anyway."

He hung up. Was the "indifference clause" a self-defeating one? Not if he can overcome the initial indifference on the part of the woman prospect; then she must give him a Sign—indicating that she alone of all her gender upon earth is magically designated for him. Then troubles vanish, his Soul is located, and Divine Light guides him and his Bride to blissful Peace, graced by such blessing that Bill Cole is Born Again, and knows such sinless wisdom as to be approximately God, though fully married, and because so. Will it happen? He'll go to further parties, to create risen chances opportune to the standard test he'll apply.

VII

One by one, he unwomans himself of all of his women with whom he played the superficial gallant, a temporarily Mozartless Don Giovanni. Now he's Don Giovanniless, too. He strips his house bare, to erect, therein, the sacred chapel. There he'll bring his Bride. Her dowry will be his Soul. Their Union will be the Spiritual even of the last four or five thousand years, leaving bachelor Christ in the lurch as a sorry shadow, a pale inferior, a bloodless imposter, compared to Bill Cole's deified incarnation in polar merger with his Soul-revealing Queen.

CHAPTER 3

I

In those fashionably frequented circles of literary, artistic, professional, social gatherings, known by dictionary definition as "parties," Bill Cole's star had not merely unwaxed itself in waning, but with a thud had fallen flat on its five pointed surfaces, blunting all his points and rubbing dim his previous elegant glitter. He was dulled of all his former glory. The point now became to avoid him. Spurning him was now a mark of "chic"ness, a "belonging" to the smart trend groups that exercise a self-privileged vanguard in the cruel conformity of snobbishly playing favorites and harrying those who have been consigned to the "out-of-favor" limbo of social nonrecognition. Finding himself snubbed by those who had esteemed him, a new "out" under the consensus of "in" contempt, plunged Bill Cole into a novel low of misery.

Men who had envied him, and played the game of inferior rival to him, were now scorning him with smug righteousness. Women who had fancied him from afar or from close, with varying degrees of hope and twitter, of longing and undaring, of pining and tender reticence, of adoration and concealment, of passionate declaration and carefully feigned unconcern, now ignored him effortlessly, by the dainty instinct of their mob, a thoughtless herd's stampeding chorus mooing a common note, identically cow-like, in the meadows of uniformity.

Benevolent pity was the note struck by some men; compassion for a fallen member of their women-chasing tribe. Bill Cole was now stamped a failure by stares and glances that marked him out for disgrace.

It was too unfamiliar: so sudden and ungradual. What consoled him, in this great crisis, was his vow of spirituality, the inner candle he had lit to faith in his Deliverer, the Female Redeemer, who'll take him from the brutal world of sordid fashion, the vicious cult of snobs by elastic conformity to trends of comet falsity and slick spurious meteors on the greased surface of the galaxy of empty values.

His internal chapel's shrine's altar's luminous abiding devout humble faith in the imminent advent—heaven-sent—of a True Bride who discovers, installs, and saves his pure cosmic Soul. Taking refuge there, he's spared the wicked barbs and darts of his petty, vindictive enemies, who, in spite's venom, jointly glee to avenge him for the lordly might he once commanded at the top of the glamor struggle in the love, lust, prestige, and influence jungle of combatants who bare civilized fangs and bristle with cultivated claws for sophisticated strife for the spoils, booty, and plunder of gains in false-hearted vanity and the brightly colored honor of empty plumage.

Plenty of women will pass the test of initial indifference to him, now, to qualify them for the further stage where all will be eliminated but one, the one who magically reveals the Sign of their Eternal Union.

His being degraded, his loss of class, guarantees the candidature of countless new entries for the mystic Bill Cole Sweepstakes, all become eligible by virtue of the great Indifference he inspires. Who, though, will surmount that Indifference, to go on to the next stage? Will they all remain just as indifferent to him in the end as they were at the start? Sealing up his Soul in its tight cell of utter loneliness, the barren, arid, desiccated, unrelieved, famished cell of sterile monkhood? His unwedded Soul, grown seedy with neglect, overgrown by rank weeds? Fulfilled by no risen Bride of Kindred Soul? Doomed merely to rot, and die?

||

He forces his way into parties where once he was gloriously awaited. He's still a book critic and reviewer, retaining his prestigious column in a national magazine as well as contributing free-lance articles to several other publications. Professionally, he retains influence and power; but on the *personal* plane, as just Bill Cole the man and person aside from his inclusion in the present publishing sphere, the commercial world of arts and letters featuring predominantly the popular but occasionally the aesthetic—as just Bill Cole, his name has officially gone downhill into the valley of mere mud, where it stagnates and putrifies and gathers a fetid swarm of flies that drift in scavenger packs to those divested of pride and glory, dying in the molding decay of their stripped might. Formerly invited to all the parties, he's currently in the position of having to "crash" parties not hosted by firms that would benefit by his article writing. Subtly or unsubtly, he's just not welcome any more; he used to have semi-celebrity status and enjoy the marked attentions of the loveliest women: now, he's called "the washed-up has-been."

Fickle fortune! But Bill Cole is geared for a comeback! He has inner fortitude. He'll be saved—by the Appointed Woman! She'll arrive on her silver steed, clad in stunning armor. She'll say, "Climb on." She on the saddle, he clutching behind her, will ride high up the mountain of Immortal Love, far from worldly storms and petty jealousies. They'll join the other Immortals, on terms of fresh equality, and share in Olympic reveling, serene prayer, and passionate pomp.

That's his program. It keeps him going. It tides him over. From it, he gathers strength.

III

It's a publishing party. Bill Cole is actually invited, thanks to his key position as a critic. It's at the pre-dinner cocktail hour, when business offices close shop for the day at five o'clock. The book celebrated is a safely mediocre novel done in a cliché-packed conventional style, dolled up deliberately for the mass market. It has, whatever, no pretensions to art at all. It's absolutely a commercial product.

Guests are milling about. The author is surrounded. Bill Cole is only spoken to by the publicity director of the publishing house. "Please review it, Bill Cole. Favorably."

"No. It stinks. It's lousy."

"But you're eating our *hors d'oeuvres* and drinking our Scotch. Won't you pay for it with a favorable review?"

"The book isn't worth it."

"Have you no gratitude? We invited you here, despite your severely sunken status in the party hierarchy. We took pity, and we demanded payment—in the form of the payoff of a glowing review, a fame-making tribute to a sincerely earnest author."

"Sorry. No game-playing. I'll leave the party, if you resent me for not complying with your dishonest stipulation."

"No. Stay anyway. But you're a punk."

Those disrespectful words, icily contemptuous, were delivered by a woman ten years Bill Cole's junior; one, moreover, who would have fallen in love with him less than a month ago, before his "conversion" and fall from social standing, to which she was acutely attuned. Instead, she played the hard-bitten, no-nonsense, cynically idealless businesswoman, hustling for her firm as its publicity director, and snobbishly bullying anyone deemed bullyable in the field's revolving turntable of altered status ranking on the pecking order's radically shifting field of hierarchy mobility that tosses reputations around in the make and break, the up and down, the in and out, the this and that.

That's a sample of the treatment Bill Cole was getting now. Word of his degradation had gotten around, and everyone was eager to jump in on the act, and do his or her little bit to drag him down. He was the latest bandwagon fad—"humiliate Bill Cole." He was open game. A general amnesty was granted, impunity for consequences, a moral immunity, an ignoble concession, an ease from conscience. The target of the season! The whipping boy of the corrupt literary racket. Everyone's scapegoat for the frustrations endemic to the publishing industry at this God-forsaken period of its occasionally enlightening history.

Bill Cole was permitted to stay. The party was at its crowded peak. He looked around, on the chance of spotting his destined future Bride. But the women belligerently, aggressively avoided him, with wounding insult. No-one had the prescribed Indifference that would prove malleable to later reversal.

His harvest for the evening: emptyhandedness. He faced a night of dark, bitter spiritual void. His Soul, with its quivering wings, would be locked in an iron cell, windowless, to wall in his despair, his wail of anguish, to drain privation of all the pain it could bear, in cold, slow drops of agonized pulse before the congealing coat numbly hardens in its mercy.

IV

He had resiliency, and would rebound. Next night—yet another party. Hope cruised anew, in his battered breast.

On past reputation, not by current invitation, he managed entrance. What a wondrous ensemble of women! Whom would they include? The One?

No more ordeals or drawn-out futilities. He'll negate negations, and relegate failure to failure. Failure can fail if death can die. Let's make good from bad. Much good can be made, from so much bad.

The bad was stacked against him, in heaps of difficulties. He had rejected all his old loves, burned his bridges behind him, cutting himself off from the multitudes attracted to him in his old days of glory as the latest Don Juan personification, the only life-link to the old legend. Then his Vow came, his reformation or conversion, and he rejected the women who craved him—a whole lot of women.

Add *that* batch of rejected women to a new batch—in his reversed reputation—of new women who'll reject him, based on current social form. Then who's left? Anyone?

One. There *must* be one. *The* one.

Only her. The complete Only.

The only from the one. The one and the only. The complete only. Only that one. *His* one. *His* only. He being hers. Forever.

V

Now it's the next party. Well, any difference?

This time, the temper tempo is calm, so that female reactions to him are unhostile. They fulfill the "Indifference" specifications of his holy hopes.

They're all so charming! Drinking his Scotch whisky slowly, he chats with one woman after another, drifting among them. Uniformly indifferent, they courteously feign interest, with transparent insincerity. They're well-bred and polite—civil. Which one, if any, will experience an involuntary development—a change, in subtle degrees or however drastically eliminating transitional stages in one wholesale leap—from indifference to the contrary, to acutely its opposite, letting some special Sign glow forth, so that one dart pierces two hearts, linking and lodging in them both, so that separate lives feed off one pulse, as utmost diversities draw inward, and to their common Center converge.

VI

Two groups of women, one *he* rejects, from the past; one rejecting *him*, in the now. From the second group must come his Salvation. The first group eliminated themselves by having been unindifferent, by current estimations of retrospect. Then, let's concentrate on the second group. Party by party. Until—

"Hello, I'm Bill Cole."

"Indeed, you *must* be."

"Why must I be, you pretty girl? Tell me."

"Because I automatically reject you. And only Bill Cole comes under that category, by current fashion, of being automatically rejected so soon as sighted, even before the identification of recognition or the introductory procedure."

"Can't you change your mind, pretty girl?"

"No. I'd be out of the social swim, ostracized by those in the know of the vogue, were I, foolishly, to behave in any manner toward you other than by standard rejection. I must keep my standing, in my gregarious circle of conspicuous emulation of the Norm's unfaltering guidance, dictating conformity standards that require only unthinking obedience. I join all those who reject you. *Not* to do so would be an unthinkable offense against prevalent good taste—tantamount, indeed, to suicide from the sanctum of civilized belonging."

"Is there *no* exception? No courageous nonconformist emancipated from mob participation, from mass animal uncritical blind adherence to the gross behavior of the so-called enlightened herd that calls the tune and rates people by gutless mere obedience? Have you all abdicated individuality, all you unexceptional women who follow these arbitrary social codes and dare no note of dissent, no rebellious assertion of the unique private soul that divides a real person from the vagueness of 'people-in-general'? Oh you spineless women! You collectivists! You cowardly combiners! Where, among you, is one who calls herself her own self? Her I'll find, and she'll find me! We'll be each other's joint and permanent reward, for daring to have souls apart, which we call our own: jealously preserved from being blunted to group measure, and lumped into the horrid heap of a rough, compact alliance of surface shells together, devoid of the animating Soul that confines and defines the true individual! I'm not speaking to any *person*, in speaking to you; rather, to some 'entity-among-merged-entities'! It's disgusting!"

"Bill Cole, you're raving and ranting in an impolite way. I'm a buddy of the host, and I can have you ejected by force from this civil gathering, in full view of those who may mock you as you whizz out. You'll be laughed to your social grave."

"I choose to be alone. Goodbye, pretty girl."

"Alone means lonely, you fool."

VII

Thus ended another fiasco, debacle, of Bill Cole's recent party-going. His tauntress proved a prophet: he got lonelier all the time, in the dark chambers of being alone. Would he become beyond reclaim? A social leper, as outcast as a street bum? Horrible prospect.

Who will deliver him, from this travail? Who will find his Soul for him, via herself, while also leading him back from fallen grace to reassumed dignity in that vicious marketplace, Social Concourse? He needs to be saved for the *world* of fellow beings in circles of culture distinction, while saved also for the *heaven* of Two Souls in Higher Love's Divine Privacy.

VIII

Such paradoxical-seeming double salvation—*for* heaven, *from* and *for* the world—must be ministered to by the same agent: a woman of worldly standing but paradisiacal rarity: *she* would be a paradox too, in and of herself.

Would she come along? She would, but Bill Cole would have to implement that occurrence through his own active intervention: he must stalk and scour the parties, as a forlorn, ubiquitous figure, scorned but persistent in the face of continual social disgrace. Such is his trial, test, or labor, by which his endurance, his faith, his worth, will be sorely tried, with pitfalls and humiliation strewn in his way. He'll survive, and come through. He'll last, and be delivered. He'll stick fast, whatever may happen, till he finds himself soaring, quite unstuck, in free flight beyond all borders that bound trivial love. The change will be dimensional, not in quantity. Sheer transcendence, into the Outer Soul, companioned on route by that consort, his Queen, with whom together, God and Goddess, they get to dwell in Love's True Realm, and rule over the Dominion of the Absolute, far from his test-and-trial-trap-of-travail-and-torment from which, miraculously, with his Bride's aid, he got unstuck, by strife, pluck, and combative fury; by patience; and by such luck as only God grants, to him elevated to equal grace in the foremost Kingdom.

CHAPTER 4

I

"Hello, I'm Bill Cole."

"Are you? How quaint! Well, that's my cue."

"Cue what for?"

"To dip into another section of the party, where you happen not to be, because, forbidding you to follow, I leave you here."

"Are you being fashionable, in rejecting me?"

"How did you guess?"

"But couldn't you come, in time . . ."

"To like you? Not a bit. I'm firm. I join the general detestation and abhorrence of you. I belong to your league of detractors."

"Well, the party contains more women than only you. All won't *equally* reject me, will they?"

"Not *equally*. But all *will* reject you. You'll see."

She was right. Not quite equally, but with general totality, he was thoroughly rejected, by all and sundry of the women guests there present.

Another fruitless party. Oh well.

II

Such dismal results multiplied, party by party. The disdained of all men, Bill Cole's Don Juan-y star had come full circle to its abysmal eclipse. By his own doing, his own will, as well as by women's prevalent wills.

He would suffer all those rejections, toward a single compensatory acceptance. Who by? The game is to hold on, to hang in there, come through, and find out.

To find her and himself, in one. The entwined Soulness of a pair. Purely brought to Heaven, and left there.

III

"Hello, I'm Bill Cole."

"Are you? Then goodbye."

"Is that proper party behavior?"

"Toward *you*, it certainly is."

"You're so pretty. Please don't *continue* to reject me."

"I *must*, if I wish to retain my social standing as a respected, up-to-date, on-the-go, up-to-the-mark woman. My reputation is at stake. Others at this party are observing us. They're watching me closely.

Please *seem* rejected, *act* rejected; make it obvious. Dramatize it to the full. You *are* rejected."

"I'm angry."

"*That*'s a good role to play, Bill Cole: it's perfectly compatible with your state of being rejected. Now, act it out. Put on a good show."

"But it's real."

"Of *course* it is. But make it *seem* so. How it *seems*, is the true game."

Everyone laughed. Bill Cole both was and seemed angry. In the theatre of life, he was the finest fool on the stage.

Perfect for the role. Glaringly himself. A little too perfect, perhaps. Bordering on the maudlin, on the exaggeratedly theatrical, on the grossly overacted, on the hysterically sentimental. Just too convincing. Soberly serious, by implication. Out of control. Too like life—too painfully so. Lifelike, to a *fault*. Not removed enough. So real, it was dangerous.

He's getting out of control. He's growing wild. Subdue him! He'll tear the place apart! Stop him! He's a maniac!

IV

Yes, he *did* get out of hand. He had become violently unruly. The police had to be called for. They handcuffed him and took him away, before the hushed, shocked, chastened, scandalized guests.

"Disturbed the peace." That's the charge. Also, maniacal fury, with intent to harm, hints perhaps of momentary aberration, or dangerous border insanity; a public nuisance, at a private party where, officially, he was unwelcome, and never invited in the first place: he had forced entry, in the undesirable role of "crasher."

How justified the host was, to have never invited him! Thus events proved.

Such property damage! Overturned tables, smashed expensive bottles of unopened alcohol and fine glassware—collectors' items, now broken beyond repair. And damage to *people!* And to the host's reputation! For having him there, despite his official uninvited status.

V

A night in jail. Morose, drunk, suicidally depressed. Fallen lower than in the worst nightmare. Quite abandoned. Unsupported. Alone to a criminal degree. Antisocial. Criminally alone, criminally antisocial.

Criminally unloved. The ex-Don Juan. Currently depraved, and crazed, in haunted lovelessness.

Abandoned. Solitary, as solitary in the psyche as in his overnight jail cell. A social outcast. Kept away from people, confined to solitude, by force, behind bars, in a steel cell.

Beyond the pale. Unaccepted socially. And *for* that, punished, *by* more of it. More of the same.

VI

Is rehabilitation possible? The editor of the magazine he writes book reviews for and a literary social column, is summoned as character witness by the magistrate to the court trial. The editor will vouch for Bill Cole, show faith in him by not firing him. That vote of confidence by so influential a literary figure will do much to repair the damage done to Bill Cole as a professional and social participant in the cultural communications world where at present he stood so low thanks mainly to the successful allied war against him by the combined fashion snobbery of women, the same gender who used to submit to his endless charm.

The law suit against Bill Cole is by his last party's host, who sues him for more money than either he has or is capable of making. Damages and reparations are asked for. The violence of the defendant reduced the apartment to a partial shambles, and damaged the host's social reputation into the bargain. Bill Cole had not only crashed the party uninvited, but then proceeded, via violence, to violate the spirit and purpose of the party itself, with his uncalled-for acts of arbitrary, unprovoked, wayward, drunken mayhem.

Bill Cole's lawyer protests that his client *was*, indeed, provoked. The prosecuting attorney had accused Bill Cole of "an unseemly display of anger."

"Unseemly!? But my client was *asked* to seem. To seem angry. By a girl who had rejected his overtures but wanted to advertise conspicuously this rejection, for the enhancement of her social reputation. So she asked Bill Cole to lay it on, to give a great display of it, a convincing performance, an open demonstration of it. That would show the other guests that the girl was indeed being fashionably snobbish in following the accepted vogue of spurning Bill Cole so completely that he could feel the full humiliation of rejection. He reacted with anger that was spontaneous. It was real, the anger Bill Cole felt. But that didn't satisfy the girl: she asked him to act it out conspicuously for the benefit of the party guests, who then would rate the girl high with honors and social esteem for reducing Bill Cole to so furied a frenzy."

"Do you mean," asked the judge, who presided with an iron gavel, "that all the damage inflicted by Bill Cole's rage was merely *show*, an attempt to *appear* as angry as he was indeed feeling, to *seem* what actually he was truly being?"

"Yes, your Honor," said Bill Cole's lawyer.

The girl was called to the witness stand, and she admitted having provoked Bill Cole to put on a theatrical show of his anger. "Yes, your Honor, I confess to having goaded or urged him to act out the violent rage. He had compromised me by making verbal overtures for my love. To regain my dignity, I had to put him thoroughly in his place, for my very honor was at stake, in the fashionable world. I stage-directed him to an angry semblance—then, though, it got out of hand. I apologize to the host for the damages I—directly or indirectly –prompted Bill Cole to make. My father, who's wealthy, has volunteered to reimburse the host for both the material damages Bill Cole inflicted and the social damages incurred as well; to the tune of the full sum of the suit demanded of Bill Cole himself—who, I may add, should now be exonerated, since I lay the guilt to my head, and soothe my conscience by appeasing both the offended host and this solemn court of law."

Ringing applause went up. Bill Cole's magazine editor boss embraced him enthusiastically. The honesty of the girl was commended. The judge closed the case, with that dramatic end. The offended host was satisfied and reimbursed. Thank God the girl's father was so wealthy and generous! Everyone got off in fairly good shape, relatively unimpaired. The reporters, by and large, wrote up the case in a sympathetic tone toward Bill Cole. This stemmed the tide of his recent series of serious reversals. It paved the way for a comeback. The worst was over. Down as far as he could get, he was now on the way up again, in the world's fickle eye. He's becoming a cultural hero. Not the Don Juan of before, but a man treated sympathetically by the press. A fallen and reformed rake; scorned fashionably by all the women, sufficiently punished, now deemed respectable again. Scarred, wounded, bloodied, but unbowed. The recipient of the honor of invitations, once more, in full standing, with restored character, to the best parties. Back in demand. Not clamored for by the women, as before, nor condemned and rejected by them so universally; in neither extreme, now; but regarded as very interesting: receiving mingled, ambiguous, mixed, ambivalent attentions. His Soul is unknown. It hungers for The One: his Eternal Bride. First she must be indifferent to him, on meeting; then reverse herself, feeling interest: then show a Sign—identifying herself as the Absolute, unique among all women, for Bill Cole's own true companion to the solid scope and depth (outside all shallow worldly levels) of their utmost Souls, combined.

In their two persons, they'll unabstract Love from its Myth: reconcile Earth to the Sublime; arrest Time; and shape Eternity to their very features, giving Being the Seeming that Art seems to demand from what merely exists in factually our old universe, graveyard to all illusions and ideals except, most miraculously, Love's.

CHAPTER 5

I

Bill Cole has rebounded. Socially, he exists once more. The girl who confessed at the court trial has been acclaimed for her courage. The loyalty of Bill Cole's literary magazine boss has also received plaudits. For a change, things are looking up again.

Reinstalled, but altered by his recent misfortunes and recovery, Bill Cole feels headed in the right direction. His confidence feels solidly grounded, now; not air-loose. He'll take charge. He'll court luck. And when it comes, he'll strike.

He's back in full, good credit. As a critic, he writes better now than ever. Suffering has sharpened his craft.

II

"The definition of beauty is that it doesn't exhaust itself," Bill Cole wrote, in his widely read magazine criticism column, apropos a first novel no-one ever heard about by an author no-one ever heard about. It was the raveliest review he had written for years. Nor had he, nor anyone else, ever met that unknown author. And why should he have? His reviews were unbiased by "personalities." Many's the author he knew personally and was on eating and drinking terms with, whose books he either didn't review or, when he did, it could well be unfavorably. That's how impartial, incorruptible, fair-headed he was. He dignified the reviewing profession. He ennobled the high office of the critic.

The author's name was Helen Whist. She's a mystery personality. What's she like? Her novel seems somewhat autobiographical. It gives interesting clues. Into, though, what?

Bill Cole craves to meet her. He's acquainted with her publishing house editor. Through that connection, a link may be forged, through the veils of the unknown, and into, at last, Helen Whist's very presence.

Is *she* the Love Bill Cole has been waiting for? Or is his hunch playing yet another false lead?

She intrigues him. She's unknown. But what a terrific novel she wrote! Such was the gist of his review.

On the back cover of the novel (or on the hardback dustjacket) was the flimsiest of biographical sketches of this author, unaccompanied by any photograph. Nor did the publicity release for the press contain any more personal information or even the usual photograph. As a person, she's a blank. She offers no opposition to anything Bill Cole may project upon her, dreaming into her his heart's ideals.

He *must* meet her. He phones her publishing house editor, whom he invites to lunch at some convenient midtown restaurant. Fitting, that Bill Cole should stand treat to the editor; the former wants something, out of the latter.

"Thanks for the rave review in your column, Bill Cole. We appreciate it."

"I didn't do it to ingratiate myself with you or your firm, Barry. It didn't matter who published it, *who* was the author, or *who* the editor; I wrote about it the way I did, in consideration only of the book's merits itself. Like a baseball umpire, basketball referee, or football field judge, I 'called it as I saw it,' without preconception, favor, or prejudice, one way or the other."

"Naturally, Bill Cole. No need to have explained or justified your high principles as a just arbiter in the public field of good taste and aesthetic discernment so far as a commercial book is concerned, which hits the market as a potential money-maker or money-loser but is nevertheless subject to universal rules of reading pleasure, objective criteria that call in the fine judgement of distinguished critics such as— indeed, Bill Cole—your very self, munching away across the table from me, in this snug restaurant where your generosity stands me this delicious lunch treat, despite the modest personal funds at your disposal, for you're well known to be poorer than you deserve to be in the light of your eminence as a writer who sheds much light on the contemporary scene of books, books, and more books."

"Thanks for your elaborate compliment, Barry—if, indeed, it is a

compliment, being so twisted and tortuously convoluted in its labyrin-
thine period-sentence clause-by-clause rambling artful overwrought
ambiguity so deviously constructed that its essential theme, if there
was one, was drowned out by auxiliary shoots off the lost main trunk."

"That was a mouthful of analysis of my own vocal mouthful, in
between our food mouthfuls of our hearty lunch here. But Bill Cole:
surely you want something from me. Why else would you have invited
me to lunch, when you've barely known me? What, then, can I do for
you? Does it bear upon Helen Whist? Are you slightly enamored of
her? You wish, through me, to make contact with her? Is that it?"

"Barry, you're psychic! How did you know?"

"Bill Cole, women were always your obsession, your true study
in life, involving extensive field research and close application to particular cases. Even more than books themselves—from which you
eke out your professional livelihood and can barely afford to buy me
this lunch—women are your abiding interest, your absorbing passion,
your consuming fascination. Though I barely know you, I know *that*
about you. Your reputation history has been fostered by gossip, rumor,
grapevine, the press, party chatter, and word of mouth. You're not an
unknown figure, you know, in these our giddy times. You've been much
talked about—even to the point of being discussed. People who never
even met you know *something* about you. And what they *do* know—the
fundamental minimal essential limit to what's basic and elemental to
you—is that your life somehow has to do with women, as centrally its
supreme theme, key subject, and paramount undercurrent. No?"

"You're right, Barry. To contradict you would be self-dishon-
esty, on *my* part. I can now appreciate the basis for your intuiting my
more-than-professional interest in this new author, Helen Whist. Barry,
have you met her? As her editor, surely you must have. What's she like,
where does she live, under what circumstances, how can I meet her,
can you set it up, can you arrange it?—Barry, don't let me down. Of
course my lunch invitation was for a purpose—you guessed accurately,
and hit the mark."

"You may be disappointed—"

"Barry, I'm completely dependent on you for my love life's crucial survival and fulfillment. I must meet, and then marry, Helen Whist. It was ordained by God, on the day before the very beginning of Genesis: He created light and words *after* designing my careful fate; through you I'm to meet Helen Whist, who at first will be indifferent to me, then later show interest and reveal the special Sign, signifying nothing less than total Love between our Souls linked by immortal destiny. Well, God did *His* bit, to set all this up. *Your* part, as a later stage in this divine process, is, dear Barry—the Introduction. Well? I'm waiting."

"Bill Cole, calm yourself. You're frothing hysterically, champing at the bit. You're in danger of acute indigestion. Tether yourself. You're wildly out of hand—carried away, almost. Pull yourself together. Listen: Helen Whist is not for you."

"Barry, you presume too much, in tampering with my destiny. One further note of interference, or unwillingness to co-operate, will result in your death even before we're able to order our dessert, not to mention coffee, to terminate our meal. In other words, your life will end before your lunch will (I'm treating you to both), unless you do as I say: introduce me to Helen Whist, tomorrow. Sorry—make that tonight. I'll wait no later than conveniently necessary in this vital urgency of this inevitable emergency with its insistent timetable of persistent immediacy as an overwhelming priority in life's crowded agenda. Do it—for me, Barry, for me."

"Bill Cole, you're so compelling, in your plea. I'll introduce you two tonight. That's a promise. Come at nine to my apartment. Here, take my card, it has my address. I can't guarantee results—beyond just the bare introduction, itself."

"Barry, you're a pip! You're my friend for life! My treating you to lunch was the best investment I've ever made!"

"Wait and see, tonight, at nine, Bill Cole, before rejoicing. You're too premature, as it is. Curb your optimism, or you run a disappointing risk, I'm afraid."

"I run *riot*, in eager expectation! My life joins heaven, tonight!"

III

You bet that Bill Cole really groomed himself in preparedness for his life's major event. He bathed, showered, shaved, put masculine perfume on, brushed his teeth with mint-scent paste, combed his hair, dressed himself in his best suit, with matching tie and shirt, and his shoes were a brilliant shine.

What more can a man do, to put himself out to appear with the best impression before his life's culminating love that brings all search climactically to completion? Yet, he realized, she must first greet him with indifference. The impression he presents should fall short of devastation.

Worries began to assail him, little nips and gnaws, tidal ripples from speculative disturbances. One was, how was Barry able to assume with such certainty-ease that Helen Whist would be available tonight, on such short notice? Was he empowered over her schedule in her personal life, beyond being her literary editor, the publisher's representative for her book? "Of course, I threatened him, at peril of death, and *demanded* tonight for introduction. He *had* to produce her, by my stern imperative, at dire ultimatum."

He wondered, then, whether Barry was Helen Whist's boyfriend. Why had Barry cautioned him against undue optimism in regard to the love-made-in-heaven construction that he was so eager to assume? Barry knew something that Bill Cole apparently didn't, damaging to the latter's ethereally prospective estimate as to his divine suitability for, with, and from the chosen lady of his dreams.

Hours remained, till nine o'clock. There was no pressing assignment to do, no review or article dawdling in the danger of an approaching deadline. He was too nervous, anyway. It calmed him to think that, at any rate, the issue was in God's hand, despite Bill Cole's lapse from long-ago Christianity into strictly non-church-attendance since skepticism ended his angelic childhood.

Helen Whist. What would she even *look* like? He prayed for her beauty; and for her being sufficiently young; unromantically attached:

free for himself.

In what was she circumstanced? She was a rare, gifted novelist. Beyond that, with no information provided by publicity press release put out by the publisher, or by the dustjacket back cover biographical blurb, he had precious little to go on, short of his all-licensed imaginings that ranged fearfully far from the factual modesty of limitations circumscribed by the actual.

He'll confront the "actual" at nine tonight. With unpleasant results? He was inflatedly buoyant in the helium-filled sphere of the puncture-possible balloon, the burst-prone bubble, the prick-susceptible bladder-ball, the jelly-quivering circle of tenuous, amorphous little hope-blob, defenselessly precariously vulnerable to the slightest assault on its unbuttressed, substance-void nonsolidity of mere mentality's nothing's air, the fragile subjectivity of desire's idea and intention's vague emotional vapor in the floating void of the strict absence of the real concrete, the tangibly empirically palpably truly actual out there.

IV

Time was ticking on. The more time went by, the closer narrowed down the interval between the shortening present and the moment, all so impending, of Helen Whist's coming into sight.

Meanwhile, Bill Cole still had to wait. All there was between the lonely now of him and the arrival of the shock and impact, the soft instantaneous collision, of Helen Whist's meeting him and vice versa at mutually the same instant on their simultaneous plane of discovering each other upon encounter, was the tedium and duration of all this waiting. Tedium? Anxiety, rather. Its tense strain. This wild surge of feeling, without an intermediary object to contact yet.

It all came down to Helen Whist. It all rose up to Helen Whist. From whence came down, from whence rose up? From past women, the successes and the disappointments, the intrigues and the disasters, the flirtations and the culminations, the wooings and the winnings, the rejections and the rejectings, the long affairs and the short-lived ones, the semi-platonics and the unabashedly sexual, the mild dalliances and the problematic traumas, the fond tenderness and the violent bouts of fury in clashes of fiery temperament, all the various degrees of bondage between Bill Cole and women-women-women in his life of women, more women, and yet *still* more women, which will radically stop when One Woman (by name, Helen Whist) ends that endless series of women in the plural, by succession, alternation, overlapping in the numerical multiplicity of plurality's proliferated female pluralism in Bill Cole's literally women-teeming life so steeped in women, so singularly steeped in so innumerable an amount of those special human beings, women, Bill Cole's favorite sex, because or in spite of his not belonging himself to that select, preferred gender, to which he's devoted his life; but now all the gender will be totalled in the person of a single representative: plurality ends with the singularity of Helen Whist, herself.

All those parties he went to! In vain, as it turned out to prove. His route to Helen Whist came via the non-party circuit. What matter the way, what matter the road—Jerusalem, Mecca, and Rome are approached and gotten to, in the devout fruitful end of *getting there*. Helen Whist is arrived at. Soon; time is moving there; a few hours only, before nine o'clock in Barry's apartment, where and when life as known before is over to Bill Cole, and his official apotheosis is at hand, deliverance to another realm, the Spirit's reincarnation, the metamorphosis of loneliness to fulfillment by Love's upper reaches for which all Bill Cole's days, prior to nine o'clock tonight, were remotely only a previous world.

V

He's still waiting. He's in his apartment, but it's not important where he is or isn't. Helen Whist is going to materialize soon, soon, she'll appear, she'll be there, in her publishing editor's apartment, she and Barry will be waiting for Bill Cole; or was she invited for nine as well? In which case, she may be a few minutes late, Bill Cole may *precede* her, he and Barry may be waiting for her a few minutes; or, maybe, she and

Bill Cole will ride up the same elevator together, from the lobby, from the street: they may meet *before* Barry could introduce them; they may chance upon each other entering the building, waiting for the elevator; he'd recognize her—*on the instant*. And in her, there would *he* be, recognized for the first time, the Self that had been dormant, the cocoon-wrapped Soul-in-quiescence of Bill Cole, submerged in its own latency, now emerging and found, *in her*, in Helen Whist's person: fulfillment, completion, dear deliverance, sudden fruition, self-realization, the achievement of existence by the revolutionary final phase to culminate the concealed development of private inner evolution into the dawn's primary light of life loftily lifted to its preserved pinnacle of infinity, where only those precious Souls are admitted, the elite and elect, those Chosen by Immortality's chillingly impersonal test that weeds out the undeserving and promotes those only when Love has deemed worthy. Helen Whist is the personal female Christ appointed to purge Bill Cole of his overwomened career, to redeem him in full for crimes and sins of an appallingly mediocre kind; to bathe him in the joyful blessing of grace, where, cleansed, purified, he'll undergo a two-in-one Salvation, at the hands of his Saviour, Helen Whist, who'll be Saved along with him, Saviour and Saved as One, One Saviour and Two Saved; two separated bodies on the world's stage, divided till they merge, on meeting, and take on new lives, not as bodies alone in the dividing world apart, but as Souls inseparable in Love's own sphere; beyond mortal conception and outside the comprehension of the doomed.

That's what he envisaged. Time is ticking on. Soon he'll leave his apartment and take a bus to Barry's apartment. What a seemingly ordinary journey! What a commonplace route he's taking! How pedestrian the way! With what unassumingness does Divinity conceal its Advent, the Holy consummation most unmiraculously come by, by a crowded city's plain nocturnal concourse.

VI

Time is going by. He's on the bus, headed for nine o'clock. Helen Whist, the final woman of a life given so completely to women. Met not at a party, but by a set-up with a go-between, by design, by contrivance, by deliberation, a co-ordinated plan involving three people. It's been fixed up, in advance. It's in the works. It's coming to pass. It's afoot. It's on its way. It's coming about. It's to happen.

What's to happen? *What*?

VII

He's getting there! The bus is nearing Barry's apartment, at the same time that nine o'clock is getting there too!

The event is working out. Everything is smoothly on schedule. It's flowing like an appointed river, keeping its proper currents in correct conduct keyed to the counsel of the given tides.

It's happening like clockwork. There's no hitch. The bus isn't stalled. Bill Cole alights at the bus-stop, the right one. He sights Barry's building by the given address. He's arrived. So has nine o'clock. So has destiny. Destiny, in Helen Whist's shape, dressed as her, looking like her, in her step, being her.

To be met. Only the meeting is left. All has proceeded as foreseen, as planned. The final step will be the meeting. Her initial indifference, her recovery, her Sign-giving, the scene of charged Recognition, and bodies bulging with the burden of Souls to be born.

CHAPTER 6

I

The elevator is empty. Helen Whist could have preceded him, and is up there waiting for him with Barry; *or*, she's a little late, and will arrive to find Bill Cole already there with Barry.

Or maybe Helen Whist has already been there a long time; maybe she was Barry's dinner guest, long before nine o'clock. *That*'s possible, too.

Well, whatever it is, he'll find out. His rendezvous with destiny is well underway.

Up the elevator, without a hitch. Smooth as silk, or flowing water, swift as thoughts of love, or wings of rhapsody on melodious air.

He's on Barry's floor. There's the apartment number. He buzzes the doorbell, just as, down in the lobby, he had buzzed the appropriate bell that let him be electronically admitted, on Barry's return signal, at the general door of the building itself.

So much for mere technology, and the security system in modern urban dwellings. Now for a more *spiritual* adventure. That's what he came for.

He's arrived. Barry opens the door, greeting him, with a prepared smile. Disappointment—no-one else in the apartment. Love, in the person of Helen Whist, is somewhat delayed. She'll arrive "shortly." Have a drink, meanwhile?

Bill Cole doesn't mind if be *does* have a drink. No, he wouldn't mind at all. It's all in God's hands, but he's nervous anyway. Nervous? He's trembling. This is fear and dread. What a foul premonition! What is he afraid of, what does he dread? There should be joy, instead: waiting Love's arrival.

"Don't get upset. You're trembling. Bill Cole, you worry me. You're riding for a disappointment. I kept *my* side of the bargain; *my* conscience is clear. But I warn you. Don't key your hopes on what you expect. As I said over lunch today (was it today? Yes, today, at that restaurant, where you treated me—it was today!), Helen Whist may not be the one for you. I cautioned you, in all fairness, but you got angry at me. You threatened my life. Well, I did my part. It's arranged. Helen Whist will arrive. But don't say I didn't warn you, when her arrival doesn't turn out to be what, with all your heart, you've so deeply planned, poor Bill Cole. Don't kill yourself, should paradise become disaster. Helen Whist is not as you foresee. You'll see."

II

Barry's kindly intended speech aroused Bill Cole to defiance, even to the pitch of wrath, while his spirits sank in grim depressed prospect. Was Heaven an illusion? Was Helen Whist not the Helen Whist so soulfully devised in Bill Cole's image of her? Was she not his Spirit's concoction? Was she altogether on a different scheme?

He gave Barry hell. Poor Barry. He was innocent, and unfairly dealt with. Bill Cole was unjust—unreasonable. He's living in another world—a world called "dreams." He'll wake up, soon.

III

"Soon" becomes "now." The downstairs hall buzzer rings, then Barry's answering signal, the electronic admission, the pause for the elevator time, now the apartment doorbell buzz, Barry's opening the door—a man is standing there. The man looks over Barry's shoulder, directly to Bill Cole. Unmistakably, the man pronounces, "Bill Cole, I presume? Hello. I'm Helen Whist." The tones are effeminate. Now it comes plain to Bill Cole, coldly, clearly: Helen Whist is the pen-name that this modern homosexual man has taken—reversing a woman's taking, long ago, George Eliot for a pen-name. Well! This is reality. Goodbye, Heaven. Hello, lost love. Only to *lost* love. It's solidly entered. It's there. It's standing there. Lost love, itself. *Him*self, rather. In the very person of Helen Whist. With whom Bill Cole's soul, after all, is *not* going to unite. As it so turns out. While destiny's ghost mocks. And dreams, before fading, are permitted to laugh.

IV

Well, that's that. Bill Cole has gone home. He didn't stay very long, after that.

What next? He's a bit tired. It's been an exhausting day. It's ended cheerlessly. Sleep is needed. And now.

CHAPTER 7

I

As Bill Cole was leaving, "Helen Whist," though not in taunting tones, had shouted after him, "Thanks for your review. It might bring me fame. It's certainly boosted sales. Thanks."

Bill Cole hadn't replied. He had walked out shocked. Numbed. By the failure of things to turn out in quite the manner hoped for. He was somewhat "lost." Shrouded in fog—that mental blunting force.

Now, it was days later. He's been, as it were, "recovering." He had had a blow to recover *from:* so his recovering had real material to work on, and was well based.

What now? Life, it's said, "goes on."

In vengeance, bitterly, he could publicly retract, in print, in his column, his previous praise review of Helen Whist's novel, saying that he had been mistaken, taken in; that on second reading it had proved itself a dud. (To parallel his own private experience, in his own secret mental discovery, with the book's very author, him- or herself.) But that retraction, recantation, would be a peevish, petty thing to do. He's above that sort of stuff. He'll forget the whole matter, and forge on.

Forge on, but for what? He had lost his dream. The bottom had dropped out. It was all an illusion. "True Love" didn't exist. There was no "Soul." And no Saviour, in female form.

He had deemed the book a good one. The quality of the book had nothing to do with his "romantic misfortune." He hadn't been deliberately deceived, by either Barry or Helen Whist. It was self-deception, self-delusion. Responsibility was his. He'd accept it.

He'd stand by his guns. It *was* a good book. He had been the victim of no-one's malice. There had been no persecution plot. He had only dreamed, that's all.

II

No more dreaming. That's his pledge.

But no cynicism, either. That's a bad mere alternative, to dreaming. Nothing too negative. But no dramatic hope, either.

What's left? A middle ground? No: he needed excess.

Passion. That's what's required. But *informed* passion, not what will turn out to seem misguided.

Women. He still needs them. But wisely, not too well; shall he control, if he can, this time, his loves?

Loves? Plural again? Back to plurality? In wide action over numerical fields, spread so far out that quantity-superficiality shall prevail, and not poignant deep swells of passion? And no True Love?

III

How sad. Has his life dwindled? He doesn't, so much, this time, dare?

He's terribly lonely. Two cures had been attempted, for loneliness before. First had been the Don Juan method; in the end, it went bad. Next was tried, but came to grief, the Two Destined Souls approach. Party after party, with his fallen reputation, and his string of rejections, often publicly humiliating. It had all "come to a head," as it were, with that shocking, scandalous rampage rage of his, his sensational arrest, and his subsequent triumphant vindication in the law court trial, thanks in great deal to the girl's courageous testimony in his behalf. That restored much of his lapsed standing in the social world. Now, *outside* the social world, this recent private matter between three people: himself; the go-between Barry who, Tiresias- and Cassandra-like, had tried in vain to warn him; and Helen Whist, who turned out very much not to be what his Spiritual Soul had supposed—not the agent of its great awakening. It was a fiasco, but it would be kept private; his reputation in the literary-social world would mercifully be unaffected by that stunning sequence of events, terminating in the huge Mistake-recognition.

Bill Cole is reminiscing in his apartment. He's accompanied by his most frequent companion of late: Solitude. He's taken to grotesque, macabre humor on this whole misfired affair. "Helen Whist can *still* be my Life's Only True Love, Our Souls Joined in Permanent Union. It's still not impossible. All I'd have to do (entailing some personal sacrifice, inconvenience, going deep into financial debt, and other painstakings) would be, although it's a bit out of my way, to take an unpaid leave of absence from my job (if granted), fly off to Scandinavia, undergo a complete sex-change operation, convalesce, return as a woman—Belle Cole—and woo the man Helen Whist anew, offering him a glorious opportunity to be reformed from his homosexual life to a brand new style: heterosexuality; offering him, as rare prize inducement, the reward of my virgin maidenhead, fresh from Sweden, totally untried, purely pure, for his maiden defoliation, our twin baptisms, as it were, under fire. If Fate intended us to be together, for our Souls' sake, who are we, just because of our previous sexual habits, to interfere?" Better we should adopt new sexual styles for our Souls' sake; best to adapt the less to the great.

"However, he might prefer the retention of his homosexuality; in which case, my expensive sex-change operation will have turned out useless, and I'd remain just as lonely as before, alas, with no Heaven-sent Bride—or Groom—as True Wedded Soul to mine.

"So I'll stay male—it's much simpler this way, nature's good old status quo, in staunchly safe conservatism. Why should I give up my Soul's Ultimate Search for True Love, just because Helen Whist happened not to be as female as his own name? Why should I remain a permanently damaged victim to some guy's populace-fooling penname; scarred and paralyzed by succumbing to that deception? My Search can work with someone else—a *real* women, not merely an effeminate male. Undaunted, I refuse to give up. I'll give it another try. There are hordes of women, new untried ones, unmet yet, who'll come to literary soirées, publishing parties, social gatherings, art gallery openings, and other formal celebrations for the commercially semi-sophisticated, for the aesthetically inclined, for the well-stocked categories of the book field meeting every description of literate, opportunistic, career-grubbing humanity, linked together on various festive occasions to drink, talk, meet, and chat. A woman will be indifferent to me, then give the Sign. It will be True Love, this time. I'm owed good fortune and fair dealing, a kind of retribution-by-balance, a moral reimbursing of sorts, a reparation compensation, for having endured—though at my own responsibility—that grim or silly, farcically revolting comedy in my foolish delusion over the mistaken identity of that romance-turned-horror story, "Helen Whist." I played, indeed, the Romeo buffoon role, and played it well. It was almost too real, for the stage it was performed on. Now let me return to playing the part of the serious romantic hero, the lead role, the hero who wins the heroine cut out to the heroic measure of his own high heroism, a character of classic nobility whose fate magically shall go untragic. The conclusion shall be as lofty as it is fortunate. The happy ending, immortal love. On a Godlike scale. Ascending the Heavens, in the Final Duet."

Such was the interior monologue, indicating renewed determination and the resumption of idealism, of Bill Cole: recently defeated, stunned, numbed; but now on recovery's bath, rebounding back to bold ardor and high energetic resolve.

He's ready to venture forth again. The former Don Juan, the all-but-Mozarted Don Giovanni, turns toward women. For where there are women, *there* may very well, amongst them, be, at last, That Woman.

Without whom, he's still as yet unSouled. But let *her* change that.

CHAPTER 8

I

For his confidence's sake, Bill Cole can't afford too many such more setbacks, reversals, as lately too embarrassingly taken on his ego's handsome chin. Being Loved by the Right One is the goal. (The wrong one, of course, just won't do.)

The Right One at first must be indifferent to him, then love him and reveal the unmistakable Sign (what it would look like, Bill Cole yet didn't know, and won't till it's actually flashed, in its occurrence that happens as an event on his felt field of experience, by and in conjunction with that particular Right One).

Of course, it goes without saying that he must love her as well, in kind and intensity of simultaneous degree. That would be natural, fair, essential, and in keeping with "the order of things": the logical harmony of a well-run universe.

What if the universe isn't well-run? Too bad, but maybe it won't prevent his own individual life from anyway itself being well-run. But what if *that*'s not well-run, either? Well, he can still aim for Divine Love. But what if *that* fails, too? (As it *has*, lately.) Well, then he can look for the perfect imperfection. What for? Well, because he's got to look for *something*, hasn't he? Yes, but . . .

II

He's in his office at the magazine he regularly writes for, at his desk, writing a book review. Sometimes he does his writing at home; this time, it happens to be at the office.

His boss, the editor, abruptly enters the small business room. "Bill Cole, I received a suspicious phone call."

"Did it concern me, Boss?"

"It sure did."

"Could you perhaps elaborate at greater length? Just to fill me in?"

"It was from a woman."

"Oh! One of those!"

"Yes, there sure are a lot of them. More than even *you* have ever met, Bill Cole."

"If the phone call from this woman concerned *me*, Boss, then why did she phone *you?*"

"For complication's sake."

"Oh yes. A worthy cause. What did she say about me, Boss?"

"What she said about you reflected somewhat on you, Bill Cole, in referring to you."

"No wonder you're telling me this, Boss. It had so much to do with me."

"That's why I thought you'd like to know about it, Bill Cole."

"It certainly does arouse my curiosity, Boss. But, now that you're on this subject, couldn't you reduce a portion of the mystery I'm enshrouded by, or veiled with, by divulging some relevant details?"

"You'd like a little more information, Bill Cole, on this matter we've been discussing?"

"Yes, why not shed some light on it? I'm rather in the dark about it. Some enlightenment wouldn't be out of place; here."

"I'm certainly willing to oblige, Bill Cole. That's why I interrupted your writing by barging into your office."

"That's no liberty, it's your right. You're the boss."

"That I am, Bill Cole. And it's your duty to keep recognizing it."

"Oh, I *do*, Boss. I defer to you in what pertains to the magazine. But back to that woman's phone call: did it have to do with the magazine, as well as with me?"

"Not directly, Bill Cole; but indirectly, since what has to do with you indirectly has to do with the magazine as well, you being a part of the magazine, a regular contributor to it."

"Thanks, Boss. But what did she say about me?"

"I'm coming to that point, Bill Cole."

"That would satisfy my considerably aroused interest, Boss."

"I *knew* this matter would interest you, Bill Cole. That's why I came here to tell you about it."

"Well, I'll listen very attentively, Boss. You won't just talk to empty ears."

"And by the time I'm finished, those ears will be even *less* empty. And in no uncertain terms, either."

"That sounds logical, Boss. Well, why not reveal what it's all about, Boss?"

"Right now?"

"The time seems just about right for it, Boss."

"You've got a good point there, Bill Cole. Granted. So, shall I let you have it?"

"Fire away, Boss. Shoot straight."

"Only if you're ready, Bill Cole."

"I'm *more* than ready, Boss. My ears have done a good housekeeping job, cleaning up all the clutter of the residue of what's accumulated there, in order to be bright and shining in preparation for your delivery, Boss. That's how fully attentive I am."

"Fine. You've done the groundwork, I see."

"Sure, a little sweeping up, getting things out of the way so that the impact of what you're about to bring in won't be lost in any dusty crowd, Boss."

"That's fine, Bill Cole. Well, is that my cue?"

"I prompt you, urge you, to speak now, Boss. You'll be heard, to the fine sharp click of a totally receptive concentration equal to the ovaries' keen egging on of sperm for fertilizing impact in the biology of reproduction among creatures in nature that duplicate their kind."

"You'll not, then, misconstrue what I'm about to say? Nor distort it in the misconception of a faulty comprehension? Nor violate its letter or spirit, by an act of confusion?"

"No, I'll take it straight in, and give it a direct interpretation, not interfere with whatever point you're making by making an error on the receiving end of the transmission you're about to impart by the language of a vocal communication."

"I'm free, then, to express myself, or deliver myself of what will be dispatched to you as to what the woman phoned me about?"

"Of course, Boss. When did she phone you? What did she say?"

"She phoned me a few minutes ago."

"Boss, that's impossible: *we*'ve been talking for more than a few minutes."

"How time flies!"

"Why? Is it a bird?"

"That's what time is, Bill Cole. A bird, but not a perching one; rather, one that's 'on the wing.' "

"I follow your distinction, Boss. So she phoned before you came here to tell me about it?"

"That's about the right sequence, Bill Cole."

"So far, so good, Boss. Well, she phoned you. But what did she *say?*"

"What did she *say!?* Ah, that's the point I'm coming to, Bill Cole!"

"You mean all this up to now has only been a preamble?"

"Yes, preliminary to telling you what she actually *said*."

"Yes, what *did* she say, Boss?"

"Well, what she *did* say is just about the crux of the matter. That's the central essence, as far as her message went."

"Could you be more specific, Boss?"

"Sure, Bill Cole. What do you want to know?"

"What she said about me, and why she phoned *you*, if it was about *me*."

"She didn't want to hurt your feelings."

"That's considerate of her. She spared my feelings, by phoning *you*."

"That's about it, Bill Cole."

"Yes, but what did she actually *say?*"

"I'm a little vague about it, Bill Cole. Hold still, while I recollect."

There was a pause, while the Boss strained his memory till it discharged itself of the burden tensely coiled within that context.

III

"Boss, before you begin, can I delay you?"

"I consider that my relaying to you what the woman told me by phone in regard to you has already undergone a lengthy delay. But if you insist, Bill Cole."

"I do, Boss. But, to be short about it, I'll be brief. I suspect that it was a crank call. May I guess what she told you?"

"What fun, Bill Cole! *Do* guess."

"She told you that she met me at a party recently, for the first time, was introduced to me, and felt complete indifference toward me."

"Bill Cole, that's uncanny of you! Why, that's precisely what she told me. But then she said more."

"May I guess what that 'more' was?"

"Do try, Bill Cole. But are you a clairvoyant?"

"This *does* sort of have an occultly mystical sound about it, I confess. I can't explain the amazing success of my ability here to guess."

"Well, guess again, Bill Cole."

"She then told you that, following her initial indifference to me, she underwent a strange transformation in her feelings about me, which she couldn't prevent, to the extent that . . ."

"You're right, so far, Bill Cole. Go on."

"Her indifference changed to love for me! But she was too shy to confide directly in me as to this strange, miraculous birth of love for me that seemed spontaneously to burst forth in her unsuspecting breast."

"Bill Cole! This is unbelievable! You're right! But how did you I *know?*"

"Well, Boss, shall I admit how I know?"

"At once, Bill Cole! Cut out the suspense!"

"When the phone rang I picked up the extension in my office because I thought you had gone to the bathroom and because the telephone receptionist at the switchboard was just leaving for lunch and hadn't yet been replaced. So I picked up the phone, at *my* end, and before I knew it, your voice and this woman's voice were already connected up on the line, and when I heard the woman mention my name, I dispensed with ethics and morality about privacy and eavesdropping, and eagerly listened in, in a blaze of fascination, as though my whole life would be altered—which it might be—by what that woman accounted for, attested to, in the inner workings of her heart, concerning her intimate feelings—which she had to reveal to you, to relieve herself of that almost painful burden—about, of all people, me."

"Bill Cole, I forgive you for listening in on my phone conversation. It's all too understandable, it's all too human. How *could* you put that phone down? So what if you committed a breach of office ethics, a violation of procedural forms, of the given code of rules customary in civil conduct for the courtesy of reserve and the respect accorded to privacy? These were indeed special circumstances, and, with all my heart, I forgive you, while also urging you to *act* on that extraordinary call. If you listened to the end, you heard the woman giving me her phone number to impart it to you. That's an invitation. To Love."

"Boss, I accept that invitation. I was waiting for you, here, to come in and tell me. But I felt shy about telling you that I already knew. I'm glad it all got resolved this way, Boss."

"Bill Cole, will you marry her?"

"Sure, but not before I phone her and arrange to see her, to have a meeting with her so that I can find out who she is; for I confess that I have no recollection of having met her: I draw a blank, as to her identity. I know which party she referred to, it was a big publishing party to celebrate the launching of a rather unimportant book last week, and I spoke to *lots* of people that night, almost all of whom, by coincidence, happened to have been women. So I can't single her out in my memory. She was 'lost in the crowd,' so to speak."

"Well, focus on her *now*, Bill Cole. She dearly begs you to respond to the opportunity. She suffers a royal pang of love for you, which, shyly, she partly concealed by phoning *me* about it."

"Boss, though I can't visualize her in any particular shape or form, I already requite her love, in a vague act of faith—like a blank check to be filled in later with all due particulars."

IV

Bill Cole was ecstatic—nothing short of that. His benevolent Boss rejoiced for him. By a resounding echo of true identification, sweetly feasting at empathy's overflowing table, the Boss dwelled, himself, in Bill Cole's great stroke of enchantment. This Love seemed unalloyed, in its strain of high purity. The rarest of good fortune was Bill Cole's, by all appearances, in the alchemy of Souls in a true blend. So, in surface, did it irresistibly seem, by some potion distilled in One Magic Beam from Divinity's endless sun, catching Bill Cole square at his immortal core, in his Spirit's Home, built only now, full-born, for the care of his attendant Bride.

V

Joy, supreme. Bill Cole's Boss embraced him, he brought out a bottle of rare old wine for special celebration. The Boss was happily married, a loyal family man. He had felt paternal to Bill Cole, despite being quite a few years younger than his bachelor book-reviewer and literary columnist whom he allowed to occasionally contribute to other periodicals. Bill Cole was underpaid, and was consequently still poor after many years of faithful service to the publication. The Boss pitied him for that, but could do nothing about it, due to the cold economy of the facts of life at the financial heart of the magazine, which, despite its wide circulation and national distribution, barely eked out a make-even profit in the statistical ledger of business; such accounts accounted for the aging book reviewer's continued marginal poverty, in spite of his fame in intellectual circles, his long-established esteem among the book-loving elite.

Maybe this woman is wealthy! That would not only solve Love's problem, but more material considerations as well! Oh, hopeful ideal!

CHAPTER 9

I

Her name, simply enough, was Jill. She'd become "Jill Cole," if that marriage, made in heaven, were to take place on the earth by some official ceremony, as though Heaven were dubious and not to be trusted in matters pertaining, strictly speaking, to the conjugal—which earth had pre-empted from its rather grand if remote cousin.

She had only given the Boss one phone number, presumed to be her home one, as if she wasn't employed in any office in a line of business. Bill Cole had jotted it down himself while phone-eavesdropping on her hook-up with his Boss, who also wrote it down on a slip of paper which he's now passed on to Bill Cole, not knowing that the latter had recorded the same number on his *own* slip of paper, along with the same name, Jill, whose part in Bill Cole's future loomed indeed gigantic, without that future being too far removed from arrival into the suburbs and precincts of the province of immediate concerns, the pressing business of the matter at hand.

II

It was now late afternoon at the office. Bill Cole was trying to complete the book review he had been working on at the time his Boss had barged into the room with a look of cunning enigma. When Bill Cole had listened in on the phone call, minutes earlier, he had interrupted the writing of the review. Following the revelations between himself and his Boss, they drank wine in celebration of a great stroke of good fortune they had assumed to be in the works, to raise Bill Cole's Love Life from nothing to everything on the graph of improvement so major as to say that the superlative had abruptly succeeded, without so much as a transition in the interim, the level of lowest minimum on the Love Life Chart of the same man, Bill Cole.

Now, he was trying to finish the interrupted review while the book was still fresh and as yet unfaded in his recent memory of reading it.

He was distracted, though, by thoughts of Jill. She had qualified by being at first indifferent to him, before beginning to feel love. Then, as he so regarded, she revealed the Sign—by confiding in his Boss as intermediary. A finer go-between couldn't be imagined, so kind and loyal, so generously good-willed, in bearing Bill Cole's best interest in mind. "That was the Sign, itself," Bill Cole considered: "Her phoning my Boss to tell him of her early indifference and subsequent change of heart. That was the unique Sign. All the prescribed requisites have been followed by this woman. She's won my Heart, by terms of my Holy Vow. Thus she's all mine, as I'm hers, by Souls Ordained. We clinch Destiny's Prophecy, which was made before the first day in the Genesis of the world, even before words and light were made by the Creator, our Lord. All is now confirmed. Such weighty matters of vast import involuntarily divert me from finishing this book review, for which there's a pressing deadline, with the issue about to go to press. I'll hold off phoning Jill till I've finished this infernal review. I'll bend my mind to it, by sheer force of will."

He finished it, brought it into the Boss'es office, but as his Boss wasn't there he gave it to the secretary, who carefully gave it a quick copyreading for any error-detection before sending it to the typesetter for conversion to galleys as a stage toward the printed magazine all glossy and new for the next issue, gleaming with black, fresh, even print on white paper of sleek but economical composition, ready for distributing to a wide readership.

Work was done for that day. Now it's time for amorous play—not lighthearted, but immensely solemn.

To phone Jill. That's the deed. It's five o'clock in the middle of a working week. There was only one number to call. It's probably her home number. But what if she's employed and can't be reached? Maybe she's a teacher in school or college, or has some office job at odd hours. She may not be home when he phones. Then again, she may be. So phone.

"Hello, is that Jill?"

"At last! It's *you*, Bill Cole!"

III

Well, it's her, all right. She's really on the phone. Bill Cole is in his office, where he dialed her. For privacy, he's closed the door.

"I got your message, which was the Sign—by the manner you conveyed that message, by way of my Boss as our go-between—that uniquely you're divinely intended as mine alone, my Soul's Match, my Knower, my Redeemer, my Saviour, my Fulfiller. By the great Spirit between us, you're already my lawful Bride. To meet you might be vulgar and redundant, with so much already confirmed in the Invisible Sphere. But let's meet and sleep together tonight by partnership of our bodies. Our bodies have to catch up with our Souls, in intimacy: they lag so far behind, that a dangerous schism might erupt—dualism between the material and the mental—which could overseparate us as knowers and us as carnal lovers of each other. We must be all in all, omitting nothing whatever, of our boundless bond of complete inclusiveness. By our abundance, we share in Nature's own bounty, whose general Source is ours as well. By all that's universal, then, let me visit you now and behold you. Love is so much in the Now, that delay blasphemes it."

"Please arrive, Bill Cole. I'm not me except that you're by me. Here's my address . . ."

"I've written it carefully down. I'll leave my office and take a taxi."

"It would be an expensively long ride, for I know that your salary and savings are indeed modest. Come by subway."

"As you say, Jill. I'm on my way."

IV

What disappointment! Coming up from the subway, locating her street as per directions, then finding the building where her apartment was, it was obvious to Bill Cole—all too melancholily apparent, though he should have known in advance from his knowledge of that area in the big city that the district was hardly first-rate so far as residential classiness went—that Jill was hardly rich.

She lived in a veritable slum! Could Bill Cole's Own True Love have turned out to be as poor as he? No *wonder* their Love was made in Heaven: only Heaven could tolerate the material basis of poverty that their Sublime Bond of Souls would have, in earthly terms, to subsist on.

Well, they'd manage to scrape by. Love would find the way. Over mountains and seas, if necessary. The way of true love is often strewn with thorns. Not smooth and easy, love's way is often rough, rocky, and unsteady. But love will find the way. What a way! And what a feat is love, to weigh the feet that trod away and win their way to Love, far and away the best way to outweigh care's burden. Love is way out in front, and has a way of staying there, to put care out of the way. Love weighs well, in heaven's way to the human heart.

V

Bill Cole was now walking up the stairs of her dingy, elevatorless building. Squalid odors came from mangy apartments. True Love was really being put to the test, now. If Love could survive *this* . . .

More disappointment. Knocking at her apartment door high up in the cheerless building—a tenement sort of affair, in the low-rent bracket—Bill Cole saw it opened to reveal his Dearest Jill as being crippled and paralyzed in a wheelchair, with a twisted face all contorted to one side in a blur of marred features, astigmatic eyes that were crossed out of all focus in a squint of intolerable ugliness. Was this Love's Trial? Was he being tested? As in a fairy tale full of childish superstition, was Jill's ugliness really a toad that would turn into a Princess if given the right reassurance of Love's dose? The Princess held captive in the toad's squat body, to be released if the hero (Bill Cole, in this case) passes this repugnance test, this loathing-endurance, by singing out the purity of his Love for that vile, loathesome-looking toad, a physical marvel for how far repulsiveness could go in a world already notable for its imperfections that strain beauty's standards and upset idealistic codes everywhere, violating aesthetic rules, mocking the precepts of good taste, repudiating all cultivated principles, defiling our civilized doctrines of higher refinement.

VI

Hideous to look at, and apparently quite poor, what attractive assets did Jill, by way of compensation, possess? There *must* be redeeming features; the features of her face were feats of atrocity. They murdered beauty by the vital organ of its ideal. They so twisted harmony, that its grotesque distortion smothered aesthetics under the mask and visage of ultimate caricature.

As once the Don Giovanni of his social set, set to music by a Mozartless hand who wrote the score of numerous loves that Da Ponte could make libretto from (though Da Ponte wrote the libretto *before* Mozart wrote the score—that should set the score straight), poor Bill Cole was used to beauty's highest standards as applied to the kingdom of women, a kingdom whose crown he'd won, whose sceptre he'd held, whose throne royally he'd occupied by the regal seat of his own well-tailored pants.

Finally, he finds his Own True Love: shaped and featured so unseemly, that Ugliness sets a new physical low to the dismal level of standards by female imperfection. Is that a joke, an irony, a puckish paradox played impishly by misfortune's genius for malice upon the completely surprised Bill Cole?

He'd expected Jill to be a rare beauty. Had they not met at a glamorous publishing party, full of ranking beauties that adorn such cultural get-togethers supported by the book industry to the high tune of powerful commercialism? He could recall meeting no-one crippled and paralyzed to a wheelchair. He must have been drunk by the time he met the woman who turned out to be this Jill he was now just visiting on the premise of acting out between them Love's highest office.

And she, a physical ugly, had the audacity to be indifferent to *him* at that party! Oh, what galling retrospect!

Then she quickly switched from indifference to Love, as though guessing Bill Cole's requisites for a woman to qualify as his Sole Love; then, too shy—or was it a ruse?—to phone Bill Cole directly, she took the detour of phoning his Boss, at the office, which Bill Cole, somewhat to his guilt, listened in on; he chose to interpret that as the Sign magically revealed, revealing that Jill was destined as Bill Cole's One and Only even before Genesis first discovered light and words, or rather caused them, via the Lord, to be created upon the face of the world-about-to-be-born, a fundamentalist invention according to the Gospel of religious faith by the ancient myth of Christianity that still gets practiced in the world of advanced machines.

Jill met the qualifications required. But Bill Cole felt less devout, now, about honoring those qualifications and in Jill's case granting her such reward that would bind him forever to her less-than-appetizing soul and skin.

He'd renege on his Holy Vow. His concept of it when making it hadn't foreseen what hideous ultimate shape it would take, the Jill it would assume, in time's prank on him, exploiting his vulnerable weakness, his obsessive craving for a crazy dream of True Love. Crazy dream? Obsessive craving? These are late interpretations, dated only since entering Jill's apartment. Before that, he was earnest and devout, in pious fidelity to True Love as the sole reality; sole and solar, for souls to the number of two, so combined that infinity results, and, on the same scale, eternity's dimension as well; which outweigh, between them, all else known by reality's outmoded name between the outer borders of our universe itself, where life and death take on their various forms in wide contention, filling in a packed ball which the lost years of emptiness surround in singular song.

Now, all that seems nonsense. Jill has destroyed his ideals. She shocks his illusions away. His dreams can't endure, by her living offense to them. Love is insulted, by her very presence. *Her* face! *Her* form! *Her* nature! Love as generality dies, when reduced to such gross particulars.

Love will never be the same again. Will it even, ever, *be* again—in the person of any other woman? Or has the future caved in? Has Love run out of time, by so fatal an example as Jill's, ruining Love's chances for Bill Cole with as yet that still-unmet woman—who, but for Jill, *could have*, in time, fulfilled and redeemed Bill Cole's lost Soul, lonely, betrayed by Jill, spoiled and drained of later chances?

CHAPTER 10

"How can you get outside in the street when you're in a wheelchair living on the fifth floor—crippled and paralyzed—of this filthy building that has no elevator but merely a rackety staircase? And you're alone, with no-one to help you. How do you get about?"

"Oh Bill Cole, do you *always* ask embarrassing questions? You, so sophisticated! Did you leave your courtesy and diplomatic tact behind you, downstairs, feeling ashamed to carry them up this awful building all rotten with the dank sweat of its own squalor? You snob looking down your princely nose! You're the *moral* cripple. Basically, we're equal.

"Am I not good enough for the likes of you, you with your airs of mighty refined gentility imposing as a would-be gentleman but now getting a tonguelashing from a shrill crippled bitch who's not what you supposed her to be by your grand foredream of romantic pastel shades that tinted me the rosy pink soft and rich and sweet, instead of the shrew I am and poor and ugly and mangled, foul-tempered, with a wicked evil tongue and a vitriolic outlook from my squinting eyes and the venom dripping from my bared fangs?"

"Why, Jill, what a monster you turned out to be! You're simply revolting. Love must have been Blind, to lead me here."

"*You* took that chance. Take the responsibility. Accept your Fate. I'm yours."

"Not so. I repudiate this whole deal. I renounce all involvement. I submit my complete resignation. I rescind all I said. I unsay it, and more."

"Wrong. It's too late to back out now, Bill Cole. You're mine forever."

"No, Jill, I made no commitment that would sign away my soul to you. My visit was not a binding one, but just that of a browser who came on speculation, a scouting mission that left me under no obligation."

"So you retract your Holy Vow of Love? You turncoat traitor renegade! I'll boil you in water and get a sour revenge on you."

"Your breath is foul. Don't wheel yourself so close to me. You offend my sight, my nose, my mind, my ears—even your touch would be revolting: but *that*'s a pleasure I'll well avoid."

"You can't get out of it. When you phoned before, you said you'd come over for sex. Well, now that you've arrived, I hold you to what now I deem a pledge. Take your clothes off. We'll have sex."

"By all that's decent, Jill—if delicate humanity has any hold over you—a thousand times no! Sex with you would turn me against the act forever, with fair creatures whose gender you drag down to degradation by the abomination of your belonging."

Jill harangues Bill Cole, to the boiling point. He can take just so much abuse; then, letting out so violent an oath that plaster coats of paint peel off the ceiling as though startled into animation, the much beleaguered man declares, "Jill, you're an uncouth barbarian."

"Enough of such pleasantries, Bill Cole. Just take your clothes off. Bare not your feeble protests, but rather your aging but still hard body, so that my lust's ogre may feast on the remnants of your ravaged manhood."

"Jill, I dread the savage fury, the demonic beast, by which your misshapen body gets driven and bounced about, though confined to that private scooter machine you depend on for locomotive necessities, by defect of your pathetic limbs gnarled and knotted by their atrophy."

"Stall no more, Bill Cole. Pander to my crippled lust, with all your hearty parts. Let's couple, you in firm health, and I writhing beneath, so lame and lost, without my trusty wheelchair."

"When I knocked at your door just before, it was opened immediately. Were you right there by the door? Or were you away, but wheeled fast?

"Your body, Bill Cole. Your body. Hand it over, please. I'll drain your feeble last manhood's ounce from it, with glee to put pain in pleasure's place, taking you erotic and leaving you neurotic, till I teach you impotence, to solve your horror by putting your copulating faculty out of commission for the duration of your remaining life on this desensualized earth. Do you have children?"

"No."

"Were you married?"

"Never."

"Never? There's always me. I have a strict hold over you. It's not too late. Marry *me*."

"No, Jill."

"I'm fifteen years younger than you, at least. Why, I'm practically giving myself away!"

"Please, Jill."

"You're fascinated. That's why you remain in my apartment, instead of opening the door and running down the stairs. Technically, you're free to do that. But you can't. Your will has abdicated, defected, to mine. I've taken you over. I've cast a spell."

"Jill, how can you get downstairs, if you must remain in your wheelchair? Are you feigning the extent of your incapacity?"

"Darling! You see right through me! Look!"

She stands up, shoving the wheelchair away behind her; it rolls and crashes against the bed. She walks around normally. She has command over her body; and not just over hers: she extends her dominion to Bill Cole's body. She undresses him. She gets him on the bed. He's passive. But potent. He can't protest. He could only protest by impotence. But she rules over him, by making him potent—quite conquering his will, annexing it to hers, taking him over, fixing him pinned helpless to her dominating desire.

He's her mascot, her special toy masochist. Her bidding, is his to obey. He's relinquished his understanding, accepting such docility for his portion that abject servility binds him to her ruthless dictates. The quest for True Love has led right here. The Souls are well wedded with harsh physical finality. He's her sexual slave: assertion takes no other form, than obedient sex, to such capacity that outdoes even youth's prime, for she's put him in a frenzy, and brought his energy to a pitch, but tamed his daring to only lust's permitted outlet. Beyond that, he dares nothing, and she keeps him there, cures him of other longings, saps his will for the world, trains him as a pet, to live for her alone. He's accepted these terms, choosing only what she chooses him to choose. He's lost to the outside. He's forgotten about his magazine boss, his column, his reviews, his renown in fine circles as an established critic and literary arbiter. He's forgotten society, the culture-commerce complex; he craves no more parties.

He's enclosed in his Jill. She has a small income, enough to keep them both in conditions of squalor. Having each other, they need barely more than just those hardy necessities that shelter, clothe, and feed them. They're completely unified. As a sacrificed individual, he's reduced to only those qualities that relate with Jill, on terms of her total ascendancy, in every aspect of their living.

He's stripped of pride. There's none left.

Dignity? Not to the point. The point is, Her. His God, Jill.

CHAPTER 11

I

His apartment is left unattended to, while he stays in Jill's. He neglects his job. He doesn't report to the magazine office or phone up his Boss. The latter is worried, not having heard from Bill Cole for days; deadlines are getting dangerously close. Phoning to Bill Cole's apartment, there's no reply, by day or by night. Other writers are assigned the columns, articles, and reviews that ordinarily Bill Cole would do.

He's missing. He's a missing person. Is it a police matter?

In this city, it's easy to get lost. The Boss imagined possibilities. Bill Cole could have run afoul of some dirty deal, as one of crime's intentionally anonymous victims. By now, he could be killed, run over, kidnapped, carried off, put away, under cover, insane, hospitalized, done in, dumped, damaged, or who knows what? Bill Cole is a virtual son to the Boss, though older by years. The Boss is overcome. He must find Bill Cole. The star reviewer has to turn up safe.

In a burst of lightning, by the pierce of a bolt, by one illuminating flash, it suddenly dawned on the Boss (he could have kicked himself for not realizing it sooner), that the key to the mystery would naturally be that woman, Jill, whose phone call to him last week about—and eavesdropped in on his extension by—Bill Cole, may have triggered off a series of events leading to the alarming, lengthy, unexplained disappearance of the crack reviewer.

She had confided in the Boss, through the invisible medium, her too-shy-to-be-directly-declared love for that man she had met at a publishing party. She gave the Boss her phone number with the request that his specified employee please gratify her by using it.

The whole conversation had been overheard by the employee himself from his own little office. Bill Cole had taken the using of the Boss as intermediary to be the revealed magic Sign that this was the woman he was destined for, as well as vice versa in this inter-destiny business, which would unite lives that had so far been unsatisfactorily separate.

The Boss congratulated him for finally finding—being found by—his True Love, after so many heartbreaking detours through Don Juanism and a period of social disgrace, fashionable rejections, party scandals, mistaken identities, false leads, and other bunglings that prepared him (through the bumpy miswisdom of fortune's permission for random accident to rule by the broken road of chance, all uneven and never predictably regulated by either divine guidance or any direct human control) for finally finding—being found by—his True Love, after so many heartbreaking detours, etcetera, in the circuitry of events unfolding without pattern on a wide scroll of human time.

Before finishing his interrupted book review in time for the secretary to look over for errors as quick copyeditor before she sent it to the typesetter with the next issue about to be pressed out, Bill Cole, with his Boss, celebrated over wine in the office this breakthrough from banal love-gropings into, at last, the realm of Love Conferred by Divine Proclamation, which excuses human will from its feeble operations.

The review handed in to the secretary, the Boss being out at that time, Bill Cole had been seen by that secretary, then, to enter his office and close the door. It must have been then that he made what must have been the most important phone call of his life, from the number that Jill had dictated by phone to the Boss, which Bill Cole, from the other extension, had himself also taken down, with leaping eager delight at grasping Love by its long-retarded but now finally present bulge of great juicy ripeness.

An immediate appointment must have been arranged. That's safe to presume. He must have then left the office to go see her right away, to kill off all further delay, now that Love's opportunity was summoning him with its unmistakable call that, *for the very life of him*, he must harken to, and with great glee, heed.

"For the very life of him?" What did that mean, now?

Then he disappeared, and has never returned.

"Never?" That's too harsh, melodramatic, and ominous a term. "Not yet" is better: he's "not yet" returned.

Bill Cole was about to get "swept away," "carried away." Yes, but just how far has passion carried him? And not one word from him, all this time!

He hadn't even remembered meeting her, at that now-fatal party. But the impact of *her* memory remained sufficiently vivid to set loose wild mating calls and Soul-cries from those people who were evidently starving for each other, as retrospect is now wisely commended and piously entitled to conclude.

Bill Cole had attached occult significance to that chain of events: her initial indifference to him on meeting, her reversal to Love for him, and, most critically of all, her indirect communication via the Boss as intermediary by phone that—at first to his guilt—Bill Cole had not unhooked himself away from, in his keen listening on secretly his own extension. Interpreting all this as favorable to his Holy Vow, seeing all this in a Transcendental light, as though God had arranged it long in advance and now the due hour had struck, Bill Cole acted in a decisive manner—and has been gone since.

A week has passed, not one word from him. Why, it's just not like him! Especially concerning work, he had been reliability itself, taking on responsibility with confidence-inspiring dependability of a very high order, in spite of such low earnings through years of faithful service.

It would have been in keeping with his character to contact his Boss. His silence is cause for serious concern. There's an alarming core at the heart of this confounding mystery. The Boss is determined, now, to get to the bottom of it.

He was such a party-goer! But now, parties have come and gone that he was invited to but never attended. That's *most* unlike him!

People have phoned the Boss asking where was Bill Cole at these parties. The publishing world, with its literary, art, and social extensions into the cultural heart of the city, has been in a whirl over what became of Bill Cole for his not being present at occasions from which he never before was absented. The Boss could furnish no explanation, but fabricated this reason or that reason, with inconsistency, to put the callers off. Now, the rumor mill is humming. Bill Cole is missing. There must be some woman behind it. It's become a mystery. Lots of versions are heard. It's reaching the papers, it's hit the magazines, there are lots of speculations. Bill Cole is too conspicuous a figure not to be missed. Tongues are wagging. It's the party conversation piece, of the current season. It exerts endless fascination. Never was he so publicized, and in the blaze of the limelight, as by his dramatic length of absence, intensified with the passing of each evening that sees his notable, marked absence from the fancy social occasions, these ritual gatherings so cunningly woven in a complicated society by the culture-commercial complex, which promotes these affairs and is promoted by them, in dizzying layers of intricacy that lay bare the machinery for endless mystique and exploitative intrigue. Bill Cole is being fed into that machinery, by the sensation—ever enlarging—of his unaccounted-for but probably woman-connected disappearance from the world that's *his* world: the culture-commercial complex, especially its literary side, the books that pile up to document the society of his time.

The anthologies that Bill Cole had compiled and edited are enjoying brisk resales on bookshop shelves as hot items, thanks to the stir made in bookbuying circles by his sensational disappearance from the scenes he had once haunted in his presence and was now haunting in an altogether different sense.

Such renewed vogue would surely bring in more incoming revenue. But how can Bill Cole benefit, if he's away? The Boss mulled it over. Feeling somehow responsibly guilty for Bill Cole's remaining so criminally underpaid despite distinguished service over years in his employ on the magazine staff, the Boss at least did one quickly helpful thing, of a practical emergency vein: he traced Bill Cole's landlord, whom he contacted to find out what the apartment rent was. The Boss made the landlord, by phone, promise not to serve eviction notice on Bill Cole, by guaranteeing to pay rent due during the occupant's absence. The Boss made out checks for two months' rent that included the next month, and sent them by special messenger to the landlord's real estate office. This guaranteed that Bill Cole's vital possessions— books, papers, documents, manuscripts, records, correspondence with people of future historical significance—will remain in proper files and drawers and shelves and folders and boxes and compartments in the apartment, rather than be dumped out on the street (by the landlord's act of dispossessing him) for the municipal garbage trucks to take up and grind up into waste pulp of totally banal uselessness.

Earlier, the Boss had done another loyal service for Bill Cole: testifying in his favor as a character witness at the court trial over the defendant's being accused of throwing the angry rampage rage at the party he had crashed, a tantrum to act out in real as well as appearance his being fashionably rejected for conspicuous social standing by a pretty girl who later then had the courage to confess her part in goading Bill

Cole. Hers and the Boss'es testimony were both instrumental in getting Bill Cole acquitted at such stage of his career of grim decline, when the wolves and vultures were howling at him in the lowest ebb of his reputation star.

"He's a sympathetic, understanding, generous man," the Boss sobbed reminiscently. "He's drudged away doing hack work, for the feeble income I've enabled him to derive from gifts as a foremost literary critic. I must leave no stone unturned, as it were, to take every possible step to rescue him from whatever peril he's in and get him back safely. I must save a good man, for a busy and brutal world, the ruthless machinery that grinds talents into slick stencil, narrow formats of stereotype, flat gray areas—but Bill Cole has resisted that successfully. I dearly love him, as a son. He's missing, and now, swiftly, I'll act."

■

Phoning up the Police Department's Missing Persons Bureau had been the Boss'es desperate solution, in his distraught agony over what could have happened—he imagined everything—to his favorite employee. But before resorting to that recourse, he had found, in his own handwriting, Jill's name and phone number on a slip of paper lying on Bill Cole's desk. He should have discovered it and used it long before. Precious time has gone by, dangerously bordering on "Could it be too late?" Now anxiety has gone acutely past the worry level into wild desperation's hysteria; he must prevent desperation—which contains hope yet—from plunging into despair, which has abandoned hope. Who else can contact Bill Cole? There seem to be no relatives, no buddies, no intimates, no cronies, private to Bill Cole's heart (beyond the open public of the party-attending world of society's culture-commercial complex, primarily concerning publishing but including aspects of mental industry as well, including even intellectual spheres to whom thought is paramount in its applications to universal problems of humanity itself and such like matters) except his Boss, who's his best friend and close adviser—perhaps, indeed, *only* friend, for all the socializing that gets done, those gatherings, the stable continuum of parties for various occasions, combining art, literature, business, and communications among people for all purposes and under so many brackets.

Bill Cole is missing; and *has* been, quite overlong. A decisive step has to be taken, before "too late" becomes the horrid state. Now is the time. The Boss dials Jill's number, from the office; he should have done it before. At least, though, he's come to do it now. The call is getting through, in that, at the other end, he can hear the ringing. The ringing is succeeded by a voice: not Jill's as he remembers hers to have been, but another voice altogether: the live voice of Bill Cole. It's not too late and he's not dead! It's him, himself. The very man.

CHAPTER 12

|

"Hello?" was what Bill Cole's living voice had gone into saying.

"Bill Cole, come home."

"But I *am* home. Who is this?"

"Don't you recognize my voice, Bill Cole? You always *used* to recognize it. Have you changed so much, since you disappeared?"

"I *haven't* disappeared. Jill has been seeing me every day since she Saved me. I've been found, since being with Jill. Before that, for all my life, I had been lost."

"Bill Cole! Are you mad!?"

"I was crazy *before*. Jill Saved me. Now I've found the Way. And the Way is Jill."

"Is she your Christ figure, in a female version?"

"Christ never Saved anyone, he was a fumbling amateur, compared to Jill, who's the Real Thing."

"You're blaspheming, Bill Cole. It offends me, despite the atheist you remember me to have always been."

"I don't remember you at all. Who are you?"

"My voice isn't familiar to you?"

"I've only been Born Anew—that is, for the First Time—since being with Jill. What my life was before that, I neither care nor remember."

"You're *lost*, Bill Cole! You sound beyond reclaim. The social-literary world is buzzing about you. Come back to this world. It's *your* world, Bill Cole."

"My only world is that of the Heaven of Jill. I'm where I am. I'm right here, in my right place."

"Where? I must come over and rescue you."

"I don't know who you are. But I don't like you, for wanting to take me away from the Heaven that Jill is. Hang up, leave the phone, good-bye."

"Wait—no, Bill Cole, wait! Stay on this phone!"

"Why? You wish to deprive me of the Heaven that is Jill. Who are you, that you interfere with my New-Born life? You're an unwelcome stranger, who meddles with my divine life. What right have you, to do that?"

"Bill Cole, this is your Boss."

"I'm free. I live divinely. I have no boss."

"You don't recall your Boss? The magazine where for years you've earned a reputation for a fine though underpaid literary columnist and book reviewer? Occasionally, you contribute to other publications, too. But mainly you're my employee for our magazine that deals with books and literature, contemporary culture, and stuff like that. And I'm your Boss. Recollect now, Bill Cole?"

"It's dim and vague. It must have been in my former life. I've put all those things behind me—whatever they were. It was all in a former life. I don't recognize anything at all from that period, now. It must have been some prehistoric dream, whatever did transpire in that former life. I don't remember having any Boss, or writing for any magazine. What you report to me—I don't doubt your sincerity—is news to me, but of an irrelevant kind. What happened before Jill Saved me means nothing to me. It's a dream that faded away. It concerns me not at all. I'm Born Anew. Jill is God. Leave the phone. You claim to be my Boss, but I acknowledge nothing of that sort. How dare you invade the Sanction of Jill's Chapel with the rude audacity of your phone call? You've called from *another world*—a world I've repudiated, if I ever *did* live there. Yours is a most unwelcome call. It violates the Spirit of Jill. You must be a kind of devil, to tempt me to return to what I never really belonged to—if, indeed, I ever actually *was* there, as you seem to claim."

"You've become a religious fanatic, Bill Cole! Stop it!"

"No, I've found my Self, my Soul, my Reality. I've been Delivered to Heaven, by Jill. She's Redeemed me, for whatever past I had—it's fuzzy if I ever *did* have one—prior to my state of Grace and exaltation that now is my life, with Jill."

"Bill Cole, you've gone mystical! It's horrible! Are you a member of some cult? Is Jill your fake guru?"

Finishing his last question, the well-meaning Boss heard a click. He'd gone too far, and offended Bill Cole, who hung up. But he wouldn't give up. He'd phone Bill Cole right back—this time, bring him to his senses, restore him to the rationality that seems to have deserted the poor deluded convert to Jill's shrine, the devout simpleton, the amnesia victim, the profoundly lost (though he claims being Found) Bill Cole. Is he beyond reclaim? The Boss will persist, and phone again. It might be a long verbal tussle, to wrestle with a lost soul who claims to be a Found Soul. With foresight that he might be on the phone a long time with this difficult character, the Boss goes, first, to the bathroom, to void his urine sacs so that he won't be physically uncomfortable during the siege, assault, and barrage he intends to wage—against Bill Cole's retreat from the world into the false Jill Paradise as the Boss so impiously sees it—on his next telephone call. It's dark, it's after working hours, his is the only office still not closed in the building. Only the cleaning women and a security guard and a maintenance man are in that towering office building, other than Bill Cole's former boss, who's intent on reinstating himself in that capacity once more. But he expects opposition. Jill must have brainwashed her resident captive. The Boss hopes to undo that. Eventually, he might have to struggle against Jill herself, in a Herculean tussle, for Bill Cole's Soul. Or is that Soul already committed—unalterably, irrevocably, permanently—to the cult of Jill, as the Boss sarcastically sees it? Is Bill Cole lost forever, to the world? Will he never review another book, never write another literary column, never compile and edit another anthology, never attend another party, never again be part of the culture-commercial complex that rules over the business-artistic-social set with a wide communications network? Is Bill Cole to forgo all that, to which he's always belonged? The very contemplation is too heartbreaking! For Bill Cole to lose all that! For all that to lose Bill Cole! Why, it's a two-way tragedy! Is it too late to cut off that two-way tragedy? To avert such an unthinkable severance, dissolving one of nature's natural bonds in the civilized form that nature's bonds today take? The Boss must head that off. It's his duty, his crusade! It's his mission, from the world, to restore Bill Cole to his lawful place. He must shatter Jill's hold over poor Bill Cole's sorely befuddled Soul. He must place that Soul right back into society. More books are being published. Some were "destined" to be reviewed by Bill Cole. The Boss must make that possible. He fights *for* destiny. Bill Cole resists, *for* destiny. Which opposed camp has destiny on its side? God was on France's side against Germany, but God was on Germany's side against France. Which one was the True God? The God whose side won?

To tug Bill Cole away from Jill, is the Boss'es task. He goes to the bathroom, to relieve himself. He comes out feeling lighter. He'll fight, now.

❙❙

For the second time, the Boss dials Jill's number. It rings, and for the second time the voice of Bill Cole is heard answering "Hello?" That's the cue for the Boss'es opportunity to go to work and reconvert Society's withdrawn citizen to social worldliness once more, brilliantly functioning as a literary critic, in which role he serves most usefully humanity's sophisticated breed.

"It's me again, Bill Cole: your Boss."

"I have no Boss but God. And I have no God but Jill. That God alone. I serve."

"Bill Cole, you've lost your wits."

"Perhaps. But I've Saved my Soul."

"*You* have!? I thought *Jill* did it!"

"We're One, Jill and I. We're One."

"How tight and close you must be then—very thick, and stuck together, you two."

"Why do you analyze us? What do you care?"

"Bill Cole, I'm your old friend—your best friend—your counselor, adviser, loyal guide, and friendly critic; not just, in the strict line of business, your Boss."

"All that is far behind me. You're a ghost from a past I disown. You're ancient history, and outmoded to obsolescence as any force whatever for figuring in my new life as a Saved Soul. I repudiate whatever came before my Great Conversion. You make no dent on me for invoking a past I've long outgrown in my current State of Grace. In vain do you even phone me. Why do you persist, a second time, after deservedly being hung up on the first time? Jill alone orients me my bearings and obedience, presiding over all that I do and think, by her Holy Office granting me my any determination. To her I turn, in all things. What, ineffectually, can you hope to do with me? My will is Jill's, and you're only an empty voice. Goodbye."

With that, in perfect timing, Bill Cole again hung up. The Boss was defeated. He'd prepared for a long battle, for fifteen rounds, but the fight was stopped in the second round, by way of a technical knock-out. But Bill Cole hadn't just been the victorious boxer; he also was the determining referee himself. Against those odds, against so compound an adversary, determined to resist, what chance had the poor Boss in a third bout? Did he even belong in the same ring with Bill Cole? So completely was he overshadowed, that they'd even be fighting different fights, from offsetting dimensions, each outside the other's framework, contending from separate spheres altogether.

III

Undaunted by his first two defeats, the Boss planned yet a third phone call. This time, he'd employ different strategy. The same tactics would court the same disastrous result. Cunning will well prepare his approach, in advance.

But will Bill Cole reply, and not Jill? The Boss dials, then hears ringing. The tone "Hello?" is again Bill Cole's. Here goes, then, the third try. By now, it's hours and hours since normal office closing. Even people's bedtime is closing in fast on the current passing moment.

"Bill Cole, it's your Boss again."

"No, it's not. You may once have been my Boss—I'll grant you that on trust of your honor in the truth of your memory. But now I'm Saved, by the Grace of Jill. You're out of date, as an alleged Boss of mine. I won't dispute your claim of the 'was'; I defy your pretension to the 'is.'"

"But am I not still your friend?"

"I don't recall your *ever* having been so. Nor does your plea of friendship, based on old times, kindle such motions of current warmth as to stir a loyal heart with beginner's ardor."

"Bill Cole, you're cold."

"To *you* I am, with chilling reserve, to keep well protected my Divine Flame. To Jill I'm bound. By her Light, life opens sight to God, and for that I renounce all that adds up to any worldly less."

"Do you, nun-like, abjure the universe for a convent? Have you turned your back, monk-like, on earthly society, to darken your days forever within a denatured monastery? Come back. I implore you."

"You've phoned three times. Twice before, I hung up on you. This third time, I haven't done it yet. No, not yet. Till now. And with this now, I do it. And loudly, too."

The receiver was slammed down hard. Three for three was the Boss's defeat record. He had planned careful strategy for the third bout. But in action, Bill Cole wouldn't let him execute it. Bill Cole crowded him, giving him no room. He tied him up; cramped his style, pushed him around, kept well ahead on every point, dominated each exchange, administered a thorough lesson, winning in a rout, giving the initial aggressor such a trouncing, as, with one-sided a beating margin in what was virtually "no contest," to discourage the Boss from further future futility. Even so, the Boss was plotting his fourth phone call. He was all battered; yet still game. Fighting was in his blood. They'd have to *carry* him out of the ring. But once revived, he'd crawl back in again. He had more tricks up his sleeve. He's no quitter. He can take any deal of punishment, and not throw in the towel. He'll keep on carrying the fight, keep forging in, ever on the offensive. Let Bill Cole make *one slip*—

IV

It was even later than before, just to give you an idea how late it was. Some people were already asleep, in that big city. The Boss was still in his office. A new assault is planned. He'll dial the number, for a rematch. He'll wear down his opponent. He'll never back down, nor ever give up, till Bill Cole *re*-converts, from Salvation at the Hands of Jill the God in the Divine Myth of Faith, to re-emergence as a pivotal, key character, ubiquitously predictable as a participant in the culture-commercial complex that rules the sophisticated jungle of fashionable literate society that promotes and pushes such products as books, more in the snobbish vein for business and prestige and standing in the hierarchy, than by purely aesthetic standards of intrinsic merit more than conspicuous pretensions as works definably of art by universal application to objective criteria.

For the fourth time, Jill's number is dialed. The Boss is a hardened old pro. He's an old warhorse, gone back to the wars. What though he lost before? Each battle is a new one. Sweep the field of corpses, to make room for the fresh maneuver, and yet another assault, whatever the odds or previous results.

Dialing completed, ringing is heard at the other end. The Boss dreaded that Jill would at last answer this one. But no, there was Bill Cole's voice again, with the same "Hello?" The Boss braced himself, before hurling himself into the thick of the fray, headlong into the heat of mortal combat, with Bill Cole's Soul at stake. Would it remain in the Heaven that is Jill, or would it be persuaded by the Boss that the *world* is its true home, where social life must be braved by relentless rites of initiation, by pagan trials of hardihood, heathen survival on frank planes of amorality?

"Bill Cole, please bear with me."

"Must I? Be grateful that Salvation in Faith to Jill my God has included patience among the broad line of improved qualities. Do you come with more propaganda, in public relations service for your worldly clients, the publicity agent whose chief account asset comes under the heading of society? You hardly tempt me to leave Jill, my God. My Soul is all wrapped up in her. *Un*wrapped, it would dissolve. For, then, my Soul's sake, kindly desist from your campaign to corrupt me back to where happily I'm delivered from in the sinless Jill of my Heaven. Don't unRedeem me, please. Does devilry need my assistance? Enough worldlings are recruited, their ranks and numbers are furnished swollen; must I bloat them further? Such dense population stands in no reinforcing need. Where *I* am, with Queen Jill, sparse Heaven *needs* a Soul or two. In great supply, the world shouldn't demand. In scarce supply, Paradise needs Jill to settle there, accompanied by her fortunate consort, myself. God's people are few. Spare us, please."

"Such angelic affectation, Bill Cole! You put on such rare airs!"

"I'm Pure of Heart. Let only Jill approve, and I dwell in God. If you disapprove, dear former Boss, my compass marks me on the right road. Virtue is ever counter to you. Keep opposing. How well I soar, by the wind that keeps you low!"

"Bill Cole, you're goody-goody. Cut it out."

"Must I hear that? Do you try my resolve? No, you only strengthen it."

"Come down, Bill Cole. Come down."

"And leave my Jill? Too much telephone dialing has addled your wits. When in Heaven, with Jill, *stay* there—by that Credo, I Live."

V

Bill Cole still hadn't hung up, on the fourth phone call. The Boss then must scarcely be threatening him. Not to antagonize Bill Cole was the way to keep conversing on the phone. Careful not to rile Jill's converted Angel, the Boss realized a moral victory by the length of time he was allowed to hang on. Far from winning back Bill Cole's Soul for the world, the Boss had at least wrested some reluctant confidence, and even conversational equality, from Jill's Captive in Piety. Could the concessions gained provide fulcrum leverage and traction toward a more crucial advance across Heaven's lines? Then the raid itself, on the Soul that the Boss assumed the world would want back from its runaway excursion to God's haven for deserters and renegades fled in dissent from Society, taking refuge in Salvation's secret retreat, where cautious escape hides in undetected stealth of its defection, living out a watchful exile from the robust responsibility, the vigors and the rigors, the perils and consequences, native to explosive earth, whose savage primitive fury drives cowards away, who fail at contemporary games of sophistication.

VI

"Bill Cole, you're dead."

"Am I? Then that's the state that I prefer."

"With qualifications, you're dead in a conditional way."

"Be plain. What do you mean?"

"I say this: To the *world* you're dead."

"The *world?* That's mere matter."

"It's all that matters. It determines Life, as such."

"No, *Jill* does that. I live, in her."

"But she doesn't exist. If you're dead to the world, you're dead to her too."

"By far, you're too clever for me. By truth I live, by Jill. I can then dispense with mere cleverness, which you, being godless, find an indispensable substitute for the Truth you're barred from. I live in Holy Light; you rot, in foul darkness."

"Bill Cole, you're going too far!"

"You haven't gone far *enough*, mere worldling!"

"Those were contemptuous tones, Bill Cole. Take them back!"

"Our fighting words are only words by telephone—a medium that won't permit blows."

"You've scored a point there, Bill Cole. And taken the round."

"What round?"

"That's boxing parlance I'm talking."

"Don't export your vulgarity, across the telephone, to Jill's Temple where I reside. Keep your filth out there—down there. The phone is an instrument for evil, when you use it. Your words liberally sprinkle blasphemy. I'll piously disconnect us, now."

Four phone calls, and four times hung up on. But the fourth one lasted longest. Some slight improvement has been shown.

VII

The Boss would declare a truce, self-imposed. He was weary. He had to marshal his forces, but rest the troops, to do battle tomorrow. He'd have to rally their flagging morale. His adversary was formidable. Possessed by Jill for his demon, put under her spell, bewitched in enchantment, Bill Cole possessed supernatural powers of resistance. He refuses to return to his senses or the world. He likes it, upstairs.

VIII

The Boss finally locks up the office, descends on the elevator to the street, where black night is too late to be lit up by the evening's early revelry. It's nocturnally peaceful, out there.

The traffic is almost empty. He flags down, finally, a lone taxi.

At home, his wife is asleep. But *he* can't sleep—he's too restive. Charged by the world, unofficially (he's taken on this mission voluntarily), to raid Heaven and wrench Bill Cole's Soul from Jill's greedy grasp, tug it loose and bring it back unharmed, intact, useful, capable, and willing, to the world—that's no trivial task or child's play. It's a tall order. The Boss would rise to it. Slight means wouldn't do. He must bring his heavy artillery into action. No, that's too bulky, unwieldy, unmaneuverable; cunning and deception might better get the trick done. *How*, though? That's the point.

That's also the point at which he fell asleep. He'd have an arduous day ahead. He could use all the rest he could get. In the world's diplomatic corps, its fateful ambassador to Jill's Heaven in dispute over Bill Cole's Soul, the Boss needs strength and energy. Sleep restores him, to the bold enterprise: to prise away the key prize of Bill Cole's Soul from Jill's Heavenly Captivity. Society is wild with wonder: "Where is Bill Cole?" It's on "everyone's" lips. Only the Boss knows the answer to that. He keeps it neatly a secret. It's essential to operate discreetly. Awful Powers are at work. Vast Forces cross uneasy borders between Earth's excitable terrain and Heaven's Lofty Majesty. Two irreconcilable factions, at traditional odds. The Boss is Earth's spy. He'll sneak into Heaven to steal back the Soul that Jill stole, the precious one of Bill Cole. But why precious? What's special about it? It just is, and must be taken as such, assumed as given. It's a vital Soul. It can't just be safely ignored. That's what all the fuss is about. Of course, the Boss is loyal to his friend and important employee. There's that *human* element, involved.

The Soul is valuable to its present owner. She erotically stole it, somehow. The thief enjoys it, toys with it, even loves it—she genuinely loves it: the loving thief Jill. It'll break her heart to lose her prize. But her prize is prized by the Boss—to the tune of Earth's value on it, which is plenty. A King's Ransom, it would command. Its worth exceeds Splendor's Estimate. Coveted by Heaven, and won and kept in Jill's portion of the Upper Realm, this Singular Soul (which formerly wore the identity of a Don Juan, a Lothario, a Casanova, a Don Giovanni whose exploits require Mozart's agile power for adequate expression) was the object of Earth's intrigue to get it back. Broader boundaries than international ones are being covered.

Under heavy secrecy, the espionage agent sleeps it over. He wakes up praying, despite his atheism. He asks for Divine Guidance, which, supposedly, is on the opponent's side. He's a sly spy who's not above (or beneath) getting ahold of the enemy's weapon, thus neutralizing, perhaps, the enemy's stronghold advantage. How sly a spy can be! To steal the enemy's thunder. To co-opt prayer to his own ends.

Deft and slick is his prayer. Will a deceived Heaven, succumbing in vanity to such flattery from an unexpected source, actually grant him what he prays for? That would be strange. But prayer's territory is strangeness itself. It's estranged from what we normally expect. It strains, for a special effect.

The wife spies him praying. "He's crazy," thinks she. "He's been strained, lately."

The wife broods this inner soliloquy: "Let normality resume. Prayer isn't normality, it's a sign of its lack. Something is wrong, if my husband prays. The prayer attempts to put it right. God, answer him. Answer my husband. In Bill Cole's concrete form. Restored. Brought back, to where my husband is once more his Boss. Then, let the usual reign.

"With no extraordinary need for prayer. Let normality resume and proceed. Let Bill Cole's Boss be my Husband. Let my children get success. Let my Husband love me always. Let his magazine business get more profit. And let me get younger. And even younger."

Such were the Boss'es wife's thoughts. The Boss got up from kneeling at prayer. He asks her to cook him a hearty breakfast. He expects a hard day, ahead. The day of winning Bill Cole back—his Soul; and all the rest. Back to where the underpaid literary hack surely belongs. Where he'll get the most rousing reception: the hero's welcome, having survived some great adventures in foreign parts. The conquering traveler heroically returns. He's home. He brings back a story, surely. A rousing tale.

He'll be paid for that tale, quite handsomely. It means so much, to the folks at home, that one of their own went away and then came back. Bearing, of course, his Tale.

IX

The Boss is at his scheming, to draw the right plan. Shrewdly, his plot takes form.

Must he combat Bill Cole, or primarily Jill—or both? How unified *are* they?

He'll divide them. That's the plan the Boss will put into action. Create dissension. Rip them apart. Bill Cole from Jill, his appointed God. Break them up. Quite slice their unity. Make them fight—*each other*. Plant discord, between them. Then, they'll do the Boss'es work. *He* won't have to fight them, if he succeeds in making them fight each other. He'll build his conquest on their division. Bill Cole, Soul and all, will be saved for the world. Were it not for the Boss spy's need to go about it secretly and anonymously, the world would well reward with fame, power, and wealth, so great an exploit: espionage heroism, playing Earth against Heaven, marshalling and deploying such cosmic forces for Bill Cole's Soul alone.

For Helen's body alone (and face) the Trojan War was fought a long time. Finally, the Greeks prevailed.

For Bill Cole's Soul alone, the Boss ascends Heaven to set strife between Bill Cole and Jill his God. That takes some doing.

The doing is done today. He rolls up his sleeves, after breakfast. He'll go to work. Using his office desk telephone. Only some cheap local calls—to Heaven and back. Worth it, at *any* price.

Cheap tools, cheap overhead, minimum expenses. But to what effect! Great deeds, from small means.

X

He kisses his wife goodbye. Now, *she's* praying.

He's on the subway to the office. Up the elevator, he's now in the office. For privacy, he shuts himself in. The secretary and staff shouldn't know this business. It's highly confidential dynamite. It crosses cosmic boundaries. It breaks theological barriers—a more wonderful feat than just breaking the sound barrier. In fact, it invades God's lair. *That* horizon's never been explored. The *Boss* is the hero—not Bill Cole. But his mission is guarded and secret. The world may never reward him. It won't appreciate his vast feat. Spies can be so unsung. That's their occupational drawback—the anonymity that's so necessary to the performance of their task: it deprives them of glory. A spy's vanity can get so frustrated. He must work in secret. His joy is private. Unacclaimed, unrecognized, he's gained his own self-respect. He's too circumspect to achieve acknowledged heroism; but he's done his job well. That he knows, that he goes by. Fame passes him by –that worldly trifle. *Spiritual* glory is the spy's lot. He gets a nod, a pat on the back, from God, for a job well done, a hidden gem of history. Behind the world's scenes: behind them, but shifting them, moving and altering them. Nudging cataclysms into place. As only God could do, did He so empower Himself. But His proxy representatives do it, in His stead. His delegates, His deputies, the ministers and agents, who are entrusted to get God's work done.

Empowered and entrusted by God to rip Bill Cole away from Jill up there in "heaven" somewhere, the Boss's mission seems on behalf of the world. Is the World, or is God, his client? Or both, by divine intervention into the secular, that high-low alliance?

Up into Heaven the Boss is prepared to go. The humble road is first an audible one: the phone. He'll discharge his High Office in his own magazine office. The latter is a front, as of now. Disguised as an Editor, the Boss has a secretly supernatural mission to accomplish. His wife vaguely suspects it; his secretary might, too. And society gossip from the literary world, from the commercial-culture complex, is rife with speculation. Cloaked in anonymity, in the guise of an editor (which anyway he also is in quite a literal sense), the Boss will make contact with Heaven, where Bill Cole's Soul is imprisoned in the special shrine of Jill's cell. To drag him away howling, the Boss might have to do.

Bill Cole would be reluctant to be rescued. He deems himself already Saved. He's quite "rescued" enough, by his Jill, from that den of evil-doing, the commercial-culture complex, which he's put so far behind him, he's forgotten ever having been in it. He's masked his past, for his own delusion. Jill loves him, he loves Jill. Their Bond is Eternal, so far. But the Boss has other ideas. Object: to destroy that bond. To create dissension. To set Bill Cole at odds with Jill, in hate. To break up that high mating match. To split them, in two, apart. To get Bill Cole back. For books, parties, reviews, society. For women, once more. For Love, on a lower level.

CHAPTER 13

I

"Whom do you love, Bill Cole?"

"You, Jill. But must our catechism be repeated? To become, hypnotically, a formula?"

"It's a stylized ritual. Bill Cole, whom do you love?"

"You, Jill."

"Your love is well invested: I love you back, with interest."

"A financial metaphor, for love? Such worldly terms!"

"Bill Cole, I won't be criticized!"

"Pardon me, Jill. I was overthinking."

"Well, don't. Think less."

"Yes, Jill."

II

"Bill Cole, am I beautiful?"

"No, Jill."

"How dare you defy me, Bill Cole?"

"I dwell in Truth, Jill. You have an ugly face-and-physical-body. But when I first visited you, at the Advent of my Revelation, you received me here in a deceptive wheelchair as though crippled, maimed, paralyzed. How foul were you to look at! So foul, that I fell!"

"You took compassion on my ugliness, Bill Cole?"

"I fell into your power, Jill. What a trap! I just loved it."

"Don't you still, Bill Cole?"

"Our bond is weaker. I'm disenchanted. One who claims to be my former Boss phoned me four times here, all last night, the last very late. You were overbearing. You commanded me to answer the phone and speak. I defied him. He wants me back for the world. I put him off— that was my stance. But the wooing took its toll. I'm seduced. I'm sorely tempted. Let me go. I'll go back."

"Stay here, Bill Cole."

"No."

Then she sexually overcame him, and they coupled. It brought him back into her fold, like a sheep into the flock. In his glow, he continued loving her. Her hold over him was sexual. It overcame his objections. It stilled his doubts. Such was their ethereal Passion.

III

"Jill, I'm getting restless."

"Stay with me. Our Bond is Eternal and don't betray it, Bill Cole."

"But Jill, I'm bored. Restore me, set me at liberty. My past is coming back. The amnesia effect is wearing off. I recollect the World, and me in it. *That*'s my place, not here."

"I won't set you free. You *must* remain. You pledged love. It's your Holiest, Holiest Vow. Should you corrupt it, I'll set Hell upon you. Love me: avoid Hell."

"That's a credo, a doctrine, a formula. I'm tired of it. I wish to stir, to spread my wings once more. You're a drug. I'm your addict. I need more of you. Love is blind. Passion binds us. But I'm restless. I hear the world's call. That Boss will phone again, this morning: I feel it in my bones."

"When he does, *I*'ll answer it, Bill Cole. I'll scold him so discouragingly, he'll leave us alone. That meddler! My nemesis! I'll cut us off! I'll scissor-snip the telephone wire. That will isolate us. It will remove us, from that Boss's persistence. We'll be safe. In Love's opiate blossom. Inhaling its sweet drug."

IV

"Jill, I forbid you! My telephone wire, connecting me to the world, shall not be cut by you! I won't be cut off from my roots—it's my umbilical cord that keeps the Source flowing into me. It nourishes me. It's my vital link, my bridge—which behind me I won't burn—to the Mainland, to the World, that clamors for me. Loosen me from your clutches. What though we Love—and we do love—what so? The *World* is my place. Our Love is too rare, too ethereal, too unreal, too sexual. It's stagnating in its own rarification. Release me. I'll answer the phone when the Boss calls, give him a positive reply in keeping with my defiance of *you*, and ask him how I may report back. It's *essential* I go back. For my Soul's liberty."

"But your Soul is already Redeemed by *me*, Bill Cole. I'm its Saviour."

"Well, I'll just lapse. My fate's in the lapse of the Gods."

"*I'm* your God—it's in *my* laps. Come lapse in my lap, where we overlap."

"All right, let's go round, for our last lap."

As things turned out—or in—, that proved to be their last bout of sex. It snapped Jill's spell, which bound him no more. He felt, finally, free.

CHAPTER 14

I

"You're leaving me, Bill Cole? I weep."

"Poor Jill. I still love you. The Boss will phone soon. Him I'll heed, to your loss."

"My hold is broken. Dear Bill Cole. I loved you."

"I loved you, Jill. Eternally so. Our love *was* eternal—while it lasted. But even—alas—Eternity ends."

"I've lost my all, by losing you. I'm getting old."

"I'm already old, Jill. We'll both be dead, some day."

"Couldn't we have died together? Spent our last years together?"

"Sorry, Jill. I don't feel like it. Once, I wanted nothing more. That's changed. The Call of the Wild—the Call of the World—reclaims me. Our silent phone will ring. The World's Ambassador, or else secretly its Spy, in the form of my Boss, will implore me to go back. I'll give him credit, but he's too late. He'll think he's reconverted me. Let him. I'll go obedient. I wasn't 'swayed' by him—it was my own internal choice."

"But his badgering you, his incessant hounding last night on the phone—"

"I was tending that way, on my own. He facilitated, expedited, catalyzed it—in *effect*. But by *essence*, my mind was made up—in its inner workings. Our love is over. I see you plain. You *are* plain; ugly, in fact. I had misgivings when first I arrived here. You were feigning being crippled in a wheelchair. That was how you chose, in deceit, to receive me. I had forgotten meeting you at a party—because you were too ugly for me. At the party you weren't in any wheelchair. You rented it or borrowed it and then phoned my Boss at the office. (How my memory is improving: I imagine, reconstruct, invent, interpret, and recall with such clarity now: the veils have fallen from my eyes. The vision opens. I can see, once more.) Your divine love for me had intuited what the secret conditions of my Holy Vow were, that enabled you to qualify and uniquely pass the test for the role of my Only True Love. And Heaven knows—God!—it *did* work."

"Yes, Bill Cole. How we loved!"

"Our Souls were bound. Forever. But forever is over now. I resume 'what was.'"

ll

"Please, Bill Cole. Reconsider. Before the phone rings. I look like a foul toad. But if you continue loving me, I'll turn into a Princess. Of greater beauty, youth, and wealth than in a fairy tale."

"What babbling, idle ranting! You ever dabbled in magic. But I've grown hardened to it—unmoved."

"Bill Cole, the Princess is locked inside the toad—release her!"

"I prefer non-fiction, thank you."

Jill wept out her broken heart. At that moment, the phone call came. This time, with jovial heartiness, Bill Cole's ringing tones replied, "Is that you, Boss? Take me back, will you? I hate it here—it's so airless. Jill is only an ugly wench. She excites me no longer. How she once did! God, what great sex! But that's over, now. I'll return. I'll leave my Love behind. My *Soul* remains, too. With Jill, I leave it."

"This is delightful, Bill Cole!, You're coming back! What great news to all the women who adorn the commercial-culture complex and go to the parties looking for you! You'll resume your mantle as a Don Juan! You can reclaim that Kingdom. It's yours again thanks to the romantic publicity about you in your mysterious, much-talked-about absence. You're the rage, once more! The returning hero! The conquering hero! Don Giovanni, himself!"

"But Boss, where's my Mozart?"

"We'll produce him! Now that *you*'re back, *anything*'s possible!"

CHAPTER 15

He resumed his high standards of at least prettiness for women, with priority on beauty. Jill was Love's extraordinary exception to that bold old law of his.

On proud terms with the World, he goes. It had been stultifying, at the end, with Jill. He mated Souls with her, most sexually. His Soul remains behind, in her squalid, impoverished apartment. He'd fulfilled

Destiny, which then ran its course. She was about fifteen years younger. She ruled him. He loved it, at first. When he couldn't bear it, he yanked his Love away, but only his body escaped, and his astute worldliness, his urbanity, his literate polish and sophistication: they went with him. But he couldn't tug his Love away. It stuck to what it was: Jill.

He'd obeyed—or was fortunate enough to find—an old destiny, created even before the Genesis of light and words could so sublimely be Authored.

Officially, Jill and he had never married. They were already Wed. An official ceremony would be a travesty of the one Nature had provided in their Sexual Souls, coupled, paired, and mated with such perfection that sterility was the offshoot or product. Perfection ceases to be organic, once formed, surrendering such vitality as was essential to keep Love's unity fresh to let air squeeze in and out. They were smothered, in their own perfection. The Ideal stopped being practiced. It stepped back, and was swept, with cruelty, into that mental shadow, the pure Past, reeking of nostalgia, devoid of all its former Substance.

The good old world! Stepping into an old shoe. The comfort of all its imperfection! It can be such fun! It's dandy for being less demanding; the soft haven for improvising, for falling-in, for projecting the right impression on impressionable fellow beings so ready to admire and (in the lower case) love. Less pressure, less challenge, less discipline. Most obliging, tamed to decency: the World, so easy-going, genial-paced, so loud and quiet, so violent, merciful, forgiving. It has alcohol's compassion. It's wild, to just our measure. It fits so well. It has the right "feel."

CHAPTER 16

The fashionable world gave Bill Cole a hero's welcome. Fame, power, money, and sex appeal are all gloriously his. His Tale is syndicated and widely published. The publicity factories create great public renown for him.

The Boss isn't noticed. He's behind the scenes. What had he done, anyhow?" Bill Cole had already changed his mind and broken Jill's spell over him. The Boss was prepared to fight. But the fight was won—by Bill Cole's own will, his decision to come back.

Jill is dead. She couldn't live any more. In a sense, she's preserved in Bill Cole. He's old now, but memory flashes sharply to the best heights, to the rare points, to the finest moments lived.

Jill "lives" while he remains. Her permanent death waits for Bill Cole to join.

Meanwhile, he's enjoying himself. Fame, power, sex, money, prestige, influence; and loads of love whose rich terror and sweetness accumulate lyrical power to such sounds of drama that only Mozart's genius is left outside that audible picture. It can all but raise Mozart. His touch would complete the right perfection: Bill Cole in the leading role, that excellent subject.

Sorry. No Mozart. Such still music. Muted and silent. The unmade opera. All but heard, almost.

High Sophistication and Simple Love

To any reader: People ordinarily don't talk the way this novel's characters do to each other and themselves. Please accept their fancy literary language as fiction's license to distort "life," negatively put; to transform "life," positively put.

Yours conspiratorially,
The Author

CHAPTER 1

I

"If all the episodes of my sex life were to be laid end to end, I'd be too laid to be a lady," Yolanda admitted. (But only to herself.)

At that point, she was called on by a visitor. So she admitted it to him, too. He was shocked.

But fascinated, too. (He only newly knew her.) In fact, his imagination was stirred.

He was worked up, to at least a frenzied pitch.

With evident longing, he looked her up and down. (Also sideways, lingering on the "around.")

All this was hardly lost on the currently observant Yolanda.

Her visitor was seated on a soft chair, slumped well down in its cushiony upholstery, which yielded a deep sag to his firm torso weight, all gathered into concentration at his plunging buttock area. Such is the solid geometry of the physics of sitting down, the gravitational pressure of living body upon fabric furniture, all concretely environed in Yolanda's living-room.

Between the two human principals representing the only two genders known, an interesting flirtational conflict was being lived out, to the full.

▌▌

"What's the purpose to your visit?" Yolanda asked, in a friendly rather than suspicious tone.

"When I met you last week, you intrigued me, that's why I asked for your phone number. Then, you remember, I phoned yesterday, and you said to drop in this afternoon, so I did. And here I am."

"You sure are. You're sitting there like you own this place."

"It's such a comfortable chair to sink in. But am I too forward in sitting back so snugly?! Would I be less forward if I sat up more stiffly, more—forward?"

"No, remain sunk in as you are back there, as a courtesy to my utmost hospitality. For were you to sit stiff, I'd feel remiss as a hostess."

"That's gracious and generous of you, Yolanda."

"Pardon; I forgot your name."

"Martin."

"Of course. That's the same name you used when you phoned me yesterday."

"I *always* use that name. It's the only first name I've ever had, and always will be, as long as there's still a me."

"Yes, names are the most consistent things about people, don't you think?"

"Certainly. People's *least* consistent points are their behavior, promises, vows, oaths, their feelings of love and hate, their thoughts, all their feelings, attitudes, mood, inclination, compulsions, obsessions, passions, concerns, indifference, interest, the whole conduct of what they do, the how and when and why, the way they are, and what comes from them."

"But in how they *look*, people are *more* consistent. Their physical face, their body structure."

"Yes, but over the years, looks gradually change, usually for the worse, as people grow older."

"So sad, so true, Martin. Then the name—Martin in your case—is the only *really* consistent thing about a person; reliable, dependable, steadfast."

"True. And also the least important."

"If you were named George, would everything that ever happened to you have been the same? Everything that you ever felt and thought been the same?"

"It's hard to prove yes or no. No test can be made on that."

"Let's drop being so theoretical, hypothetical, and conjectural."

"Yes; where should we drop them?"

"Oh, anywhere. I *told* you to make yourself at home."

"You're very free with what's yours."

"Mine? What *is* mine? What do I really own, to be free about, and generous with?"

"I'll answer that, but first may I pour myself some more wine?"

"How blind of me not to see that your glass is empty. How long has it been empty?"

"Ever since my last sip."

"How drouth your parch must be!"

"Yes, but only thirstily."

"Don't lean forward to reach for the bottle, it'll upset the indolence of your equilibrium. I'll pour you some."

"You're kind, Yolanda."

"No more so than average, in these circumstances."

"It's the custom, to be civil to a guest."

"That's barely the base, from which the gradual process of an intimacy unfolds, as things might turn out."

"Let's hope they do. I like how you look . . . But I like *you*, too."

"What's the difference? One is me outside, the other's me inside. Or are you referring to lust, abstracted in the impersonal, as a highly selective, very excluding reaction to a partial aspect of me?"

"You're very point-blank. If I directly answer, it would inhibit the actual action of a possible seduction."

"Do you intend seducing me, Martin?"

"Yes, but not by direct means."

"How then? By inveigling *me* into seducing *you*? The coward's ploy."

"It's not necessarily cowardly to be successfully expedient."

"Martin, there'll be no seduction today. So stop optically caress-ing my soft round surface bulges, slopes, inclines, gradations, and such sculpture snares for your yearning gaze."

"I will, but could you make it a little easier for me, Yolanda?"

"Gladly. But how?"

"Put more clothes on."

Yolanda glanced at herself, appalled at her indecent absentminded-ness, shocked by her own forgetfulness, a most misleading neglect.

She was in her underwear. That's how she had opened the door to Martin's doorbell buzz, led him to the chair he was now reposed in, offered him wine and poured out a glass for him, and sat herself some yards away in a wooden, no-fabric chair. And conversed and conversed, listening and speaking, in an educated and civilized alternation.

III

She returned, fully clad. For indoors. Not for *bedroom* indoors, but for living-room decorum in conversation with a guest she had only met once before—for half an hour; though as recent as last week, their only previous meeting took place on so obscure a social occasion that, when he phoned yesterday, she had forgotten not only having given him her phone number, but even having met him at all. To overcome that men-tal lapse, she had been quick, on the phone, to invite him to visit her on the morrow, Saturday, giving him her address and the afternoon time, in a casual but definite appointment. When they hung up, she wondered who the stranger would be. Then, vaguely, she even forgot the appointment for the rest of the night and for the next day right up to the afternoon doorbell buzz by a totally neglected man's finger.

IV

"It's soothing to see you so fully dressed. Now why don't you *reverse* the process, and undo all that dress-up, and get yourself even more unclothèd than before? That could accelerate our growing acquaintanceship into the rapid familiarity of truly loving friends, having jumped over some preliminary stages and cut across intermediate ones, into the full blossoming and finished culmination of high, privileged intimacy, exquisitely polished."

"No, that's like electric-battery-forced hens unnaturally coerced into laying premature eggs under a constantly simulated daylight of artificial manufacturing illumination. That infernal machine practice stunts the organic ripening process of pure, unhurried growth, with diabolic rapidity that literally forces the issue. Let's retard our unseemly haste, for slow nature's course of love."

"Well, if you put it that way, all right. Have you noticed?—my glass is empty again."

"You'll get no refill, this time. I don't want a drunk stranger, on my hands. I barely know you, so be polite."

"Does polite mean sober?"

"It helps."

"Soon it's Saturday night, with this afternoon declining. Am I forwardly too presuming, if I ask you be my dinner guest at some restaurant tonight—assuming you have no prior engagement, of course?"

"Your invitation both flatters and tempts me. But I decline. It would be too much, too soon."

"*Have* you, though, an appointment tonight?"

"You're brash and boldly premature, too personal. It's none of your nosy business. Get up from that chair, now, you're taking root there. You seem suctioned into it; from the knees to the chest you've grown invisible. Go on, get unstuck."

"There's your rude departure from manners. Here's *my* angry departure."

He struggled out of his seat with an upward jolt, in a gush of violent force.

From his suddenly straightening lap, his lately empty glass dropped unbroken to the floor, at a widely flung arc. The rug softened the uncracking impact; there was a peculiar bounce: the glass came to rest, by odd improbability, at a standing position! Startled by that quirk of chance, Yolanda unfroze and started giggling. Transformed to mirth from his bolting anger by this nice domestic surprise, Martin panted with laughter, richly encasing his recent bouts of sexually frustrated rage and an embittered, embarrassed disappointment of his pride. He and Yolanda, in one joined stride, fell mutually into meek hysteria's helpless grip. That humbled them both, for love's rash stroke, by humor's ancient grace. Flung together, they wouldn't separate: glued to one shrieking embrace.

After wildly outdoing itself to intensifying repetitions and reaching an insane, inhuman pitch, their spun-together double bolt of hysteria subsided from its incredible peak in gasps and moans, almost sexual.

An abrupt understanding, between this man and this woman, had advanced itself, taking a short cut, nipping corners, into an undeniable existence. It towered over the man, the woman. Cowered by this understanding, they were its trembling servants, like two horses yoked together as an old harness team, dragging a large-wheeled carriage on the dust-raising road, clobbering out a stretch of hooved history at places lit up to eyes that long ago went dark.

They broke apart. "Go now," Yolanda ordered.

"But I didn't finish answering a question."

"What question? Was it even this lifetime?"

"You told me make myself at home. 'You're very free with what's yours,' I retorted. But you countered; 'Mine? What *is* mine? What do I really own, to be free about, and generous with?' Instead of answering, I asked if I could pour myself more wine. There was more talk, and you poured *me* wine. Then *more* talk followed."

"And more. Leading to more."

"So here we are, Yolanda. You're throwing me out."

"Certainly. It's *my* house. Or rather, flat."

"What *is* yours?"

"*You* answer, some *other* time. Meanwhile, quit this *place*."

"Directly?"

"Even sooner. Let our next now be two nows, not one: mine, alone; and yours, alone."

The door closed: he was out, she in. Each with a separate series of thoughts, containing the other. Mental presence, during physical absence.

CHAPTER 2

Martin worked in an office. Somewhere else in the same city, Yolanda worked in another office.

It was now Monday, at their respective offices. Martin hadn't phoned since his interesting Saturday visit. He had phoned her Friday evening at her home, and she had invited him to come the following afternoon.

If he wanted to phone her now, could he? Yolanda forgot whether she had given him her office number in addition to her *home* number. She didn't even remember giving him her home number, when she had met him the other week at what was to her, now, an obscure social occasion. In fact, she didn't even remember having ever met him in the first place, at that now obscure social occasion. (In addition, she didn't even remember the social occasion itself, vaguely fogged up by its own obscurity in her oblivious recollection of it.)

Included in not remembering having even met him was her not remembering having even given him her *home* phone number. True, he did use her home number successfully, as proof that he had it. But how did he come by it? She had given it to him; or someone known by them mutually had given it to him, following or during that social occasion (voluntarily, or, more probably, at Martin's own request).

Or she might have told him her last name and her address whereabouts, enabling Martin, with sufficient information, to look up her number in the directory.

Or someone known to them mutually could have (voluntarily, or, more probably, at Martin's own request) told him her last name and address whereabouts, enabling him, with sufficient information, to look up her number in the directory.

What Yolanda didn't remember was Martin's telling her from her soft living-room chair that he had asked her for her phone number on that occasion when they first met. Not remembering that, she had the trouble of all her wonderings now.

He had said "your phone number." Did she then give him both her numbers, or one?" She didn't remember anyway, no matter *what* happened.

Did he have her office number too? Had she herself given it to him, or else had someone known mutually by them given it (voluntarily, or, more probably, at Martin's own request) to him?

Or had she given him her last name and the name of the firm she worked for, so that all he had to do was look up in the directory the phone number of the firm, dial it, and ask for her? Or had someone mutually known to them given him (voluntarily, or, more probably, at Martin's own request) that information?

On the phone on Friday evening—the only time they had ever had a phone encounter—he could have learned her last name for the first time by her supplying it to him then as a necessary accompaniment to her address, enabling him to make his following afternoon visit; or perhaps just the apartment number could have sufficed for him to successfully make his visit and buzz the right bell with his finger, for the bells in the lobby hall were under apartment numbers instead of under last names.

Once in the apartment, if Martin hadn't already known Yolanda's last name, he could have learned it by seeing it on a paper somewhere, such as on an envelope addressed to her, lying about, here or there.

But the last name by itself would still have been insufficient for his learning the name of the firm she worked for, and—if he wanted to— using it.

It was mid- to late-Monday morning at her office desk, while she pondered all this—at the same time earning her salary by mechanically doing part of her overall required work.

She could phone *him!* That would partially solve, or anyway rub away, all those doubts, contingencies, conditions, provisions, qualifications, and problems.

But why should *she* take the initiative? *He* should.

But he already *had*—by phoning her Friday.

But *she* already had—by promptly inviting him, on his Friday phone call, to visit her the following afternoon.

It was so complicated when they were apart! Wouldn't their being together be simpler?

Maybe, but it would introduce *other* complications.

What? Well, wait and see. First, let them be together.

It was now near Monday lunch hour. Either Martin had her office number but didn't want to or bother to phone that morning; or, he *would* have phoned, but didn't have her office number and didn't—or didn't know how to—get it or the name of Yolanda's firm from anyone mutually known to them who *did* have the number or at least know the name of Yolanda's firm—as well as, of course, her personal last name if Martin didn't already know *that*.

To cut short the spread by spread of such confusions, Yolanda made a snap decision: *she*'d phone *him!* But she'd have to hurry, for it was now almost the time when office workers of whatever firm throughout the city would have already gone off for their lunch break.

Hurry, then, was urgent. But it soon became useless, when she realized that she didn't know Martin's last name or have it written down somewhere; nor did she know what firm he worked for, or have its phone number anywhere.

If she knew the name of his firm, or had it written down, so that she could look up its phone number, it would have to be a *small* firm for her to reach Martin on the phone without being able to give his last name. As it was, her not knowing the size (comparatively speaking) of Martin's firm was a mere extension of her ignorance, which already included her not knowing his last name or the name of his firm, or having it or them written down anywhere, as well as not knowing whom—mutually known to her and Martin—she might ask.

She had no association of Martin with anyone else she either knew or didn't know, since the obscure social occasion where they met in the first place, evoked the recollection of no other person (nor did it even evoke the recollection of itself, so lost was it to memory, altogether).

For such reasons, she didn't phone Martin. She didn't have his *home* number, either, or know how to get it, in case she would want to phone him that evening, following an afternoon at the office of being unphoned by *him*, for whatever reason.

But *he* might phone *her*, at *home, tonight*—as he did on Friday night. What day was today? Monday. She had no appointment—or desire—to be out tonight.

She'd stay in—and wait for him to phone: reduced to passivity that was in acute disproportion to her would-be-active inclination, which, unable to assert, she'd fall back on passivity, by her phone, tonight.

But an actively waiting, receptive passivity: an eager and alert one. It would assume an active form. It was dependent passivity: to pounce on a ringing phone, and meet Martin's mechanical voice with her own warmly replying one.

The old human voice instrument, and the new telephone instrument, in simultaneous service of that old emotion, love, felt by two of today's undead people.

All this thought chewed into her lunch hour. She hurried out to take a late lunch. But the elevator was slow in arriving at her floor. Her legs were twitching. In miniature, waiting for the office building elevator to take her down to a delayed quick lunch, corresponded to somewhat, or reflected, a longer waiting period: for tonight's phone call, at home, from Martin.

Before that, the elevator will have taken her down to eat, then back up again for afternoon office work, then down again for the subway ride home, and Monday's darkening sky into night.

Her future seemed centered about Martin. He determined what

time was, and how.

The elevator took her down for lunch. It was half crowded. She was late: for lunch, for Martin.

Or rather, late for lunch, but too *early* for Martin.

For his phone call, tonight, at home.

Hours and hours away. Hours and hours, of thought, ahead. Of Martinized thought.

Films and films of imagery, scenarios, fantasy, dream projectory, starring him in the leading role, and co-featuring herself, the equal-billing heroine, in this modern mystery romance.

Just who was he, in fact? He was so unknown, down to so many essential details.

For that matter, who was even she herself? She was being remade, and in a new process of becoming, relative and variable to Martin as absolute and constant.

But *he* was relative and variable, too. This unstable flux of two people in identity-doubt. Suspense quickened. Mystery was mixed with a phone call.

But *would* he phone? Even *that* was unsure.

Yolanda slipped through space. Nothing held her up.

For firmness, she needed the solid marriage institution. With him.

A stable footing: having him permanently, in a state of constant love, regular and guaranteed, for her.

Would he agree to that? Such dependency! Such true uncertainty! Such empty-bellied now, famished in passion for the fullness of a devout devouring, that swallows love itself, devouring its own devourer.

Down the elevator; work is done for the day.

Down into the subway, up out of it at her station, then up to her flat, and while it's getting dark, she does little things while waiting for the phone ring.

It's dark. Here's the waiting.

The night grows later.

At eleven o'clock. Still no ring. Not even from anyone else. No ring. No ring.

Now! It's next to midnight!

Still not. *Still* not.

It's too late for him, then, to ring at all tonight. He's too civilized. He's too courteous. He's too refined, to ring at *this* late hour.

She's gone to bed, and is asleep. The alarm clock rings. Hello, Tuesday.

Today is Martin's voice-day. If not at the office, then back here tonight.

Future is only desire. Fulfillment stops time.

There's no future, but Martin.

The arrival of his voice will let the next now appear. The now that announces a new life.

CHAPTER 3

When Martin left Yolanda early Saturday evening at her own firm command, he was full of love and lust for her, and full of calculations of restraint, to play it "cool," to refrain as long as possible from phoning her, to build up the puzzle and tension in her that would approximate love for him, in its wondering doubt. He dared to put his hope on that cruel method of silence. Cruel? Only if it worked. Only if it *could* work. Successful surgery also required some sharp measures.

He hoped she wasn't *too* promiscuous, as he recalled her admission, on his arrival at her flat, in the form of a rather rank pun: "If all the episodes of my sex life were to be laid end to end, I'd be too laid to be a lady."

The way she said it, it was not a mere joke. Had he, then, already, so many predecessors to be retroactively in jealousy of? He was new on the scene, and he'd supersede them, shove their shadows into the long-dead past.

Yolanda. He ached to phone her. At the social gathering where they met, the other week, he had requested both her home and office numbers, and wrote them down on her spot dictating of them. She seemed absentminded at the time; even more so last Saturday afternoon when she opened her door to him in her underwear. He had soon seen that it wasn't intentional on her part—just an amazing feat of forgetfulness. He had neglected to inform her of her omission until dramatically later on in his visit.

Excitement, surprise, novelty—even astonishment—totalled a part of her meaning to him. To figure her out would spoil it: he hoped never to.

His visit was two days ago, it was now Monday morning at the office. He took stern precautions against phoning her. He worked along at his desk. Along with the business forms, the phone was handy on his desk. It shone with invitation.

It was so easily within reach. The ruthless resistance of self-discipline clinched him knottily to a staunch restraint.

Phoning her tempted his fingers in spasms, and pulsed crazily through his wrists. His hand was being yanked mentally back, when the object of his self-denial started, on its own account, ringing.

It yanked him back to businessmindedness. The love-bubble burst, as he went through a business matter on the phone, perfunctorily.

That's what he was there for: to earn his salary. To work, to better himself. To gain promotion, to improve prospects, carve out a secure career . . . and marry Yolanda?

His resolution to win her by the tactic of delaying the next contact with her gave *him*, at least, torture.

But he let Monday afternoon slide by, at the office, still stalling himself. He buried himself in work: there was a heavy press of it, at this period, granting distraction to the lovelorn.

"Lovelorn" implies a pessimistic hope prospect. For which, mercifully, he had as yet no grounds.

She *had* rejected his offer of dinner that would have prolonged their eventful Saturday together, adding the night to an afternoon that had culminated in hysteria.

But it wasn't a rejection of *him*. It was probably a coy gesture of modesty and proportion; enough had happened already, so soon.

That night, he engaged in a social activity that began right after work and prolonged itself in sessions and extensions that kept him absorbed right up to midnight—which would be too inconsiderate a time to take the risk of waking Yolanda from . . . was she alone or with another? A hot stab of jealousy almost melted his resolve to desist from a discourteously late phone call.

He decided, in compromise, to end his non-Yolanda-contact agony on his office desk phone tomorrow morning.

It would be, for them both, the same Tuesday morning. That, already, was a link between them. Their phone talk would forge further links, and advance their love to an actual, renewed meeting.

Tomorrow evening itself, perhaps, might meet her convenience agreeably.

But what if, when he phones her at work tomorrow, she's too caught up with duties to linger for long at the phone? Then he'd press her, quickly—coming straight to the point—for an appointment.

The time and place would be set up, as the vital data leading to . . .

On those calculations, Martin, who had now gotten home to bed, stumbled at the halfway post between the weakening thoughts of wakefulness and the dimmed consciousness which we call sleep.

He woke to the clock's alarm performance. It was officially Tuesday morning.

The day returning Yolanda's voice to his life: and, if all goes well, the actual presence of her entire person, that very evening.

The real Yolanda, the body itself behind the disembodied voice for which the telephone was specially invented.

If she lived with him as his wife, the telephone would be just another background instrument in their own apartment—secondary to the two people, who'd dominate the foreground as the central living figures, setting the stage that relegates other things to mere functions on a graph of use.

People come first. Yolanda is foremost. Love's the final step: served this morning, by an ordinary telephone call. The formal channel, in organized society, in our phase of civilized history, for communication's intimate reduction to two: love spoken in private universal tongue in the heavenly concord of hearts at one.

"Yolanda's and my essences, to mingle, at every daily commonplace level. That magnificent institution, marriage.

"I'll propose, if all goes well, tonight. But first, a trifling preliminary procedure: a morning phone call.

"But I'm barely out of bed. I'll hurry my dressing. I'll go to work and phone my fate. To drag my future out of hiding, to join it to Yolanda's time. To place our bodies in regular communion, in the same residence. To establish love's domestic independence from the necessary phone."

The subway, the elevator, the office. The morning's work. The phone on his desk.

To take up, on this early Tuesday, the heart's unfinished business of last Saturday.

Dialing from the number on the paper. (Not the home number; the other one, below it.) The call gets connected. Yolanda is asked for. "It's her voice! It's charged with joy! She's greeting me!"

The phone wire buns with joy. The voices charge up and down the same wire. To and fro, like eager mice in a narrow corridor, scampering back and forth, racing into each other, in nimble, vibrating dashes, nibbling on the fare of air, the surging feast between them, in open currents, in blazing waves.

CHAPTER 4

I

Suzi had gossip for Jasper. "What is it!" pleaded the latter. They were having tea in her living-room. As old friends, they had occasional meetings, with slightly decreasing frequency in the recent years.

(Despite Suzi's strenuous efforts, Jasper was letting the relationship lapse somewhat, or sag apathetically. Suzi repeatedly strove to revitalize it. Mightily would she try again, this afternoon.)

"Yolanda? No! I don't believe you!"

"Jasper, I swear, it's true."

"Are you drunk? Are you on drugs?"

"I insist."

"Where did you hear it?"

"Yolanda told me, herself."

"But weren't you invited?"

""No, it was one of those minimum ceremonies, no religion to taint it. A simple City Hall license, a civic formality, with his mother and her father as swearing-witnesses and co-signers on the secular, municipal forms."

"But is it *official?*"

"Jasper, you malign me, by even now withholding your total credulity from my report. This is a report, not a tale."

"But Yolanda—the longer I knew her, for these so many years, the more it became positively apparent that never—I mean never—I repeat, *never* – would she relinquish her unmarried status."

"Well, here's your chance to change your opinion."

"Who is he?"

"Naturally, you were going to come to that. Indeed, yes, who is he?"

"Suzi, I'm asking you."

"So you are, Jasper."

"Did you meet them? What's he like?!"

"No, I only saw *her*. She phoned to tell me—after, not before."

"After, what?"

"The marriage."

"That's disloyal. Yolanda's a close friend of yours—and an old friend of mine. But *you*, she should have told before. She was unfaithful not to."

"It was whirlwind. It was private, between them. Other people didn't enter into it. It wasn't a deliberately kept secret—they didn't conspire to fool anyone, especially not their friends. It's just that their world excluded everyone else, during their uniquely magic period of lightning courtship. It was no dark plot. It was just a sensationally spontaneous stripping of the world to nothing but each other."

"*Mutually* spontaneous? That's rare!"

"Rare, but duplicable."

"Who by?"

"Us?"

"Cut it out, Suzi. So?"

"They weren't even *thinking* of their friends; much less than who to announce their love to."

"Is love antisocial to the degree that it's pure?"

"It simply thrust its power inward—and dwelled between them, as a pair."

"That's morbidly to cut themselves off."

"It was their gentle and violent duet, you see: with no instrumentalists, no conductor, nor an accompanist, nor audience—just each other."

"The enchantment of the perfectly reduced world—or the wildly expanded one—of themselves."

II

"Suzi, you're frothing. I never saw you so carried away."

"It's thrilling, it's marvelous. A classical case of pure romance, of ideal, absolute love; happening in our own age of cynical decadence and the 'realism' of no illusions, pre-disenchantment from the start!"

"You look like you're a convert to a new cult."

"I am. Now I'll look for what *Yolanda* got."

"Where did she tell you all this?"

"The essential headlines on the phone. We made a lunch appointment, and at the lunch she sketched in some detailed"

"Like a Saviour enlightening an apostle. Now, as her devout disciple, guided by her exemplary divinity, you'll emulate her holy miracle."

"Don't sneer, Jasper. Don't degrade all this."

"But *you* degraded it, once, *for* me. You summoned me to tea this afternoon, with your urgent phone call this morning, tempting me with 'gossip.' That's the term you used—'gossip.'"

"That was a ploy for surprising you. You came here expecting 'gossip.' Instead, I bowl you over with grandeur."

"It didn't work."

"Evidently not. But it remains, for me, grandeur."

"How exalting! Let's come down from it."

"You never rose to it."

"What's there to rise to?"

"Jasper! For *me*, at least, don't spoil it."

"You're tedious. Well, who is he?"

"He's called Martin."

"How enlightening. Why, you're a mine of information!"

"Please! Don't mock!"

"Sorry."

"And something else."

"Yes?"

"It's personal."

"Go on."

"It might surprise you."

"Go ahead."

"It concerns *us*."

"How?"

"It's a request."

"Yes."

"An important one."

"Suzi! Stop this!"

"Well, what is it?"

"You're ready?"

"Don't be silly. Go ahead."

"Very well, Jasper. Are you ready?"

"You're crazy. Yes."

III

"What Martin is to Yolanda, you be to me!"

"Suzi, you're being outrageous."

"Look, you've been homosexual for long enough. Mainly, mostly; it's made you rather miserable. Have you ever even *tried* a woman?"

"That's *my* affair. Keep out."

"Well, let's become lovers. I love you."

"This is schoolgirl nonsense. Are you to set me up in the semblance of this Martin, while you go masquerading as Yolanda? Are they an epic pair—Tristan and Isolde, Romeo and Juliet, Adam and Eve?—the very paradigm for us to make ourselves over as?

"Suzi, we've known each other a long time. I dearly value your friendship. We see each other less now than formerly. We may be, even, drifting apart.

"Don't sulk. This may upset you, but I'm content to be gay. I'll never be caught naked with anyone but a man. And don't get a change-of-sex operation. You're not my erotic type—in *any* case."

IV

"I've loved you for *years*."

"Why did you pick *now* for breaking silence?"

"Yolanda stirred me—her true love."

"Was *Martin* gay, then, too?"

"No, probably not. That made it easy."

"Easy? Who for?"

"Yolanda."

V

"Suzi, I'm going home."

"No. Hear me out."

"No. You're using the shock of Yolanda's marriage as a way to jolt me from men to you. I don't need a 'cure.' I've had sad breakups with my lovers, I've suffered from their infidelities, but that's no reason to switch to women!

"You want to 'reform' me! You insult my whole life!

"I'm all right gay! I'm *fine* gay!"

"Jasper, those screams—"

"You created them! Let the whole neighborhood hear! I rise to these screams, to defend my way of life from your 'reformist' insult."

"I only wish love."

"*How?!* If I'm gay!? You must ungay me, to get love from me!"

"*Remain* gay. But love *me*."

"I can't live a contradiction like that."

"Then abandon gayness. Try *me*."

"You're pathetic." Hurling that, Jasper gave it an underlining finality by rising and leaving, so that Suzi, hearing the door slam, had a whole field of solitude to crumble in.

"He's not *my* Martin," she thought. "Martin loved voluntarily. Yolanda didn't beg.

"Jasper was so emphatic, that I'm cured of my love for him. What a therapeutic plunge I made! With decisive certainty, I *know* I'm not his!"

She was dry-eyed, smiling. She's purged! Her heart is clean, and empty.

CHAPTER 5

I

"Suzi and Jasper have fallen out!" David told Marguerite, in bed. They were having a love affair without quite loving each other. Nor were they living together. Usually they slept at David's house: where they were now, late at night, following sex. (They were in no hurry to sleep, since the morning before them was of the week-end variety, when their respective office buildings would be firmly locked.)

"Fallen out!? But they were only friends! Jasper only goes for men."

"Despite those true outward facts, Marguerite, which had been plainly evident to everyone else beside your own astute self, Suzi had confided in me some time back that her friendship for Jasper was unaccountably deepening—growing, as it were, love-blossoms—without Jasper at all keeping pace or even knowing what he was not keeping pace to."

"Why, Suzi's an idiot. It was obvious that no woman could divert Jasper from his confirmed homosexuality. His reputation as a poet and avant-garde novelist has been bound up with his private sexual taste. His literary career was even partially predicated on his sexual identity. Not that fame and ambition would corrupt his honesty from a change in bedroom preference—he's just never wanted women, that's all. That's plain for all to see. It was *perverse* of Suzi, to fall in love with him—so self-defeating, so simply self-destructive, it makes me doubt Suzi's maturity *altogether*. Being a renowned fashion designer hasn't exempted her from childish emotional stupidity. David, you're almost asleep."

"I like to resist drowsiness and keep talking. I feel, somehow, detached and floating."

"Weightless?"

"Half ethereal, and half here. Let's prolong it, Marguerite. The dimensions are blurring, yet my communicative clarity is conversationally all intact."

"You're extraordinary, David: a business executive, an art fancier, a gourmet cook, a conscientious father, a devout womanizer, an amateur gardener, a socially prominent host, a connoisseur of high culture, a crack collector, and the most untragic of widowers."

"I'll modestly leave your catalogue, as it is, incomplete. But there's one glaring inaccuracy. Why call me a widower, knowing that I'm only divorced?"

"She's dead to you, dear David."

"Oh."

"But what happened with poor Suzi? Did she suddenly jolt Jasper with her shocking declaration of long-pent passion pouring suddenly forth like a gush out of the blue?"

"She led up to it, and then let him have it."

"What chose her to seize *that* moment?"

"She lured Jasper to tea on a gossip pretext. Yolanda's sudden marriage was her bolt of inspiration. She wanted to singe Jasper with that divine flame."

"To infect Jasper with the same germ of pure love, like the contagion of a social disease, an epidemic starting with Yolanda, which Suzi hoped to spread and carry—a precious, flaming example—to Jasper's stubborn breast?"

"Yes. His 'no' was full of rage, for he felt an insult to his homosexuality in Suzi's missionary fervor to convert his currents from men to her. To uplift and reform him, he saw it as. Defensively misreading her love for contemptuous condescension to 'cure' him of homosexuality, he became furious; though be suspected her love to be true, as well. He refused to join Suzi in getting fitted to the unique Yolanda-Martin mold. He's Yolanda's old friend, and had just been told by Suzi of the marriage; Suzi herself having been informed by Yolanda only the day before."

"What's Martin like?"

"I've never met him, nor has Suzi, nor has Jasper.

"Yolanda's keeping him to herself, till the first blush of their blazing romance dulls its shining bloom."

"Did you *have* to raid botany, for your metaphor? . . . Sorry, dear, don't pout. I'm affectionate, not critical . . . What of Yolanda's promiscuous past?—you were once prominently included, in the series. Did you love her? Did she love you? How did it break off? How did *all* her affairs break off? And will this marriage last?"

"Marguerite, at this late hour I can't find simple answers to multiple complexity. Yolanda is complicated beyond even complication."

"Did she reject you, at the end? Or did you tire of her? Don't pursue motives; you can describe the bare events themselves; no need for analytical explanations."

"I'm overwhelmed with sleep. Let's wait for tomorrow night, when I pick you up to take you to Suzi's for dinner. Now, a big blur is sweeping me away."

"I can even hear it. Sweet David." She kissed him tenderly.

She gazed at his sleeping face. "Has the Yolanda disease caught *me* now? I never felt this love for David before.

"It's pure revelation. Suzi was *bound* to fail with *Jasper*. But David —he's another story. Can *our* story match the pattern of Yolanda and Martin? I feel ecstatic. Yolanda's magic—I want that formula. So would Suzi. We all do.

"Let *David* catch the disease. He and I will invite Yolanda and Martin to dinner. It will rub off.

"I'm tired of this endless modern round of love affair after love affair that lead nowhere except to merely another love affair with somebody else. They all seem to begin in love's hope, then decline into mere physical routine and formal banality.

There are even overlapping affairs, even simultaneous ones. For all its abundance, the actual sex turns into mechanical sterility, a coordinated form of tingling repetition, a lively habit between bored partners.

"Cynically tedious expedience. But does *any* love last? Mine for David is just beginning.—If I *do* rouse him to love for me, on the example of Yolanda and Martin, how long would it last—on my side, on his?

"And why do Suzi, David, and I all comfortably fall into a conspiracy of assumption, almost a religious credo, a joint act of absolute faith, that the incredibly begun blending of Yolanda's heart with Martin's is destined for permanence, in contradiction to broken matches everywhere observed? Are we colluding in the fabrication of a Myth-in-our-midst, to the choral chimes of a sacred grandeur?

"We *need* to believe in it, just as Christ and Catholicism are needs for some, or Communism, or Zen Buddhism, or astrology.

"We need gods, or deities. We need divinity, a miracle mountain to climb away from the base commonplace that steeps our lives in cynical corruption, in dreary daily habitual decadence, bleakly making necessary our brightest ideals.

"We've made Yolanda and Martin heroic, in the immense blessing of their love. We rewind our watches to their timelessness. We set our sights anew, and alter our horizons accordingly. We put on another rhythm, to the tune set before us. Our lives are made, somehow, of finer material, woven by higher hands than the stuff we're accustomed to.

"We dare, now, to dream. Thank you, Yolanda, and you, whoever you might be, Martin. I aspire with David to your sublime workings.

"Under your influence, Suzi brought to a head the realized impossibility of her Jasper-obsession; she took it to its logical conclusion, openly before Jasper, and has become conclusively purged of the manifest illogicality, brought into the open, plumbed, examined, and brutally exposed.

"Thanks to Yolanda and Martin, Suzi can think clearer now. It's been clean therapy. Now, she's ready, for a likelier prospect; no longer is her network choked with static, with rust clogging her channels.

She's open and free, for Love, whoever it might be. She's fled the trap of her own devising, that bound her to fruitlessly pursue the grotesquely impossible.

"David, asleep by my side: I'd pour a love-potion in his curling ear, or place it under his delicate eyelid, that now flutters to some trembling internal dream.

"I aspire to be the permanent second bride of David's life.

"He has three children by his former wife. They're in boarding school, and they visit her, and they visit him.

"I'll be a pure second mother to them; and purify David, in the process.

"By all that's holy, I vow this. By dear Yolanda, and the unknown Martin."

▌▐

These meditations took up time. When Marguerite fell asleep, David was already chugging away toward the halfway point of his own sleep.

He rose long before Marguerite, made himself a brief breakfast, and set up painting materials.

He set about painting a lovely scene from his window. He was serene. He had a free day before him. Marguerite would wake, dress, and go home, leaving him alone.

Later that night, he'd fetch her and they'd go to Suzi's for dinner.

Suzi was a great friend of David. He bled for her tormented heart over Jasper's definitive rejection of her; but rejoiced that she made a clean break, a successful surgery of a lump of love-cancer.

Suzi deserved bliss. She's been terribly lonely. Her fame as a fashion-designer is world-wide; yet Love, that ideal little sprite, does persist in impishly eluding her.

III

David felt, somehow, a warmer tenderness toward his dear, sleeping Marguerite.

(He *assumed* she was still unstirring, for acutely he could hear no sound from the bedroom that adjoined his makeshift painting studio.)

It was so peaceful, just painting away like this; leaving his business cares forgivably forgotten over a sustained sweet weekend.

He began to get carried away, thinking about Marguerite. At this rate, he would have to propose to her soon.

The phone rang. It was Jasper, inviting him and Marguerite to a party next week to celebrate the publication of Jasper's newest book; a novel that bordered dangerously on the naughtily autobiographical, even to the inclusion, in fictional disguise, of all his closest friends.

"*You*'re in it, David."

"*Am* I?" Flatteringly, I hope."

"As well as Marguerite."

"In connection with me?"

"Naturally. And Suzi's there, too."

"Treated how?"

"I've made her fall in love with a lesbian!"

"How quaint! But will it upset her?"

"My conscience is clear. But we recently broke off being friends."

"Yes, she told me."

"She proposed love to me!"

"I know, she told me."

"We had a falling-out."

"Not irreparable, I hope."

"It depends. I'll only resume friendship with her if she limits our friendship to friendship alone; I've set definite restrictions on it."

"She's *cured* of love for you—she told me. She brazened it openly, and learned a sharp lesson."

"That's encouraging. Well, David, *do* come to the publication party next week."

I will, and I'll tell Marguerite. When can I get a copy? I'm dying to read how you've dealt with me."

"I'll give you one at the party, David, and inscribe it to you."

"Are you more engaged in fiction now than poetry?"

"Both equally. They set each other off, and balance each other out."

"Lucky they don't *cancel* each other out."

"Oh, don't be facetious, David. I love you too much. Not seriously; but I've been infatuated with you for years.

"I *know* it's hopeless; you'll *never* be gay.

"I'm glad I've confessed it. I feel purged of it, coming clean like that."

"That seems along the lines of *Suzi's* cure by confessing to *you*. All this love is in the air these days. We're all a bit delirious. Yolanda's magic with Martin, I guess, has set us all off."

"It's even hit *me!*"

"Who for, David?"

"Marguerite. We've had a long affair, and finally I feel love."

"David, what does Marguerite have that *I* don't have?"

"Lack of fame as an author."

"But she's no author to *begin* with."

"No, but she's lovely."

"I'm jealous."

"Set your love-sights on a man who dotes on *you*, Jasper. Get requited, get reciprocated. Join the love wagon. We're all on it!"

IV

"Well, I hope Marguerite returns *your* love."

"I'm confident she will."

"Who will *Suzi* love, and be loved by?"

"According to your novel, a lesbian."

"But the lesbian doesn't love Suzi back."

"Maybe that's just as well. Who does the lesbian love?"

"Read the book, dear David."

"Dying to, Jasper. I'm in the middle of painting a window scene, so I ought to hang up."

"You're uncouth, David."

"I'm hardly abrupt. We've been talking for ages."

"Marguerite and I will dine at Suzi's tonight. Shall I convey any sentiment or token, or tidings or apology, to old Suzi?"

"Not from me. It might seem petty of me, but *she*'ll have to make the patching-up overtures, I'm afraid, to me. I was the injured party."

"But *she* was the *hurt* one. *She* bled from love; not *you*."

"I'm unappeased. I stand firm on pride."

"Narcissist!"

"Shut up! Anyway, if she shows up at my book party, we can repair the split on new terms outlining friendship's bounds, so that they won't be exceeded next time by an inopportune bout of Cupid's measles."

"Now that I've rejected you, Jasper, who will *you* love?"

"I'll love the one I'm loved by."

"*Who* by name?"

"We haven't met yet. But we will, soon."

V

"Jasper, we *must* hang up. I must put down the phone and take up the paintbrush again.

"And I hear stirrings from the bedroom. My life's only love is dressing herself.

"Goodbye, Jasper. Oh, wait—did you invite Yolanda and Martin to your publication party?"

"I tried, but can't get a-hold of her. Her old home phone is disconnected, and when I tried phoning her office they told me she was 'on leave'—for some unspecified duration."

"But she has so many friends!"

"They're all equally in the dark. She hasn't contacted *any* of them—except Suzi, just after the marriage. Since then, she seems to have disowned her peopled past."

"She's incommunicado. I've tried tracing her myself, with discreet investigations to that effect. But nothing lingers, to clutch to. She left only love's intangible behind; an immense power, that grips us in its waves.

"But she's been spirited away. In bare spirit, does she remain.

"All else is our darkness—and light."

"Lost to us."

"But what she's found!"

"But we can't see it."

"Nor that familiar being, in our midst."

"Gone."

"Without the slightest farewell!"

"Mysteriously so. But she'll unearth herself, and come forward, hand in hand with her dark abductor."

"Yolanda is your oldest friend, in our big city. Surely *she's* in your novel, somehow."

"It was my stroke of genius. I was prophetic."

"You mean you *predicted* the advent of Martin?"

"Suzi surprised me—*shocked* me—telling me about Yolanda's escape from the vagrant rounds of aimless promiscuous drifting from indifferent arms to indifferent arms, to a fairytale admission to love's ultimate cloud-castle. I, Jasper, the human being, was shocked *genuinely* when Suzi broke the news to me. I, Jasper, the *author*, however, had long ago forecast Yolanda's superb love-stroke. Read it, in my book."

VI

"That was Jasper on the phone, Marguerite."

"I eavesdropped, and found the bits fascinating. More tonight, on that. I'm going now. "

"Your respect for my solitude-needs convinces me that you understand me altogether. "

"Love assists comprehension, in this depth. Meanwhile, goodbye."

They kissed, and she let herself out of the door, waving from the street as she passed David's window-view, on her way out of sight.

David painted, but soon sighed.

"I love her, with such a love as I've never felt since childhood."

His sigh subsided. He attached some brittle strokes to his growing canvas.

The world seemed to contract. It shrunk. In perfect detail.

In a rare vision, he saw it entirely.

It was lit by inner love. This mystic penetration subsided, the world regaining its usual size.

CHAPTER 6

I

Modern, but tasteful, the interior decoration and fine functional furnishings, as befitting the foremost fashion designer's own private home.

She never worked at home, but had an office and studio for the purpose, conveniently located quite close.

Suzi had hired a girl to help with the preparing and cooking, but once everything was ready, had dismissed her; she would take on the serving duties herself, along with the hospitality.

A momentous change had just happened in Suzi's life. It was so sweeping, that nothing remained from before.

It was so drastic, it carried all before it.

Arriving slightly late for dinner, as was the custom in their fashionable circles, David and Marguerite noted the change instantly.

The whole atmosphere, in every particle of the interior, eloquently bespoke the transformation. Every object, each cunning corner of space, reflected it equally.

The place was charged, permeated, suffused, lively, with the splendid feeling. It radiated continuous currents, in a steady dazzle.

Suzi was not alone, in receiving David and Marguerite. There was a conspicuous fourth person—the radical agent himself, of the dynamic new picture. Possessively introducing him as "Gil," Suzi arranged the quartet of seating at the lovely table laden with luscious food.

Each course, each dish, was queenly. Gil co-presided, as the lordly surprise host.

The distinctive tone, all around, was "love."

Two couples, in amorous symmetry. But how had Gil—so David wondered—arrived so opportunely as Suzi's saviour, as her golden knight in shining armor, so timely on his prancing steed, decked out in Suzi's true color?"

As the swiftly swooping antidote to the romantic fiasco, the dispiriting debacle with Jasper, was this a mere *temporary* flash, or stopgap, in Suzi's luckless existence?

Or was Gil the finally found, monumental answer to Suzi's almost despairing longings? Was David a witness to love's permanence?

He felt himself to be a *participant* in love's permanence, with Marguerite. To find himself a witness to *Suzi's* completed happiness, added the complementary angle to the rampant, rounded blessings that played a free riot with four souls.

II

With subtly obvious redundancy that broadly bordered on the comic spirit of the ludicrous, Gil, indicating Suzi to the visiting pair, asked, "Do you mind if I love her?"

Silliness seemed to descend. David replied, "All right, but remember, I loved Marguerite first."

Suzi turned frivolous too. She gaily dropped her nonsense into their giggle pool, while hilarity managed to inflate itself into a quivering jellypuff empty of any supporting substance.

Aimless ennui next entered. A vapid hysteria grew from the very absence of mirth.

Lightheaded, dizzy inanity grew on space; as the two couples consumed superb wine in quantities of heroic abandon.

Marguerite proposed a toast to "love."

Four sparkling glasses were raised, in the wild rapture of their rapport.

"Who are you, Gil?" David asked, flushed with the giddiness, "beginning, let's say, with your occupation."

"I'm an occasional dabbler in art criticism, but mainly I review books. Tomorrow's paper carries my favorable review of Jasper's semi-autobiographical venture into poetically condensed fiction with gently vicious portraits of Suzi, you, Marguerite, Yolanda, and other adornments of our social set, generational era, and cultural environs. 'His sympathetic malice refines raw friends into crystalline characters that bear distant but poignant resemblance to the real-life originals,' is a phrase I recall having constructed."

"Have you an advance copy of the review here?"

"Alongside the very novel under review. I'll get them, David, wait."

Gil scurried off to another room. "How dull of me not to recognize his face and name instantly," confessed David to the two women; "his fame is so obvious, that it slipped me by, in this atmosphere supercharged with the glow and languor of moody love. How did this suddenly happen between you?!" he asked his hostess.

"Last night, without warning," Suzi explained. "We'd been casually acquainted, of course, for years, on amiable terms of meeting by accident at social gatherings, commercial promotions, cultural affairs, that mingle us seasonally in and out. At a cocktail party yesterday, We prattled ever so superficially—oh, you're back, Gil, with the novel and your review. I'm telling our sweet guests—or trying to—what befell us yesterday."

Gil resumed his seat, in a momentary silence with scuffling. He took over Suzi's narration, which ran into inertia difficulty which threw its stalling mechanism into high gear that used up the remains of the empty fuel supply.

"While gossip took its ambling course from 'him' to 'her' to 'her' to 'him, making rounds and circuits among business connections and light social rambling, our talk in passing stumbled on and entangled with our new local sacred legend—the vanished Yolanda and the Martin whom nobody knows.

"Love now had overtaken our discourse, in the element of its mystery.

"The subject itself, then, violently united us, under Yolanda's enchantment. We jointly yielded, to the amorous pressure, which gently swept all other influences aside, and blew us in such sway, that the bond between us doubled into separate selves—but such a Suzi, and such a me, that in this doubling a single bolt shot through us, and we were one."

III

Marguerite was moved to reply, "We four owe Yolanda the unpayable debt—if these loves do last."

"I protest," exclaimed Suzi, "that you yet have doubt. Pluck out the doubt: it's precisely the wrong note. It accuses our harmonies of servility to brevity itself, the decay-breeding worm with its crippling load of poison rot."

"Love has crumbled before," Marguerite maintained. "We make

a religious mountain of Yolanda's example in superstitious fear—or rather from the terror of experience—that love, by time's stern standard, fails."

"In *all* cases?" Suzi challenged, the vivid marriage broker of love's legitimate union with the eternal.

"Excepting the two pairs present here," Marguerite relented, "and also excepting that immortal contemporary prototype of our hopes, the heaven on loan, the very model of earth's conjunction with the divine: rarest Yolanda, and her airy deliverer."

On that note, they prayed with fervor—all four, in trembling unison.

IV

When the prayer concluded its fourfold solemn rumbles of high, helpless silence, Suzi inquired, "Has anyone else ever heard from Yolanda? Do I remain the only one known to us to get a phone call and be favored with an actual meeting with her, as happened some days ago?

"Has she not circulated another word anywhere?

"Dropped out of sight? Ascended to heaven, handlocked to her soul's earthy redeemer?"

"Jasper tried, I tried, others have tried, to trace her sources and follow her baffling whereabouts' unknown next moves," David reported, looking so confounded that Marguerite laughed in reflex compassion.

"Her parents can't be located; she's left her job—leaving no forwarding number with her former colleagues; she's moved out of her apartment—leaving no forwarding number with her former landlord; she's vanished ruthlessly from her friends; has she betrayed us, now that she's inspired us?" David whined, dramatically underscoring the pathetic, while doing equal justice to the merger of the futile and the desperate.

A spell of silence drooped among the friends.

David's dearly loved one broke through this pall, with cadences of incantation:

"She's had the most uplifting effect on us, heaping pure magic on banal lives, conjuring divinity from closed skies," Marguerite wailed. "And now that we don't need her—for she's given us firm romantic grounding on slopes of solid bliss—where can she be found? Have she and Martin gone the saintly path; for which plain geography has no earthly tool whatever, for the surveying chart and the map's miniature scope?"

Gil admitted perplexity. Sheer bewilderment opened a gaping vacancy, and four people's groan of gloom loosely fitted in the vacuum.

"Without Yolanda, our love may not last," Marguerite remarked grimly, in swiftly blatant contradiction to her previous contention that now "we don't need her—for she's given us firm romantic grounding on slopes of solid bliss." No, the footing must be shaky for they missed her so, the lost Yolanda, love's divine provider.

V

To supply badly needed hope, Gil suggested that prophetic clues could be found, as to Yolanda's ultimate destiny—cryptic leads to her Martin-associated, wedded fate—in Jasper's great new novel.

It, with Gil's review of it, were on David's blind lap. David and Marguerite hadn't yet read it. Suzi had, so she opened a discussion with Gil about the Yolanda-based character, and the Martin-approximating figure, woven through his book by Jasper's cunning craft.

VI

David lashed out: "How dare we deify them? We're craven supplicants to a cult's shrine of our own devising. Why, weakly, should we cringe with religious feeling? Why owe our loves to Yolanda-Martin? I rebel, that we must credit them so."

This was a sharp reversal, from the previous sentiment shared and agreed on. All four gasped, at such a swerve. Love seemed shaky, deprived of its support. Could two lovers buttress their own love, themselves? *Must* they appeal to stout outside bolstering, to the gods that fortify and confirm?"

VII

David demanded of Suzi, "Couldn't we trace Yolanda through her husband's job, her husband's last name?"

"She never told me where he worked or what her new last name had become. I regret not having questioned her. At the time, such questions didn't occur, seeming completely inconsequential, even trivial, in the grand blaze of their romantic blur."

VIII

Nearly drunk, very sleepy, David couldn't well follow (nor could Marguerite, so fuddled and exhausted was she) the intricate discussion of Jasper's novel, especially Yolanda's role in it, and Martin's mysterious presence as love's circuit-completer, two equal souls in one holy jointure.

Not having read the book—or even Gil's review of it, still lying there unread—David and Marguerite let Gil's and Suzi's literary analysis go by unneeded.

David drooped. Marguerite sagged. They got up to take their leave.

They'd all meet at Jasper's publication party in a few days. Suzi was eager to demonstrate how completely she had recovered from her wrong-love-altercation with the proud celebrant of the party's occasion. She'll proudly display her new-found Gil, arm in arm, to Jasper's humble inspection.

Jasper will be effusive in thanking Gil for such a glowing review.

The leavetaking formalities were concluded. The last "goodnight" finally was said, and finally given back.

David staggered out, entwined with Marguerite, to the night's bracing air, outside Suzi's now-closed building. "To your place or mine?"

David asked.

Barely managing an "Either," Marguerite slumped in David's unsteady support. A cab had been summoned by Suzi by phone. Its back door was open, to receive them.

It wasn't the bed itself, but the last stage in getting there. A brief ride, before permitted oblivion.

CHAPTER 7

I

The days went by till it was time for the big party. Jasper had called it "my" party, but it was a party *for* him, *by* the new book's publishers, at a specially-rented bookshop space that could amply contain not only all the guests that the publishers invited, not only all the guests that the esteemed author invited, but all the crashers as well, who had heard about this "top party of the literary season" by grapevine excitement and the well-worn routes of rumor's grinding mill. Mostly, people from the "trade" were there: book review editors from magazines and newspapers, radio and television interviewers, literary agents, authors, publishing editors, promotion and publicity representatives, hacks, free-lance journalists, columnists, feature writers, dealers, go-betweens, talkers, everybody commercially concerned with books through whatever angle.

It was at the "cocktail" hour, between the hour of office closing and the hungry time when people go about getting dinner, on an ordinary workday of the well-worn business week, in a colossal city that serves the high industry of commercial mass communication. It was no rural hamlet or bucolic backwater, but a cosmically global metropolis where democratic culture concentrates the marketable exploitation of popular products, Jasper's novel fit that category, though written purely for aesthetic excellence.

The party was a publishers' investment, intended to boost the book's sales appeal and make broadly public the author's fame, getting across the wide idea of the book being all the rage, commonly in demand by a stampede of eager, conforming tastes held by the conventional thrall of fashion's latest value, for herd consumption that dearly unites the separate lonely cells of individuality, stamping out the latter but enforcing a collective bandwagon of obedient choice, selective and distinctive, superior to those who don't join.

Jasper's publishers were backing him with handsome faith in this corporate investment.

It was expensive, the waiters' fees, the bookshop space renting, the security precautions, the promotion material, the tasty *hors d'oeuvres*, the gin, the Scotch, Bourbon, wine, and other commodities to induce the intoxication of euphoria to be associated with the product sold: in this case, Jasper's novel, so psychological, poetic, fascinating, and readable.

"It's all about love," said a senior critic to a young, pretty editorial assistant.

"I know, having read it," she sweetly replied, undecided whether to flirt with him or to present her coy sexiness to other men of power and glamor who wolfishly roamed the cluttered, open market, the exotic jungle, of flesh and commercial contacts, the predatory circulation of men and women "on the make" with sharp-weaponed prowl, bartering experienced charm for further gain, for spontaneous intrigue casually prepared for impulsive exploitation on the mined field of chance encounter, pursuing personal advancement on a scrambling carousel of precarious culture economy.

Jasper was so surrounded that David and Marguerite made no effort to compete for their honored friend's well attended company that currently included dignitaries whose cluster of prestige was accessible only as the occasion dignified it, so that ripe connections had situational availability, which ordinarily would be immovably removed from tardy opportunity's clutch.

Suzi came up to greet David and Marguerite. "I hear snatches of quotes from Gil's review all around the room on roving people's lips," she proudly accounted. "Gil's attention is in high demand here, so I'm letting him circulate freely about as a glittering lion in this motley-caged business zoo that's opened the gates for inmates and outmates to mingle and imbibe the pungent juices and mixed brew of voices and spiced concoction brought to odd assortments in a jamboree of overflowing." Waiting for Suzi's description to unwind itself, David, when it did, asked, "Has Jasper been too busy to notice that you and Gil are . . ."

"Precisely. There wouldn't be much impact now. I'll flaunt it when he's less occupied."

"Anyone sight the missing Yolanda and the Martin nobody's seen?" Marguerite loudly asked in the voicy oceanic din.

"Their presence would create a conspicuous sensation were it not for their absence," Suzi declared with a sad sigh.

"I fear they're lost to us forever," David delicately despaired, but his words were whirled up unheard in the open-throttled roar of the throng's prevailing inaudibility, so combined were sounds in a dense block, allowing no separate words to slip through.

A prodigious drinking rate reached the alarming stage. Wanting desperately to express themselves in circumstances ideally created for social communication, and finding this desperate want crowded into corners of frustration as mobility space diminished, people radically clamored for richly antisocial beverages that stultified discourse to lonely levels of inebriation.

Noise and drink shattered delicate equilibria of conscious distinctions. The beast of a uniform blur grew ill-shaped, from unconnected, unpieced-together, fragmented conscious splittings-off; as minds were pierced functionless by a coarse mob force, brute, numbing, cut off from the civilizing sphere of inhibition's humane grace,

Suzi was sucked into the vortex, in a nightmare search for Gil.

Glazed and stuck, David and Marguerite, who were dying to leave, stayed. Some inertia of fascination bound them there. Their will had been sucked away, and they joined physical presences with the other human objects pressed bodily together, to the swelling sway and surge of gross inanimate existing, blunted of any articulate refinement.

II

The party did love no good. It degraded everyone there, erasing people's worthiness as objects of love, as well as sapping people of love's large and generous power.

David and Marguerite would resume their love later, somewhere else, after the party. They were merely together in the way that a table and chair might be, in a warehouse cluttered with objects worthy of storage but not of use.

Their human will was suspended, until privacy will thaw and restore it, in respect to each other, themselves, and the universe of original marvels.

III

Suzi looked all over. She couldn't spot Gil. Was Gil still aware of her? What a place this would be, to misplace love!

IV

Gil was in an inner circle close to the party's heart and source. Jasper was its center.

The usual vacant pit of his narcissism was now solidly filled with acclamation, affirmation, substantiation; Jasper's love was complete. Self-love stood grandly realized, and enjoyed an immense sufficiency.

Any other person would spoil his love-life. It beamed, on himself alone.

This party crowned his book a success. Into it had gone David, Marguerite, Suzi (miscast as being in love with a lesbian); and love's luminous Yolanda, joined to the fictional Martin of Jasper's divination, a poetic prophecy turned downright true in the world where *people* roamed—the ones who are there despite, or because of, art's invention or discovery of them.

The characters withdrew from the book, and took on people-roles.

The people flattened out, and turned into characters.

Reality went tricky with art.

The party was in full session. But where was love?

CHAPTER 8

Like a stormswept coastal town subjected to mighty oceanic siege and a sky turned wild, love had been battered.

Under a returned sun in the mellow mercy of peaceful skies and calm ocean, the damaged town surveys itself, planning restoration, reconstruction, and a prosperous future.

David and Marguerite are married, living in David's house. Gil gave up his apartment and moved in with Suzi, in love's other form: unmarriedness.

Jasper has lovers, but his lasting fidelity is settled solely on himself. Yolanda? Where is she? Clung in legend, forever, to a Martin who remains faceless—but sturdy, and Yolanda's—to the official legacy of imagination.

They don't return. They left behind enough love (taking their own with them) to keep going three pairs.

The third pair is one Jasper. His book is outdoing success. Fame is art's truest reward.

The book portrayed David and Marguerite in such a vein, that they're pleased with their fictional selves.

Suzi's Gil-fulfilled life shows up Jasper's error in depicting her. Jasper adores Gil's review of his book.

They're all on the best of terms, and frequently see each other: the two couples, and their brilliant author friend.

Not just love, but friendship prevails; good feelings, all around.

Yolanda has disappeared for good (not for bad, they hope) with the Martin nobody met.

Jasper's novel can't track them down. She was absentminded, but not absent from five, at least, minds. She was forgetful; but is unforgotten.

She's in the book, with Martin. She left behind her love. It's taken good shape; it's in fine form. Marguerite is expecting: her first, David's fourth child.

Suzi and Gil remain locked in love.

Jasper expects Yolanda's return, hand in hand with Martin. This newest theme is being done in verse.

Annually, the five friends celebrate the future return of the fabulous pair with a party whose ritual is the thought of love's eternity. Love, as life's only absolute against time's steady death.

Love, that delights us in and out of books. A human invention that surpasses all truthful discovery.

Love at the College Level

CHAPTER ONE

I

Love was over. No, not really.

Certainly in the *general* sense, it was very much potentially active; looking about, preparing, getting ready; comparing, receiving "messages," keeping available, opening up little hope-nibbles, here and there.

In its particular sense, love had rolled over and died. Don was still there, as a presence, as her official husband, and official children's father. They owned a fine house together; old customs perpetuated themselves, stale but still spry. Domestic habits clung to objects and familiar places. Traditions and usage go with family and ownership.

The settled life, established bonds, possessions, possessiveness, and all those duties and observances.

Don remains, keeping to rooms that she avoids. The house is large enough for both of them. They keep up appearances, and play down their separate lives. Their decade-old daughter keeps to herself what she suspects: that something is up. Their two-year old doesn't have enough to go on, just yet, she has fewer parental memories with which to compare the current set-up of married life with the partners apart. Such is what matters have come to, in that private house with its sweet, old-fashioned back garden kept delicately uncultivated.

Four residents in a comfortable house; not to mention lots of visitors, guests, and hired help that come and go.

Baby-sitters are in more frequency, for Fiona goes out a lot on her own, as Don has been doing for years. Dead love brings alive thoughts of new love. Romantic escapades abound, to escape dreary home facts. Fiona is newer at this; she has beginning fantasies, soft and fluffy, like springtime's return; Don, the veteran, has had some hardened campaigns; he's been to the wars, and would bare scars and tales, but that he's secretive.

Fiona has stopped caring. His first infidelities hurt, for love had still been there to be hurt. It converted, quickly, to hate.

Now, no more love, no more hate. A nice, clean, economical indifference, with free outlook, and the roving heart.

The heart's open road, fancy free, the second youth that precedes middle-age. With money enough to indulge the whims that do materialize, and carry caprices beyond mere mental shadows, to follow up the windings that come about, to see where they just might lead, if taken to

. . .

These appetites are affordable. They're fortunate, as divided pairs go, with means to make division work, to multiply opposite ways.

Money for hired help, baby-sitters, separate cars, enabling one to get around. Social life could be a constant carnival, an arcade of fun, glitter, and intrigue, the amusement park of hidden delights; an exotic fair.

Fiona throbbed. She was fortunate. Others might not know where their next meal would come from; Fiona's doubt was on a higher plane: where would her next love come from? She was a tramp, a bum, in the heart's vagrant slum.

||

Her definitely blond hair was never peroxide bleached, dyed, tinted. Nature's always premature decay was dulling her bright locks; subduing their brilliance to lackluster off-canary gray—in minority flecks that slowly took toehold, small inroads that foretold the overwhelming avalanche.

Wrinkles made inroads around her eyes, the blue of which seemed sadly somehow to be fading, when environed by dents of tired facial surface, the linear links to ultimate decrepitude.

Well, if Fiona wasn't the beauty she once was, the men now appropriate for her would themselves be correspondingly older.

The scale was just updated, that's all—or downgraded?

Maturity is an asset that can't be helped. It's a blessing that's accepted with quiet resignation. It's a virtue that's offered so gracefully, who are we to decline? It's a reward which, for all humility, we just can't dodge.

The slow approach of distant death came about in gradual signs. Love, with its eternal ring, corrects that grave fault, all at once. It alone commands equal power to hurl death heroically back in grand full Olympian combat. Temporarily, love wins: it's livelier.

III

Fiona was assaulting youth for the second time, from the other side.

She had that weird feeling; she'd been through all this before—but in an earlier way.

The differences parted to reveal similarities. The similarities, though, bore inherent differences.

An odd tilting of light-shade angles, of cold-hot, of wet-dry, of up-down, thick-thin, round-flat, soft-hard, out-in, stuck-loose, heavy-light, empty-full, slick-coarse, stretching-slack, powdery-firm; in common ranges that adjust incompatible planes and almost combine dimensional opposites through a scale compromise that rings out registers along the far-flung arc, through sliding folds connecting sides and ends, under one disjointed rule. Order, so chaotically come by, is still, of some sorts, order. The mind that so perceives this order, however, pays a derangement fee, a displacement price, dissociation from fellow minds, a dislocation, disorientation, distortion, and likely words prefixed by "dis-".

So there she was (or rather, not "there," but "when"). Slipping everywhere outside between. Lost with so many founds. Endlessly sailing along in the discontinuous, turned up and tossed about, home safe among reversals, risen literally to the point of down.

She kept recovering from all this, close and far; and had further recovering to do, from her recoveries.

Radical instability, everywhere. Love, religion, art and peace, poetry and purity, faith, eternity, absolutes, beauty, harmony, perfection, truth: all these were healers. They restored, purged, cured, and cleansed. They clarified, simplified, composed, related, organized. They reconnected original continuities that had fallen into disrepair, disruption, disarray, and other "dis"-prefixed words disgorged from any dictionary, at large, like fluttering feathers from a plucked old pillow.

IV

Her patriotic nationalism; her solid-core Christianity; her humanity-idealistic socialism: all had disbursed their ingrediential components from crumbled seams and remained, ever after, unreassembled. Her come-apart organisms, once rent-through, were broken up for good. And went unreplaced.

Now, "where" was she (it was "when," really)? Searching for love. All fresh, a second-time-over fresh, searching again, from her later position. Conditions are altered; the repetition is hardly identical, in this renewed search. The earlier search was both better and worse. *This* search is both worse and better. It somehow seems like another sort of search, altogether.

The love she seeks will be stamped with a whole new man, of his own distinctive brand, as yet unknown. When he's identified—brought dripping wet into recognition's net of the known—the search is ended . . . And a new sorrow begun? Joy preliminarily to give way, once joy's taste will attest to sorrow's suffering aftermath?

She braced, to meet the future; or went slack, to make *it* aggress.

She and the future are slated, always, to come to terms and meet. She and her own future: a doomed clash of armies, that grope, fumble, slip, and slide, in the ignorance of the night; grim and gripless antagonists, in clumsy slant of converging; bungling up their rendezvous by degrading destiny into accident: heaping on fate the deep indignity of trivial chance.

V

Her patriotic nationalism; her solid-core Christianity; her humanity-idealistic socialism; add to these the marriage unit, the family system, the clear-cut imposed order, the organized institutional socially prescribed traditionally solid rearing of children in the conjugal household: this sacred bond also collapses, falls apart in anarchy and disenchantment. Discarding the wife and mother role, Fiona is on her own again.

She's acting out of order for her age. A full-time governess is employed for the kids. Fiona's become a kid too: she's gone back to college! She's a student, again! And dresses cute and young: a pony-tail, tight sweater, scrubbed cheeks, junior jaunting shoes, an elastic step.

It's autumn, the term has started. She's not at home, but at the local university, where she's enrolled. She's going for her degree! The air is bracing, the leaves are turning; the men are handsome—the older students, and that ageless body, the faculty.

CHAPTER 2

"The glory of the universe, and the love of life: the things most heartily recommended. Before we go any further (if it's *possible* to go any further), I should pause to explain (if explanation is needed) that the opinions expressed in this classroom may not reflect the doctrine, if there is any, of this virtually global university.

"A university—even one as large as this—is only yet just a tiny fraction of the universe at large. And I, now lecturing before you, am only one professor, of only one department, sectioned off so departmentally, in this department-store-resembling university, where knowledge is acquired competitively by grading.

"Our university, even conceived as a whole if your minds can get around that far, is nevertheless but one of a great number.

"But it's the university we're closest to, as we're inside it.

"All of you listening to me in rapt silence are my students for this singular course; I'll assign grades at semester's end, which will contribute to your academic records—or, in some cases, alas, detract.

"This is not the nearest university for by far most people throughout this immense universe.

"Well, we locally must consider ourselves, in our current classroom here. That's our immediate concern, as a group unit in an academic cell.

"Let's leave other units to their other places. To us, they're merely academic, as abstract entities, remote from us.

"I'm trying to *place* us. Here we all are—those of you attending this course, and I, its instructor.

"Well, our hour's up, the hell's shoot to ring, today's class has witnessed my monologue and without including any vocal participation by you, the passive but attentive scholars. We'll correct that in full at our next meeting. Adjourned."

The class filtered out of the door; Fiona too, carrying books like a schoolgirl. She was attending the "Unlimited Advanced Education That Includes Adults" Session Branch Program at this, her local university, tardily to make amends for neglecting to complete college to the extent of a degree earlier, before marriage and motherhood, in this her life that was so rapidly going on.

She was matriculating through credit accumulation at a part-time curriculum aiming for such a diploma or certificate as would qualify her to eligibly compete for a teaching post at professor rank through the gradual instructor title, at the conclusion of her interrupted and now resumed career as a student duly registered for this, another term.

She hugged her books to her breast on leaving the classroom. She looked so cute!

So schoolgirlish! Her still-blond hair tied behind in ponytail. Wearing a tight sweater to advantage over other women students who hadn't enlarged themselves by past breastfeeding to dangling infants as a motherly pastime or urgent bond between the female begetter and her recent begotten, which extends such breasts as were there to begin with, to such milky plumpness as forwards a mature growth.

Her two daughters are governess-cared-for. Her husband is who-knows-where? and who-cares?

She's free, for an affair. However bookish is the campus, there's an autumn tang there. The air is rare. Intellectual learning excites the blood and sublimes all lust.

It's exhilarating. The football team is practicing. Men walk the campus, through cross-sections, to various buildings, to appointed classes.

The tingle in Fiona's loins. Don hasn't slept with her for two years—he's only nominally, now, a husband.

There's a pulse. It's in her dear organ, between high legs. It wakes, and yearns for its next mate.

Men. But who?

CHAPTER 3

I

Her mathematics teacher, though full of higher quantum, total-dimensional geometry, mystic-equationed algebra, and vast velocities of massive energy, seemed meekly submissive to Fiona's charming field of radiance. In fact, he fell under her spell, as they consulted quietly together after class.

Fiona had a free period, and so did he. Usually he went to his office, at such a time; now, in the abandoned classroom, he sat on his desk while Fiona sat nearby on a chair. Their conversation was intent. It included the constant intermingle of their stare.

Their dialogue ran smoothly between topics. Rambling, discursive, yet swift. Keen, but mainly impersonal.

Now she described her recent philosophy class. She was able to quote hunks of verbatim from that lecture which paired the universe and the university in terms soaringly universal: "The glory of the universe, and the love of life" . . . "A university—even one as large as this —is only yet just a tiny fraction of the universe at large" . . . "This is not the nearest university for by far most people throughout this immense universe . . . broadly narrow statements, the focus off a far range.

"Professor Flood's reputation is spiralling right across the campus into the outer world at large," affirmed Professor Keld, the numbers specialist, to his mature stray student he's gladly stuck with after class. "He's published first abstruse tomes, which only experts of metaphysics could grapple up close to; now, he's popularized without compromising, and is reaching a wide range of eager laymen who thirst for keys to locked mysteries."

"Do you know him personally, Professor Keld?"

"No, only by sight, reputation, and some of his works. His Philosophy Department and my Mathematics Department ought to bisect with interdisciplinary penetration; they're kept, however, too strictly apart, despite inherent mathematical substances in philosophy, and the intrinsic philosophical nature of mathematics."

"If they belong together," Fiona declared, with surprising brashness coming from a mere student, or else spectacular boldness, "I'll join them."

"That would please me. But where would you get the power?"

"I'll merely apply the power I already have," said Fiona, audaciously.

"But Miss—"

"It's Missus; but call me Fiona," said the student whose age approximated, at a glance, her professor's category. "Were you accusing me of arrogance? Dear Mister Keld?"

He blushed, with perplexity. His mouth stood open. She closed it, with a kiss, completing his surprise.

▌▌

"She had simply walked over, and kissed him. She'd already been standing for a while, while he leaned on his desk. Her act closed their talk, not only his lips. The bell rang, ending the period. They parted, he to teach a new class, she to attend a different one. They walked out of the room, and at a silent signal, went separate ways. In fantasy's steps.

Each merging into the other's dearly lit absence.

▌▌▌

Though lacking an appointment-excuse, Fiona went down the Philosophy corridor to knock on Professor Flood's closed but unlocked office door. It was opened by another student, who was in conference with that eminent luminosity, who motioned that Fiona be seated to wait, across from his desk.

The other student belonged to the very same sex as Professor Flood. Such an extraordinary coincidence, in this tiny world!

Fiona listened, with fascination. She was enthralled by the Professor's erudition, logic, vision, looks, and eloquence, though in no special priority of sequence.

The student was younger, blander, colorless by comparison, put nondescriptly to the shade by Doctor Flood's distinguished brilliance.

Would Fiona have compared them that way if she had been the student's age? Maybe not. Attractions change as the person does, keeping perfect pace together.

Two professors had come into her ken. One had already been lured into her personal life. The other might be, as she sat in his office.

Doctor Keld was Fiona's own age, while Doctor Flood stood slightly older, but only by chronology, not by spirit.

In spirit, he had no age. He was for all the ages in the civilized pageantry of humanity's endless thrust.

Doctor Keld had won Fiona's heart—though by her aggression, as she had thrust it on him. Was she about—awesomely, suddenly—to become fickle? While discharging a favor, a duty, a mission, for the man she's now betraying? Such impulsive abandon? She had years to make up for: ignored by Don. The inattentive husband had made her too lonely. Suddenly her heart does double-duty, in its greed to redeem the lost years. It lurches at two top professors—with what success?—in desperate compensation's dire devilry.

IV

Now the male student had left. The door was discretely closed on the remaining two: that toweringly intellectual professor and this student who, no longer young, nevertheless filled up the entire office with the subtle intoxication, the delicate scent, of allurement, of rarified seduction, of love's elaborate enticements.

The Professor had been seduced before, in his star-studded career from his undergraduate days, to his post-doctorate sessions, to his instructorial apprenticeship, thesis tutorials, and lord high professorship with his campus-transcendent rise to cultural renown wherever the cloistered circles were in all outposts and international realms official to truth's pursuit.

He had seduced, and been seduced. He was at the end of his second marriage, on the very verge of a mildly notorious divorce, peppered by the odor hum of some juicy scandal.

Fiona, though, was his match. Professor Keld had felt meek and helpless in her mature, trouncy grip. So too now did Professor Flood. Fiona had amassed her mastery, as a student, as rather a woman, over mere faculty males.

"Yes, Miss . . ."

"Missus; but call me Fiona. Professor Flood, there's something I want."

"I hope it's me. You'll have it, if that's the case."

"We'll regard that later. Something more immediate is pressing now."

"How extraordinary, what is it?"

"Professor Flood, I want you to join your Philosophy Department to Professor Keld's Mathematical Department."

"What! In the same university?!"

"You heard me."

"But it's totally unprecedented!"

"Create a revolution. Innovate."

"Me? I should do that? But why?"

"I want you to."

"That's a cogent reason. But why else?"

"The two Departments are related."

"Sure. But is that sufficient for merging them?"

"I declare, that it is. Furthermore, Doctor Keld thinks so, too."

"Who's he?"

"The Mathematics Department Chairman."

"I'm jealous. Do you love him?"

"Of course. But I love you more."

"In that case, I'll cooperate, to my full authority."

"Considering the extent of your authority, that should be sufficient."

"How should I go about this radical procedure?"

"Leave it up to me, Doc. I'll do the arranging. I'm setting up for you to meet tomorrow, on neutral territory, with Keld himself. You yourself will also be present; and I, to arbitrate. Us three alone. The respective members of your Philosophy Department, and Keld's Mathematics Department, will, of course, abide by, and not object to, nor in any way block, the joint decision of decisive jointure. Is that clear?"

"No colleague interference, I guarantee, from my side. Keld had better control his. Meanwhile, back to me. I'm taking a risk, out on a limb. The Chancellor, Dean, Provost, and President of our University might somewhat look askance, perchance."

"We'll present it to them as a *fait accompli.*"

"Still, I'm sticking out my neck. I'm jeopardizing a great career."

"Not with *your* fame: *any* university would want you."

"But would *I* want *them?* No, I want to stay here. I'll make a supreme effort, to join the departments, under the joint jurisdiction of Keld and me, whose coupled autonomies will constitute virtual tyranny—even at defiance of university policy. All this is for you. What's my reward?"

"Me."

"You? That ought to be enough, to gratify any fiendish sacrifice. But am I to understand that reward of you includes all of you?"

"All, but especially the part between the waist and the knees."

"That would be a preferred concentrational area to delight my senses and soothe my mind."

"Doctor Flood, though formidable, you're agreeable."

"That's much of your doing, dear Fiona."

V

Flood was caressing Fiona, fondling her. He had come around from his desk to sit closer to her, the better to articulate her surface regions within handy access to his groping hands. He massaged and manipulated her swelling thighs and outer haunches, up to that throbbing crucial meeting point between the torso proper and the dividing legs, above and in front of her rearing bottom, and protruding ever delicately below.

His professorial dignity was cautiously being compromised: such an excruciating conflict was well under control.

His lust, however, was getting out of hand. She had to curb it, for they were in his office, with staff secretaries, colleagues, and students waiting outside.

Their breasts were wildly panting. How flavorsome, with what cunning pungency, university life had proven to be!

CHAPTER 4

I

Fiona's two daughters were going away on a day-trip: a school expedition for the elder, with the younger and their governess given permission to go along.

In addition, Don was to be away that day. The man of the house, estranged husband and negligent father. Yes, he'd be away. To a woman, no doubt.

Or else, pursuing his occupation. It was either work or a woman. One or the other.

So the whole house would be Fiona's, for that day. She had no classes that afternoon. By fortunate coincidence; the schedules both of Professor Keld and Professor Flood happened to be open and free, for that time.

It was a gorgeous autumnal day. They'd have a late, leisurely lunch—but with of course important matters to be agreed on, in the working course of their lunch—in the delicious back garden of that ample house.

The garden was kept in delightful disarray, in keeping with a carefully cultivated air of informality.

Sweet nature abounded, in small units. An early afternoon sun parted the clouds (or rather, the clouds parted for *it*). Soft warm air gaily danced about. A mild dalliance. Such murmurs, in the scented air. Fluid ripples' melodious liquidity. Love, all but audible. Sounds and sweet airs. Roving shadows, overhead. Wine below, birds above, and leaves of lovely lassitude.

Professor Keld was in awe of Professor Flood. Flood was widely published and well known, not cheaply, but with esteem, an honored place held in lofty intellectual circles.

Professor Keld was, also, in love with Fiona. His wife need never know, nor his teen-age children. It was merely Fiona's affair, and his.

No, not only theirs: it was also of great concern to Professor Flood—potentially, for he didn't yet know it.

On his part, Professor Flood, though not quite in love, was physically under the infatuation of Fiona's influential sphere.

It had been intimated, in his office, By Fiona herself, that something was amorously afoot, perhaps; involving Professor Keld. How, though, serious was it? This furrowed Professor Flood's brow, under his white, patrician hair, that now swirled to the wind's languor and the teasing breeze.

Keld's awe of Flood blended with envy. Flood was respectful to Keld, but aloof, and just barely condescending. Keld resented this. His love for Fiona got the better of his veneration for Flood. He was determined to wage battle. Fiona was the stakes they'd play for. University warfare, in a private garden.

II

A hired woman had cooked their outdoor food. Limitless wine to escort the tasty fare down.

A tree dappled them, with its motley assemblage of leaves. Its lower twigs wafted their upper hair. Here was a love triangle, but off campus. Two married men and one married woman. Three creatures, the latest along evolution's line except for their juniors that overlapped their lifetime in lower age groups fresh from the birth factory.

Generational coincidence, and other coincidences, brought the three together. Miraculously, there they all were.

In the same garden, eating lunch. A late lunch, but all three were there.

In a privately owned patch of cityfied nature.

Under a common sun, that least expensive of necessities.

Three figures, sitting round a table.

An outdoor trio, under Fiona's own tree.

Splotched all unevenly, in passion's intrigue.

Three highly polished intellectuals, two top men in their fields, and one aspiring to be a top woman for knowledge transmitted by education.

Keld loved Fiona, Flood wanted her but didn't quite love her yet, and Fiona: whom, if either, did she favor, with excelling luxury of choice?

She suspended as yet a decision. She wavered, in plastic neutrality, between them. She cautiously refrained from committing herself. Flexible palpitations would go either way, between her ardent pursuers, whose academic standing would stagger her women friends to angry gasps of envy or clasps of admiring applause.

She was dangling them; they reached the harder.

The issue was supposed to be Departmental merger. Underlying that ostensible reason for their meeting was the accidental flaring of contention for that rarely privileged student's choice favors.

Birds twittered down, with their songs. A cat curved between legs like a snake. Hearts were entwined, in ponderous suspense.

Love flickered madly. Its jumping beam alighted alternately on them. Sun-shade mottle shifted, in wide switches.

Fiona's breast heaved. She loved both, or either. Or all men, or life itself, the totality-containing world, represented by her two suitors: green passion, in a green shade, tinted to autumn's roving medley, in nature's decay of assortments.

Three adults in their own lives' autumns. Biologically doomed, yet immortally attuned to Love's Universal: given, for local habitation and name, a university setting transposed divinely to a private garden. Evil's garden, of temptation. A tongue emitted forked, from fair damnation's exquisite snake.

III

"Keld, what do I get for consenting to the merger?"

"That's a virtuous reward in itself. You will have done a good thing."

"Thanks for the morality sermon, Keld. How pure it would be, to merge our departments! But if I consent, leave Fiona alone."

"Is she the price I pay, Flood? We're foully bartering, and defiling pure love. Why 'deal' for her heart? Let it accord one of us its priceless benefits. Not under contamination of a bribe, a sullying 'deal,' the duress of interestedness outside its sphere: let love go radiantly self-guided, in its own true light."

"That's poetic, Keld. But love has worldly persuasions, both acquired and given. I want her. Merge our Departments. But Fiona goes to me."

"What a gap in your idealism, Flood!"

"Enough so, to get what I want."

IV

Bogging down in stalemate, in vanity-bickerings and tough exchanges of self-puffery rhetoric with quaint turns of phrase tossed ornately in to flourish out a gallant male effect, these top-level deliberations sputtered aground in rancor, recrimination, and wounded pride. What was Keld's purpose in attempting to unify their University's Philosophy and Mathematics Departments? Was it a dark motive for personal gain?

He felt mathematics to be limited all by itself, even with algebra, geometry, trigonometry, and solid kinetic borderline physics of mass and velocity, energy and relativity, to play around with.

But unified with philosophy, mathematics would be strengthened by vital connections and organic joinings, gaining thereby a huge influx of significance to prop up otherwise shallow technical resources and bring them in to life's outward flow.

He wasn't personally to gain by the merger. It was for truth's enhancement, for deepening knowledge, for a greater splendor of meaning, that he thought up the idea, confided it to Fiona, and let her arrange this meeting—proving now awkward and abortive—with the Philosophy Department's eminent Chairman deluxe.

Complicating it all was his love for Fiona and his defense of this love by rising in wrath and rivalry against Doctor Flood's own designs on their mutual student.

Her own attitude fluctuated in breathlessness. She swaggered with humility. She was hysterically calm about it all. She shattered all dreams with realized pride.

Flood or Keld? Which?

Fiona couldn't handle it. Love wobbled. It fluttered with indecision like a stunned bird who ruffles to gather her wings together in a throb of panic. She shuddered. She shivered. She was in frail miniature, caught cold in the ice cube of a gleaming dream.

V

Doctor Flood seemed cynical about Keld's and Fiona's project to get him to agree to a Departmental merger. Philosophy had to do with everything, by nature, already; its province extended into every discipline and study, with admission automatically granted.

Science, art, psychology, sociology, every single subject naturally fell into philosophy's all-encompassing domain, came within the sway of a boundless philosophical empire that kept stretching out to bring tamely into colonization the rugged remoteness of any conceivable horizon.

So why accord mathematics a special preferred privilege that linguistics, anthropology, genetics, law, ethics, archaeology, biology, and other respectable branches are not to be granted in equal favor? Thus reasoned the thinker, Flood.

But, when gripped by powerful lust in his office for Fiona, he had yesterday made a pact with her. In return for her body, he had pledged to cooperate in that pet project of hers. This afternoon, though, in her garden, basking in the lyricism of the occasion but murked down by bitter personality strife, Flood was reneging on the vow he had sworn yesterday. Why should he consent to an active love rival's pet scheme and fond dream? Why should he back Fiona's loyalty to the man who would thwart his desire for her? No, the agreement was off. Fiona should support *Flood's* schemes, not Keld's. Fiona should transfer her loyalty, bodily, to all that ever Flood thought and wished. Such conversion should start right away, and the training set up for Fiona's abiding faith and obedience to Flood's dictates.

Devotion, submission, he required of her. And the way to get it was not by accepting this bribe. He'll play clean. She must want him unconditionally. To have her on her terms that would gratify a rival's scheme, even if by so doing he defeated the rival's claim for her love, would be not really to have her, clean and pure. So, the "deal" was off.

And anyway, Fiona aside, so far as philosophy was concerned in a departmentalized university, it should be yoked and harnessed to no other department, but keep a private stable for itself. Not for ivory tower isolation; on the contrary, it already contained every other discipline, with infinite extensions all subservient to its central network.

Everything, mathematics included, was grist to philosophy's endlessly active mill. It was the radiant hub and center to every human activity and enterprise.

It stood, then, in no need to lower its immense stature, its pre-eminent status, by joining departments with one of its own subsidiaries, or tributaries, or components: dear little mathematics. Why should a towering Whole join equal rank to but one of its parts? That's like The United States admitting Idaho as equal partner, granting it the same rank as the federal entirety of the Government itself.

This "argument" was reasonably stated by Flood, with confidence and patience, to Fiona and Keld. The afternoon was shading in lengths to the gathering chill.

Lunch was long over. Late tea was now served, by the hired woman, along with sweet-cloying pastries short of nutrition but long in instant pleasure.

Keld hung his head, submissively. His professional plan had failed. But what of his amorous one?

Would Fiona add her rejection of his love to Flood's humiliating rejection of the combined-Departments idea? Then Keld would retreat to his wife and carry on as the numbers head of the university as if nothing had happened. But shame would attest that something had happened. He'd resume his husband and career duties, as always, as before, but bear within an ignominious burden. The stink of defeat, in love and work.

VI

It was getting cold. The dusk was coming. The sun was down. But the grouped figures remained there, as the hired woman cleared the table they were grouped around in the gloom of their uncertainty.

No departmental merger. There, *that's* settled.

But one matter remained to be settled.

The choice of the student hostess.

Her two professors waited. Well?

Indecision wedged her in panic.

No, gentlemen. No choice, yet.

VII

Leaving the garden behind, they went through the house and down the front steps.

In front of the house, three cars were parked. One remained there: Fiona's. (Don had driven *his* where he went today.) One was Keld's, who got in. The third was Flood's: he got in.

The rivals made no handshake gesture; no friendly pretense: no shallow courtesy.

Each, from his respective car, waved goodbye to Fiona, and drove off, in different directions.

Fiona waved to them both, in both directions. Her heart was, as the cliché goes, "torn."

But rich. Rich with two men's care about what she now did, said, thought, or felt.

It was now night. The children would soon come home, with their reliable governess.

Would Don come home? Why care about that? She had cares enough.

She also had homework to do. College was not just for love. There was responsibility, too.

CHAPTER 5

I

She decided: why choose? She chose, then, not to decide. She'd commit, then, double adultery. That surely would keep her busy, what with two lovers (both in grand positions but one enjoying renown far beyond their college), and her serious work toward a doctorate degree and post-graduate specialization.

Her mother duties were light. They were well delegated to a responsible governess who discharged them with conscientious exactness and even maternal warmth. That was fortunate for the two- and ten-year-olds, nice daughters, but Don's more than hers, though of course she had been technically their own and only mother, from the birth point of view: which shouldn't be underestimated in importance. Were it not for birth itself, how would *any*one get born?

Since the birth of the younger, no more sex with Don. Lots of making-up, to do.

Don? Write him off and forget him. Why waste a bother over *him*, with two great new men to not choose between?

Let choice come later. Now, enjoy both.

II

Eventually, "later" came. Who—Flood or Keld? The great philosophical author, or the mathematical genius?

Let her brood that one out. But lightly, meanwhile, get smoothly bruised and battered, lovingly pommelled, orgiastically trounced and pinched, pushed and pulled, pumped and worked over, by each in his own turn.

By now, Flood loved her as much as Keld did, in order to keep apace. If he had been her only choice, Flood might have neglected to go so far as to love her. But being in contention, he got desperate, and took care not to take her for granted. So much care, he's now "in love."

Fiona loves being loved by both. It quite improves those bad times when, for too bitterly long, a gaping vacuum stood at her heart's empty ache, open wide with that appalling terror, loneliness.

III

Was it immoral to be alternated over by two men, Keld for two or three nights, then Flood for two or three nights?

Yes, but delightful, too. Such variety couldn't but prove stimulating and entertaining. The men got increasingly desperate. Their love turned violently competitive, which gave *her* more and more sexual pleasure, and drove *them* into wild, lost depths of complete love, ferocious passion, the depraved darkness of insane romance.

These are torments of the damned. Each wants to be the unique possessor of her. Each craves to be her only one.

She loves, now, the idea of "two." Any reduction of that to "one" would fall beneath adequacy to the contamination of the incomplete.

The more each of the men wanted to be her only one, the more (perversely, even spitefully perhaps) Fiona needed no less than both. She gorged on such erotic greed. As a *pair*, she loved them. In the arms of one, she thought of the other. They became the *yin* and *yang* of her pulse rhythm.

IV

Driven to desperate stratagems by Fiona's wilfull vacillation, Keld and Flood wildly tried to outdo each other in new boastworthy achievements, to be steeped in academic glory and win great honor. For the first time, Keld published: "Mathematics and Mankind," a book that ranged far afield into speculative metaphysics of human destiny. On the dedication page were the simple words, "To Fiona—the Muse who always remains more admirable than even the work she admirably inspires."

When Missus Keld saw that, she sued for divorce. Her grounds for suspicion had long been proven correct. Three or four nights each week, for months already, her husband hadn't returned home. Their marriage had been so happy, till that started happening.

At first Keld had apologized with hugely complicated fibs worthy of his mathematical standing. Then, he sketched only rough explanations. Finally, none at all.

His teen-age children were saddened. They'd always preferred their dad.

Not to be outdone, Flood, who had already been widely published, came through with a new book that made him, overnight, a national celebrity. He made guest appearances on the well-known television talk shows, and was extensively interviewed in the periodicals.

Flood's sensational best-seller, which doesn't stoop below the most rigorous standards of scholarly perfection nor make concessions to cheap modes current in popular vulgarity, is comprehensively called "Life, Mind, World, and Truth": an ambitious title, but the text more than fulfills those grandiose pretensions, justifying a critical rave from the book review column in *The New York Times*, heralding Flood as "finally, the second Socrates, Plato's logical successor, Aristotle's eclipser, Kant's annihilator, Hegel's master, Spinoza's more-than-equal, Schopenhauer's superior, Nietzsche's nemesis, Kierkegaard's exceller, Heidegger's outdistancer, Sartre's surpasser, and Dewey's outdoer."

The dedication page of "Life, Mind, World, and Truth" contains these simple lines:

"To Fiona, whose existence on earth is history's most beautiful mystery and evolution's master stroke so far.

"Without her inspiration, not a single word of this book would have found first dawn within the modest brow of the author, whose gratitude to his Muse falls short of adequate expression save by the sacred intimacy of secrets shared with our holy bed in nights of love's eternity."

On publication day, Flood's divorce at last came through. Too long pending, it was now thoroughly uncontested, and made the culture hero a free man. He was that anyway, but now his freedom was technically official, and even legal.

The strenuous struggle between academic titans for Fiona's elective preference moved her and gratified her no end. But was she satisfied? No. She urged them on to greater heights.

CHAPTER 6

She was now the campus marvel. She was known by sight over the whole college; pointed out, whispered about, spun by multiple gossip into patterns of assorted legends.

Her age was exaggerated. She was said to be a witch; an occult priestess of the black arts, the resurrected votary of an ancient form of pure evil, of voluptuary magic that removed men's senses and drove them to frantic animal extremes, even sometimes into vegetable excesses, and once to the absolute mineral level, or even to the verge of annihilation itself, to the outward limit of all nonexistence.

She was said to be the reincarnation of a peculiar essence of witchcraft that bedevilled scholars from the straight path and infinitely multiplied their sexual resources to the point of prodigious proclivities of biologically impossible potency, turning in performances of supernatural power borrowed in part by barter arrangement from a soul-salesman of Death.

"With all the younger women around, who would gladly worship at fame's shrine with their offered bodies on shared cots heroically to couple with the hero in and out of any temple, how does Fiona do it? What's her secret? Keld of great mental deeds, and Flood far-flung in fame, are her body's own private slaves, spinning orbits of frenzied obedience to Fiona's bidding; they create marvelous works of delicately structured monuments of enduring consequence, historical breakthroughs in the organized rampage of truth; and dedicate such masterpieces to Fiona!

"What does she have that other women of her age never dare to hope for any more? How is she able to keep Keld and Flood in double thrall? What wicked spell does she lasciviously weave; what enchantment's potion of alchemic brew, what crystal drops from mixtures never told, does she use with unscrupulous compensation for her beauty's corrupt decline and time's brutal punishment?

"With all the pretty students just half her age licensed to roam this Eros-studded campus, all young and eager to enjoy academic privilege and bask in the wilds of intellectual discovery with great female liberty in the first flushes of a vigorous freedom to pursue knowledge at the feet and in the arms of a patient male faculty body, how does Fiona—handicapped by her wrinkles and hair hideously graying—*outcompete* the nineteen-, twenty-, and twenty-one-year-old flesh of soft sweet limbs of the entire university female enrollment, the matriculated student body of that division's gender, let loose in the curricula jungle to learn first-hand in an open market of bold competition for faculty favorites; with the greatest premium of priority, the cream of choices, being the numerical wizard Keld and that reigning Pope of philosophy's Vatican'd hierarchy, Flood, Apostle of pure thought and the darling chosen Saint of the carnal paradise, whose private tutorials are the dreams of each girl's attainment but admits precious exclusive few, by appointment only, of impeccable academic record?

"Flood picks Fiona alone; and Keld does too; both ignore all the younger women, whose barrage of ardent charms the great professors resist in easy and total dismissal. Each has only Fiona on his whole mind. Neither alone, however, would do for Fiona. She controls both, and toys with them in turn.

"Twenty girls would gladly share Keld; thirty would share Flood. But both are in the fold of Fiona, each being only a half of all her own ownership, exclusive property off bounds to any trespasser, her body's private pets and twin subjects held bound to her spirit's whimsy as she sees fit; how does she do it? What secret succeeds in unfair competition to spoil the odds of youth and beauty, and overturn all advantages known to custom and nature in unequal erotic combat?

"She's truly a marvel. Does she have a secret? Or is her secret uniquely just herself, being Fiona?

"Unfoiled by decay's onslaught, she's the possessed creature of some demonic art. Held in tight check by it, in turn she subimprisons Keld and Flood as deputy tyrant beneath her own captivity.

"We marvel at this mystery as to a new truth not yet explained. We envy her and pity her victims and her outstripped rivals; We're in awe. Magic is only undisclosed truth."

Such was the whispering consensus, the deep legendary tangle that clustered about her. She had dark powers that eluded normal light. Two spreaders of light, Keld and Flood, were bound body and soul to the campus witch. Ancient evil was unleashed, in a modern sanctuary of science and sanity. The sober stronghold was invaded by forces long obsolete. Fiona was their conveyor. Enchanted, the enchantress used sex to enslave, love to benumb, fascination to devastate, and mystery to seal it all up.

Thus the aura grew about her. Myth returned, in her own figure, form, and face, to the liberal university that admitted women. Myth wore Fiona's feature, and walked realistically there. In living detail, art merged with that scene. There were plenty of campus beholders. They, in those years, saw it, clearly.

Later, they would wonder. Doubt would efface those former impressions. Belief would become void of confirmation. Absence would vacate the senses. Was it true? Was there a Fiona? A Keld, a Flood? A universe-enclosing university, to attest to all that?

If real, how? Later years would lose their faith. Presently, though, it's true.

CHAPTER 7

Fiona grew as the campus legend. The rumor spread and reached off-campus too. It was no rumor: it was true.

Don heard about it, and was mystified. He had held his wife as no special prize, disowned her in conjugal contempt, spurned her body as stale and overridden with the palling familiarity of a thing once owned and lightly discarded.

He had gone for younger women; But *was* his wife so tarnished? She was now excellently valued, by Flood and Keld. What rare rebirth had restored bewitching magic?

Having advanced from domestic dullness and dismal marital neglect to double triumphs in the glamorous outer world of amorous escapade, Fiona looked behind her and saw the danger of regression to tedious former disaster. To resume what had long ago failed was what Don now wanted: all avid for a fresh return, he pursued her anew. He had placed too low a value on her: the world's gossip reproached him for that.

If Keld and Flood loved her, why—she was lovable! Don had thrown away a gem worth more than all his tribe in successive adulteries. He'd reform; he'd claim her back; legally, they had never divorced. She was, by rights, still his. His eyes were opened up by amazing true rumor, off the campus. And he owned her!

He owned the wonder loved by great men—or one, anyway, Flood, who was surely great, by spread fame. Keld was great within his special field, and owned a local reputation compared to Flood's. All that, though, is no more than academic. More to the point is that Don now will exercise his option, and own that owner of lofty souls, in her own lofty right. He'd remove the Myth from her great conquest scenes, and restore her to her proper roles: wife and mother. She'll be a God-fearing Christian at home; her wild magic tamed; her bewitching powers for great love now harnessed to strict domestication, and convention's old duty.

CHAPTER 8

Outright, Fiona said "No."

"I mean to have you back. I'll put such pressure on you, till you yield."

"You have no real hold over me. In the law court I could declare lots of reasons, citing your negligence and so forth, your string of adulteries, your general contempt, neglect, and dismissal of me as a true and proper wife, as even a person in my own right. I'd win the case; and get custody of our daughters, too. Not that I truly want them, but you'll have to be proven unfit, and so you'll have to lose them. And lose me: whom you've already lost forever in all that went between us. Your *legal* loss of me will follow in more technical detail, meaningless in the true human sense of what bond of understanding exists between us.

"You can't tie my soul down. It soars aloft, on unclippable wings. I'm beyond your ever knowing any more.

"You won't reduce me, to *your* shallow measure. I have independent means. I need no alimony from you—child support only, but you'll have visiting privileges, and our daughters may stay with you on weekends—perhaps intruding on your love affairs, but so be it.

"In emphatic terms, we're finished. My lawyer will set things going today. I'll keep this house, please: it's mostly mine."

"I'll fight you through every legal loophole, with loads of testimony and witnesses to support my claims. You've driven two distinguished men to the disgrace of the divorce courts: you've broken up a happy marriage and family unity in the case of Keld. Flood already had a pending divorce before you got your claws on him, adding scandal to scandal to expedite it, his second divorce from only his second wife. But you're driving them to distraction—the Mathematics Chairman, and the great Philosophy Professor."

"To distraction? No. To the opposite of that. To do their work so well, that they've published books inspired by me, books putting them pre-eminently even further along in their respective fields. I drive them to great works. To wider fame for Flood, and new recognition for Keld.

"It shows that I'm a force for the good. What evidence will you put against me, in the trial?"

"That you're a practicer of witchcraft, black magic, occult demonology, and love alchemy. Your campus reputation has widely flung itself into mythic proportions outside. You're possessed by an obscene devil. It must be exercised. I'll have scientific witnesses of psychic phenomena to give expert testimony. You'll be put to death—burned at a stake, like that old Arc-Joan.

"But our marriage will be reaffirmed, its sacred institution upheld, before you make an ash of yourself. Even as the flames leap at your dress's hem, we'll renew our marriage vows, in our daughters' presence, before a full and deeply moved audience. A minister will preside, you'll become a new-born bride, while receiving, at the same time, your Last Rites.

"You'll die a Christian, in the fold; you'll die a dutiful wife; a devout mother; a patriot of America; a humane, practicing socialist: you'll die in the glorious sanctity of all our unbroken institutions: marriage, motherhood, the whole Christian religion, political nationalism for our great Republic, and the true idealism of the democratic process of our magnificent future institution, Socialism.

"You'll die, under the protection of such conventions. You'll die— gone up in flame like that French lady saint—in the full and preserved odor of our family unit, intact.

"Flood and Keld will be barred from your execution. Only abiders of goodness will be admitted: preservers of social forms of law and order, of the good bonds of custom and tradition, the eternal verities, the continuities of the collective cohesion of our race, human civilization in public practice, not fragmented into private anarchistic factions of group-fracturing into isolated pockets of morbid romantic independent individual insane unrooted solipsistic atheistic selfish lonely eccentric subjectivity. We want mass coherence, not the chaos of dangerous individuals.

"Such is what I plan for you. Redemption and salvation, but punishment too, through death.

"I'll be a noble widower. I'll be brave and stoical, in the great hour of my bereavement.

"Farewell, Fiona. My attorney will speak to you tomorrow, to instigate a law suit that charges you with such serious crimes against society as evil, uncooperativeness, and making of yourself a campus spectacle, the *femme fatale* vamp who breaks up her own and other marriages by immorality on scandal's grand sexual scale."

"But Don, that contradicts your earlier stated intention to domesticate me back into roles of tame wife and mother, forcing me home to leave my amorous triumphs behind."

"I had to change my mind when you stated your own determined defiance and threatened a horrid and insulting countersuit."

"Suit against suit. We're not suited for each other."

"Your behavior is unsuitable."

"It suits me to continue it. Tonight I'm visiting Doctor Flood to sleep with him, as well as tomorrow night. The night following, Doctor Keld will come here to sleep with me: he hasn't quite settled yet into his new divorced bachelor quarters."

"Very hospitable, Fiona. You're a tramp."

"But you preceded me with your sexual liberties. Are you any less a tramp, then?"

"I'm a man. A man can only be a tramp by being a homeless vagrant loitering hobo of a bum."

"Grant me my liberties, please."

"No. I own you."

"Move out. Move out of my house."

"It's *our* house."

"By mortgage deed, it's mainly mine. I evict you, Don; and will sue for divorce."

"Your suit is suitably unsuitable to show how unsuited we are. But the family is sacred. For our daughters' sake, and society's, we must stay together, and renew our marital bond with a deliberate, self-sacrificing sense of duty. We must behave according to principles. We must uphold the law."

"Don—you're crazy."

"Is that your latest insult?"

"No. It's merely a spot observation. I'm doing field study, for my course in Abnormal Psychology this term. You're my case for research. And what a case!"

"I'm your husband."

"That's why I'm leading my current life. You drove me to loneliness. I'm getting old, but I developed powers to unlonely myself with twin bouts of love—that long may linger—with men of extraordinary achievement. They love me. I own them. You can't own me. I won't let you."

"We'll see. The law, you know."

"The law is *my* protector. I'm the injured one. You drove me to this."

"The law. I insist: the law."

"The law cuts both ways. It will judge *me* the aggrieved party. And find *you* the offending one."

"The law. That ancient body, the law."

CHAPTER 9

I

The law, after due deliberation, adjudged Fiona innocent of all of Don's charges, and Don guilty of every accusation levied by the smoothly expensive attorney that Fiona had the good sense to hire.

It was a sensational court case. Keld and Flood were two of the notable witnesses.

It was highly publicized. Fiona's anonymity as a private citizen was shattered forever. Her reputation had now extended from university to universe, but there, due to spatial limitations on the outer cosmos fringe, had, perforce, to stop.

The jury was fair and impartial, in turning in the one-sided verdict.

The presiding judge, however, was secretly a friend of Keld's.

But the secret was stealthily kept. Even from Flood and Fiona herself, as well as from the battery of lawyers employed by the embattled married pair.

Flood and Keld had found themselves allies, on the same side for the first time. They collaborated well, much to Fiona's attorney's surprise, relief, and gratitude.

II

The trial was considered a triumph of liberal enlightenment over the reactionary upholders of old forms of order and the outmoded systems of individual suppression and public normality in conventional molds and creaking but approved customs that hold tottering old society together.

Fiona was now the heroine of liberal causes, added to her previous role of occult queen of legendary magic. She was a university symbol, or symbolic cluster in simultaneous representation.

She was now a *national* heroine, as well. Her name became more widely known than Flood's to the nonacademic majority of the commonplace world.

She was a controversial figure, over whom people took sides in frenzy, with passionate advocation or, depending on viewpoint, with disapproval that included a role for Don as the martyred victim of injustice.

The court victory vindicated Fiona's double brand of love as a lifestyle alternative that many trendy people tried in vain to emulate.

The sharing of Fiona by Keld and Flood was now brought into argumentative justification by liberal defenders of unrestricted sexual license, as well as by more moderate or even timid advocates of variety in erotic fare. These represented Fiona's side, that is, the person with two mates. Those who saw it from Keld's and Flood's side maintained that half love satisfaction was better than none, despite the jealousy factor involved and the constant pressure to compete.

III

Everything turned out Fiona's way, whatever she wanted she got, following the court case. The divorce was on her terms. The big house with the lovely back garden was hers alone. The rooms in it that Don had frequented were fumigated of his last remaining trace.

The ten-year-old daughter, meanwhile, had become eleven, by the process of passing a birthday. The two-year-old daughter, in much the same manner of living by the same mechanical calendar rule of socially observed time among contemporaries occupying the same universe, was three years old: estranged from her father, as was her elder sister; seeing him only on weekends and other designated times that the Fiona-dominated settlement mercifully allocated to the crushed, annihilated, overwhelmed loser of that celebrated divorce case which brought in its train and sweeping wake so many issues pertinent to the day, showing history hard at work changing the social scene, or rather, social forces splattering a new rate of surprise on the historically changing face of all the peopled globe that roared around with its emotional load inside a vacant portion of space.

The population generational to the times got to know, directly or indirectly, about Fiona's two lovers and her unloving husband. Fiona, meanwhile, kept on aging. But death had a long time to wait. Love was too busy, with complications, to give death much attention. All that living had a retarding effect on decay.

CHAPTER 10

I

Keld decided to stop this nonsense. He plotted to find a way to force, somehow, Fiona to decide.

He'd bribe her daughters' governess, or her daughters themselves, if he could find out what to bribe them *for*.

He had already connived to somewhat rig the court case by having the magistrate be, by coincidence, an old friend of his—a secret never revealed. But what bearing that had on the outcome—who could tell? He'll never know, anyhow.

He wanted to force Flood's hand, force Fiona's hand, to stop this endless, endless sharing.

"Now that Don is gone and the coast is clear, Fiona," he said in her ample house, "let's call a summit conference for the back garden with Flood, you, and me to meet at top level to decide."

"*What* to decide, Keld?" Fiona specified.

"Oh, just *decide*, that's all."

"For its own sake?" Then the decision would lack substance, cause, reason, meaning, issue, and significance. A rather shallow decision, I'd call that. Empty of all but academic exercise."

"Nevertheless, Fiona, a decision *must* be made."

"Being imperative makes you look so solemn and pompous, Keld."

"It would be a joint, three-way decision."

"Really? About what?"

"Well, about the nature of this triangle."

"Triangle? Oh, there you are, being mathematical again, Keld. Can't you leave shop behind you, and forget about your professional vocation when you pay me a pleasure visit? Get into bed."

He did, and she joined him there. They made a deep imprint on the mattress, that night.

▐▐

Flood wondered how to get rid of his rival; to put a stop to this nonsense, to make Fiona his own monogamous wife, a model of old, virtuous, steadfast fidelity, totally his, the simple one-to-one relation restoring a secure foundation for love's aging sexual comfort.

"Fiona, oust Keld. Be mine only."

"No, I'm too used to the standard of the two of you to relinquish one and spoil the fun of being spoiled."

"But it's no fun for me. Or him."

"No? Sometimes it is. Should I show you how?"

"Yes."

"Then come here."

He did, and that night some coils from the bedspring snapped. But they were too wrapped up in each other to notice the accident below. They went on with their business at hand, or pleasure, with an innocent singlemindedness, a deep withdrawal from circumstances outside the compact one, the all-inclusive one of each other, that widely excluded anything extraneous to the everything that, between them, converged into utter condensation.

III

Keld persisted: "Fiona, make me *only* yours."

"No; I like Flood equally well."

"But I'm jealous."

"So is he."

"It's unfair."

"No: it's *very* fair."

"Well, it's unfair *equally*, for *him* and *me*."

"Keld, can't you *ever* leave mathematics alone? Must you always bring your symmetrical measuring machine with you?"

Chafing under this reprimand, Keld reacted in a strange way: impotence, in bed.

He got scolded for that performance failure: "If you keep it up (I mean down), then I'll favor Flood, over you."

That warning wasn't lost on Keld. He resumed his loving ways, forcing Fiona to withdraw that clever threat of hers.

IV

"When will you graduate, if ever?" Flood asked, with concern. Fiona's studentship had become prolonged, course by course, credit by credit, to practically a lengthy career in itself.

"I like campus life," Fiona admitted. "Higher education obviously suits me. Being on close terms with two of the leading faculty members tends to bring the university right to my own home, so to speak. It's an easy car drive between here, my big old house, to and from the college grounds. The governess relieves me of responsibility for bringing up my daughters, so I'm free to lead a contented student's life forever. Why not? I have ample means, and no work to do except to live and learn, and find love in your and Keld's ever-replenishing arms.

"Why should I hasten to graduate toward post-graduation? I'm in no hurry to become a teacher myself. Why earn a living, when I don't need to?

"Meanwhile, I'm aging gracefully. My decline is in a lovely state of suspended procrastination. I linger in the endless hush of an Indian Sumner, the deep rich Autumn that remains forever.

"Death can wait. You and Keld have lots more loving to do, for which my appetite, no sooner spent, revives again. Satiety quickens, surfeit awakens, what they've just quelled. Can you demonstrate that, Professor? This is no lecture hall. This is my bedroom, where sleep is done by night. Will you oblige to show what other function this room might have by interior architectural design? I know it already, but would like a reinforcement lesson, to drill it home and make firm the memory. What can you say, to this special request?"

He replied by deed, which far out did what words could only have done. The bed sagged, by the wordless weight of that dual, usual deed—dual because Fiona's participation, a subtle blend of the active-passive, that quite went to Flood's head through the passion zone to inflame his smarting ardor, firing his game to ever harder serves.

Then he collapsed. Was he dead? Only in the sense of being spent. He still wasn't finished teaching Fiona philosophy—first-hand, from his whole supply of a lifetime's work.

Or philosophy, there's no end. Fiona kept learning it with love, and the more Flood taught it to her, the more *he* learned about it too. They set a co-education record, of sorts. The university wildly resounded with contagious love campus-wide. A love epidemic, mingled with formal learning. The student body, the faculty body, all joined in the act, warming life with lots of lovely learning. It was all the rage. It was the fad that season. It was the key for fashionable conformity. It was the herd instinct, at work. The group outweighed the individual. It was the massive height of the higher education's democratic mass application regardless of age, rank, class, status, or even sex. All were admitted, in that open enrollment program.

Seniors, sophomores, freshmen, upperclassmen, graduate students, postgraduate students, doctorate candidates, nonmatriculated auditors, student teachers, adjuncts, part-time personnel, instructors, assistants, professors; lecturers, department chairmen, provosts, deans, chancellors, board of directors, associates, secretarial staff, registrar, bursar, payroll, library, personnel, cafeteria, publicity, maintenance, security, all offices, crews, staffs, departments, divisions, sections, of that multi-organized university that had to do with human people: these caught the love-germ, all caught it, their fever in common.

Fiona was their leader: the pace-setter. Keld and Flood were co-apostles. Love spread, and caught fire. It raged, consumed, maddened, and devoured.

That was the plague year. It still hasn't subsided.

Love is so infectious! The social disease well set in the university's culture colony: education is a swift conductor. The campus community is so easily exposed, link by link, to touch off love's stampede and pass it along as though this were a college of medicine, turned into its own hospital for endless intern practice.

CHAPTER 11

I

Final exams peacefully put to bed the spring semester. The summer vacation period had now officially begun. This precedes the Fall Semester, by the seasons' academic cycle.

So far as more money went, Fiona and her two lovers could easily afford a holiday anywhere abroad.

For delicate personal reasons, all three couldn't accompany each other: the two men might get in each other's way with abrasion, friction, irritation, awkward misalliance. How, then, could a holiday be arranged without an unpleasant scene taking place between professional gentlemen over a former student in common?

But why not take a holiday from love itself? Love was university-associated, and the summer holiday should leave university cares behind. Such cares included, by essence of recent terms, the joys and agonies of Fiona's shared love with the polarized antagonists, Flood-Keld.

Shouldn't they all leave each other alone for the two hot months and go separate ways altogether, a trio of three different directions corresponding to the number of principals involved?

Love had gotten too gnarled with intensity, due to its shared quality that made jealousy an inherently flaring component in the tightly stitched together closely knitted compound destinies of three separate individuals.

They needed breathing space. They needed spatial distance. To be torn asunder, to grope for private thoughts in solitude's travel opportunities.

Fiona was agreed to this plan. Keld conditionally agreed, if Flood would. Flood would, if Keld did.

Thus, the plan was passed by unanimous decision once suspicion was abated that there would be no trick, deception, treachery, on any member's part of that three-way pull-push.

Keld was assured that Flood would absolutely not see Fiona once, anywhere, even by accidental encounter, by traveler's chance, during quite separate holidays abroad.

Flood was assured that Keld would absolutely not see Fiona once, anywhere, even by accidental encounter, by traveler's chance, during quite separate holidays abroad.

No cheating! It was sworn, on sacred foolproof honor. The word and soul of true gentlemen and a lady.

II

Then flared a bitter disagreement. Each of the men wanted to spend the last farewell night with Fiona before the two-month absence. Only one could be so favored, but which?

They couldn't agree on a schedule. Each man absolutely wanted to be the last one she would be with before her morning embarking abroad. How could that be settled?

The answer was, it couldn't. Fiona, as judge and arbitrator, could no more find a solution than the embattled rivals themselves.

This was a sticky problem, that could only get uglier.

The time was rapidly arriving for the night of farewell—or rather, of two-month adieu. They'd have to think of something quick.

They were now in a position to understand the difficulties that the big nursery, the United Nations, had in reconciling and soothing the hurt, petty, spiteful, jealous, begrudging factions of countries bound tight together in childish disputes, eruptions, altercations, spying, meddling, and serious playfulness.

It was so serious: it was deathly. Neither rival would concede a single advantage to the other. They would rather bicker forever than generously give in with noble self-sacrificing magnanimity, when the bone of contention smarted on their respective vanities.

Neither would let go. They were stubborn with love as grim as death.

III

Two or three nights with Keld, then with Flood a similar number of nights. These alternating series had been going on long enough to establish that system as a tradition that bound the trio together by virtue of acceptance; however begrudging and often depressing it would be for the man whose turn it was to have to sit out a couple of nights knowing that his arch rival was "in possession" of his true love while he himself was serving the allotted banishment term as a lonely exile of the heart.

The one whose turn it was to be Fiona-deprived could, of course, find various ways of amusing himself and need not at all be lonely: on the contrary, Flood's or Keld's company was very popularly in demand by lots of convivial souls who offered all sorts of entertainment, hospitality, drinking, parties, gourmet feasts, sporting events, and amorous dalliances, as well as concerts, operas, ballets, films, cosy television viewing amid comfort, weekend excursions, tennis, golf, sailing, car rides, and the light romance of sex without commitment. These sugared the pill of going through a few Fiona-devoid nights; they cushioned the term of exile and softened the banishment harshness, to ease the hours away from true love with light diversions and well-constructed distractions.

Love still pined and ached. Being without Fiona, for however brief a term, was distinctly worse than being with her—not that being with her was at all bad. The contrast was appreciable.

If a little knowledge is a dangerous thing, then partial possession of a loved one, equally incomplete, is dangerously unsatisfactory. The tortures of Keld and Flood alternated with their joy. It all depended on who "had" Fiona on the given night, and who, therefore, didn't.

Occasionally, but rarely, she'd have neither. The men were important, and there were complicated demands on their time. It was agreed that if the one scheduled to "have" Fiona on a given night were prevented by illness or professional obligation or private matter or for whatever reason, his rival, who was *un*scheduled that night, could not on that night replace him: which would have been unbearable for the one whom circumstances—unforeseen, unavoidable, in the contingencies of complex society for men of consequence—prevented from the happy and fair exercise of his carefully allotted claim on his darling's time that evening. The right and privilege to Fiona was valued above life itself; jealously guarded and vigorously defended. To be with her was preferable. It was not easily deterred or deferred. The right to her company couldn't be contested, for a given evening. It was *that* man's right, and in his default or reluctant forfeiture, the time must go vacant and no one else fill it. That was their "property" arrangement.

Sometimes Fiona *wanted* to be alone. So she would shift and juggle their schedules, in order to be so.

It was understood that she'd never betray *both* Flood and Keld, with any third man, whatever. This was an unwritten pact, but sacred. It united the rivals in a common bond of security, and mutual protection.

Fiona could have "fun" on her "nights off": there were endless social possibilities. But her amusements must stop short of sex. That was a firm code, binding her jointly to Keld and Flood.

IV

Who would have her the night before her holiday journey abroad? It was an open date in the schedule. It couldn't be both. It could only be one.

The night was drawing close. There would have to be *some* compromise, *some* agreement. But on terms of whose favor? Luck wouldn't be neutral, that night.

CHAPTER 12

I

Keld had her for the two nights before the eve of her departure—which would be the eve of Keld's departure to another destination, and of Flood's in a third direction.

The eve of everyone's departure was an open night. It was the final day of June, with no appointment marked on anyone's calendar.

A meeting was hastily arranged for lunch of that fatal day. Fiona's back garden would be a beautiful setting. The first time those three had lunch there, which had been the only time till today, it had been a late lunch all afternoon to the dusk, on a gorgeously idyllic day of unconquerable autumn. This time, it was early summer, with term ended, three pairs of luggage packed for three separate early departures tomorrow morning for two months in different parts of Europe—the great cradle for many American ancestries, including Fiona's, Keld's, and Flood's, as it so chanced by hardly startling coincidence.

The same lady was employed to cook and serve the lunch and wait on the table under the garden tree. She had done such a fine job the last tune, that tradition decreed she should again serve the same trio, whose lives had now become knotted together in a knot of indissolubility. On that autumn lunch occasion here in the same garden, the knot had just loosely come to be.

This last day of June hadn't just come by itself: a whole spring had gone into its making. This was well demonstrated by outdoor natural evidence. It wasn't terribly noticed, though, by the three middle-aged college people. The following night they'd be in different parts of Europe. But what are *tonight's*, meanwhile, crucial sleeping arrangements?

▌▐

The point was, which of the two men would, and which would not, be left out of Fiona's love chamber, this last available night till September ushers in a new college and love term, with Europe left safely behind to true Europeans?

Another way of putting the sticky problem is by rhetorical reversal of interrogative sequence: so rephrased, the question would go:

The point was, which of the two men would *not*, and which *would*, be left out of Fiona's love chamber, this last available night till September ushers in a new college and love term, with Europe left safely behind to true Europeans?

Thus rephrased, the problem remains unchanged. Manner can only affect matter-presentation just so far.

(But manner *is* matter-presentation. But what does that matter? In a manner of speaking, we're where we were before, but bogged down by word-placement's over-fussed-over drapery.)

III

Time seemed to slow down, in the garden: to a stately, dull old standstill. It seemed hours before the serving woman placed their plates of lunch on the table. But no-one cared, since time's slowdown occurred during general unhungriness at the stomach's sensation center.

All three stomachs felt the same way: indifferent.

Meanwhile, they drank expensive alcohol: Fiona sipped gin-and-tonic, Flood had Scotch-and-water, Keld Scotch-and-soda. The two men were on their third drinks, Fiona. on her second. The portions poured had been substantial. Giddy lightheadedness began to reveal even rates of intoxication for the two men, and inebriation's lesser pace in their belovèd hostess.

The day was blandly sunny, with a droop or sag to nature's creatures, which included grass, bushes, tree, flowers, birds, and family cat, not to mention insects, both winged and creeping.

That last time here when the garden was autumn's, there was wine before and during the lunch. Now, the powerful drinks were portentously lethal of dosage. Lunch was kept at bay by all this guzzling on sadly reflective stomachs. Fiona kept putting off the signal for food to be served. Three hearts were being drowned, in pools of sadness.

IV

The two men weren't hating each other. They weren't merely polite: they seemed even on good terms.

As rivals for the one thing they loved more than anything in the world, they were surviving jealousy and substituting mutual respect. Well, Keld *always* had respected Flood, and been in awe of him, having read his books before he knew the man. Flood had seemed patronizing of Keld, in their first garden meeting here. Now, they identified with each other as good men, not merely adversaries. As solid, good men. Not merely in academic attainments and excellence in given field, but in themselves, for what they "were." Yet, can what they "were" be, in fact, so readily isolable from achievements, attainments, professional work and honors? Those too go, to make the "man."

V

"Say, why are we so gloomy?" Fiona asked in a tone of that same gloom. "We'll only be two months apart, which hardly adds up to *one* lifetime, let alone to *three*. Shouldn't we have great joy at the prospect of Europe? It's got a lot of history going for it. There's so much culture there, you'll spit it out in your soup, and pick it out from your nose, and clean your ears with it, and strain your eyes from it, and store some away in your mouth—and *still* you'll never exhaust it!"

"What's that got to do with love?" snapped Flood.

To which Keld added, "Culture all around you, but loneliness in your heart: you're not warm enough to do the culture justice, then."

VI

Time had *altogether* stopped. But signs of life continued, one being the sipping of strong beverages from glasses that periodically went "ice-cube-clank."

Still given no cue, the hired lady went on replenishing ice and drinks, but delayed with the food-serving. The hour was already half way from lunch to dinner. But the sun remained high, at the just-past-midsummer light; far away, up there: close not to Europe, but to heaven—if there *is* one.

Europe, everyone knows, is really there: geographically undeniable, as well as historically packed solid with precedence. As to heaven, people are less sure: it's theologically still under dispute.

There are *maps* of Europe, but none of heaven. That's a further hint of proof of Europe being "there," but there being something insubstantial about heaven: a little too ethereal, perhaps.

Europe would be gone to by them tomorrow; but would Flood,

Keld, or Fiona ever go to heaven? If so, by what combination—of two, of three, or by singles?

Heaven hardly approves of a love triangle: too much passion, right there. Heaven's fragility couldn't bear it. Fiona *had* been a Christian, but her faith had sputtered, lapsed, and then gone inert.

Flood, in his early days as a philosophy student, had *flirted* with heaven, but only as a concept: heaven flirted back, but it was strictly platonic between them. They met, but Doubt always chaperoned them.

Keld, as a mathematics student, couldn't see heaven, for numbers kept getting in the way. He never *did* arrive at that great Equation.

VII

They were drunk, but finally hungry. Fiona signaled to the serving lady, who had kept the food hot all that time. In a trot, she brought it out, and under the garden tree that trinity of intimates began to eat like starved animals.

While eating, they were sobbing. That illustrated the "parting-being-sweet-sorrow" school of theory, with unanimous evidence.

As the food shot in, love poured out. Swilling by mouth, and copious eye-deluge.

Love broke up their composure. The violin-strains of sentiment swooned them away, to the high wail of melancholy and the low dirge of grief. They were mature adults, yet gave way to infantile helplessness at time's gulf of impending division. That gulf looked all one way. Admitting passage over there, its sickly thickness took up blockade, with dire grim distance; against hearts clamoring to return, souls soaked in solitude's grief, mates kept apart, the rejoining never reached, the sweetest agony of love, that perishes in the dark, and only the dark remains, but not the love that went lost in there, the love that dearly never returns, it went away, it never came back, there's dark there, but not the love again, the dear thing went out of sight, went dark, stopped.

VIII

"It's *Europe's* fault! If it weren't for Europe, we'd remain united," reasoned Keld, with a burst of logic.

"It's the summer vacation's fault—if it weren't for that holiday between terms, we'd all still be together," Flood reasoned, in a swift bolt of logic.

"It's *love's* fault—if it weren't for love, we'd all be happy and free, and romp off to Europe in great glee," was Fiona's contribution to the rational radiance of pure reason carved out with gleaming logic's incisive blade.

IX

They seemed to be having misgivings about leaving each other for two months. Haunts of regret tried to reclaim them from that plan.

The point of this meeting *was* to have been to figure out which of the two men would sleep with Fiona tonight. That issue was shunted aside, as unimportant; unbearable premonitions of loneliness had been inserted instead as the agenda's primary item of priority.

Oh, they'd miss each other! Love bloated to the poignant point of bursting into squirts of grief.

"No! Let's *not* leave each other!" was the impassioned plea of Keld. "Let's rescind our plan," Flood warmly advocated. "Death alone should have the power to part us—not our own wills!" proclaimed Fiona, in a gust of heroism. They all ecstatically embraced. The serving lady was amazed, to see that. The hour was saved! Love came flooding through, in high choral immensity, thundered by a thousand angels. Hallelujah! This triumph pierced heaven. Salvation was at hand. Exalted, they praised God, and repealed their atheism.

Was Europe their destination? No, a map of heaven was unfurled. It was written all over the stunner sky. Love, its capital city, blazed forth. Love, cut three ways.

CHAPTER 13

Travel plans were quickly altered, tickets, reservations, and schedules changed, just before the five-o'clock closing of the airlines office and the travel agent office; to the effect that all three, on the morrow, would fly off to the same place, and remain together from place to place on the same European itinerary, although two rooms were ordered for all the hotels they'd be staying at. These adjustments, though complicated, were confirmed at the airlines office and travel agent office: passing, by a few strokes, from desperate plan to impending reality which the morrow would start realizing, through an intricate summer process over two mapped-out months. Love was made practical, and kept going over a whole summer tour, a well-balanced trip with all the particulars worked out in the cool sweat of thoroughness, down to the least change of trains, airport transference, or even catching a bus. The computer facilitated these future connections. The electronic age, with its vast technology, simplifies modernity's complexities, and can even minister to Love. The same love, but new means.

Love, in the grand vacation style. Love's high holiday, soaring in the clouds, accommodating the odd number of three. Love and money command the instruments, and miracles modestly get done.

CHAPTER 14

I

Jealousy has given way to friendship, rivalry to fondness and affection. That's the new Flood-Keld arrangement, that fell into place. Their first stop is London.

Fiona doesn't approve. She feels deprived, as the three walk over Blackfriars Bridge, with the Thames rumbling below.

"Are you two getting homosexual with each other, at my expense?" she vented her suspicion.

"No. One or the other of us sleeps with *you*, my dear," said Flood, soothing her alarm. "We're certainly not inclined to go gaily *physical* together, Keld and I. Friendship; not lust, is what beams forth, in our new relation."

"It certainly *is* new," added Keld. "I could have killed him before, over you, Fiona. Now, I don't mind his having you, when he does. *He*, in turn, doesn't mind *my* having you, when I do. Who could have foretold this harmony? Not I, not Flood. It was pure hate, before. Now, great rapport."

▌▌

On a bench in Kensington Park. Fiona is scolding them. "Whenever, for a moment or two, I absent myself from you two, I come back to find you talking together. How dare you do so, when I'm not present!?"

"You don't *own* us, Keld replied. "We do what we like. We're not plotting against you, just because we talk. Your paranoia suspects a conspiracy against you, but we only like to talk together, by all that friendship holds innocent. Topics pop out, out of everywhere. It's not *you* we're discussing. Are you only morbidly suspicious, or are you tyrannizing over our acts, forbidding us to do or say what you're not there to control?"

Flood then chimed in: "We won't tolerate your interference! We're free men!"

Fiona wept, bowing her head into cradling arms, as she sat there. Ignoring this outburst, the men went on talking, getting up, in so doing, to pace about Kensington Park, stranding Fiona on her lonely bench, abandoning her to the horror of feeling unloved after so long living in the double reinforced comfort of love's constant blessing.

Keld and Flood were purging themselves—and each other—of their Fiona-demon? Their alliance was Fiona's alienation? The bond between them snapped the bond each had with Fiona? These were the victim's meditations. She felt terribly old. Ancient. Discarded. Useless.

Abandoned. Banished from love's exotic garden. Vulnerable, mortal. Frail. Alone. More alone than with Don, when he had closed shop on her.

Flood and Keld were walking out of sight, animated in discussion, between trees of the park. From her flattened bench, sagging, Fiona followed them with only her legless eyes, hollowed with resignation, broken passive in despair.

III

No, it wasn't that bad. Restitution of normality at their Hyde Park hotel: Flood was scheduled to be Fiona's sleeping partner, while Keld had a single bed in another room. It all turned out as usual. Nothing *really* was wrong. Not in the vital sexual sphere. No transference of love *there*.

But in the morning, it started all over again: the men's talk, designed for each other, the friendly incessant dialogue that always left Fiona out.

She was the third party. She was phenomenally excluded, considering that their love was supposed to be focused on her. Was it? Only in bed in the hotel room at night, by appointment, but not spontaneously in the day ever, no, they preferred each other, even their silences were directed to each other, as they toured London with two in communication and one left to wander by herself.

In pride, she stopped going about with them. They'd go off to one part of London, eating and touring together; she was left to her own choices. She'd have to wait till night to see one of them again. And only till the morning. Her world was shrinking. She lived for love. And love grew less. It dwindled only to its sexual minimum.

Stripped down to its sexual essential, what is love? Not what it used to be, by Fiona's famous university success.

Was *London* to blame? Let's get out of there, quick. Maybe it was only the *place*. If so, try another.

(Their computerized itinerary dates and connections allowed for optional improvising with the flexible mechanics of last-minute whims and the impulsive fancy of choice, for which then the schedule of bookings, reservations, and transportation facilities was accordingly adjusted by the well-paid services so alertly in the ready to expedite the notorious traveling changeability of people on the move; subject to fluctuations by mobile hazards removed from stabilities of stationary habit.)

They flew to Dublin, all three. But the same thing happened there. The men *did* prefer each other. It wasn't due to place, but to their own preference. Their friendship flourished. Fiona withered, in her shrinking world of love.

IV

In Paris, Fiona tagged along behind the two friends. In the winding paths, they soon lost her.

In Toledo it was worse. But it wasn't Toledo's fault, or Spain's in general. Fiona's company seemed undesirable. She was bothering them. Keld would see her in bed that night; can't she amuse herself till then? "Stop being a nuisance," Flood outright said. Keld had been spoken for; he didn't add a superfluous word, but calmly nodded.

In Venice, spending the day by herself, Fiona decided to put up a challenge, bring things out into open test, to see where the weather lay, and how far things had actually gone in her monumental twin ruins.

When they returned late to the hotel, she was there waiting for them, to catch them both, not just the one scheduled to share her room that night.

"When you leave to Florence tomorrow, I'm not going along."

They took it calmly. "You're staying here?" Keld asked.

"No, I'm going elsewhere."

"Where?" Flood asked; but his tone was dead: it was uncaring.

"It doesn't matter," she replied.

"Well, have a good trip," Keld wished her.

"See you at the college," Flood added.

And it wasn't even August yet!

V

Fiona was traveling alone, but her heart wasn't in it. She idly took in sights, but so what? When she had left the Venice hotel the final morning, for the train station, Flood and Keld, rather than attempting to persuade her to change her mind and continue traveling with them, made not the slightest gesture of regret or demonstrated the least sign of missing her. They gave her a happy sendoff—happy for them, with the relief of the unburdened; with all that had gone before, that was an insult.

It was a slap on the face, but with a slack hand, with flabby, unfeeling apathy. Where had their famous memories gone? Could love so easily dissolve within their pair of genius breasts?

Or had love undergone such transformation, transference, that left each other the object, and cast her off—her, the flaming source itself, the true cause and origin of altered lives?

As her train was entering Vienna, she contemplated vengeance. But that would be in September. At the university.

She was a university cult heroine. She had started an enduring love fad last term; or the term before—her college career became blurred.

Wasn't she too old for college? What was she doing there?

She was a divorcee, with two children she'd delegated to mother's care.

Her children were both daughters. Did that contain any significance? Could any symbolism be found there?

She had gone searching for love, with great scoops of double success, at the institute of higher learning.

Her success was such, she had assumed its lastingness. Her powers were famous, to hold bewitchingly her love-prey in willing subjugation that made her the sacred object of eternal passion.

Well, passion had proven itself to be non-eternal. On a plain of flux, with everything else. Subject to bad games in the art of chance.

Going to Europe, all three together, had been a mistake—and no small one, either? It was a venture of unforeseen consequences which now could never be rectified. It wasn't Europe's fault. There *was* no fault. No blame attached, not even to "Fate."

Fate is a myth anyway. There are just incidents and accidents, tendencies and inclination, imposed order on the erupting chaos of chance.

VI

What was she doing in Vienna, alone? Mozart had been here once—or twice. Or was he somewhere else?

Was *Cosi Fan Tutte* composed here? *The Magic Flute* or *Don Giovanni?* She had loved all three. That's a different sort of love than loving a man or being loved by one—or even by two; and loving two.

Did she love Flood and Keld as they had loved her? Not as much, perhaps, as she had loved being loved by them. Basking in their love's alternate onslaught, each switching on, in turn, a competitive ardor that the other then strove to surpass, in a spiralling heroism of entwined vines locked in a choking ascent for light up a wall that twistingly they climb in rugged hardihood of combat.

She was that wall. They had scaled her, together. Now, the wall could drop off, mortar and all, for the vines had already insured their own firmness, by their mutual support, locked in their death-grip of tightly clenched love.

This allegory, or parable, startled the reverie-dreamer of it, Fiona. She snapped to. Now, her bearings to take. She's in the Vienna opera house, waiting, between acts, in her orchestra seat, for the curtain to rise for the resumption of *Cosi Fan Tutte.*

She was wearing an opera cloak, befitting the occasion. She herself was between acts—her own legendary acts as the college queen of the occult. She'd strut her magic anew when the September term starts. It would be a new act. Its theme: revenge.

Here she was, in August, far from campus—almost as far as were spiritually possible.

Unescorted in the Opera House. Strains from the orchestra pit. The curtain rises, to resume Mozart—the genius who preceded Keld and Flood, and who was unfairly dealt with by monetary debt and poverty, leading to rotten luck and an early death, fittingly unsuitable for framing his later gigantic stature in Fame's posthumous hall of high brutal irony and paradox. Flood and Keld are better off, in their living portions. Well, Fiona will redress that. She'll bring about their brutal downfalls. That will serve to remind them that they loved her once but stopped. A steep price she'll put, on that stopping. So unpayable, they'll spend their next lives climbing up the impossible arrears and slipping back down, scaling and sliding and scrambling with an endless pit below them, where descent (reversing the entwining vine climb) shall plunge them quite beyond pity's repair.

This nightmare was dreamed for them by Fiona. She'll soon put it into pure motion.

VII

That night she lies in bed alone. Alone! No Keld, no Flood: that's "alone's" definition, at the moment.

Mozart's opera is resounding in her head. It ended only an hour ago, with the grand finale. But her head keeps fidelity-time to the waves of voice and instruments that pile cascades of foam on her wild, frothy, banner-waving beach.

She's in a Viennese hotel room. How quaint to be alone! Keldless, Floodless. Such chastity ill-becomes her middle age, which should be rigorously in the flush of second youth's renewed pursuit.

This abstinence—was it really hers? Was this really Vienna? Had she become so divorced, that Don was a tiny dot in her past? Was she actually attending the university, toward that nominal old degree? Were Keld and Flood no longer hers? Had love utterly stopped, from their suddenly combined hearts? Stopped the bounty of their flowing from fruitful fountains that sprayed her with those continual drops of praise so carnally proved in passionate repetition's ripe pure patterns of sky-written self-replenishing?

Not a drop more? Down the empty drain of time?

VIII

Those traveling companions, the Professors: did they love each other, or just exult in beautiful friendship, the bond of their joint emancipation from Fiona's despotic rule?

Their love for her had outlasted eternity—once.

Did love have a mortality-clause in it? If so, how sad.

Surely, this was August now. It was past midnight, in a Vienna hotel room.

What was she doing there?

And later, in September, what would she be doing at a university? —which she set fire to, as its exalted resident arsonist in the art of high love?

Would Flood and Keld continue to disown her, next term? She'd become a campus disgrace, by that dramatic reversal. To fall so low, from her two-pronged pedestal erected and sustained in garlands of ever-renewed glory by the university's two most eminent men? Well, easy come, easy go. What's given, is then taken away, by the One who gives: the Lord, or someone equally up in the ratings, the capricious dispenser of fortune's low, unstable pranks that promise and confer hope, furnish expectation forth with proof, and then—when the going's good—snap it away! like that! bang! you're dead!

Or *symbolically* dead, of sorts.

IX

They yanked the love-carpet from under her feet.

They plucked the sun itself from love's sky.

They'd attended her Advanced Love Tutorial, and passed with high grades.

She'll teach them some hate now. They don't know its meaning, yet.

X

Those arias are still haunting her, as *Cosi Fan Tutte* gets another performance in her sleepless head on a Viennese pillow, as her hotel window starts the light of dawn rolling, bringing forward a new day in August.

Deception, treachery, love's cynicism, high betrayal, tricky cunning of Neapolitan aristocrats (aided by a sly serving-wench), deceit, conceit, romantic frenzy, the playacting of sincere love. These are some of the Opera's literary themes, abstracted from the music itself.

Fiona saw Keld and Flood in the male romantic roles, while casting herself in the two corresponding female roles.

She was dreaming. The dreaming wore for clothing Mozart's own language. That's the well-dressed dream, for you!

Mozart swept over Flood and Keld—and herself as well. She slept— in pure Mozart.

XI

She woke up to the banal, however. The tawdry, trivial, and trite. It was a day in Europe. She's a traveler not lacking for money. She's an American tourist—of the middle-aged breed. A divorced woman travelling alone, with two daughters in different-age-bracket summer camps along the American countryside.

She's a sophisticate, educated, cosmopolitan, metropolitan—but manless, momentarily. In that category, she'd gone from "two" to "none," in the number of men, without passing "one" in the sheer drop.

How banal, to be in Vienna in August! With what disgust she feels —anywhere at all, Vienna or the moon for that matter—that state of loneliness: the frustrated dependency on the benevolent disposition of others to single her out for devotion's earnest submission, risking the rejection agony in so venturing such feeling that expects her to respond in kind.

Loneliness is need: which *others* must fulfill. How abject, to place your needs at their disposal!

Fiona is proud. But loneliness ridicules pride. Pride would stand away. Loneliness would crawl up close, to abase pride, and beg. Loneliness is pride's traitor. But pride is too proud to proclaim itself too loudly against that cringing worm, loneliness.

XII

She's wandering Viennese streets. But she doesn't meet Keld and Flood. This city hadn't been on their itinerary. She'll wait for September, at an American university: she'll make her presence known; ruin them, through and through. Destroy them both. Possessed by the wrong demon, she'll cover the whole university—especially the Chairmen of its Departments of Mathematics and Philosophy—in a conflagration of hate. She'll practice its occult magic—the language of hate. She'll be hate's witch, goddess, priestess, messenger, and ambassador. She'll be perfect for the job. She's well qualified, from the opposite post.

A renegade makes the best spy; the former alcoholic the best reform preacher against alcoholism; the most militant atheist becomes the most valuable convert. Love's apostle turns perfect as hate's key exponent, well versed in their polarity's peculiar grammar and dynamics, and best qualified to exploit such related tongues in translation's skilled language that works from both sides toward whatever object.

XIII

Hate will fill the campus. Viennese citizens are startled to see the look on Fiona's face—all clenched in the theatrics of malice—as she passes them in the streets, walking there but quite positively being precisely elsewhere in the churning fury of driven determination; At a certain American university, subtle curricula conditions will be imposed. Everybody shall major in—or be required to take courses in—a new special subject: hate. An extensive study program will be built around it. A Degree in Hate will be mandatory, as a graduate fulfillment. It will be the end product of education. Workshops and laboratories will be set up, for further investigation. Other subjects will be geared toward it. So Fiona determined, in Vienna. Her body was there, expensively clothèd. Her mind dwelled in quite another realm: in abstract hate's higher education. In concrete hate's applied daily station. She went into hate's heart. Her vision was complete: *Love* stood there: of all places, at hate's heart's center.

CHAPTER 15

I

Autumn starts the university season rolling again. Footballs fly, and studies begin.

A merger is announced. The Philosophy and Mathematics Departments are new combined, under the joint Chairmanship of their two former separate heads, Professor Flood and Professor Keld. Flood, of course, is the university's star boast, for sheer outside reputation and fame universalized. Keld is considered the top man in his *own* field, though less a figure in world popularity, by virtue primarily of his being less well known in the commonplace daily round of the everyday sphere of the ordinary realm untouched by special fields of scholarship, academically consecrated circles, areas along intellectual lines outside normal interest on a mass average.

Presented as a *fait accompli* to the university's Chancellor, Dean, Provost, President and venerable Directors of the governing Board, this departmental merger of Philosophy with Mathematics (called now Philomatics or Mathosophy? No, that's too officially undignified) was formally accepted by the ruling Body because the most glittering stars of its faculty firmament were both behind the merger and at the head of it. The radically unprecedented innovation would be substantially established as soon as inaugurated, thus institutionalizing the teeth out of change's terror, taming it down to the docility of what's fully accepted.

Time is a known change-bringer. New changes are soon old institutions staunchly defended by conservative tradition.

The *real* surprise, this September, was something else: Fiona is missing! No-one has seen her. She's not attending any class, she hasn't registered for any course. It's too delicate a matter to ask Flood or Keld about. They don't seem to be worried, or pining for her or missing her. Maybe they're secreting her, in protective jealousy, in suspicious possessiveness, from campus view or from public view at large? They're seeing her privately at her grand house or in their own homes, but don't allow her to venture out too openly? As their mistress, she's too valuable a property to risk exposing to the wayward chances of the lust-charged campus atmosphere—an atmosphere which she herself in great part caused to come about. Love-dust, of course, filtered through the lust. Passion combines them, as a neutral word. People's need for each other down to the deepest intimacy, which takes the clothing off and makes for fierce embracing, tight clutching, hopeful groping, greedy grasping. The beholding, and then, behold!—the holding. For holding is close to having. And the having holds us close, to another's heaven.

II

Flood and Keld were closest to her; "everyone" assumes that they of course are still alternately seeing Fiona, which plainly implies that they know just where she is. They don't. *They*'re puzzled, too.

She hasn't reported back. She's been in contact with neither. Last thing they knew of her, she was leaving Venice and wouldn't tell them where to. Nor had they really cared, then.

They're in their new departmental office, facing each other from opposite sides of their mutual main desk, each seated comfortably back on a sturdy chair expensively semi-antiqued.

"You phoned to her house?" Flood asked. He himself hadn't.

"No, let's do it now," Keld suggested. They were only mildly concerned, but felt a vague guilt. If any harm had befallen her, both would feel uneasily responsible, in some way.

It was during an afternoon when neither had office hours, scheduled conferences, or scheduled classes.

The phone was at a desk corner nearest to Flood, so he—from somewhat fading memory—dialed the number of that house, that well-remembered house, without having—as yet—to resort to his private phone-number book for handy assistance.

There were a few rings on the opposite, invisible end, then a girl's voice answered: Fiona's older daughter.

"My mother hasn't come back from Europe yet. We haven't heard from her. She didn't send any letter all summer. I assume she just prolonged her travels. She warned us before she went off with you at the beginning of July not to worry about her in case we didn't hear from her. How was she? What happened?"

Flood, who had phoned to get information about Fiona, found himself in the position of being asked for it himself, by her own daughter. Such motherly neglect appalled him—was she so uncaring to her own offspring? The neglect seemed compounded by the daughters' father's being forced by divorce and custody law and court ruling to stay away from them for unparently long stretches of time. Why, the girls are orphans! Poor little girls, in their big house, with their mother so love-obsessed and self-servingly devoted to the final recapture—or belated discovery—of an idealized sexual prime which is youth's by right but anyone's by the plots and stratagems, the thickly laid devices or fortunate encounters in the open mating game's wide court of play.

Before, at least, their mother was technically there, with the daughters. Now, she's irresponsibly absent from the household, unaccountably overdue back from a European caper that began with two lovers in tow, the jaunt of a queen with her twin entourage of noble lords with access by divine privilege to the permitted intimate parts of her regal person; but less than halfway through the summer, the holiday lark collapsed from her flying reign; abandoned by her dual gallant escort, she turns into an aging well-to-do divorced American female tourist alone and mysteriously unaccounted for, her unknown whereabouts veiling her absent presence from home and university view both.

A surrogate or deputy mother, the governess, is very capable; serving Fiona's daughters with truer love than Fiona was ever willing to bestow on them. And father Don has weekend privileges: they visit him then, for by court edict he's forbidden from setting foot in his own former house. At other set times he's permitted to see his daughters as well; but at distant intervals, carefully doled out in the begrudging charity of parsimoniously precise justice in portions barely meager to appease the paternal breast.

Aunts, uncles, cousins, and other relatives, for unknown reasons, just didn't appear. But the daughters had at least abundant friends for consolation, with whom to exchange rounds of formally playful visits.

They miss mother-love. Which they never had anyway, but at least they used to have her presence. Now, not even that. Until how much longer are they without at least the figurehead of maternal love, meaning her actual physical presence, however lacking *inside* Fiona is in tender warmth for sweet innocent daughters, to the number of two, successful fruit of Don's defunct union with her, in the pre-Flood-Keld days, before her renewed onslaught on youth's second prime to pour a double dose of decay-deterrent, age-exterminator, over her extended body that serves love from lust, ekes out lust from love, with death-defying passion, the loneliness-killer?

III

From his co-chairman's office, overheard by Keld across the desk, Flood told his former shared mistress's older daughter over the phone what little or, actually, nothing he knew—nothing, it turned out—about what became of Fiona since an early morning goodbye in Venice in July with Keld there to also bid goodbye; and this being October, and no sign whatever of her since, there's grounds for worry and maybe a detective should be assigned, if that could do any good. Next on the phone came the daughters' governess, who was worried to despair and begged Flood to tell her what he knew, but Flood could only repeat what he had told the older daughter, and in the end the governess was weeping, out of sight, while in the office, across the desk, Keld made signs to get off the phone by now, since conferences were scheduled and classes would soon be held, while just outside the office, students and an instructor were waiting and a staff secretary with urgent official business.

Keld and Flood were of one mind about their little Fiona affair: it's all over now, and should be filed away in the inactive index, belonging to the past proper in the tidy clutter of archives academically out of use. Remorse of guilt, the conscience of their responsibility, kept the matter current, however, as a spasmodically recurring preoccupation of regret and scruple.

Why no word from her? Not to her own daughters or their governess, nor to her two lovers whose love stopped. Her non-contact opens up the gruesome doubts of mystery and speculation, grim awe at the unknowable fitful stabs of baseless conjecture, swarming vistas of boundless possibilities loosely tinctured with guilt's awful aroma: how far are Keld and Flood responsible for the events of her life after their neglect forced her to leave them in the crushed vanity of their double rejection, their defection from the bond and constitution of love fully fledged and declared?

She had voluntarily left them, but they had pushed her. That was on a July morning in Venice. Now the campus of which she was a legend, a love-goddess, a witch possessed of ancient demons, the holy keeper of passion herself, magic's latest incarnated queen, is singularly silent to her footstep.

From where emanates her silence? Still in Europe? Or hidden nearby somewhere here? Or is *death* the source of that stillness? Is her silence death's sound, across the grand remove?

That silence accuses. Flood and Keld find it unendurable, oppressive, in open-ended reproach to be filled in by horrid images of guilt, confessions of responsibility by morbidity-crossed conscience pleading for forgiveness in doubt's unchecked motion of wild self-accusing wonder, given no clue, no directional fact in a perpetual bewilderment.

Is she dead? Or is her silence planned? Or a combination, of planned silence by death? (Planned beforehand, of course, prior to death itself, a state of final planlessness.)

More months go by, without relief. The Christmas vacation, then final exams. Then a between-terms period. New registration, and the Spring semester.

Silence from abroad. Snow falls. Snow covers the university. So does Fiona, in a harsh glare of white silence.

Silence, and the unseen. Deliberate, by revenge?

The Spring term is ending. Soon June. Sumner holidays. The year's cycle. But no Fiona.

CHAPTER 16

I

"She couldn't just *disappear*, Keld."

"Yes she could. Moreover, that's what she did."

"Yes, but where did she disappear *to*?"

"At an extreme, maybe death."

"That *is* extreme, Keld: a harsh one. Couldn't you tone it down a little?"

"Tone *what* down? Death?"

"No; your conjecture of it."

"Flood, at *this* stage, what other supposition could there be?"

"That she's alive."

"In the world of somewhere?"

"Or in somewhere's world. But *this* one."

"*Our* world?"

"Broadly, yes. But not specifically this city or university."

"This mystery is stale. I'm *sick* of it."

"So am I, Keld, *sick* of you. I regret having agreed to merge Departments. I now renege, however belatedly. I withdraw my Philosophy Department, intact, from the merger."

"I could kill you, Flood."

"Don't, Keld. If you do, I might find myself with Fiona. I prefer to stay a world away, at least."

"But you *loved* her."

"So did you, with disastrous results for your harmonious marriage, Keld."

"Well, we *both* loved her."

"That's universal, as well as university, knowledge. That we did. We loved her."

II

"Flood, *please* leave our Departments united. Under my Chairmanship. You resign. Go away. Out of my life."

"Keld, *you* go out of *my* life. I'm remaining here, at the University. I'm arranging, before the summer vacation, that when the Fall term begins our Departments will be separate once more—and remain so always. As before, our Departments will be in separate buildings. We're in my former and my future exclusive building. You and your colleagues will have to vacate it. And leave my life for good. I want no more of you."

"I'll kill you, Flood."

"Don't. Instead, let *me* kill *you*. That will dispatch you to Fiona, maybe. Take up with her again, on terms of love that leave me out."

"Sorry. We're in dispute over that."

III

Hatred was in the air. It infests the two Chairmen. The university is spared, for it's summer vacation. Will the hate still be there, infecting the campus, when September starts the Fall term?

In July, Keld goes abroad for a European holiday, with a female student for companion. Flood also travels in Europe, with one of *his* female students. Their paths, by design, never cross.

Neither encounters Fiona, either. In separate itineraries, they go all over—but never run into her.

Maybe she's not "there" to run into?

Her daughters haven't heard from her, or seen her for over a year. No word to anyone. Silence, with death's own stillness—or a *living* stillness, but having much the same effect on those who knew her in familiarity's various modes.

What's become of Fiona? The University's Fall term has begun. The Departments of Philosophy and Mathematics have reverted to the custom of being distinct from each other. There's no plague of hate to infect the campus. Fiona had thought of leaving that for a legacy, but it just hasn't taken place. Was her will thwarted? Her will was proved fallible by Keld and Flood. Anyhow, maybe she retracted the hate wish. Or added love to it, to chance out the right balance.

IV

Flood's' married for the third time: the female student he traveled abroad with.

Keld's second marriage is to the student *he* took abroad.

Keld and Flood have been spared Fiona's curse. She was to take revenge on them: to destroy them, by every possible way. It hasn't, however, happened.

Fiona's daughters have given up on their errant mother. The governess is doing an inspired substitution job.

Don went back to the divorce court, cited Fiona's lengthy absence from her daughters' needy sides, and has won permission, for the girls' sakes, to move back into the house in full paternal resumption and responsibility. He seemed repentant and humbled. The court awarded him conditional custody, contingent on Fiona's return, explanation, behavior, and intent.

V

International detectives had searched for Fiona, but then given up. Her bank reports no withdrawals since last year on her steady account, which, by provisional law, has become settled, estate and all, on the daughters she had no love for, in her frantic search for love from men.

Is she alive or not? If alive, she's aging toward death anyway, by decay's independent process.

Love filled out her life, in the varied fortunes of intention, and by the will's adventure.

If alive, is she in love or has she inspired any? Is any love left? She spent her life pursuing it. She achieved mixed success.

She depended on others to fulfill it. Some did, then didn't. If she lives, with her remaining biology, given her character and disposition and all, what man, if any, is she with? And what's *he* like?

Just picture him! The adored ideal of Fiona's whole life.

However, he may leave her. He liked her for a while. But he doesn't truly love her.

She'll have to try again.

If, that is, there's any Fiona left. Is there?

If not, love remains. It's always going on. Others have it. Flood and Keld have it, with young recent student wives. Don probably has it, by some manner. The older daughter will have it, soon; the younger, later. The governess, at least, has *them, now.*

The campus is *full* of love. And all departmental faculty.

And *off*-campus, love is spread. It fills nonacademia, everywhere.

There'll *always* be love. Fiona had her share. She was sung and celebrated, for it.

But what of love *now?* Is she there, to have it?

She may be there, and not having it.

Would that be worse than *not* being there?

She's so old, by now.

Love gravitates to the young. It welcomes them, in throngs.

All flock for love. All cheer it. Educated, or not.

Love is still here. So might Fiona be, but not just where love is, despite a sentimental theory that has enjoyed popular currency since ancient times: "Love is everywhere."

Maybe, but at different times. If Fiona has any time left, there may be some love there, and maybe not.

However, she'll never graduate. All those courses! All her collegiate activities, resuming a former youth to double up her lifetime with healthy helpings from love's open feast, at her local university buffet.

In love's whole lifetime, there was once a Fiona. What happened to her has gone into the whole history of love. Love's entire human career.

THREE QUESTIONABLE AUTHORS

Posing for a Novel:
A Rigid Sacrifice Staked for a Dubious Case
(A Silly Tragedy)

(Two characters: one relaxed; the other in the stiff attitude of a pose painstakingly held despite limbs that ache for mercy. Latter speaks first:)

George is writing a new novel these days.

What happened to the old one?

There *was no* old one: it's *always* been new.

How perennially recharged is his literary creativity!

A freshly potent, but unrealized, threat!

And when is George's new novel due to be finished?

Never! For it's too *new* for that!

How unfadingly current he can manage to remain!

He's a *practising* novelist, for he's never fulfilled!

Ah, leave George to his undoubtably sincere pretensions.

Yes, in time, they appear so *natural* in him!

But enough of him. Tell me, why are your back and limbs so stiff, that neck and legs all betray the tenacity of an ache?

Because I've been *posing* for George's novel. He told me to *hold* my pose, so that the character I'm enacting won't be disjointed, or go represented in amorphous fragments to weaken the narrative.

How *long* must you hold you pose?

Forever, unless he *finishes* his novel some day.

Then your stiffness will increase, till your joints freeze in their various attitudes, and your posture harden into permanent immobility.

(Disgustedly:) And all for *what!?* For a less-than-mediocre novel, being non-written by an aspiring dilettante!

It's not worth it! Then why do you go through with it?

I promised him. It was my favor to him.

And he holds you to it?

He does, in this unbreakable mold of my pose.

The Publisher Defending the Author to the Character's Protesting Original Who Resents Having Been Too Misrepresented to Survive

(Characters: Novelist's character victim; and publisher. Latter speaks first. At beginning, neither knows identity of the other; character confesses early; but publisher's identity as publisher isn't revealed until much later.)

The critics consider Alan Morris to be the top novelist of our day.

That's very controversial of them. I disagree, I say it's not true.

Taste and judgment will decide. Why don't you like his books?

Alan Morris is known for one great, major novel. I personally hate every page of it.

That's a very subjective opinion. How are you qualified to be so critical?

Because I'm in it. I'm the central character of that novel.

You were lifted from real life?

No, I was *brought down* from real life. I was debased.

The author took liberties with your character?

Considerable. I would never have permitted it.

Had he known you well? Were you friends?

We moved in the same circles. I was always being *observed* by him. He didn't dare become my *friend*, for his characterization of me in the book would have been a betrayal, an abuse, and more offensive for us being friends. So he coolly kept his distance, noted what I did, how acted, what I said and how I spoke. Little did I know that I was an author's victim. My slightest foible or aberration would be grotesquely stressed in his monstrous rendering of me—or *rend*ing of me, for I was wrenched from what I was, and sunk by assassination into a horrendous portrait that detailed my faults with microscopic distortion into telescopic caricature as the chosen fool of all ridicule. It's not a role I'm suited for, and I resent being handled that way. I was falsely depicted, and would sue him, but in the book's foreword there's a note to the effect that his work was fiction and resemblances between real people and the novel's puppets could only be caused by coincidence. So I can't take him to court. But to *task* I *will* take him, and man to man challenge him to a grudge fight, whereupon I'll beset him and submit him to an awful beating at the hands of my own two fists, which will spare no inch of his exposed person in a fair contest, just as *he* spared no inch of *my* open surface in that novelistic slur and insult he handed to me under the sanction of its being "art." If that book is art, then I'm a page and not a person, and he's an artist rather than a scoundrel. He has dealt with me in so offhanded, vicious, inexcusable a stroke of public malice, that I'd as soon pardon him as *become*, in actual cold blood, the contemptible being he made of me in his novel's slanderous plot. I have a score to settle: I'll go drag Alan Morris into a printer's press and rub his nose in the vile ink. And I'll have him set into type, and locked into the infamy of print. And smudge his name on every bandied sheet or giveaway rag inflicted on public outrage to promiscuous scorn. Alan Morris personifies revenge; my wound will heal when this vengeance rectifies, by penal equation of retaliation, the damage he did me in flinging my good name and character to the muddy villainy of the mocking readerdom.

But the public doesn't *know* that the character was drawn after *you. I* didn't know it, until you *told.* And the name has been fictionally changed altogether. You needn't make a public *confession.* No one would be any the wiser; just shut up, and admit to *nothing.* You *imagine* being suspected; but you're not associated with the character drawn after you. Only Alan Morris, you, and now I, know the truth. It will remain a deep secret.

But you're assuming that his portrait of me was *accurate:* it's *not!*

Don't worry: *I* forgive you: I'll forget I've ever read the book, I won't recognise in you, or identify you with, the fictional counterpart of your own character. You're *clear*, in *my* book: you haven't been vilified: I'll protect you, with the stubborn bond of loyalty in guarding the terrifying secret; despite those creative insights by Alan Morris into you, his symbolic penetration of laying your heart bare, his ruthlessly perceptive analysis of all your failings. Oh, were you captured! Feel flattered, that he based on you the stupendous masterpiece of his lifetime genius so far. You're immortalized by such distinction! He must have sensed a "rightness" of you for the role, with that unerring, uncanny, poetic license he invoked on rarest inspiration's airy wings. You're his finest creation! How can such realism ever die? Literally, it's your making. Art alone can make a dull type like you permanent. How well you've been cast! What privilege granted; he *loved* you, to shower this favor on you!

You're misinterpreting; you're confusing my complaint; vindicating his crime, turning the issue upside down, twisting clarity, reversing justice, and abolishing truth. You're compounding the injury done by *him*; and my hatred must include *you*, as well: also my revenge.

You're being silly, with infantile spite and innocent incomprehension. Suspend your critical faculty—or that midget excuse for it. Allow me to shed the gracious sense of your gradual enlightenment.

You seem in collusion with author Morris, his defender, apologist, and fraternal spokesman. I'm *convinced* by what I suspect. Now go on, in your elaborate pardon of him.

Your life has been artistified. The *role* sparkles; the author imbued it with his vitality, caressed it into shape with the robust patience of a nimble, contriving imagination. Tell me, now: outside of this character you were generously donated, what are you in your miserable self? Nondescript negligibility would you be left with, for boasting of who you are. Acknowledge Morris to be your divine Saviour, if nobility bids you to afford to. Your nonentity has been charged with life, wrought into a realization more splendid than you could achieve by yourself in unassisted futility. How transformed you are into the real image truth and art would brew! It's stunning!

I don't appreciate it. You're making this up.

You've been brought out by the work Morris did. I'm not making idle talk! Listen sensibly. Take this in with care: as *Morris* gave care to filling you out, given the skimpy material you had to start with. I'm showing you: now you're recognizable. He's defined you into hewed form, where before your existence grazed the amorphous! You're rescued from vagueness, and supplied with the bold body of an abstraction. Concrete, with an inner assemblage of blood. This was *done* for you! How holy is your obligation! Show your gratitude; wrath has no place, and is a gesture of spite's ego. Kneel before Alan Morris, who, gratuitously, and quite disinterestedly as a master of artifice for art's own sake, happens to have granted you a sweet reason for justifying the banal accident of your existence. He's authorized you with the very means to your identity: the license and permit you need to claim your higher independence. You have the concession and franchise to literal being, by right and decree, by sacred deed, entitled to you by literary endorsement; backed by the reputation and professional sponsorship of Alan Morris, whose solid weight supports you on a well-based flight in humorous fantasy as an etched figure for satire in full force. You ought to be glad. Are you?

I'm not convinced. Persuade more, against my blast of skepticism.

Before he put you in his book, or drew his book on you, a dim-witted scheme of flimsy skin gave threadbare soul to your clothing's fabric. What more was contained in you? Behind what you wore, what hollow surface was your life's deep core? Now there's substance in you. Alan Morris put it there. A gift unmatched by your little vote of thanks. The novel proclaims you as a *man:* laughable, but a man. Would you be that otherwise?

You insult me worse than he does!

You're not even dignified, without *words*. Words provide life with all its significance. And if the words are Alan Morris-written, so is the greater life conferred. It's a rare endowment.

I don't *feel* so special. It's *me* to judge.

Don't be arrogant. All is owing to the author, and is the author's property. What distinguishes your life from its own dead state incidental with cells that move without meaning? The verbal genius of Alan Morris, without question, simply put. You complain of being Satire's victim? You should rejoice! Enlarge yourself imitatingly into its enormity. There it is, your mold. Grow into it, don't wear it with baggy looseness, but fill it roundly out, *become* the shape you're stoutly fitted to, according to the tailor's pattern. The form of your birth onwards is all his doing! It was imposed by his brain. He's redeemed you from insignificance. He's poured hope into emptiness. His sympathy springs you alive. The grace of mercy to be fathered through the medium of his compassion. Heaven's supreme benediction is immortality; the deputy in administering this blessed honor upon you was Alan Morris, none other but him. His mission was divine; you were his creature; the critics extol him; doesn't that content you?

You speak in a wicked way, to weave a spell and use words under false pretenses, attributing greatness to mediocrity and honor to insult. It's time I may ask you: who are you?

Other than as his spokesman?

Yes, you yourself.

Is your question relevant?

I consider it is.

You're not coercing me?

No, merely requesting.

Such personal information?

Yes, you mustn't deny me. This is imperative in nature.

Alan Morris is your man. Stalk *him*. But I'm hardly concerned, and not involved in the case.

That's for me to decide. Again, I urge you.

Are you practicing extortion?

Don't compel me to. Submit by peaceful means. What have you to do with this avouched genius; this fabulous creative personality, Alan Morris?

The author, do you mean?

Who but? Don't stall.

I *am* his publisher. His books bear my imprint, on dust jacket, on title page, and in advertisements, as well as publicity releases. You see, I'm directly concerned, with vested interest, in how well his books do. I profit from his being a best-selling author. The literary merit, aside from the sales value, of his novels, is of course the province of critics. I *trust* his work is great. And stake my money in it.

(Sarcastically) How courageous of you to back up your "opinion" so solidly! What risk-taking! You confuse popularity with artistic excellence: such a confusion is endemic to your position. You stand to gain profit by keeping this confusion intact and preserving it dogmatically. A business man has to be pragmatic. "Art" is another matter. *Exploitation* of art is the enterpreneur's practical domain. I see your game. You pimp for Alan Morris, don't you?

You're being harsh.

How can I spare you, when I wasn't spared by your hired henchmen who rubbed me out with arsenic from a poison literary pen? You still try to sell him on me, after the way he sliced me up? You must think I'm a martyr with nine lives, each life donated to sadistic whim forgivable in the name of art according to commercial gospel. You must admit to its unreasonableness.

I advocate your change of viewpoint. You inveigh with weighty self-defense against literary purity. Aim for bigness of soul, not personal animosity. Dispense with your ego, that incumbers you so to rule out a noble approach.

Oh, the persistence of rot! What are your recommendations?

Appeal to Alan Morris directly. I'll give you his unlisted phone number to be rung only on a private appointment by exclusive permission. He'll be impressed by that!

So I'm to "win" his approval?

He's so humane, it's quite possible. Forgiveness is in his nature. He's done it before.

He won't hold his having victimized me against me?

Beseech his forgetting. Implore contritely. Be the humble suppliant. He's apt to consent, if your sincerity gives earnest evidence. That will soften him.

It's his mercy I'm to beg, in the candor of my proven guilt? The tables of accusation seem overthrown, and incrimination countered in the reproof of stunning reversal. Justice is shocked into a coma, and anarchy may dance until the ancient convalescent recovers,

Ask Alan Morris the following favor: he should inscribe his autograph, in indelible tattoo pen, around your winking navel, "Alan" on top of it, and "Morris" below. He's umbilical to your second nativity, and has authored your resurrectionary rebirth, to set the animation going on the pyre of apotheosis. He perpetrated your perpetuation, invisibly beyond what you natively offered to begin with: the actual seeds, factual occasion, of your literal source. He's made dregs of your origins, and dredged the remains, shelved the abandonment, discarded all the shells of outward truth. Your literary deification has arrived. It's in public print. Utilizing those comical means that swell the breath of satire and surrendered your folly to entertainment. That noblest of literary endeavors, Satire, you've earned a sainthood for fueling, tied to the stake of flames. And Alan Morris staged the *crucifixion*, with his own *crucial fiction*. In your own *crucibled friction*. What an act of cooperation on all sides!

Aren't you building it up?

The flames were heaped up plenty high. Alan Morris does a thorough job. He's not slack in his craft. Once he's hot, he piles it on. In the cold clarity of his discipline.

Fitting praise from his publisher, words that pack a pure professional bias!

Your criticism is the puny measure of you. Can you *deserve* to have been created by him? He based his creation on your pure nothingness. His skill nullified your being a total nil! Birth is no mean gift, to offset the non-birth of your usual deadness. Only by remote luck can you conceivably merit it. Is it for that boon that you wish to punch Alan Morris in the nose to fabricate some imagined revenge over on him, on the bloated pretense of petty cause? Your shallow narrowness is narrow and shallow. But he's magnanimous. As a produced creature, you must appreciate it. Go on scolding, and you're *still* forgiven!

What's incredible is hard to believe. Therefore, I'm still not convinced. Limp and lame, let your explanation stumble on.

I'll try, though with exasperation. What an obstacle to communication is your obtuseness, making my job of defending Alan Morris perilously difficult!

I *need* too much pity to award *you* some. Go ahead.

Back to Alan Morris, though he needs no defense, but I'm a bungler, and must redo what has had no persuasive effect, to probe your density upon reiteration, and hammer persistence to batter down your buttressed wall and ram through and storm the fort with the oily torch of light-shedding illumination to drive sense through your thick skull bent on defensive nonsense, and to tap on your inner stronghold of understanding by budging a bomb through.

What are you getting at? Put your words in a cryptic vault.

I'd rather encapsulate them in a pill, that you swallow.

I'll puke it on you. And watch it counter-explode.

Drive back your violent imagery. I won't have my tongue crippled by the insecurity of a threat. Do you retract your harm?

No intention inferred, of malice or less. Resume your apology of your favorite money-making author, who made of me a monkey; in making money for you.

You make light of the whole deal.

That's what it is: a *deal*. I thank you for defining it in the light of a true confession.

I won't be trapped. What's your game?

To vindicate my clear name, of sullied honor.

The character had a *fictional* name, nowhere resembling yours. That takes care of *that*. What *else* are you protesting?

Stop patronizing me, you sinner! You abettor of another's sin! You mongrel cur sin-monger! You in*sin*uator! You *sin*ister man! You *syn*dicated sinner! You *Cin*derella of all in*sin*cerity since—oh, since I know not when.

Don't get carried away. Go back to yourself, and hold on grippingly. Be consolidated. I need a becalmed audience, to be my star author's pleading advocate, and present you with the means to award me the verdict, against your own gracious loss, which unprotestingly I would have you accept; to end the ease and forestall an expensive appeal in suit. Grant me your judicial ears.

What elaborate description have you prepared? I'll listen with generous consent, while you tirade me aghast. Have your words out.

(Grandiloquently, as though by frenzied rote in the teeth of whatever irrelevance the situation may plot against him, but rigidly upholding his message with fanatical zeal like a lawyer defending an unpopular cause while justice waits to trounce on his impassioned rhetoric and tear it coolly to fits and shreds whipping wind that gusts open the courtroom doors and crackles through the windows to parody the oration in progress:) He's compounded of bigness of soul; by his own vast stature, he's measured *you* in your making; your traits have undergone immortalization through his alchemical welding of the special properties of ironic exaggeration with the magical nature of precisely realistic portrayal down to the exacting harness of the least detail. The result is *you*,

turned vivid from the nebulous. Art has chiseled you entire; by what audacity, therefore, do you accuse *him* of being a chiseler, in the pejorative sense? What monster has ingratitude fancied, dislodging decency from nature's feathered nest that harbors righteousness from indignation's calumny and the outlaw rebel of pride grown into perverse spite? Reflect!, before your shifty, evasive answer coyly refutes truth's ego-dethroning denunciation! What feeble gropings can reply put together, now that you're beaten down, and your untenable view destroyed?

Alan Morris wrote a bad book. It's no good as a novel. Aesthetically, it's rank with faults.

(Incredulously:) You must have read it in the *Braille* version! Go on.

Next is a *grave* condemnation. Brisk yourself for it.

Should I duck, or dodge?

Either one. Or both.

Your warning is timely. Go on.

He made me by *type*, and left out my *individual* characteristics. I'm only a stock comic fool of a character, and no longer *me*, in that falsely praised, miswritten fornication of a fiction he aborted. As a *tale*, it's only an appendix: a *dog* can have a tail, too.

You're embittered. Apparently, he "hit home." He scored. You admit it, for being hurt. The truth *does* sting, doesn't it?

You're wrong, as he was. How wide a combination are all the possible *twistings!* To make you seem right.

I'll let you rent. Go on.

Before him, I had a soul. Now, it's molested. Not nullified, but wrangled. To meet popular demand, or anticipate or to create it, you published a huge edition of a rotten novel. Based on me, like a misprint.

Dispense with your value-judgments. Stick to the facts. We'll thresh out this case.

I doubt it. I doubt you, and I doubt him. The wrong I've been done is irreparable. Dim melancholy aches softly, since anger is inactive for an outlet, and it's hard to express hate otherwise. So my hate is subdued. For you and him.

Are you the injured party?

Justice soothes me to believe I am.

All due to a misunderstanding, undoubtedly. Let's examine this matter freshly, untattered by a personal smattering of subjectivity to invalidate the fair crystal of an appraisal in the smudge and grime of self-seeking.

How righteousness replaces right, in your case! You're a cunning fool.

Don't stoop below a subsistent level of dignity. We must conduct ourselves like gentlemen, not scoundrels. With that accord to base our search on mutual soundness, we'll sound the reaches of our *discord*, and iron the differences out. Are you amenable? Be at least *amiable* enemies, to be agreeable. We don't want *ugly* combat to divide us.

Those are gentle rules you're making up, after you've made it rough for me! I add hypocrisy to your evils. It fits you well, and joins all its friends, in that assembly for the workings of hell, that convention hall and meeting place and congregational zoo for those beasts of abstract crime so well united in you that they've illegalized guilt and go on unpunished. What a convenient prison that is: the indefinite parole of free culprits and criminals at loose, at large, in liberty, unconfined to do their worst without obstruction. What a permissive society! What encouragements and enducements to run up the breaches of law and indulge crime in the undetected splendor of its openness! Truly, these *are* modern times.

Unfairness reigned *before*, too. But let's get back to what we're about. Where were you?

In my fault-finding crusade. Compiling reasons; to back me up. I was wrongly portrayed in a novel.

Or, so you say.

What do *you* say?

(Haughtily, in condescension:) I *am*; I don't *need* to say.

You say you're a publisher? How suitable for Alan Morris to be your author! How well you conspire together, to find the right downfall to fit my ruin! What a pair!, redeeming each other of conscience, through combination-immunity. I detest you both. Where is *he*?

In your present mood, brooding retribution, I won't endanger him by revealing his location. A publisher must *protect* his author, from unwarranted intrusion and privacy's vile violation by a reader plagued by dissatisfaction; whose vendetta against art seeks to wound the artist himself as literal scapegoat in abstraction's animosity. Currently, you're insane. Therefore extreme safeguards are requisite. I'll not expose Alan Morris to the strain of your wrath, till restraint take calm hold of you again; and Reason's democracy recapture the lost government. Your unruly ravings rant without rule. First overthrow chaos; install some sense; and dispute through Order's moderate terms. Till such a happy revision take place in putting your wits together that now operate separately, let's suspend this fruitless argument, Halt debate while futility detains it. Otherwise we blast our sounds to noisy waste and get back loud nothing in sonorous echo.

But we want to feed the echo.

You mean nourish the *ego*?

Oh! I'm confused.

So am I. But you were first to confess.

I was only *trying* to complain. Why must such an effort be held to my discredit? Alan Morris did a large crime, singling me out to falsify my character. I can *feel* how exploited I am. The *victim* can tell best. He's in the position to know. It's on *him* that the effect has been made. He's intimate with it. As the recipient. He's the closest.

You don't *sound* like you're suffering.

No, I keep it a closely guarded secret. I wouldn't give you the satisfaction. My torment you'd only gloat over.

I haven't an ounce of sadism. What are you attributing to me?

Sadism.

But I haven't an ounce of it.

No, you have a pound.

Then I'm a *heavy* sadist?

No, for I'm making *light* of you.

You make light of me? How?, for your tone bespeaks gravity: and gravity bears *heavily* down, not *lightly*.

It depends on what it is that's coming down.

Oh, I *fell* for *that* one.

And your downfall is a low drop, for you're low to *start* with.

You debase me even *further*.

I *tread* on you, you're so low.

Then I warn you: watch your step.

You watch it: you're *closer* to it.

You have grounds for saying that.

And you *lie* on them. So there.

That's the lie of the land.

You've landed yourself in a grave for a plot.

So gravity is gravely destined.

There's no levity in *that* notion.

Hardly conducive to *light*heartedness.

Not something to be borne aloft on.

A grave old man, no longer in infant b(u)oyancy. Alas: What an end!

Not *only* the end: his *head* goes there, too.

He has a head for where he's going.

He's heading there.

But can he *face* it?

That's another matter.

Another matter is what he *faces*.

What else is matter, but a man's *faeces?*

What a loss of face, in his headlong fall!

For that he's fated. Heads over *feetsies*.

And so he's faded. He fetes the worms.

They squirm through him. What a base feat!

He's brought to lowliness.

But you're already low *now:* you're a publisher.

I'm embarked on a business venture. Alan Morris is my head writer.

How can he be your *head* writer, if he writes *tales (tails)?*

That's a *toss*-up, and I'm dazed.

Why? Is he still *tossing* his salad days?

He's a veteran. Experience bids him write well.

What can he *right*, being so *wrong?*

You're *left* with this fact: he does *write (right)*.

I'm left without recourses: he's branded me with infamy. He's slandered honor, and reduced me ignobly to the low, demeaned proportions and base deeds of a revolting character, directly inspired from me! No recognition would apply to me but what *his* terms have made instead. He took an unlicensed liberty on the mistaken claim of his genius. Whether malice was intended or not, I *have* been harmed in an awful way. *You* make it worse, by maintaining that *I* owe a debt to *him*, by virtue of his creative power. Creative? It has destroyed me.

It's your choice to interpret yourself as a victim, instead of the availer of great opportunity to *borrow a life* which *reality* stingily withheld from you, but which Alan Morris invites you by vicarious proxy to be the liver of. How amazing the harsh angle of divergence that pries our minds apart on this obvious, undebatable point. If you don't *have* the sense, where can you borrow it?

Not from the fiction Morris made me into. A dolt like that!: Not me at all!

(Looking at own wristwatch:) It's near time for an appointment, and I won't stand here arguing with you. I've done all I could, but you refuse to be happy.

Stay! I'm not done yet!

I'm a busy publisher, my time is valuable, I can't squander it in nursing a psychiatry on a poor problem-child like you. Be brief. What's your contention, now?

It concerns Alan Morris.

You've been harping on him all day! Can't you leave him alone now? Give his ghost a little peace, while it's still alive and writing books that profit my publishing business. Haven't you had your fill at taking cracks at him, poking imaginary blows at in fact your benefactor? Justify that!

Am I to praise and thank him for setting atrocity on a path of plunder under cosy sanctions? He's plunged authorship into the degradation of all honor, for which his fraternity of scribblers owe him a drubbing. I'm one character *outside* his book, and another *in*. Which one is the true *me*?—certified by God's inspection as being—if this word has meaning for you—*real*?

Let's not trouble ourselves with "real." I offer to compromise by regarding your portrait as a take-off on you as a model, a rendering loosely based, if you like, on a point of departure, not a strict literal version. It was a vague study of you, you were only sketched, it was a variation on some theme you suggested, rather than a mirror-image exactly filled in with meticulous imitation. Let's put it *that* way; and end our jointly unmutual pondering. Or is my solution too simple for your urge to take the stultified and hopeless end of all your self-mortified bargains? You're addicted to mental complaints. I don't blame Alan Morris for using you: as comic material, you were a "natural." You lend yourself to be interpreted as all possibilities of a fool. You *ask* for what was done to you. By what you were.

My complications didn't need a photographer to record them into an abstract poem: Or a sculptor to versify my stilted prose. Or a choreographer to graph my drafted pose into a smeared oil painting. Or a water-colorist to musically compose my pastel tints into a huge work of architecture. I was transposed, and deformed. I was *de*posed, and *trans*formed. A novel ruined me. It took me away. I want me back. Tell Alan Morris that.

I'm joining him now, in an appointment. No, I can't invite you along. It's a confidential business talk. About very private matters. No, nothing to do with you. *(Making motions to go: impatient; beginning to move:)* I must shake you off. Don't cling, like a character without an identity. Go read the book again, and find yourself there.

(Miserably, meekly and weakly:) I'm lost. I'm too weak even to read. Where can I be located?

What an abject specimen you are! Alan Morris will *never* use you again; for there's nothing to use.

I'm a broken man. I'm a defeat. I'm what was beaten.

Stop pitying yourself. *Misery* won't improve your condition.

No, but might it not *express* it? Your scorn *proves* how low I am; dignify me with your contempt.

(Glancing quickly at wristwatch:) My urgent meeting with Alan Morris, a top-level conference of the utmost priority, is soon upon *now*. Haste has taken me over. Goodbye at once!

Spare me your conclusion, please.

From it?, or for it?

Give it, is what I beg.

While on the run, here it is: when you're soon dead, the novel based on you will still please posterity and have reprinted editions. You're converted into a valid myth, by the necessary distortions that you say "violated" you. The author did his job. You've been exploited for the *good*, like raw oil being tapped, for a well built on it to realize the resources. But you were *unpromising* material: a tribute to the *author's* resources. Your banal truth has been transformed. The worthless man that you are, having only a *fact* to go by, was well transcended: a literary character was made, who lives. A fiction that dwarfs you. That shames you. But that you should praise; be proud of; whom you can't *emulate*; but who has replaced you, and who picks up strength even while you weaken. No, you weren't sacrificed; for what *was* there of you to sacrifice? You decline, just as though no word of Alan Morris had ever been printed. Go down, peacefully. Be rubbed out from your forgotten mark on earth. Go into inconsequentiality: which is only a short trip, you needn't even budge an inch. Who are "*you*"? Don't even *try* to answer, and you'll be spared embarrassment. (*Other is slowly crumbling to ground from standing position.*) However, I'll cheerfully send along your regards to Alan Morris; I'll set something up socially, for you two to remeet again. (*Wagging a stern, insolent, mocking finger at finally fallen character:*) But no animosity, I warn you: he'd be appalled, the gentle soul that he is. He's finicky. Edgy, at times. Only your impeccable behavior would do, at my proposed dinner. I'll mail you your invitation, in due time. Do your best, till that time, to save your dwindling life from stopping *altogether*. We don't want a *corpse* at our table. It would mock the whole proceedings. (*Having worked himself up to increasing indignation; ruthlessly shouts:*) I will not be made a fool of. *Forget* about our social meal! You can starve alone, can't you?

(*Steps on or over—careless as to which—the prone character, strides quickly offstage, leaving the victim in a breathless, moldering heap or flattened out like a straw, as devoid of life as the empty page of a non-written novel. He's as still as furniture or a small rug. Then the curtains close in; and what they cover is seen to be nothing. An empty stage is all the curtains can cover, in closing the play. It's the audience's cue to stir; it has been brought home to them: that it's time to go home. And as one body, this is what they do: program in hand, and play in head. The dead drama is borne away.)*

A Reverse Television Interview, and a Power Takeover, a Harrowing Tale, in a Way—but True to Life's Ruthless Opportunism, at Trials for High Tide

(An interviewer and guest author on television:)

I enjoyed reading your book.

Well, that makes us even: I enjoyed writing it.

Were the thoughts in your mind before writing it changed in the course of your writing it?

Of course.

How do you feel about it now?

About what?

The book.

Oh, I hope to market it, I'm trying to publicize it by being interviewed by you on this program, so that its sales will be great and earn me some fortune and some fame. But I already forgot what the book was about. *You* read it, just recently, to prepare yourself to ask appropriate questions about it and discuss it intelligently with me, its author. But I haven't really read it since I wrote it—which was years ago. True, I proofread the galley sheets to make corrections for the printers, but that was only a mechanical process, and my mind wasn't on what the book was *about*, but just on the words and punctuation marks themselves, as tiny marks of black type that led no further in meaning than themselves in lines of shapes in visible comparison against the manuscript, letter by letter, line by line. Then the typesetters made the corrections and the sheets were printed and then bound and the books were distributed and the publicity editor of the publishing firm arranged for me to be here interviewed by you, so here I am, in my best new suit (my *only* new suit in years), well groomed, shaven, shining on this occasion. Isn't it time now for a commercial?

Yes, here's a brief pause. This interview will be continued shortly. *(Pause.)* Well, here we are, back again. The author forgot what his book was about. But he hopes new minds—readers who've purchased the book—will be impressed with its contents, and the style suitable to those contents. What do you *think* the book was about?

At a venture, I'd guess that the book dealt certainly with people. That's what I of course recall. Am I right? You've read it recently, and are well positioned to confirm my hunch, or, as the case may be, refute it.

Oh, it's about people, all right. It's *definitely* about them. People are at the heart and soul and core of what your book is simply all about. Of that, there's no doubt.

Well, in that case, there's a natural bridge between book and reader. Since all my prospective readers—bar not a single one, not even a sole exception—are people; and since people is what the book is all about, then there's an inevitable link: of people reading about people. It all fits into a harmonic pattern. I'm delighted at this simple revelation of harmony. Concord between reader and subject matter is an auspicious coincidence that's bound to boost sales. The publishers will make profit, and I'll garner lots of royalties, and establish a firm reputation. This interview has taken a turn to the rosier. I swoon to be on your program, sir.

Glad to have you aboard. You raise the tone of this program, just by being on it. But now, about the book.

Yes, of course, the book.

Surely we must go into more specifics about it. We must make a finer breakdown than just to analyze broadly its being about people. Just *what* about people is it about? Surely, our audience deserves to know *that*.

My memory draws a blank, on that score. Since you've recently read it, suppose *you*—the interviewer—tell, on your own program, the audience about some particular themes, topics, scenes, and incidents, within the book proper.

Haven't we reversed roles? *I'm* supposed to be interviewing *you.* But now *you*'re drawing *me* out. I hope the *producer* of this program, or the network directors, won't object to this twist of format.

On the contrary, they're probably fascinated. This may be an innovational breakthrough in all televised history of the traditional interview, or talk show, as a stock-in-trade *genre* of this comparatively new medium—newer than radio, and *much* newer than periodicals in print. Surprises are possible—the human element—unpredictable—in the television dimension. We've participated mutually in a novelty. We're improvising, inventively. We've broken with accepted procedure. We've blazed a whole new trail, or stumbled upon one, by undeliberate spontaneity. But haven't we exceeded our time? Surely commercials are due, following which, the next scheduled program, following this one, is due to succeed ours, according to network schedule. *(To audience:)* Thank you for listening—I mean looking—I mean both. We've enjoyed having you—or you us. The opinions expressed on this program don't reflect anything but our minds. I'll be back next week, displacing him, who was the interviewer. I'll have my first regularly scheduled guest next week. Who, I wonder? I'll prepare it and plan it, with the cooperation of the program director, or producer, whoever he may be. I like television. It's a change from authoring. Buy my book. And tune me in next week. Goodbye. *("Click" is heard: program goes off the air.)*

Hey—wait a minute.

Too late. We're off the air. I've deposed you, replaced you, I've taken over, It's my show.

But how will I make a living?

Turn author. Write a published book. Then, I'll ask you back, as my guest.

How do you set *about* writing a book?

Oh, let the words come. Pour them out, and write them down. Be disciplined, as well.

You've deprived me of my living.

But I've provided for your next one.

With mere, cheap advice.

Take it. You'll wind up like me.

But if I lack the talent?

Then you fail. I have talent for both authoring *and* television interviewing. You may have talent for neither. But talent, like truth, will out. As I've demonstrated. At your expense. I'm afraid.

You've *certainly* taken over.

I've proved my strength—and caught you by surprise, wrenching the initiative from your formerly professional grasp. Sorry. We're animals, you know.

A sordid excuse.

Take it like a *man*, then.

You took it—you took my job away. And you already had a lucrative one as author, to boot.

My talent, my luck, my aggression—greed too, possibly. You're a little too weak.

I wasn't before you made me so.

But you are now. My strength, ascending, confers on you your new weakness, I just simply won out.

I hadn't planned a contest.

Nor had I. Improvising works out splendidly, in life—for me, this time. At your poor expense, I'm afraid. Your demise, is my glory. Fail. I thrive.

Your takeover was brutal, I'm deprived of livelihood.

Fall back on your wits and resources. The field is open—all fields. The better man won. You'll win, too—in a comeback, with new conditions. Recover from your fall. You'll bounce back. You'll accumulate will, and strike. As I did, now.

Thanks for the pep talk. I'm duly inspired.

Don't be sarcastic. Be a man, some day.

I'm downcast.

Then don't broadcast—or don't telecast. Go out, strike up a career. Use your connections. There are other openings – on television even. Ambition and enterprise are yours, if coupled with opportunistic cunning. Your dog's day will come—and you'll bark, a bold bark, not your current pathetic whine. Recuperate. Recoup your forces. Come back, driving.

I'll topple *you*, yet.

Don't threaten, I've just taken over. Give me time, to consolidate. I, too, must have my fling. Let me get established. *Then*, go constitute a threat.

All right. Meanwhile, fear me.

But not just yet.

But in time to be.

All right. But take your time.

You took my time—right off the television air.

Goodbye. I'm glad you liked my book, I liked writing it, too. And it led me here, I'm all-consuming. Well, I've got to prepare for my show next week. Any tips?

I won't help *you*.

You're so begrudging. You're a bitter, sore loser. You *deserve* what I've done.

So you justify.

The winner has become righteous, and points a moral—I can afford it. You, you're out.

In the cold.

Did the show increase my sales?, I wonder. I'll study the ratings. And the royalty returns, I've got two jobs. Life is busy, at present.

And empty, for me.

Go home.

This *was* my home: this studio.

Go to where you sleep.

I feel sleepless.

Then drink at a bar. Drown yourself. We'll meet again. *(Closes door on loser.)* Now I'm alone. To increase my power. To solidify, constitute, what I've grabbed, today. My future sings. It's my high note, I'm buoyant, with optimism, I'm free, with joy. Will my life peak down, from here? Is my crowning moment just past? I'm crowned, now let me rot? But so slowly. I'll slide, I'll decline gradually not like my defeated rival. But now, my moment's still high, *I'm* high. New popular author, new television celebrity. Let me ride my crest. On this "long-may-it" wave, that glistens to the sun, and whitely leaps in foam. Success will drown me, I'm in it deep, it's over my head. But delight was eternal, just now, I'm plunged in, I'll ride out my song's slow decline. And drown, in such heady stuff.

About the Author

Marvin Cohen is the author of a number of episodic novels, volumes of verse and dialogues, a play anthology, a book of essays on the nature of baseball, and several collections of shorter pieces—stories, dramas, parables, and idiosyncratic essays. His work has also appeared in more than 100 publications, from the experimental to the mainstream, including: *Ambit*, *Antaeus*, *Assembling* ("a collection of otherwise unpublishable writings"), *The Beat Scene* (alongside Kerouac, Ginsberg and Corso), *Chelsea*, *Fiction*, *The Hudson Review*, Thomas Merton's *Monk's Friend*, *New Directions in Prose and Poetry*, *The Transatlantic Review*, *The New York Times*, *Harper's Bazaar*, and *Vogue*.

His work has been performed on radio and theatres in the UK and the USA, including readings at the Poets at the Public Series, featuring, amongst others, Richard Dreyfuss and Wallace Shawn.

Cohen was born in Brooklyn, New York City on July 6, 1931, He has described himself as one who has "risen from lower-class background to lower-class foreground." He studied art at Cooper Union but left college to focus on writing. He supported himself with a series of short-term jobs including mink farmer and merchant seaman. He later taught creative writing at various New York colleges including the New School, the City College of New York, C.W. Post of Long Island University, and Adelphi University. He is married and currently lives with his wife in the East Side, NYC.

Acknowledgments

Profound thanks are extended to the following for their generous financial support which helped to defray some of this book's production costs:

Thomas Young Barmore Jr, Suzie Blaut, Matthew Boe,
Brian R. Boisvert, Alex L. Bozzi, IV, D. Bradley,
Shannon Leigh Broughton-Smith, Chris Call, Elaine M. Cassell,
Scott Chiddister, Chelsea Clifton, Jangus C. Cooper, Sheri Costa,
Michael Costello, Dr. Alan T Critchley, Parker & Malcolm Curtis,
Robert Dallas, Victoria De Maria, Daniel Dion, Isaac Ehrlich,
Frederick Filios, Thomas Fuchs, Deanna Leonie Gabb, Justin Gallant,
John M. Gamble, Stephan Glander, GMarkC, Damian Gordon,
David Greenberg, Ethan Hawkins, Aric Herzog,
Peter and Deborah Jackson, Neil Glenn Jacobson, Erik T Johnson,
Fred W Johnson, Sergey Kochergan, elif kolcuoğlu, Alvin Krinst,
Paul Kuliev, Dylan Lackey, Mark Lamb, Jonathan Mack,
M.E. Mancini, Jim McElroy, Donald McGowan, mdtommyd,
Dr. Melvin "Steve" Mesophagus, Jarrod Milne, John Miyasato,
Spencer F Montgomery, Geoffrey Moses, Gregory Moses,
Clyde Nads, Michael O'Shaughnessy, Andrew Pearson,
Logan M Porter, Philipp Potocki, Stephen Press, Waylon M. Prince,
Joshua Ragan, Patrick M Regner, Kara Roncin & James Wheeler,
Rebecca S, George Salis (www.TheCollidescope.com),
Yvonne Solomon, Martin Stein & Scott Saxon, K. L. Stokes,
Leah Sylvester, Sydney Umana, Christopher Wheeling,
Isaiah Whisner, Karl Wieser, Charles Wilkins, T. R. Wolfe,
and Stephen M. Wolterstorff

9 780578 899633